GONE TO SEA IN A BUCKET

ALSO BY DAVID BLACK

*Triad Takeover: A Terrifying Account of
the Spread of Triad Crime in the West*

DAVID BLACK

GONE TO SEA

IN A BUCKET

THOMAS & MERCER

Text copyright © 2015 David Black

Published by Thomas & Mercer, Seattle

www.apub.com

Amazon, the Amazon logo, and Thomas & Mercer are trademarks of Amazon.com, Inc., or its affiliates.

ISBN-13: 9781503947498
ISBN-10: 1503947491

Cover design by bürosüd° München, www.buerosued.de

Printed in the United States of America

To Margaret and Davy

'There is no branch of His Majesty's forces which in this war have suffered the same proportion of losses as our Submarine Service. It is the most dangerous of all services.'

—Winston Churchill, the Prime Minister, in an address to Parliament.

Author's Note

The Victoria Cross is Britain's highest honour for valour. Of the Royal Navy's twenty-two VCs awarded during the Second World War, nine were won by submariners.

Of the 238 Royal Navy submarines to sail on war patrols between 1939 and 1945, 76 were lost.

My technical adviser on *Gone to Sea in a Bucket* was Captain Iain D. Arthur OBE, RN, a former Captain (S), Devonport: the officer commanding the Devonport submarine flotilla. Captain Arthur guided me through all the technical complexities of an operational submarine, explaining procedures, tactics, and submarine lore. Without him, this book would not have been possible. However, I must say this to my expert readers: I know you will have found errors. But they are my errors, are deliberate, and have been dictated by the momentum of the story. This is, after all, a work of fiction. I hope you will forgive me.

Foreword

When I was first given the opportunity to read *Gone to Sea in a Bucket* by David Black, I was very busy and I put the manuscript to one side. However, when I did finally manage to pick it up, I was glad I'd cleared my in-tray first – because I could not put it down!

Speaking as a submariner, I found this tale of submarine life in wartime a genuine pleasure. It is technically extremely accurate from an engineering/equipment point of view, with regards to how a submarine of that era was operated and fought; and the detailed description of life on board (even down to 'Train Smash' and 'Cheese Oosh' – always popular scran!) and all the associated atmospherics one might encounter are most authentic. There are a couple of instances where I felt nomenclature was different to that I have used – for example, I would say 'All Round Look' as opposed to '360 Look' – but these are tiny; and the author may have it right: in 1940 that may have been the expression used.

I found myself easily transported back to the time I joined my first submarine 50 years ago – built in the closing stages of World War Two, so not different from the submarines David Black describes. I was in total empathy with Harry Gilmour, his hero, when he joins HMS/M *Pelorus* as the junior watchkeeper on board; in my case, and at a similar age, I went aboard my first boat as 5th Hand, and Harry's experiences scarily mirrored my own, right down to having a CO known for his liking of the hard stuff – though happily in my situation he indulged ashore and not aboard, where he was a formidable and skilled attacker. And when Harry joins HMS/M *Trebuchet* . . . well, what can I say? I too had a wardroom steward just as much an eccentric character as Harry's 'Lascar' Vaizey.

The insight into the relationship between 'the Trade'[1] and General Service (the surface navy) is also absolutely spot-on – and an element of that still exists in modern times between submariners and 'skimmers'! (It was certainly powerfully in-being when I joined my first boat – Vice Admiral Wilson's words live on!![2])

And the insight also captures perfectly the ethos and professionalism of the whole crew beneath the waves:

'Thing about the trade is, Mr Gilmour, unlike that lot upstairs, with us, if every man knows his job and does his duty exactly right, then there's a good chance we'll all live. If he don't, then we don't. It's simple as that.'

'There isn't less discipline in the trade, Mr Gilmour. If anything, the discipline here is the hardest of all. Self-discipline. You look after yourself, your mates and your boat. At all times.'

1 'The Trade': the Royal Navy Submarine Service's name for itself.
2 In 1901, when the Royal Navy was first considering commissioning submarines into the fleet, the then Vice Admiral Sir Arthur Wilson VC described them as: 'Underhand, unfair and damned un-English.'

Life in a submarine was a unique experience. On a big ship, hierarchy prevailed. On a submarine, it was different. You had to rub along, mainly because it wasn't safe to do otherwise.

The fear of 'friendly fire' from the RAF also lives on – or at least it did until the Government got rid of the RAF's ASW Maritime Patrol Aircraft in the 2010 defence review (incidentally, a crass decision – in general ASW terms!).

The book's closing adventure is indeed the stuff of Hornblower and Jack Aubrey; it's the singeing of the King of Spain's beard and 'Crap' Miers[3] (I knew him personally, and my father served under him) winning his VC in World War Two rolled into one – and the exciting way it is told helps to sustain credulity! All the aspects of submarine warfare are brought into play: the surveillance mission is extremely authentic, and once the shooting starts . . .

I could go on – there is so much to parallel with my own experiences as, I suspect, will be the case for anyone who has been in the Trade, even in today's nuclear submarine fleet – but if I did I would end up making this foreword longer than the book with my own quotes and personal reflections from every page!

Yet I do hope that anyone reading this book who is not a submariner will gain as much enjoyment as I have taken! I say this because I know that out there is a huge readership with no experience of Nelson-era Ships of the Line, yet who find the works of C.S. Forester and Patrick O'Brian hugely readable in spite of their delving deeply into the technical detail of their day.

In the same way, *Gone to Sea in a Bucket* reflects the submarine service in World War Two, with the same attention to detail. And that is why I believe that, in its hero Harry Gilmour, David Black

---

3 Rear Admiral Sir Anthony Cecil Capel Miers VC KBE CB DSO & Bar, who won his VC commanding *HMS Torbay* in 1942.

has created a Jack Aubrey for the modern age. And set him at the heart of a tale as epic as those of O'Brian and Forester; a tale that encompasses not only the same thrill of action, but also the same compassion and understanding for the true heroes of our nation's seafaring traditions – the sailor warriors then, as now.

—Admiral of the Fleet the Lord Boyce KG GCB OBE; former First Sea Lord and Chief of the Naval Staff, 1998 to 2001; and Chief of the Defence Staff, 2001 to 2003

Chapter One

Like all young men of a certain age, Harry Gilmour had grown up with his own notion of how a naval battle should be. This wasn't it.

Six hours ago he had still been naive enough to be excited; tensed for the roar of the guns, braced against the heel of the ship at speed beneath him, as if he were the central figure in a heroic tableau. Like that remembered painting from a *Boys' Own* annual: the 16-year-old boy seaman, still at his post while all the other members of his gun crew lie about, decorously dead, as the Battle of Jutland unfolds somewhere beyond the smoke and twisted metal. Stirring stuff.

Of course there was no doubt that he was in a battle. The Captain had said so, his staticky monotone crackling out of the tannoy as they had settled into their posts after the Actions Stations bell at 05.15. And yes, there had been the roar of guns. And bloody loud they were too. But hardly the rippling salvoes of his imagination. Every now and then there would be an air-quivering *BUDUD-DDUMMM!* as the main battery sent off another pair of 15-inch shells sailing over that bloody great anony-mous Norwegian fjord-wall, filling the night with rock. If he shut his eyes, he could see it now. A looming silhouette in the pre-dawn darkness, rising up almost to the sky itself, glimpsed as he and the rest of his damage-control party had descended into the fo'c'sle.

But the sailors slouched around Harry now were anything but decorous. And his ship, HMS *Redoubtable*, had done nothing more than circle round all morning at a stately five knots, as befitted a battleship of her antiquity, lobbing her shells over into the next fjord, to plummet down on a battered squadron of German torpedo boats. The fall of shot was being directed by that lanky, deeply stupid spotter pilot and the two comic grotesques he called his crew. They were up there now in *Redoubtable*'s Swordfish floatplane, watching the shells splash, telling the Gunnery Officer, 'Left a bit, right a bit,' in their smug gunnery jargon. Trying to plop the huge shells on to Jerry in his diminutive little tubs. Jerry called them torpedo boats, but they were more like the British corvette: proper steel-hulled ships, near on 1,000 tons, not the marine-ply and glue jobs that the name suggested, and armed with three 4.1-inch guns and six 21-inch torpedo tubes. Dangerous-enough little buggers. Harry had looked them up in the wardroom copy of *Jane's Fighting Ships* last night, when the talk was of nothing else among the officers off-watch. It gave him something to take his mind off never being invited to join in their conversation.

That spotter pilot had been there too. Lieutenant Turl-d'Urfe. Could anyone actually be called that? An accent to cut glass and a sneer as if there was a permanent smell under his nose, insisted, 'yes'. The Lieutenant had never once spoken to Harry, but he'd managed to make it clear that as far as he was concerned, Sub-Lieutenant Gilmour was just plain wrong. Wrong class, wrong country, and wrong bloody ring on his sleeve. For Harry, the son of a Scots schoolmaster, was 'wavy navy'. His single gold ring was not the solid band of the Royal Navy but a gold squiggle that said 'Royal Navy Volunteer Reserve'. A bloody civilian in a hostilities-only uniform, pretending to be a sea officer. And he was in the pilots' wardroom. Horrid little oik. The pilot wasn't alone in his opinions. Not by any means.

BUDUD-DDUMMM! Another salvo.

The deck lurched, and the world went out of focus again in another shock wave. Paint flakes fluttered down like snow from the deckhead low above them. Harry's stomach felt like it had just been punched again, and his brain rattled like a pea in a tin can. He looked around, letting his eyes stop dancing. The more fastidious of the dozen or so ratings under his command were brushing the paint flakes off their duffel coats before returning to concentrate on puffing at the cigarettes that Harry had allowed them to produce two hours ago.

He shouldn't have done it, of course. The ship was at Action Stations, and any activity which might distract you from your total concentration on killing the enemy was a violation of the Articles of War. Also, there was another reason. The damage-control party was up here because right under that bloody great hatch in front of him, with its winch capable of lifting the two-ton lid atop it, was the well that led down to the paint locker. And old First World War veteran R-Class battleships like *Redoubtable*, fresh from two decades of peacetime spit and polish, carried a lot of paint. Which as any schoolboy knows is highly flammable. And the damage-control party, of which Harry was in charge, was now smoking.

Harry had propped himself against the hull, slumped deep in his reefer jacket, his watch cap pushed back to cushion his head against the steel. Beside him were two ratings in huge puffed-up white asbestos firemen's suits, with the tops off, looking for all the world like the wrong end of a pantomime horse. The rest were in overalls and duffel coats – April up here, off Narvik, was still bloody freezing. About them lay fire-fighting equipment and a medieval arsenal of bars and wrenches.

The party looked small inside the vast, bland, white steel box which formed the capstan flat, a compartment that stretched away forward, interrupted only by the chains and machinery that entered and departed through it. The deck stretched the width of the ship, tapering forward towards the bow. A big space. Down through the middle came the capstans – huge metal cylinders that raised and lowered the anchors. And then the anchor chains themselves, passing down through holes in the decks above and below, into the bowels of the chain lockers. Huge, limb-thick links. A hit here on the machinery that controlled them could release those chains and send them thundering out of the locker, dragged by free anchors weighing god knows how many tons, over the side, checking movement, slewing, damaging the ship, dragging her out of the line of battle, if there had been any line of battle or indeed any battle to speak of.

The damage-control party were the ship's defence against whatever mayhem enemy ordnance might wreak. It was a critical role that the men of the damage-control party might have to perform under Harry's resolute command.

They were all older than Harry: peacetime sailors, who'd been 'in' for years. Balding pates, smokers' teeth, noses lit by rum, sea-weathered and battered. Regular Royal Navy. 'Jack', to themselves, and all around them. Career sailors, whose latest inconvenience, in a long line of inconveniences, was to find themselves at war. But then 'Jack' had long been wise in the ways of inconveniences, and wise in the ways of officers. Especially a kid like Harry.

The Petty Officer, who was Harry's leading hand on the party and who had a good 15 years on him, had persuaded Harry that, seeing as there wasn't that much happening, and as Jerry was actually on the other side of a bleedin' mountain, it seemed only fair to let the boys have a gasper. I mean it was cruel to deny 'Jack' his smoke for the equivalent of a whole bleedin' watch when there was nothin' happenin'. He had appealed to Harry's sense of what was fair.

Exasperated, Harry knew it was a fatal mistake even as he'd said, 'All right then, but . . .' and all his caveats were lost in the fumble to produce the cigarettes and light up.

Harry, about to turn 19 years old, was not a happy Harry these days. It wasn't just naval battles that were not living up to his expectations. The whole navy lark, he was now coming to realise, was somewhat lacking in the glamour and esprit de corps he had envisaged when on Tuesday, 5 September, 1939, just two days after the prime minister had announced 'this country is at war with Germany', he had walked into the Royal Navy recruitment office in Glasgow to sign up.

He'd quickly found himself at the other end of the country, rolling up to a recently requisitioned municipal swimming pool and sports pavilion on the shorefront at Hove.

'Have you ever been at sea, done any sailing, messed about in boats?' asked some ageing instructor officer, not even looking at him.

'Yes, actually,' Harry replied eagerly, 'I've done quite a bit of yachting.' A tick on a form, and for the next three months, the pavilion became his home. That was where they tried to turn him into a naval officer.

Nearly all his fellow officer trainees had gone on to little ships: corvettes destined for the inglorious slog of defending convoys against the U-boat menace, or minesweeping trawlers, requisitioned to keep the harbours and ports clear. The navy was facing a huge mobilisation challenge, and with a near-impossible task of manning all the ships they'd need to put to sea. And that was before losses.

Harry knew this because an unlikely, ageing sea dog called Captain John Noel Pelly, the training establishment's CO, told him so – him and all the other 140 aspiring officers on the course. But pretty soon, predicted Captain Pelly, by necessity if nothing else, Royal Navy Volunteer Reserve officers like them, johnny-cum-latelys here only for the war, would find themselves posted throughout the service, to plum jobs as well as the glamourless. So they were starting now to siphon off a select few into the real navy, the big ship navy.

And that's how Harry had got his 'plum'. Someone who knew someone, who knew someone, had passed the word. A chain of sage nods all the way back to the clubhouse of the Royal Northern Yacht Squadron in Harry's little town on the shore of the Firth of Clyde, at the bottom of Harry's road, where the membership had included America's Cup challengers like Sir Thomas Lipton and Sir Tommy Sopwith not to mention numerous naval officers of flag rank and lower, some serving, some not. This was where Harry had spent sizeable chunks of his youth scrubbing and polishing, and latterly even crewing. 'A sound lad' had been the verdict on Harry. So he got the wardroom of a capital ship, a clubhouse in its own right, in peacetime; an ante-room for preferment for the chaps from Dartmouth Royal Naval College. A 'fly-the-flag' beauty like *Redoubtable* was their territory. She was tantamount to a grey yacht, and within her wardroom was the opportunity to make oneself known to senior officers who would themselves one day command; to forge alliances and distinguish oneself in lounge lizardry.

Redoubtable had spent the previous seven years cruising the Med, acting as bar and ballroom to an endless calendar of diplomatic engagements. But now war had come, and she had sailed home to once again defend Britannia against the Hun. Her wardroom, no longer a focus for fripperies, was a place where serious men sat down to address their noble calling, sanctified by 300 years of unbroken tradition: to keep the sea lanes open, defend the Empire and its trade, clear the oceans of the enemy, and as they were indeed doing now, to carry the army to the enemy's backyard and keep it there, supplied and supported, until victory was won. The talk would be of tactics, gunnery drills; serious stuff. At least that was what Harry had envisaged. He saw his posting, not as an entry to some floating club, but as a pass to the front row of the coming war at sea. He would sit down with these men, share their deliberations.

The reality had been somewhat different. For a start, everybody was half drunk most of the time, singing songs round a piano like extras in some vaudeville revue. Except here the parody was real. Even the backdrop seemed a mockery. The ship might be sailing to war, but the wardroom hadn't lost its flotilla of plump floral-patterned sofas or its ornate tables for games of bridge. No concession had been made to more functional, warlike furnishings. And beneath the jollity there was the pecking order, the jostling for position and the undercurrent of bullying. That Harry could read this etiquette easily was no particular testimony to his intuition. It was simply because he was not remotely part of it. There was a French word which summed up the manner in which he was treated better than any English phrase: *froideur*. Not even his teenage ingenuousness could cocoon him from the front of cold air every time he walked in to this bloody sixth-form common room.

It was being on the outside that allowed all other insight to follow, let him read their thoughts. *Nothing personal, old chap, but you just don't belong. Fine on the bridge of a minesweeper tootling about some remote estuary, or on a motor gunboat in the Channel, or in charge of a gun crew aboard some newly refitted armed merchant cruiser, but not here in a capital ship's wardroom.* So it had been a pretty lonely life for Harry, these past few months, aboard *Redoubtable*.

There was a movement out of the corner of his eye. He glanced up and saw the Petty Officer opposite rising with that expression of naval blankness that always presaged doom, and heard his hiss, not even a whisper: 'Christ! It's the Bloke and the Jaunty!'

Harry jerked his head round, and there, in the distance, striding up the length of the deck from behind the A-turret barbette was indeed the Commander and the Master-at-Arms. Oh dear. Behind

Harry, in a flurry of seamless movement, cigarettes were being extinguished and palmed for a later date, as the damage-control party shot to their feet and attempted a semblance of naval readiness.

The 'Bloke' was Commander Maitland, a tall, stooped, imperious figure, who breathed from a rarified atmosphere. He was the executive officer, second only to the Captain, and his job was to be the Captain's representative on Earth; to know the Captain's will, and make it so. Beside him, the 'Jaunty', Master-at-Arms Beddoe, seemed equally tall, but with a scrawny, more menacing mien. He was the most senior non-commissioned officer aboard. Technically, Harry was his superior. The Jaunty's rank carried with it responsibility only for the crew's discipline, but it would be a truly foolhardy junior officer who would cross him. This one had a reputation for being a right hard-horse, even by naval standards. From Commander Maitland's gimlet glare, and the Master-at-Arms' openly smug fury, Harry knew he was in trouble. His throat went dry and to his surprise he began to feel a cold bead of sweat developing along his hairline.

BUDUD-DDUMMM!

Another salvo, as if to announce their arrival. The same physical shock wave blow hit Harry, but the Bloke's and the Jaunty's strides never faltered. And then they were on them.

Unprompted, Harry's Petty Officer called the damage-control party to attention. Salutes were snapped . . . then followed a contemptuous delay before either Commander or Master-at-Arms responded. Not a word was spoken. Mainly, even Harry realised, because there were formalities to be observed. Harry was the officer in charge, and so could not be bawled out in front of his men. Equally his men could not be bawled out in front of him. Commander Maitland, in his gold-braided cap, immaculate watch coat with its three intimidatingly gleaming solid-gold rings, wrapped in his white muffler, surveyed them all for a long moment, before turning on his heel and walking off a few paces.

'Mr Gilmour. A moment if you please.' It wasn't a question.

Harry leapt after him. The Commander stopped, so that Harry had to get around him to make his salute.

'Sir!' said Harry in his best naval clip.

Another silence, then: 'This is one of His Majesty's ships,' said the Commander, each word snapped off in steel, 'at Action Stations. Engaging the enemy.'

Harry could tell he wanted to go on. But he didn't. This close Harry could see for all the impervious formality of the man, he was really not that old, but he was very very angry and struggling to control his anger. Harry managed a quiet 'sir', while remaining rigidly at attention.

Eventually the Commander said: 'Stand easy.'

A pause.

'We will speak later. Meanwhile you might consider your dispositions, Mr Gilmour.'

'Aye aye, sir.'

The Commander had not finished: 'Should this part of the ship be hit, Mr Gilmour, your men of the damage-control party must inevitably go up with it. And therefore be in no position to control any damage that might ensue. Might I suggest that you remove the men into the cover of the A-turret barbette.'

The A-turret barbette was the armour-plated cylinder linking *Redoubtable*'s forward 15-inch gun turret with its magazines below decks, and therefore excellent cover in the event of an enemy hit on the fo'c'sle.

'Aye aye, sir!'

And again Harry leapt to comply. As he marched up to his men, the Petty Officer was turning away from his conversation with Master-at-Arms Beddoe, and not looking at all as discomfited as Harry had been expecting. The Jaunty was looking, well, quite jaunty. The sailors as ever, were po-faced. Something important had passed between these men of the lower decks, and more than ever Harry felt judged and humiliated by this new world to which he had been condemned.

Chapter Two

HMS *Redoubtable* turned her bow down the fjord, and with her gaggle of escorting destroyers fanned out ahead, she began piling on the knots, making for the open sea. Her vast grey eminence swept through the faded light that passed for night at these latitudes, as her crew secured from Action Stations. In five hours she would rejoin the powerful covering force that had been dispatched from the Home Fleet at Scapa Flow to cover Anglo-French landings farther south around the port of Trondheim, scheduled for two days time.

Following her to sea was another battleship, HMS *Warspite*, and her destroyer escorts. Between them they had chased and cornered a substantial German naval force of destroyers and torpedo boats in the labyrinth of fjords around Narvik, and reduced them to half-submerged piles of mangled metal. In a series of gun duels the German threat to the landings had been removed, and the German troops their warships had carried to Narvik had been stranded ashore, cut off without ammunition or supplies. It had been a successful operation, and the atmosphere aboard *Redoubtable* was distinctly upbeat.

After almost twenty-four continuous hours at Action Stations, hunger and the dire need for a drink were enough to numb Harry's mortification over events in the fo'c'sle. So after seeing his party stood down and all the equipment stowed, he made straight for the wardroom.

It was already heaving when he got there, with every other officer aboard bent on a similar task. Harry squeezed in, excusing himself to a succession of disapproving grimaces as he sought to navigate through the throng nearer to where the stewards darted in and out of the galley area with their trays of beers and gins and steaming bacon and sausage sandwiches. Harry wanted beer and bacon rolls and after all these weeks aboard *Redoubtable*, he wanted just for once not to be at the back of the bloody queue. It was a forlorn hope, but he was taking it anyway, even though he and all the other junior officers, the 'Subs' and the Midshipmen, did not figure. In fact, they were lucky to be in here at all. Aboard a capital ship, the place for 'Subs' like Harry, and 'Snotties' – as the Midshipmen were universally known – was the gunroom. But it had been cleared months before Harry had joined *Redoubtable* and was now a makeshift infirmary in preparation for casualties, when they eventually came. A generous relaxing of the rules had been approved, 'it being wartime, and all that', so the 'Subs' and the 'Snotties' got to mess with the gentlemen.

It wasn't the only mess rule being relaxed that night: dress code had gone by the board, and he was in a sea of crumpled watch jackets and even the odd duffel coat. For once he was unlikely to be picked up on some obscure breach of etiquette by a bored mess senior. The sense of relief, coupled with hot wafts of fried food, was beginning to intoxicate him to the point where he was forgetting the speed at which news could move through the ship.

Harry hadn't known the Bloke and the Jaunty routinely toured the ship at Action Stations to make sure the ship was closed up and ready to fight; but he should have known that talk of his disgrace would have preceded him. Despite the mere matter of weeks he'd been aboard *Redoubtable*, he should have been prepared. He wasn't. Instead he was listening with a certain amused detachment to Lieutenant Turl-d'Urfe, that imbecile Swordfish pilot, as he recounted his bird's-eye view and critical role in the past action. The pilot was at the far end of the throng, leaning against the piano, snifter in hand, in full flow, describing the tight little side fjord where the Jerry torpedo boats had been holed up.

'A proper troll's quarry, the place was; the way in was through a pinch of channel, then into a dogleg before you hit any open water,' the pilot drawled with affected schoolboy sangfroid. 'Far too risky for *Hester* and *Hecate* to try and force.' HMS *Hester* and HMS *Hecate* were the two destroyers sent to act as 'stoppers' in the bottle-shaped fjord where the Germans lay trapped. 'They'd have been coming at Jerry from the bowler's end, and of course, cunning little Hun that he is, he'd thrown out quite a nifty little fielding plan. There was one of his tubs at Square Leg, another two at Gully and the rest at Third Man. Jerry wasn't going to make it easy for us, buggers didn't have the common decency to lash themselves all together alongside the bunkering jetty . . . so that a couple of good straddles would have blown the whole lot to buggeration.'

But *Redoubtable* had sent her shells over anyway, and the Swordfish's observer, perched in his bit of the cockpit, behind his preposterous pilot, had observed the fall of shot, each shell forming little clusters of white blossom bursting from the dull black waters. And with each blossom, he'd radioed back his corrections to *Redoubtable*'s Gunnery Officer, instructing him to march each salvo across the anchored enemy, until each ship was left split and burning.

The Swordfish had circled too high for the German's piffling anti-aircraft guns to threaten her, and Narvik had been too far away from the German forward fighter strips for the ships below to summon fighter cover. It had been a very one-sided action but the wardroom didn't want to know that, they wanted more glory. One of the pilot's audience – a Gunnery Officer – said, 'Stooging around up there, you're lucky one of our 15-inchers didn't tickle your fanny on the way past.'

'No chance, old chap,' said the pilot, with an elegant sweep of his gin glass, 'could see 'em coming. Ups-a-daisy, like a ruddy great dustbin, and plain as day, hung about a bit right at the top, just like they was getting their bearings, and then downs-a-daisy. Ka-boom!'

One torpedo boat had apparently tried to dodge the leisurely, systematic smashing of the big shells. 'Whipped up her anchor and went off like a scalded cat,' said the pilot, 'but Binky did his observer stuff' – he gestured at his fellow airman, a curtailed saturnine youth – 'called in a tight little salvo right on Slips, and the bugger steamed right into it, stately swan to ruptured duck in one easy wiggle!'

Everyone laughed, and as the pilot surveyed this further triumph, Harry was foolish enough to let their eyes meet. The pilot smiled, and then in a stage whisper said: 'Well lookee here, it's "wavy"! Jerry didn't trouble you much from what we've heard. A little smoko and a snooze, was it? In the face of the enemy? They shoot you for that, you know. Says so in the Articles of War, as enshrined in the Naval Discipline Act 1866. Obviously not done it yet.' His grin broadened. 'Still, plenty of time, eh?'

Harry let his eyes drop. He couldn't help it. It was instinctive; but anyone thinking he would turn away as usual like the silly little boy they took him for was about to be disabused.

When Harry had walked into that Glasgow recruiting office a couple of days after Chamberlain's speech, he had wanted to serve, to do his bit. His motives were pure, patriotic and moral. He might not have been long out of school trousers, but he was well-read, sharp, bright, and able to see for himself that Mr Churchill's warnings of a new Dark Age threatening to engulf Europe were far from empty rhetoric; and he was determined to step up, to be one of those to stand against that evil tide. Yes, it would be a lie to say his resolve was not without all the attendant dreams of youthful derring-do, the flights of fancy, the movies running in his head of himself aboard white-hulled warships against a tropical ocean, hunting down some German commerce raider; of himself against the background of a bridge, sextant pressed to a keen eye, 'shooting' noon; bent over a chart table, pricking the chart; the Captain asking, 'What's our position, Mr Gilmour?' And him pointing to that tiny nick in a sea of featureless blue, replying, 'Right here, sir.'

But Harry Gilmour was not just a romantic fool, nor was he some inadequate, unformed youth, unequal – and never likely to be equal – to the challenges the war and the navy might throw at him. The real Harry Gilmour *Redoubtable*'s officers chose not see was at heart a serious, self-possessed young man, prepared to learn, eager to learn the duties expected of him. And right now, in Harry's eyes, if anyone was failing in their duties and responsibilities it was this wardroom full of hide-bound clowns, who should be training and preparing him to lead his men and fight this ship, instead of behaving as if they were still in the common room of some English public school, still lolling in their little rituals of bullying and oppression. Harry had had enough.

Indeed, if any of them had been paying attention to their unwelcome interloper, the officers of *Redoubtable*'s wardroom might have spotted a certain stiffening in his stance. Harry's new resolve had been spotted, however, but not by a wardroom member. Not all the officers were in their Action Stations' kit; one, behind the piano, a Lieutenant, was in his dress jacket, on the shoulder of which he sported a little braided cord confection called an aguillette.

Peter Dumaresq was a Flag Lieutenant; aide-de-camp to a Rear Admiral who flew his flag of command from *Redoubtable*'s foremast.

Harry had never actually set eyes on such a mythical creature as a Rear Admiral, who lived on the flag bridge, because flag officers were not part of any ship's company where they flew their flag, nor were their staffs. They had no authority over the day-to-day running of a ship. Their job was the tactical command of a squadron, in this case, made up of *Redoubtable*, her escort of destroyers, and any other naval unit that might come into its area of operations. Which was why Lieutenant Dumaresq might be in the wardroom, but he was not part of it.

He'd been only half listening to the pilot, whom he found tedious, but his head was up now, alerted by a sudden subsiding of the general hubbub; and he couldn't help but observe that some kind of confrontation was taking place between the damned flyboy and some junior officer by the galley door. He leant to see that the butt of the intrepid aviator's joke was that RNVR 'Sub', foisted on *Redoubtable* several weeks ago for reasons known only to god and the Admiralty.

Since they'd sailed from Scapa the Lieutenant had been watching the young man with a mixture of curiosity and compassion. The lad had been making heavy weather of fitting in, and it had been apparent for all to see that only a little of the heavy weather had been of his making. You couldn't help but notice how his mere presence had divided the wardroom; the officers who hadn't ignored him, had baited him. Not surprising really; the lad had arrived with a sort of insouciant, self-deprecating manner that was too contrived, trying to hide his obvious assumption that he had a right to be here. He was here, that was true, and he was quite charming if you took the time; but it was his assumption that he expected to be accepted. Well, none of it washed on the *Redoubtable*; this particular band of brothers had earned their places in this berth the hard way through the rites of passage as administered by Britannia Naval College, Dartmouth. They were career officers, one and all, bound in a Masonic-like hierarchy, with all its attendant codes and obligations, and as far as they were concerned, this whippersnapper, this arriviste, hadn't earned the right to breathe the same air.

Indeed, the Lieutenant, from the same school, could see their point, but there was a bigger issue at stake over this RNVR youth's presence; before this war was over, there would be a lot more like him in the ranks of the navy, and how the navy was going to fit them in was likely to be crucial as to whether they were going to win this war or not.

On hearing the pilot's outburst, all the officers in the piano corner, had followed the line of his sneery gaze, and his sneery words, and were now looking at the young man, their own faces starting to sport contemptuous smirks too. The Lieutenant had heard some muttering that the lad had yet again fluffed his duties somewhere on the ship during Action Stations. Alas, this 'fluffing' was nothing new: the bits of the ship that the lad's 'clean ship' parties had cleaned were, on inspection, never quite clean enough; when he did paperwork for the Paymaster Lieutenant Commander, it was never quite right; he kept asking why this and not that? And suggesting, 'Wouldn't this way be better?' And when he was sent on errands, he always seemed to get lost. The contempt his shipmates dished out in punishment was nothing new either. Until now, this lad had taken all their brickbats with a sort of resigned stoicism. That was how it had appeared to Dumaresq. This time, however, something was different. Instead of turning away, after a hesitant flutter, the lad held the pilot's stare, and with a composed expression that looked all the more dangerous for its suggestion of polite inquiry. And now he was shouldering his way through the crush of officers, and his shouldering was anything but polite. My god! The thought flashed into the Lieutenant's mind: surely he isn't going to hit him!

The navy would forgive quite a lot, if necessary, but striking a superior officer put you way beyond any prospect of mercy. The two were now standing nose to nose, the lad definitely in the flyboy's personal space. Dumaresq had no idea what was about to happen, and he would have been even more alarmed to realise that neither did Harry. There followed a moment when those just beyond the immediate vicinity also began to notice something was up, and the noise levels began to drop. Then the lad began to speak, with just a hint of his soft West Highland lilt in otherwise perfect received pronunciation. He wasn't loud, nor was he sarcastic or aggressive in any way; he might have been complimenting the other on a new suit.

'Thank you, sir,' said Harry, 'for your constructive comments.'

And then there followed another pause, with Harry's open gaze still locked on the pilot, whose own eyes were visibly swelling with affront and outrage. Then Harry added: 'I would welcome any further instruction you might offer, sir, in order that I might improve my performance and more effectively discharge my duties. If you would be so kind. Sir.'

'Performance? What performance?' said the pilot. 'So far as anyone has been able to work out, the only performance you've been able to perform with any observable level of competence is to draw your rations and convert them into shite! You perform no other function aboard this ship. You are in short, a shiteing machine. And what gives additional offence to your betters is that you are too stupid to know it! As thick in the head as the thing that made you and about as much use as the hairy tits that likely dangled above it!'

The pilot continued in this vein, and at first the gathered officers grinned and sniggered, and whispered to each other behind hands. Beyond the immediate circle, others craned to see and gave running commentaries to colleagues not sufficiently bothered to shove their way to eye-witness positions. The youth was still nose to nose with the pilot, who was spluttering abuse and spittle, and the youth took it all without a flicker, his face flat and calm, as if he was listening to one of the padre's sermons. Well perhaps not quite like that, seeing as he was still awake. But the Lieutenant started to sense it, and see that others were sensing it too, that the flyboy was going on too long. The smirks were wilting and people began to study their shoes. And still the young Sub stood there, silent, unflinching, a mirror to their less than noble prejudices.

When the pilot, the corners of his mouth flecked with froth, began to run out of invective, the majority of his audience began to turn away and a somewhat artificial hubbub began to rise. Attention shifted. The rest of the wardroom remained as it had throughout, unaware and indifferent.

Harry remained on his spot, well into the silence, still gazing impassively into the pilot's now-puce countenance.

Finally, the pilot said: 'Your manners leave much to be desired. If it's instruction you want, I suggest you learn not to impose yourself on other officers, when it is obvious your presence is . . . is . . . is a bloody affront!'

Harry came to attention in a military fashion and said: 'Sir.'

He turned on his heels and marched through a swiftly cleared alley and out of the wardroom.

Dumaresq watched him go, oddly cheered by everything he had witnessed. Well, well, well, he said to himself. Nothing of the whipped cur about you, young man.

⌣

Harry lay on his bunk in the junior officers' cabin he shared with two other Sub-Lieutenants. He'd been staring at the deckhead for several hours, unable to sleep despite his deep weariness. *Redoubtable* was butting into a quartering sea at close to twenty knots, but she was a big ship, over 600 feet long and over 30,000 tons, so Harry barely felt the motion. What he felt instead was claustrophobia.

19

Redoubtable might have seemed a big ship from the outside, but below decks she was an interconnecting maze of diminishing spaces. She might be 600 feet long, but she was also home to over 1,000 sailors and all the materiel needed to sustain them and the ordnance required to allow them to wreak bloody havoc on the enemy. Stuff and crew were squeezed together and below decks *Redoubtable* felt tiny, almost subterranean.

The other two officers were on watch, so the cabin seemed marginally larger. Four bunks, four sets of drawers, a washbasin and spaces for four personal trunks. The steel was painted the same brilliant white as the porcelain of the basin and splashback; the fixtures, brass and a dark varnished hardwood. Personal clutter was all chased away, apart from Harry's watch-keeping duffel coat hanging from the cabin door. There was no scuttle. This was an internal cabin with the deckhead bundled with cable runs and ducts, any light having to come from a set of light fittings, like toy steel and glass sarcophagi, bolted on to welded brackets. There were also small strip lights above each bunk for reading.

Right now, Harry lay with the big fittings off and only his bunk's light illuminating the cabin; a pale glow that only added to his feeling of being entombed. Being alone, the gloom allowed him a relapse into the adolescent luxury of wallowing in misery. For it has to be pointed out that despite all the mature resolve he had shown just now in the face of his tormentors, Harry was still at an age when such slights as the one he had suffered at the hands of the pilot were the end of the world.

He revelled in the unfairness of it all. Since he had come aboard, he had never been given a chance to show what he might do. He was nimble and competent aboard small boats, he was comfortable in coastal navigation; he could hold a course, reef, wear and tack a yacht. But here, he was little more than an ocean-going charlady, his naval duties consisting almost entirely of standing over lumpen sailors doing housework. He'd stood in companionways, on mess decks, maintenance spaces, weather decks, hands clasped behind his back and a look of feigned diligence fixed to his face. A posture ingrained by constant reprimand from the First Lieutenant. Just standing, doing absolutely nothing, while the men performed tasks no less ingrained: cleaning, polishing, scraping, brushing, painting; and all the time a wall of dumb indifference between him and them.

That he had once entertained such notions that he might stand a bridge watch aboard a ship of war, command a gun crew, even one day learn celestial navigation, let alone anything else remotely, properly naval, seemed now so mockingly naive he could feel the tears in his eyes.

He looked at his watch: he had a couple of hours to go before he was back on duty. He wished it was never, and that he could spend that 'never' here, forgotten. But he hadn't managed to get a bacon roll back in the wardroom scrum and hunger was pinching at his innards, made worse by fatigue. If he moved now, there would be few about. That was the decider. He swung his feet on to the deck.

It was well into the forenoon watch, and the previously crowded wardroom was almost empty. A steward was sweeping up, his bent figure small in the hall-like space. Empty, the wardroom looked huge, a hangar; except that it was decorated throughout as a Home Counties' drawing room. All the wood panelling and soft furnishings were bathed in a crystal northern light streaming through portholes framed by chintzy little curtains. The homely effect was spoiled, however, by the ranks of little picture lights bent over blank spaces on the walls. The paintings of sea battles, past alumni and the photographic record of more recent glories were long gone. Like the plate and the silver from the now empty display cabinets, they had been all struck down below, beyond the reach of enemy bomb or shell.

21

Harry finally managed to attract the steward's attention and ordered a corned beef sandwich and tea. That was when he noticed the back of a head peeking above one of the easy chairs. Harry sat down far away, not even thinking about joining the other officer. The sandwich and tea arrived and he pounced on them with a vengeance, his misery suspended while he stuffed his face. The distraction of food was sufficiently great that he didn't notice the other officer had joined him. One second, the chair opposite was empty, and the next, there he was; that smooth cover of a Flag Lieutenant with the prissy little braid thing draped over the left shoulder of his uniform jacket. Dumaresq, that was his name, and he was sitting there cradling a very large pink gin – at this hour of the day.

Harry and Dumaresq were already on vaguely familiar terms; had had the odd chat about yachts, which Harry knew about, and stalking deer in Argyll, which Harry didn't. In fact it was fair to say that Dumaresq was the only man in the wardroom who had been more than just passably civil to Harry since he'd come aboard, despite the fact that Dumaresq wasn't just Royal Navy, but old navy, to boot.

As others were quick to point out, lest Harry should be in any doubt in whose presence he had sometimes found himself, the Dumaresqs had history. His father had commanded an armoured cruiser at Jutland, his grandfather had been with Codrington at Navarino Bay, and his great-grandfather had served at the Glorious First of June and the Battle of the Nile under Nelson, for god's sake!

'The scuttlebutt has it that the Bloke caught you throwing a drinks party . . . in the fo'c'sle . . . for the lower deck . . . in the face of the enemy,' said Dumaresq, with an amused insouciance that poor teenage Harry could only aspire to. To compound his shame, he felt himself start to blush. The Flag Lieutenant didn't wait for a reply: 'How splendid! Your first action, too. You should have a portrait painted.' There was a genuine smile on Dumaresq's face. Harry realised he wasn't being mocked. The opposite, in fact.

'So where is it?' Dumaresq inquired.

'Where is what?' said Harry, puzzled.

'The Commander's pickaninny. He must have had one when he stumbled on your festivities,' Dumaresq stared squarely at him, before guffawing. 'Gawd, I'd have paid my bar bill just to have seen the look on his face.'

'I just let them smoke, there was nothing happening, I didn't think it was . . . the Master-at-Arms and the PO seemed to find it funny.' Harry had rediscovered his indignation.

'Did they now? Well there you are. You learned a lesson?'

'What?'

'The hand that wanks the Jaunty rules the ship.'

'That's disgusting,' said Harry. 'I've no idea what you're talking about.'

'An old Navy bon mot, but none the less true,' Dumaresq sighed. He was a prickly little sod, this young RNVR Sub. But no wonder really, after all his travails as he toiled to learn his trade in the teeth of *Redoubtable*'s tribal prejudices. He had put in a creditable performance in facing down that bullying oaf Turl-d'Urfe last night. It showed that he probably had the 'bottom' to make something of himself, his single wavy ring notwithstanding, and that he was of a type the navy would soon sorely need. It was why Dumaresq had decided to take an interest, for he had things to say that this young man seriously needed to hear.

'Now stop pretending to be a prude, Gilmour, and listen to your betters.' Dumaresq made the taunt in a consoling voice. 'Of course they found it funny. You made an arse of yourself, and the Bloke saw it.'

Harry snapped back: 'All of them, the PO and all the ratings, they knew what they should be doing more than I did. Why aren't they on Commander's Report?' He was indignant, having at last found a vent for his spleen.

Dumaresq maintained his calm, let the sparks fall to earth, and then began: 'This little village of ours has its "us" and "them" like all little villages. There's "us" – the officers – and there's "Jack". We each have our own little rituals, dos and don'ts. Take the Jaunty. He's the ship's most senior non-com. He bestows favours; his powers amuse him. He has his favourites: that PO of yours was obviously one of them. To him, having you appointed as the damage-control party officer was like presenting a classroom of tearaways with a student teacher. We both know the Jaunty has no responsibility for assigning officers. Of course not. But the Jaunty can suggest. And a good Jaunty is always on hand to take the strain off an over-worked Commander. You were obviously a gift from him to his boys, someone for them to torment.' Dumaresq gestured to Harry's single wavy ring. 'Especially because of that. You were their sport, and they not only got away with it, they managed to drop you right in it, to boot. It's a wonder you can't still hear them laughing all the way from the mess deck.'

With that, Dumaresq finished his gin, leant back and called for the steward. Harry had been impressed from the start how the Flag Lieutenant addressed the wardroom stewards with a politeness that was not common. The logic of his approach was now obvious, seeing as wardroom rules said the bar was closed right now. Truth be told, Harry was impressed, period, with this young tyro who had always seemed a cut above the herd on this ship in every way.

If you were to look at the two sat there in cosy confab you might have thought them an older and a younger brother, for in certain ways the two young men looked very much alike. Both were tall, with angular features and flops of dark-brown hair. But Harry was still all legs and elbows, his hair refused to take a comb, and his neck stuck out of his shirt collar like an unfinished plinth. His face was too mobile to suggest any hint of gravitas behind it, and the pasty skin still held vestiges of a pimply past at the edges. Dumaresq on the other hand, had the residual shading of a deep tan. The face was taut, full of subtle nuance. His ice-blue eyes didn't dart, like Harry's soft brown ones. Also, Dumaresq was in his late twenties, and already very much a man. Harry, on the other hand, aged nineteen, with his extensive repertoire of expressions that varied from vacant to unbridled enthusiasm, gave off an overall impression of a yet-to-be-broken-in gun dog; he was still too obviously a boy.

The steward brought two gins. Harry hadn't asked for one but didn't have the nerve to refuse. He looked at it with trepidation as Dumaresq proposed a toast to the Bloke.

Harry could not help but be aware from wardroom banter that the young Flag Lieutenant was on a fast track to command. His job as a flag officer's aide spoke volumes. He'd be getting his half ring soon, promotion to Lieutenant Commander, probably a berth as second-in-command in a cruiser. That he was being so affable was not at all usual, and that was why it was so discomfiting for Harry. He remained silent and sipped his gin under Dumaresq's steady gaze.

'They haven't a bloody clue what to do with you, Gilmour, you do realise that don't you?' Dumaresq said eventually, smiling his confiding smile. 'You're an intruder in their world: "Jacks"' and the Commander's. And what makes it worse is this is war. It means everything is all-change. We don't like change in the navy, don't even like to think about it. But war means that come it must. "Jack" and the Commander and all the gold braid from Admiralty Arch to the China Station can't win this war on their own. They don't know how. They're peacetime, bullshit-baffles-brains officers, and bullshit-baffled-brained matelots. They don't want you on this ship, because you are most definitely not one of them. You're a civvy in a blue suit, an ordinary chap plucked off the street and tricked out in the uniform of an officer in His Britannic Majesty's Royal

Navy. Except you don't see things the navy way. You are an intelligent adult from a world where there are no blinkered traditions or pointless procedures, salute this and polish that. You're going to see through all the folderol, the things they're doing wrong. In other words, you represent change. You have opinions they don't want to hear. Ideas and, god help us, innovations. If they're going to save their world they need to nip you in the bud. Dismiss you, start laughing at you before, god forbid again, you start laughing at them. Of course they're quite right really, if saving their world is what this is all about. But it isn't. If we're going to win this war, they're going to need you.' Dumaresq looked into the distance: 'You could almost feel sorry for them.'

Up until this moment Harry had been quite buoyed by Dumaresq's interest in him. He almost dared to hope he might have found a friend and ally in the older man. But those last words deflated him. Harry was conscious he was expected to say something, but he couldn't think what. Dumaresq was watching him closely, waiting for him to speak up for himself and stop sitting there looking like a whipped cur. Harry had to say something. He settled on, 'So I don't belong?' Lame, he thought, stating the bleedin' obvious, certainly, despite having attempted to disguise the fact by putting an edge to his voice.

Dumaresq didn't deign to notice. 'Yes,' he said. 'But not for the reasons you think.'

Suddenly Harry really did feel indignant: 'I volunteered for this. I'm here to do my duty . . .' He was spluttering and he knew it. So much he wanted to say, and the words wouldn't come. Dumaresq leant forward, and in softer tones began to speak with measured gravity.

'There are certain things you must understand before you are much older, young Gilmour. And the first and foremost is this ship. She's only good for frightening natives. She's too slow, too old, and is about as manoeuvrable as a broad-beamed Pompey whore with gin aboard. She's a has-been. You take any of the modern capital ships on the Kriegsmarine's order of battle. *Redoubtable* can't catch them if she's chasing, and can't run away if she's being chased. She's vulnerable to air attack, and as our sister ship *Royal Oak* so tragically demonstrated, a sitting duck to submarines. *Redoubtable* is no longer a major fighting unit. She's a target. This war will be fought in the North Atlantic against the U-boats. Lots of small ships and aeroplanes and nasty little battles. In the Mediterranean, keeping Hitler away from the oil. Small ships and aeroplanes and nasty little battles. In the Channel, keeping the armies supplied until they turn Hitler back and break him once and for all. Lots of small ships and aeroplanes and nasty little battles. That's why the navy is going to need officers like you, and thousands more of you. To man the small ships, to have nasty little battles. The only thing *Redoubtable* and her type are going to be good for is being escorted to the enemy's back door just like we're doing up here, so she can lob bloody great shells at anyone silly enough to wander too close to the beach. And now we have to be escorted away again before the Luftwaffe or an *Unterseeboot* turns up and blows the arse out of us. Otherwise, all that *Redoubtable*'s fit for is sitting in Scapa, grounding on her corned beef tins.'

Dumaresq sat back as if to regard the impact of his words, while Harry contemplated the image of 'Jack' throwing generations of corned beef tins overboard until the ship itself was resting on the pile.

Dumaresq took a folded sheet of paper from his pocket. 'So what are you doing in this museum then, Gilmour?' he asked. 'When there's a bloody war to be won?'

Harry spluttered, 'You've got a damn cheek!'

Dumaresq laughed and offered Harry the sheet.

'One of the advantages of being in a staff job is that you get to see all the signal traffic first. That there,' he gestured to the paper, 'came through while we were under sailing orders at Scapa. I brought it with me in the hope I might find someone for whom it might be of some use.'

Harry ran his eye over the paper. It was to be posted on ships' notice boards, a request for any junior officers interested in an accelerated training programme to make them proficient in celestial navigation. Harry suddenly felt his heart pounding. This wasn't a class on basic coast-hugging, the stuff he'd picked up crewing on rich men's yachts. This was real, this was deep-sea stuff, the stuff that would take you round the world. He would at last be able to use that sextant for what it was meant, instead of just shooting church steeples and lighthouses. The one Sir Alexander Scrimgeour had given him when he signed up to become a sailor. Harry looked up at Dumaresq, who had a little conspiratorial smile playing about his eyes.

'As you rightly surmised, young Gilmour, you are in deep trouble with the Commander. Very serious trouble. So my advice to you, as a former "Snotty" myself, who came up the hard way, is that you head him off. Now I want you to listen to me very carefully.'

Chapter Three

Harry stood on the Portsmouth Harbour station jetty and watched the Gosport ferry chug through the April drizzle towards him. It was getting late – 20:00 hours – and the wet gloom was giving way to proper darkness. Two old First World War vintage V & W-class destroyers wallowed, lashed together out in the fairway off Burrow Island, and a motor gunboat puttered in the distance, angling in towards the base proper, obscured behind North Corner. On the skyline, the masts of HMS *Victory* and their tangle of rigging stood out against the lowering sky. To seaward, a low clag of sullen cloud hung over Fort Blockhouse and The Point, retreating to merge with the narrow band of sea that was visible from where Harry stood. At his feet was the oily wash of the harbour, sluggish, moving the harbour crap with a slothful languor that Harry found almost mesmerising. There was little of interest within Britain's premier naval base on this night, but looking at what there was took his mind off the events of the past two weeks.

The ferry nudged up to the jetty in a welter of churned water and the gangway was shoved aboard to allow less than a dozen sailors, buttoned up in macs and toting kitbags, to disembark. When they'd filed off, Harry quickly adjusting his collar against the rain, hefted his own kit and joined the small gaggle of dockyard workers going aboard. Until now, it had only been by concentrating on the small and the mundane that Harry found he could cope with life, but as the little ferry nosed away from the Portsmouth pier, he started picking over the events that had propelled him here.

Harry had indeed listened to what Peter Dumaresq had told him in the wardroom of HMS *Redoubtable*, in that other lifetime. He had gone back to his cabin and completed his transfer request, careful to employ all the phrases dictated by the Flag Lieutenant. He had personally handed it to the Leading Writer in the Commander's office, before going on watch again.

Events had moved swiftly after that. Harry had expected a summons to see Commander Maitland over his handling of the damage-control party once *Redoubtable* had cleared the Norwegian coast and rejoined the covering force. And he expected it to be rough. He was not alone. One of the other Subs who shared his cabin, and who was not as resolutely hostile as some, had grimly commiserated: 'At school we used to tell chaps up before the Head to stuff a *Collected Shakespeare* down the arse of their flannels. But I fear the Bloke might be going to hit you with something a bit more substantial than a cane, old chap.'

When the first Lieutenant came for him to deliver the expected summons, he was curt, precise and scrupulously polite. Not a trace of his customary flowery abuse. It boded ill. All the pre-prepared constructions Harry carried in his head on how to play this were shouldered aside by the nausea-inducing vision of how his parents would react to his court martial. His remote, austere, academic teacher father – his wholly, resolutely pacifist father – would find Harry's disgrace comic. Harry could almost hear his low, sardonic laughter. And his mother? Her solace and endless understanding would be much worse.

His mind was so a-swim he didn't even notice that the first Lieutenant, after delivering the summons, had immediately swerved away, heading for the wardroom bar, showing no intention of accompanying him to the Commander's lair, as would have been the case if some formal ambush awaited him. In fact, so circumspect had the first Lieutenant been, that instead of Harry's departure from the wardroom being followed by gallows-stares from the assembled officers, no one noticed him slip out to go and face his destiny.

The triviality of his offence, in the real world, compared to its gravity seen through the prism of military discipline, had brought a stasis to his thought processes. He entered the Commander's ante-room and told the Leading Writer who he was. The sailor had risen at once to rap and then push open the door, announcing, 'Sub-Lieutenant Gilmour here to see you, sir'. He remembered hearing 'Send him in', and then himself squeezing past, still not yet ready to face the Commander; thinking to himself, almost panicky, what do I do now? A voice in his head answered, Come smartly to attention and snap off a salute. He was already at attention, his right arm on the point of rising, before he saw that the Commander was not wearing a cap. Naval custom dictated that he could not salute, must not salute, as the Commander, not wearing a cap, could not return it. Harry stilled his arm.

The shock of such a close shave with yet another naval indiscretion stopped Harry from noticing at first that there weren't any other officers in the Commander's tight little cubby. He saw a tidy, compact space filled with a desk, and behind it, the angular, doom-laden scowl of the Commander, who looked a little too big for the cabin. On the blotter in front of him was Harry's transfer request.

Later, Harry remembered being told to sit down and take his cap off. After that there had been no preamble. The Commander just launched right into him.

31

'Our nation is in a war for its very survival,' he said. 'HMS *Redoubtable* and her crew, the only thing allowing them to function as a fighting unit, in wartime, at any time, is discipline. There is a lot of rot talked about discipline. Rot. The truth, the essence, the only thing anyone has to understand is the rigid responsibility of officers, and their insistence on all duties being carried out in a military fashion, by all the crew, at all times. Nothing else matters. Failure to understand that and comply can lead to only one consequence: defeat.'

And then a pause. Harry remembered the pause, dropped in as if to underline the fact that the ideal had just been nailed to the mast. It was a pause in which the Commander's baleful gaze announced his disappointment.

He then began to tick off the long list of Harry's failings; exactly how he'd failed to measure up to 'the requirements of the service'. Chief among them was Harry's almost stubborn inability to comprehend the concept of 'in a naval fashion'.

But after that the lash went out of his voice, and this gave Harry hope. Everything seemed to point to clemency: the softening of the tone; the fact that the Commander was bare-headed, behind his desk, and no one else was present. Could the Commander's rant be 'more in sorrow than in anger'? A good wigging, then his request for transfer to the navigation class to be approved? There was a moment of relief before the other possibility occurred to Harry: that this wasn't a 'let's clear the air and start again' moment; this was in fact Pontius Pilate speaking. The Commander was washing his hands of Harry. The realisation came as a thump.

He'd felt as if a void had opened up beneath him; that the Commander was not only about to tear up his transfer request . . . he had decided Harry's conduct had been far more grievous than he was prepared to, or indeed competent enough to, adjudicate on himself, and that Harry was about to be passed up the chain of retribution, to be dealt with by a higher authority. A flash of the woodcut of Admiral Byng being executed aboard his flagship after his failure to defend Menorca from the French in 1756 passed before Harry's gaze. If they could shoot Byng *pour encourager les autres*, what might they not do to a sloppy Sub-Lieutenant? The Commander fingered Harry's transfer request, seemingly lost in thought.

In fact, the Commander appreciated the Royal Navy's urgent, nay, chronic need for junior officers. He understood that it could only be met by cramming civilians through a sausage machine, and he was resigned to the fact that, one day, in an indeterminate future, many of those hostilities-only officers would end up aboard the service's major fighting ships. That one day they might even command. But what the Commander did not understand was any need to accelerate that process. He had no doubt this war was going to last as long as the last one. Plenty of time for those wavy-navy chaps to learn the ropes in smaller ships. Yet they had foisted this hapless young man on to his ship, practically from his mother's tit. The lower deck had ragged him, the junior officers had ostracised him, and the Jimmy, the first Lieutenant, hadn't a clue what to do with him. The young man was utterly devoid of any kind of naval gumption. And then there was that bloody shambles with the fo'c'sle damage-control party.

Their lordships had sent this young man to the *Redoubtable* as an experiment and he'd ended up being made a fool of by that martinet Master-at-Arms and his coterie of favourites. They'd set the lad up for a fall. What a jolly jape! Except the Commander couldn't just leave it at that. Because it wasn't just that silly little bugger Gilmour who'd been the butt of their insubordination. It was *Sub-Lieutenant* Gilmour. Because it wasn't the man you saluted, it was the rank. When they stuck two fingers up to Harry, they did it to every officer in the *Redoubtable*. And that was conduct prejudicial to naval discipline, and in the face of the enemy to boot. It could not be allowed to pass.

Except that their lordships would be looking for progress reports on Sub-Lieutenant Gilmour, not to read his name in details of a court martial. They would be looking to read of the success of their experiment, to see how best to integrate this new caste of officer into the fighting strength of the fleet. Alas, the report that the Commander had been faced with writing was that Sub-Lieutenant Gilmour was in serious disciplinary doo-doo . . . right up until this little piece of paper had landed in his in-tray. No longer. A way out had presented itself.

From the moment he'd picked up Gilmour's request, the Commander had wondered who had written it for him. It certainly wasn't his own work. There had been a seasoned hand behind it. And for that, the Commander was truly grateful. With this request he could now salvage the reputation of HMS *Redoubtable*, her wardroom and his own career. Sub-Lieutenant Gilmour was seeking advancement, and to achieve it meant he must leave this ship. The Commander was not about to stand in his way. He could then deal with the Jaunty in his own good time.

Harry, of course, suspected none of this. After his royal dressing-down, he had emerged from the Commander's office having suffered nothing further than a homily on how he must apply himself more diligently to the cultivation of officer qualities, and an assurance that his transfer had been approved. His necessary orders would be cut and awaiting him here in this office, the minute *Redoubtable* had picked up the buoy in Scapa.

Meanwhile, the war went on. On the run south, stories of their 'battle' were told again and again. Harry remembered the unreality of listening to the talk; a battle that he had undoubtedly been in, but personally knew nothing of. No one mentioned the German sailors on the end of those 'ruddy great dustbins'. Wonder as he might, Harry couldn't even begin to conjure what it must have been like for them. Their experience of this engagement must have been completely different from his. The whole war was like that. According to the BBC news, the army and RAF bods ashore in Norway were fighting toe-to-toe with Jerry. Yet, in what must inevitably be, sooner or later, the main theatre, in France, armies faced each other across defensive lines the likes of which the world had never seen, doing nothing, their air forces bombarding each other with leaflets. And here was Harry, one of the victors of probably the most significant naval engagement of the war so far, and what story did he have to tell? He hadn't even seen a Jerry yet, let alone prevailed against one. That fact, however, hadn't stopped him becoming the centre of attention when he'd finally pitched up at HMS *King Alfred* again two days ago.

Harry had gone ashore on the first crew launch after *Redoubtable* had entered Scapa. Safe in the inside pocket of his Number 1C jacket were his orders and a clutch of travel warrants authorising his progress all the way from Thurso railway station to the south coast – the length of Britain. A daunting journey at the best of times, but in wartime, a Homeric epic. It had taken over fifty hours, umpteen different trains, and endless battles with overworked, unhelpful RTO officers, who were camped out in every station for the sole purpose of ensuring that every man-jack in uniform was in possession of every necessary military authorisation for his, or her journey, in triplicate, and with every proper stamp that regulations required; with woe guaranteed to betide if you didn't, and sometimes even if you did.

And then finally he was there, exhausted. The broad, squat brick and concrete block on the seafront that had once been a local council leisure centre was now a ship, 'sailing' under RN colours as HMS *King Alfred*. It still dominated the promenade, towered over only by the tall Victorian terraces of St Aubyns Gardens, but the whole area was now much more militarised. The terrace's windows were zigzagged with white sticky tape to stop them shattering in bomb blasts; barbed wire roiled the beach. Sandbags sat in entrance doors. The two naval tailors were still there, though, right across the road from *King Alfred's* entrance, likely doing brisk business among the growing number of 'officers under training' beginning to come through.

It had been only a matter of months since Harry had 'graduated', but the commandeered pavilion had become a different place when he walked back through its doors; a much busier, more organised place. He'd arrived as the cadets were finishing afternoon classes, the entire building filled with a surge of blue serge and, very young, pink, scrubbed and beaming faces.

And then at last he'd found himself standing in Captain Pelly's staff office, where everyone was far too busy to bother with the minutiae of his paperwork, and where a sprightly 60-something Lieutenant Commander told him to pack himself off to the Peverill Guest House where a hot bath and a bed was waiting, and to report back here at 08.30. As Harry had turned to leave, the older man, obviously First World War vintage and here for training purposes only, had called after him.

'You're just posted from *Redoubtable?*' He was squinting at Harry's orders, held three inches from his nose. 'You were at Narvik.' It was more a statement than a question.

'Yes, sir,' said Harry.

'Bloody marvellous!' barked the old man, and lunged forward to pump his hand.

It was to be the first of many such encounters in Harry's short stay back at HMS *King Alfred*. He could take no pride in his brief celebrity, however. He was tired, but also being back had brought on an uneasy sense of dislocation and loneliness. Seeing the cadets – their camaraderie and bands of new-found friends – had rammed home how lonely the past few months had been; that, and his sense of loss, sharp and un-dealt with, over Clive Sells, his friend of three months and now no more.

Clive had been one of his band: there were seven of them back then in October 1939, all having joined up at the same time, arriving at *King Alfred* together: Clive, Jim, Gilbert, Howard, Zack, Ron and himself. All in the same division – eating, studying, square-bashing together – separate from the 'S' men, the yachties who had signed on to the navy's version of the TA years before. (They were all older, and kept to themselves; easy since they did only ten days refresher training before being bundled out to the fleet with their new commissions.)

Harry and his chums, all university boys and as confused as they were keen, with three months training ahead of them, had gravitated together. Gilbert, taller than the rest, whom for weeks had been forced to turn out on parade still wearing the pinstripe trousers from his days as a stock-jobber in the City before someone could find him a uniform; Zack, the Manchester Jew, with his exotic olive skin and matinee-idol looks, who wasn't safe from womenkind on their infrequent runs ashore; Jim and Ron, the engineering students from the Midlands, whose life-maintenance skills left a lot to be desired; Clive, like Harry the son of a teacher, an amiable, easy-going lad whose rugby prowess had already attracted the attention of team selectors; and Howard, the son of a gentleman farmer from Hampshire, whose artistry with an iron made all their shirts presentable. A tight bond of friendship had formed among them as each in turn had their first encounters with naval discipline, the rigours of training, and the unforgiving eye of Chief Petty Officer Vass, HMS *King Alfred's* senior training NCO.

They had all passed out eventually. Gilbert got a billet in Whitehall which was never quite explained. Jim, Howard and Ron went to minesweepers, Zack to a motor gunboat, and Clive, poor Clive, to an armed trawler; dead now, somewhere off the Blackwater Estuary, blown to pieces by a German mine within sight of Mersea Island; and Harry, the experiment, to that bloody battleship.

On his way to his berth in the boarding house, Harry had gone to look at the vast boarded-over swimming pool which had become the main hall for HMS *King Alfred* before he left for the night; it was there that the drills and the lectures and the exercises happened, and it was where, on the first day, the entire intake had filled the hall, standing to attention, as they recited the Royal Navy's prayer for the first time.

'O Eternal Lord God, who alone spreadest out the heavens and rulest the raging of the sea; who hast compassed the waters with bounds until the day and night come to an end; Be pleased to receive into thy Almighty and most gracious protection the persons of us thy servants and the fleet in which we serve . . .'

Every echo of levity and youthful cynicism had evaporated before those words, delivered in a deep bellow that filled the vast space of the main hall. And in their place came the sobering sense that here, now, each and every one of them was being assumed into a great and noble enterprise; the humbling realisation that it was now their turn to share and shoulder the full majesty of that unbroken tradition, and with it, the first sense of just what it would mean to hold a commission in His Britannic Majesty's Royal Navy in time of war. He had felt a pricking behind his eyes then, and he felt it again, now.

The next day he was in Commander Granville's office. Granville, the 62-year-old destroyer Captain, and veteran of numerous scraps with Jerry in the 'last lot', was all paternal smiles. Harry remembered him well enough. Hard not to. He was Captain Pelly's second-in-command. But unlike Pelly, Granville always seemed to be everywhere. You knew Pelly was there, Harry recalled, even if you didn't see his ponderous, imposing features about the 'deck' very often . . . oh, and that was another thing you had to remember. To an outsider this might be a pavilion, but the navy called it a ship; when you went through the door, you weren't inside, you were 'on board', and what you walked on was no longer a floor, but 'the deck'. Pelly had that way of stamping his presence on the place without you actually having to see him. Granville, on the other hand, was always appearing round the corner. He was a tall, skin-and-bone creature with a pointy nose to match the point of his thinning, greying hairline and a smooth, chamois-like skin that looked as if it had worn well despite adverse weather conditions. He was never seen without his uniform jacket and a perfectly knotted black tie, and his shoes were so polished it was said that if he was standing close enough you could look up a Wren's skirt in them. When he passed, it was always in a whirl of wise advice and un-forced bonhomie. But he had a knowing edge: always keeping his eye on the cadets and the instructors alike. Minding the shop, in other words.

'Sit down, sit down.' Granville gestured to one of the metal and canvas chairs on the other side of his equally functional metal desk.

The office was cluttered with filing cabinets and paper piles, and decorated with a class timetable chart and several enemy aircraft identification posters. The desk offered no concession to Granville's personal life. In tray, out tray, three phones, and beneath Harry's file, a blotter. The pens and pencils were in an old Ovaltine tin.

Granville opened the file. Gilmour, Harris John. Born, Dunoon, Argyll, 19 May 1920. (Harry had been named by his parents after the island where he'd been conceived. Many a time growing up, Harry had thanked every god he didn't believe in that they hadn't chosen Rhum, Eigg or Muck as their favourite Western Isles holiday destination.)

Educated at Dunoon Grammar School and the University of Glasgow. An undergraduate MA student, Humanities. Abandoned his studies before entering second year to volunteer for service as an officer in the RNVR. An only child. Father, a teacher, head of modern languages at Dunoon Grammar. Mother, a housewife.

Granville remembered Harry well enough. There had been a few who had stood out at the beginning. Now the fresh faces passing through tended to blend together. Anyway, here he was again, with a battle under his belt, and complete with that look. The look the ones still under training didn't have. It had always been thus, he supposed. He certainly remembered it himself, all the way back to the last lot; young sailors returning from their first operation. Didn't matter what their role had been; standing on the bridge amid shot and shell, or cowering under the mess deck table, counting out wound dressings. It always showed, like an excessive leeway. As if they had been pushed off course and had yet to apply a corrective helm.

'You were at Narvik, I see,' he said with a warm smile.

'Yes, sir.'

'Splendid effort by all involved. Congratulations, Mr Gilmour. And well done.'

'Thank you, sir.'

Granville smiled at Harry approvingly. At least the young chap had learned brevity. For step one in the making of an officer was curing the little sods of the need to endlessly explain themselves. He eyed Harry appraisingly. A striking-looking young man, exactly the sort you remembered. Silly flop of hair though, needed cutting; far too affected for a junior officer of such negligible significance. But it wasn't the look of him that had made this Gilmour fellow stick in Granville's mind. Unlike many who had and would pass through here, Gilmour hadn't been a moaner, more a jolly-along type. Granville was fond of ear-wigging telling chatter from his constant patrolling of the halls and messes. It was a technique he used, listening for the phrase that would define somebody. In Gilmour's case there was no phrase. It was where he turned up. Granville had noticed that if anyone was falling behind, Gilmour had a knack of turning up, scooping them up and bundling them along.

Three months was a long time in a hothouse place like this. If you kept your ear to the ground and your eyes open, you could learn a lot about a cadet. Get a feel, not only for his character, but for how his fellows reacted to him. Gilmour had been the one his fellow cadets turned to for advice, had talked to; been a listener. Nothing major in itself but a handy attribute for a leader of men, if all the other attributes were there too.

Granville referred to the file. Written work: good. Concise. Gets to the heart of problems quickly, able to articulate workable solutions quicker. Good, but not entirely uncommon. A nice chap, Granville remembered thinking at the time, but if he was going to make a good officer he was going to have to get used to not being liked all the time.

'Your request to join this special navigation class . . .' said Granville, opening proceedings proper, '. . . let's see. Approved by your former captain, signed by the Commander.' A pause, and then a growing, knowing smirk. 'Now what does he say? *An unusually enterprising officer . . . but one whose talents and zeal find little outlet under the necessary routine of a capital ship.* Good grief, Mr Gilmour, whatever did you do?'

Harry thought of coming clean, but Peter Dumaresq had been very specific on that point. 'I cannot think, sir.'

Granville let his eye flick to the single wavy line of gold on Harry's sleeves. 'I can. But not to worry, where you will be going the beggars won't be choosers. Now, I take it someone has spoken to you about the exact nature of this posting?'

'No, sir.' Harry was getting to like this monosyllabic cut and thrust. It made life so much easier when talking to big shots like a Commander.

'I beg your pardon?'

'No, sir.'

'Well that's . . . unusual. They should have. Before putting everyone to a lot of trouble just to have you get here, blanch, make your excuses and leave. It's submarines,' said Granville flatly.

'Submarines, sir?'

Harry felt a distinct loosening in his innards. He had never thought about submarines, had never seen one in real life. He knew nothing about them, except that they were cramped and smelly; everyone knew they were very dangerous and prone to killing their crews in any number of particularly nasty ways. The obscene news-reel shots of the stern of the new T-class submarine HMS *Thetis* sticking out of the waters of Liverpool Bay, sunk in a stupid accident just over a year before, were fresh in everyone's mind. *Thetis*, bow down in the mud 150 feet below the surface, stern in the bright fresh air, with rescue craft fussing around her while ninety-nine men suffocated inside their steel coffin. Harry had refused to dream about where the navigation class might take him, lest he tempted fate. He hadn't, in so many words, said the word *destroyer*. But to be punished so, for daring to dream!

'Their Lordships are expanding the submarine service. They need properly qualified officers as a matter of urgency,' said Granville, still smiling, despite being conscious of Harry's shock. 'Of course, you would have to undergo certain acclimatisation pro-cedures, so the submariners could see if you measure up.'

'Measure up, sir?'

'That you don't get claustrophobic, can stand the smell of sixty pairs of sweaty socks, and are imbued with the right amount of piratical spirit as is permissible in a Royal Navy officer. In return, Mr Gilmour, I think the service can guarantee you all the action any young man of adventurous spirit might crave. After all, submarines don't do convoy escort or harbour patrols. They only go in one direction. Into the enemy's back yard.'

And often never come out again, thought Harry.

'Do you wish for some time to consider this, Mr Gilmour?'

Bloody hell. A long day and night spent brooding lay ahead if he said he wanted more time. And what if his nerve should fail him and he withdrew his request? All this for nothing. The thoughts winged through his head too fast for him to properly conjure up the moment of his own drowning in a dark oily steel casket, far from the surface and the waves and sky. All he could see was himself walking back into the wardroom of HMS *Redoubtable*.

'If I say yes now, sir, I can go on the celestial navigation course? I get to do that?'

'Subject to you not proving overly offensive to the submariners, yes.'

'Then I don't need to think it over, sir. I want my request to go ahead.'

The Commander smiled a crinkly, satisfied smile. 'Excellent,' he said, thinking, No faffing about there. Then, after more consideration, You're still just a boy, but you'll do.

And that was how Harry came to be walking up the gangway of the Gosport ferry on a drizzly spring night, heading for HMS *Dolphin*, the shore establishment headquarters of the Royal Navy Submarine Service.

Chapter Four

The three of them stood by what was little more than a plank, which extended from the jetty over the bloated belly of a submarine on to its preposterously narrow steel deck. Sub-Lieutenants Brown, Hardesty RN and Gilmour RNVR, in their dark-blue watch jackets, hats perched jauntily on heads; all identical, save for the geometry of the single rings on their jacket sleeves; mufflers against the early morning chill. Brown stood ostentatiously apart and Hardesty sort of tried to bridge the gap between him and Harry, who was sat on a bollard opposite the plank. No one spoke.

Harry, now heartily sick of this RN posturing, had his gaze fixed on his very first submarine, in all its gimcrack glory. She was an old girl, another legacy of the last lot. *H57*. No name, just the number, and she did look very very small, and not a little shabby.

They had been told to report to her at 06.15 sharp for their mandatory 'acclimatisation' dive. No point in them signing up, going through the six-week training programme only to shove off on their first patrol, and then find they had the screamin' hab-dabs the minute they shut the lid. Or so said a rather lugubrious Lieutenant with a leather fist for a left hand and a scorched left face, who'd met Harry when he walked through the door at HMS *Dolphin*, briefed him on where he was expected the next day, pointed him to where he could disturb a steward into doing up 'a couple of wedges, and a mug of tea', and then directed him to his billet for the night.

Harry had arrived in the dark at HMS *Dolphin*, and had no perspective on the place until his walk down to the jetties. In daylight, the whole place looked lashed up. An encampment whose occupants had just arrived and did not intend to stay. HMS *Dolphin*, née Fort Blockhouse, was an old fort, and from where they stood now tucked in behind its bastions, the jetties abutting a little kiss-curl of oily water, it was like looking out through the mouth of a victim of chronic tooth decay. The glorious sunlight of a beautiful spring morning, the gulls soaring overhead, had to be viewed through a foreground of rusty cranes, open workshops and random little collections of stores that disappeared up the sides of sheds of varying vintage. The dockyard workers' morning shift had yet to start and the deserted area seemed the epitome of neglect. Certainly, it was far from 'military'. And the submarines themselves didn't help. None possessed the majesty and presence that one might expect from a king's ship.

There were several different shapes and sizes of submarines in the creek. But this boat – his boat – was by far the relic of the gang, and none held his attention more. She looked, on the surface, barely more than 150 feet long, her deck pocked with symmetrical holes and a recessed hatch arrangement which seemed to pose a danger rather than any useful function. Her flanks angled out to saddles running along either beam. Smooth, wen-like protrusions, looking for all the world like afterthoughts. And behind the gun was a tacked-on oval bridge structure with a thin, bevelled steel cowl on top, sheltering its fore-end before appearing to be bitten off and replaced by a run of stanchions. Poking out were the periscope housings and a steel mount, probably for the submarine's anti-aircraft Lewis gun. She looked like a designed-by-committee tub, and she was going to take him on his first voyage beneath the waves.

He was thinking, What have I done? when suddenly a face leant over the little bridge a bare few feet above them. A grinning youth with an impossibly battered watch cap perched in a distinctly un-regulation fashion on the back of his blonde locks – locks being the first word that came to Harry's mind to describe this chap's hair.

'Morning gentlemen!' he boomed. He was wearing a white polo-neck pullover and no insignia of rank. 'Brown, Hardesty and Gilmour, all aboard for the skylark, eh? I'm Andy Trumble, the Jimmy. Nice and early chaps, the Skipper will be pleased.'

As *H57*'s first Lieutenant addressed them, the forward hatch swung open and a string of sailors in similar pullovers, bell-bottoms, and ratings' caps, ribbons embroidered with 'HM Submarines' came bustling on to the deck, heading for the mooring lines. Another head appeared on the bridge, fresh-faced and suspiciously young to be looking so grumpy.

'You lot!' he barked at Harry and his chums. 'Stop standing about looking spare and get ready to cast off fore and aft!'

The Skipper, Harry concluded. Did Skippers really come so young?

Sub-Lieutenants Brown and Hardesty looked aghast, but Harry, used to taking barked orders from his years on a yacht's deck, turned and ran along the jetty towards the after end of *H57*. He was already bending to the bollards as her Skipper yelled, 'Single up on springs, fore and aft!' The springs were the lines running from the bow to the shore bollards at the after end of the sub, and from her stern to the shore bollards opposite her bow; the tension in them prevented her ballast tanks surging forwards and backwards off the brickwork. The other lines held the submarine hull snug against the jetty. Harry had bent to free the after line, ready to throw it aboard, when he noticed the two ratings who had come aft were doing exactly that from aboard *H57*. Harry realised they were going to cast the line ashore. Well, there was a thing; they didn't take their mooring lines with them on submarines. But there was no time to argue. Not under the watchful eye of *H57*'s Skipper, who would no doubt be making an assessment of their conduct once the day was over.

Harry caught the after line and was coiling it down before Hardesty had even begun to move to the forward line. Brown on the other hand, seemed rooted to the spot, a scowl on his face. Harry could see the mental turmoil behind his eyes: an officer being expected to personally handle lines? Could such an order have been given? *H57* was now secured only by the fore and aft springs. Hardesty caught the fore line and coiled it so that now only the aft spring ran from his bollard, towards the stern of *H57*. The Skipper yelled again, 'Cast off after spring!'

It was obvious to an old yacht-hand like Harry what the Skipper intended now: to go slow ahead against the tension on the for'ard spring, to swing out his stern, and then back off the berth. Hardesty looked flummoxed, and turned to Harry, who mouthed to him silently, 'You're on.' Hardesty immediately bent to take up the slack as the two ratings from the after end walked back the spring, and threw it to him. While this manoeuvre was being performed, the black-scowling countenance of the Skipper swung towards Brown. 'Don't just stand there! Get aboard if you're coming!'

Brown, stung, skipped up the gangway. Hardesty, once he'd coiled down the spring, ran to follow him, and it was with a feeling of deep inner contentment that Harry came behind in a series of long strides and pulled the gangway smartly ashore. The Skipper, looking down, grinned at him, then raised his eyebrows in a question. Under his gaze, Harry stood opposite the two ratings on the deck aft.

With his big grin expanding, the Skipper yelled, 'Cast off for'ard!'

One of the ratings, with a deft underarm lob, passed the spring across the widening gap to Harry as *H57*'s hull was swinging out. Harry gave it a turn round the dockside bollard, stepped smartly along the jetty to where the bow still touched, and leapt nimbly on to his first submarine.

'Welcome aboard, Mr Gilmour!' said the smirking Skipper, with a leisurely salute, to which Harry made a smart return. The Skipper turned and called down into the submarine's bowels, 'Motors half astern together!' and Harry felt a tug as the submarine gathered way, moving astern, out into the harbour fairway.

Grins all round as he was ushered by the sailors down into the maw of the for'ard hatch. One of the older ratings murmured, 'Very seaman-like, sir, if you don't mind me saying.' Harry didn't mind at all. Then he was in the submarine, and there were other things to consider.

His first impression was that she was not as cramped as he had feared. Even a tall chap like himself could stand upright. But she seemed narrow. The next impression was how bright she was inside; there was a positive glare from the deckhead light fittings. There was the clang of the for'ard hatch closing behind him and he was ushered aft along the tunnel-like interior, following the back of a sailor, watching how to negotiate the several watertight bulkhead doors – no more than shoulder-width holes – copying him crouching and then swinging himself feet first through the gap. There was a blur of bunks, curtains and storage spaces, and everywhere ran pipes and cable runs, junction boxes and inspection panels, all but masking the bright white-painted steel of the hull's interior. There was even linoleum on the deckplates, he briefly noted; the thought flashing into his head that you could walk about in your socks without too much discomfort. And then they were in the control room, and that was where Harry's heart sank.

He stood upright, and to his left, so close he could have whispered in his ear, sat a po-faced rating of indeterminate age, dressed in uniform dark-blue overalls, tucked in behind a console bolted to the bulkhead. The rating clutched a small brass wheel, a miniature of a traditional ship's wheel. A large pipe dropped down from the deckhead with a flared speaking trumpet affair welded on to its upturned end, half obscuring the rating's face. Beside the man was another miniature; this time of a ship's telegraph, the two handles ready to signal and respond to all the traditional commands writ small on its face: 'Full Ahead', 'Slow Ahead', 'Astern'. The full list anyone familiar with a bridge of any sort would recognise. There was a scaled-down compass head too. Harry stared at the man, horrified. Not by him personally, or indeed the Lilliputian displays he was controlling, but by the chaos he could perceive in the periphery of his vision.

As he slowly turned to take it all in, he was aware of a small space no bigger than a car garage. Behind the rating at the wheel sat two more men, facing the hull. Except you could not see the hull, hidden as it was by two huge glass indicator gauges. Lesser versions cluttered around them, filling the spaces up to where the cable and pipe runs began, tracing the length of the compartment. These extended over the deckhead. The ratings sat in front of two more wheels, looking more like bicycle wheels.

In the middle of the compartment were two huge brass tubes, one behind the other, coming down from the deckhead and disappearing into holes in the deck at his feet. Between them stood Trumble, the Jimmy, holding on to a vertical ladder that disappeared up through another, more commodious hole. Behind him was a rather delicate scaled-down version of a chart table, surmounted and surrounded by docket holes and miniature cupboards. The array covered the after bulkhead, its door open, through which Harry was aware of the work of the rest of the crew carrying on apace.

The port side of the compartment, however, was where the true horror lay. Rank upon rank of valve wheels, control levers, a huge fuse panel, and a cats' cradle of pipework of wildly varying dimensions, woven in and out of the faces of indicator dials, all nestled snug to the hull like the boundary of some jungled sunflower plantation made of steel, brass and glass. Another rating, with an oily rag stuffed into his blue overalls, stood over it proprietorially.

Harry experienced a sure and certain conviction that the mastering of this machine would be forever beyond him. He felt a familiar hopelessness well up to engulf him.

The Jimmy beamed with that repulsive, relaxed air born of familiarity with one's surroundings and the confidence it brings: 'Flummoxed by the mooring lines, eh? We don't tend to stow 'em aboard if we can help it. We've got boxes on deck for 'em, but one good rattle from a depth charge close aboard and the box'd be sprung; they'd be wafting about wrapping themselves round the prop and the planes before you'd know it.'

The Jimmy paused to dazzle him with another grin, then: 'Your chums are topside with the Skipper, so it's a bit crowded. Stay down here and I'll show you what's what . . . cuppa to be going on with?'

Harry moved across the control room gingerly, so as not to touch anything, fearing that even to snag a lever on his jacket might send them all plunging down into the depths. 'Yes please,' he replied, as he squeezed past the periscopes to bend himself into the nook made by the chart table beyond.

The Jimmy yelled through the aft door: 'Snobell, make that another char please!'

A muffled 'Aye, aye' was cut short by a tremendous explosion. Harry's heart stopped and he gripped the chart table until it hurt. No air entered his lungs. The explosion was followed by another in rapid succession, which instantly retreated into a full-throated percussive roar. Harry was aware of muffled commands coming down the voice-pipe to the rating on the miniature ship's wheel. Harry was also aware of a gale coming down the hatch into which the vertical ladder disappeared.

The Jimmy must have noticed Harry's alarm. 'That's the diesels starting up,' he said. 'Noisy buggers, aren't they? That wind is them sucking in air. You know, to feed the combustion.'

Harry attempted a smile and nodded, trying to give the air of someone all too familiar with the physics of internal combustion engines – and failing.

'We came out the creek arse-end first, on our electric motors,' the Jimmy continued. 'Easier to manoeuvre. Less racket.' Seeing Harry still looking unconvinced, he added: 'We're in the fairway now. So that's us on main engines, both ahead, and out into the Solent.' A pause, then he gestured round the compartment: 'As you probably gathered' – Harry hadn't – 'this is the control room. I know. It's all a bit strange and alarming at first. A lot to take in. But you'll get used to it in no time.'

Then the tea arrived.

Harry hadn't 'gathered' anything because his mind had been swamped by impressions. He leant against the chart table, steadying himself as *H57* began to ride the swell, cupping his tea and reluctant to open his mouth.

'What do you know about submarines then, Mr Gilmour?' the Jimmy asked.

'Ah. Um.' Harry decided to stop before he made a prat of himself to this open-faced, friendly chap before him. 'Nothing, sir,' he said, thinking, If he's the Jimmy, he's probably a Lieutenant, so give him his title.

'Call me Andy,' the Jimmy said. 'We're too small to stand on ceremony down here. Except the Skipper. The Skipper is always "sir". So, where shall we start?' He gestured towards the rating at the ship's wheel. 'That's the helmsman. Steers the boat. But then even you'll know that! Ha-ha! Two chaps behind him are on the for'ard and aft hydroplanes. The hydroplanes are those overgrown table tennis bats you saw bolted on to the outside of the hull. Once we dive they get extended and act like aeroplane wings, sort of horizontal rudders, a few deft twiddles on the wheels by Ahearn and Hannah here' – the two ratings turned and smiled at Harry, an unheard of gesture aboard that bloody battleship – 'and we're nose down, arse up and swooping away like an underwater ballet dancer. Aren't we?'

One of the ratings yelled above the noise of the diesel, '*Swan Lake* ain't in it, Mr Trumble!'

'Petty Officer Ahearn is notorious for his deftness of twiddle,' Harry's new friend, Lieutenant Andy Trumble, confided to him. He pointed to the brass tubes. 'Eyes of the boat. The main periscope, thick as a drainpipe, capable of swivelling all round, and up and down, giving panoramic vistas of sea, shore and sky. We use it for checking who's up there when we're down here, thinking about going up there. Use for navigation in shore, all that stuff. And that's the attack periscope, with all the latest sighting and bearing notches to tell you where and how far; and thin as a whippet's prick, guaranteed never to be spotted by even the most eagle-eyed lookout.

'And over there', he gestured to the steel sunflowers, and the sailor with the oily rag in his overalls. 'That's Petty Officer McKeown. Our "outside ERA", otherwise known as "the Wrecker". The engine-room artificer who gets to work in the comfort of the control room, instead of back there among the din and grease, isn't that right, Mac?'

'All this luxury? I could be getting ideas above my station, sir,' said McKeown. There was an Irish brogue behind the smile. McKeown was older than Harry, as were all the other sailors he'd so far encountered aboard. As in *Redoubtable*, they were all obviously regular RN. Except there was something more self-possessed about these men. None of them was anything special to look at, or out of the ordinary. Same set of faces you'd encounter on a bus anywhere. But there was a seriousness of purpose, and an air of competency that he had not noticed among the huddled, dragooned masses of *Redoubtable*'s mess decks. Harry recognised this difference with a thrill.

'Mac works that pleasing little confection of valves and levers you see there,' grinned Trumble. 'They operate the main vents and compressed air blow valves. Those are the devices that take us down, and bring us up. Do you know the principles of how it . . .? No. I can see from your horrified stare.'

Andy turned and slipped a notepad on to the chart table, flipped it open and quickly drew a profile and a plan view of a submarine's hull. 'This sausage-shaped tube is the pressure hull. That's where we live, sealed up and snug. All the rest of the hull is open to the sea. These bulges along the length of the hull are the main ballast tanks. They are permanently open to the water below, and have a series of control vents along the top. When we want to dive, we open the top vents to let the air out and the water fill up the tanks. We lose buoyancy and sink. Simple.

'Now, all along here, and here,' Andy said, stabbing at little boxes he had drawn along the keel, 'are the trim tanks. All those valves there control the water in those tanks, and together with the hydroplanes we can keep the boat on the level when submerged. That's my job and Mac's job. Skippers get very irate if we don't keep trim. It's very disconcerting for the crew if we suddenly find ourselves plunging to the depths. Equally, it's very embarrassing if you suddenly start going up, and end up wallowing on the surface like a breeched whale. Especially if there's a Jerry up there looking for you. Red faces all round. So we have to watch out for the balance of the boat shifting, people moving about fore and aft can do it. Any movement of weight. Firing a torpedo plays hell with the trim. One of those two-ton buggers shooting out the front end means we have to compensate at the arse . . . actually they're nearer one and a half tons, but what's eight hundredweights between friends? Anyway, to compensate, you have to bring the water in at the bow into the torpedo-operating tanks to replace the difference in weight between a tube with a torpedo in it, which would be your "trim" when you started, and a tube that is now full of just water, which actually isn't much, but enough to screw your trim . . . and bloody quick too, Mr Gilmour or else! Especially with a salvo. You could be twenty degrees bow up and on the roof before you could say "I've lost the bubble" . . . and Jerry would be having a good pop at you before you could regain. Follow? The rest of the time, for everyday ups and downs, we use those valves to pump water from one tank to another to keep her in balance; in other words, in trim?'

Harry wasn't so sure but he grinned anyway: 'Sounds really easy.'

'Falling off a log, old chap,' said Trumble with a sardonic squint. There were suppressed grunts from the sailors. 'And for when we want to go down really fast, brakes off and arse in the air, there's this.' He stabbed at a big hole he'd sketched forward. 'Q tank. Five-hundred gallons of liquid lifesaver. We open the cocks on that, and we're gone.

'Now, when we want to come up, the Skipper yells Surface! And I inform Mac that the commanding officer wishes to take the air. He makes sure these levers on the control vents are shut, and then twiddles these valves here. That blows compressed air into the main ballast, forces the water out the bottom of the tanks, and up we go like a homesick angel. And that's the up and the down of it.'

Harry settled down to soak up the atmosphere of the control room as they chugged down the Solent. After a while he began thinking it might not be quite as intimidating as he'd thought, and had just started to relax when there was a commotion on the ladder. Brown, then Hardesty, clambered down into the control room, filling it to bursting. Andy leant back and yelled through the aft door, 'Snobell! Be a good fellow and park these gentlemen in the wardroom,' he said as he applied a palm to their backs and gently shoved the two Sub-Lieutenants aft. Harry made to follow, but Trumble's hand stopped him. Harry started to speak but was deafened by a klaxon going off in his ear. From above there was a booming voice: 'Diving Stations!'

The control room exploded into action. In quick succession, Trumble, with a surprisingly equal boom, repeated the order: 'Diving Stations!'

Two other ratings slipped into the control room. Mac was at his valves, arms moving in a flurry of twiddling. Indeed, everyone was twiddling. Then the racket from the engine room stopped abruptly. Two lookouts came tumbling down the ladder and there was a thump from above. The voice of the Skipper could be heard calling, 'One clip on! . . . two clips on!' The hatch was being shut. And then the Skipper too was in the control room, handing his binoculars to a rating who had appeared from nowhere.

Grinning at the Jimmy, he barked, 'Periscope depth, number one!'

Harry felt the boat begin to slip away from under his feet. Christ! he thought. This is it. We're diving! As they went, Ahearn and Hannah turned the hydroplane wheels. Harry watched the needle on the huge depth gauge creep slowly round, and was dimly aware of Andy Trumble giving further orders to Mac, who in turn was working the array of valves. Harry's mind, however, was out beyond the hull, imagining the sea around the submarine . . . what was it like? . . . marine life, fish, seals? Who knew what was out there? He fantasized what it would be like to see the water around the submarine. What the submarine would look like moving through it. His reverie was disturbed by the call: 'Thirty-five feet, sir!'

The Skipper said: 'Level off, bring her round to one-six-five. Group down, half ahead together.' Harry guessed one-six-five was the course, and half ahead, the speed. But 'group down'? Even the language was new.

The Skipper turned to him and held out his hand. 'Lieutenant Jeremy Penn, CO of His Majesty's Submarine *H57*. Gilmour, our very first wavy navy.' He pumped Harry's hand. 'And the only one who appears to know one end of a rope from another.' He turned away abruptly and with a gesture commanded, 'Up periscope!'

The big brass tube shot up with a hiss, revealing a complex sight and eyepiece. The Skipper popped down two handles and did a delicate little 360-degree pirouette. 'All clear up top.'

The Skipper began fixing *H57*'s position through the scope, which involved him calling out sightings: 'Nab Tower . . . the bearing is – that!' A Petty Officer stood behind him, calling the actual bearing off a bezel above Penn's head on the periscope stand. The process was repeated until the lines drawn on the chart crossed and *H57*'s position was fixed.

Penn then stood back from the scope and gestured to Harry: 'Want a quick look before we test the dockyard's handiwork?'

Harry stepped forward, his eyes wide. Penn's offer had been unexpected. This was straight out of a boyhood dream. It seemed almost too soon. The chance to look through a periscope was something that should have lain far in the future. Like a goal to be achieved, or an evolution to be undertaken after long training. To just step up and casually put his eye to the lens and look up from under the ocean seemed too sacred a ritual to entrust to someone like him, someone so inexperienced. But he didn't intend to let it pass, or even hesitate. He grabbed the handles and crouched to bring his eye level . . . at first he saw nothing, a plane of darkness, as he settled his eyes into the viewfinder, then the world leapt into his vision. First, the confusion of the slap of a wave against the lens, droplets, and then the ruffled surface of the sea. A low coast in the distance, two fishing boats rising into view, and dipping. The throat-catching excitement!

'That's the Isle of Wight,' said the Skipper, leaning in and turning one of the Bakelite knobs on the stand, 'and that is the sky. See any Jerries?'

In a flick Harry's view was rolling skywards and he was staring at high drifting clouds. Not even a gull was in sight, let alone a Jerry. He grinned like an idiot: 'All clear. No aircraft in sight.' His vision began to roll back.

'Aaaaand the Isle of Wight again. It's over a mile off, but if you wanted a better view, say, to look in a young lady's bathroom window, then all you do is . . .' Penn flicked another knob, and a beach, and a row of low bungalows leapt into view as if they were mere yards away. Crystal-clear. Harry was entranced, captivated by the clarity of the image and by the mesmerising slap of wavelets against the periscope's lens. He found himself eagerly wondering if he lowered the scope a few feet, he might actually see fishes swimming by, wishing he was a child again so he could ask to try it. But in the distance he heard someone say, 'A hundred and ten feet under the keel,' and his hand was removed from the handles.

'Interesting, isn't it?' said the Skipper, taking over the periscope, and sending it down again. He led Harry to the chart table and stabbed at a point that must have been five miles off a dot in the Solent with the name Nab Tower. 'It's an old Great War-era steel and concrete fort they built to guard the approaches to Portsmouth. The pongoes have it now . . .' Penn noticed Harry's confusion. 'The army. Coastal defence. We're heading to a deep water hole right here,' he said, and he stabbed at the chart again.

H57 began its run. Harry, lost in the mesmeric efficiency of the people and machine, had no idea how much time elapsed, and then there was a bark in his ear.

'Down periscope! Right, everyone! Beginning test run. Make your depth one hundred feet, steer one-nine-zero, group up, full ahead together.' He turned to Harry. 'We're going to carry out some bouncy underwater manoeuvres to make sure the port-forward hydroplane repairs have worked. Stay and watch if you want, but make sure you're hanging on to something!' He gave Harry a big grin, and then turned back with a sudden look of innocent excitement, like a child playing with his favourite toy. The incongruity, compared to Penn's hitherto stern mien, made Harry want to laugh out loud. This man was about to start having some serious fun.

For the next hour, *H57* plunged and rose and yawed, coming up to periscope depth, checking its position every few minutes on a bearing to Nab Tower, then diving away again. The hull strained and the engines surged. She lurched and she rolled. Orders were barked and responses noted. Her gyrations and course changes were scrupulously recorded, and another junior officer, staggering and bumping Harry with every leap and bound of the submarine, tried heroically to trace her convoluted course on the chart. Harry clung like grim death to anything that looked substantial enough to hold his weight. The babble of orders passed way over his head, and he quickly lost all notion of what was going on.

Not so the crew of *H57*, who fell to with a preternatural concentration, performing duties and tasks, without orders, their roles and responsibilities already understood. It felt good to be in their company as they worked with a sure and steady dedication to make *H57* perform to her Commander's will. And then suddenly it was all over.

The Skipper ordered, 'Midships! Group down! Half ahead. Make your depth thirty-five feet. Pilot, lay us a course to the trawler rendezvous. Mr Trumble, how long have we got?'

'Rendezvous is seventy-three minutes from now,' replied the Jimmy, checking his watch against one of the chronometers above the chart table. He glanced down. 'We've only got about two miles to run. Plenty of time to stooge around.'

'Jolly good,' said Penn, again turning to Harry. 'Enjoy that, Mr Gilmour? You were certainly grinning enough. Thought you were going to let out war whoops. Which would have been acceptable.' He laughed and slapped Harry on the arm.

'Yessir!'

'You probably want a little sit-down after that. Go back to the wardroom and get Snobell to sort you out with something. And send Flanagan and Allen up here,' he added, referring somewhat acerbically to the other two aspiring submarine officers, Brown and Hardesty. Harry had completely forgotten about them. 'I have to give them a shot on the toys too,' added Penn, with barely concealed resignation.

Brown and Hardesty sat ashen-faced in the little cubby-hole that passed for *H57*'s wardroom. Brown still gripped the table with white knuckles, Hardesty leaning on it as if breathless after some great exertion. Their eyes darted about, barely acknowledging Harry as he slid in beside them with a mug of steaming tea and a sardine sandwich. Brown got a whiff of it and looked as if he might retch.

'Skipper's asking for you chaps,' said Harry, poised to take a bite. 'He wants to show you the control room.'

'He's a bloody madman!' hissed Brown. 'What in bloody hell was he doing? You were there, did he go berserk? A king's ship isn't a bloody toy to be flung about! Was that performance some kind of punishment for us? Because we wouldn't tie his stupid little knots for him? What does the bloody navy enlist ratings for, eh? Answer me that? The man's an overgrown child. Not fit to hold a commission!'

Harry, in mid-bite, was halted by the sight of Brown's face twisted in scorn. He looked at Hardesty who had the common decency to at least appear embarrassed by Brown's tirade. Even so, he made no effort to distance himself from Brown's remarks. In one of those little epiphanies that prove with hindsight to be turning points in our lives, Harry saw everything with a super clarity: Brown and Hardesty had been frightened. And as that fact dawned, Harry realised with a jolt that despite all his earlier trepidation, he had not.

Exhilarated, yes. The atmosphere in the control room had been electric. He had felt himself in the presence of men who together were doing something extraordinary. Something he felt proud to witness and wanted to be part of. He tried to imagine what it must have been like for Brown and Hardesty sitting back here, being thrown about as the submarine had been wrenched through its paces by Penn, as he tested the limits of his newly repaired hydroplane. Sat here with nothing to listen to but an entire orchestra of cooking utensils rattling out their protest from the galley across the passage, they would have known nothing of the reasons for the manoeuvres. But Harry surprised himself by feeling no pity. Instead, all he saw in the two young men before him was a mirror of the wardroom of HMS *Redoubtable,* and in that instant the possibility of a future in the Royal Navy where he might belong, became real. All the risks of joining the Submarine Service were still there, yet for the first time he wasn't the butt of someone else's joke. Here was a world he could inhabit where things would be expected of him, where he would have a role to play. What had Dumaresq said? 'Lots of small ships and nasty little battles.' God. He'd be in for it now all right.

'Sub-Lieutenants Brown and Hardesty!' It was the Skipper's voice booming through from the control room. 'When you've got a minute!'

H57 surfaced shortly before 3 p.m., a mere hundred yards or so away from the small armed trawler that had been sent out to meet her. Protection, not from the Luftwaffe, but from the RAF, said Penn, who went on to explain that there was now a firm and unshiftable conviction abroad that any submarine, unless secured alongside or in company with, a Royal Navy warship, was German.

The two vessels made their sedate way back into the Solent at a comfortable eight knots, past a busy pattern of shipping movements. Merchantmen and minor warships, all part of the sea link to the British Expeditionary Force, were now arrayed, shield-like, across northern France. Just as in the last lot – except that at the moment, nothing was happening.

Brown and Hardesty were back in the wardroom being humoured by *H57*'s midshipman, a bad-tempered-looking youth, worldly beyond his years, who was plying them with some of the boat's stash of genever, purloined off a neutral Dutch tramp that *H57* had stopped in the Kattegat a few weeks before under suspicion of running contraband to the enemy.

Harry was on the bridge with Penn and Trumble and the lookouts. The sun was up, dappling the slight chop, making the air warm despite the whisper of a breeze. The trawler led off the starboard bow, her long sleek hull carving little in the way of a wake to trouble *H57*'s smooth progress. Lounged across the out-of-place industrial construction of housing and funnel that passed for the trawler's superstructure, her crew were goofing around *H57* in singlets. Gulls soared, and the intermittent strains of a dance band on the radio wafted back to them above the diesel thump from both vessels. All seemed well with the world.

Penn completed a perfunctory sweep of the horizon with his binoculars, then turned to drape himself casually against the thin steel cowl that formed the bridge wing and regarded Harry frankly.

'Met the Hun yet?' he said.

Harry, wanting to respond with equal frankness, did not know how to respond. His inglorious role aboard HMS *Redoubtable* hardly seemed to count. He certainly didn't want to waffle some convoluted explanation peppered with yeses and nos and on-the-other-hands. Then inspiration struck him: 'My last ship . . . my first ship . . . was *Redoubtable*.'

'Narvik,' stated Penn.

'So I'm told. I didn't exactly see much of it.'

'You don't tend to "see" much of it in this mob, either. Unless you're me.' Penn mimicked snapping down the periscope handles. 'For everyone else, it tends to be "noises, off". Preferably a long way off. Lots of thuds and bangs. Not much waiting to see the whites of their eyes, I'm afraid. It's a funny old game, this modern warfare.'

Then with his eyes still fixed on Harry, Penn fired a question to Trumble who was draped with equal sloth over the opposite bridge wing: 'So, what do you think of him, number one?'

Trumble, smiling broadly at Harry, said with report formality: 'Not afraid to muck in. Distinct blood lust in the eyes when you were taking the old girl over her fences . . .'

Without a hint of rudeness, Penn butted in: 'I'm reminded of Admiral Wilson's words . . .'

Trumble butted back, as if on a point of information for Harry's benefit: 'Controller of the navy, 1902, didn't like these new-fangled submarines.'

'Underwater weapons, they call 'em,' said Penn, with a heavy larding of mock solemnity, obviously mimicking the sonorous Admiral Wilson. 'I call 'em underhand, unfair and damned un-English!' A pause and then back into his easy drawl: 'That's what old Wilson actually said. True.' He turned to Andy: 'I can't answer for underhand, Andy, but his hair is definitely not "fair", and he's definitely not English. Two "uns" out of three isn't bad. What do you think?'

'Oh, I think he'll do.'

'What say you, young Gilmour?'

Harry was laughing at their sport with him. He composed himself: 'Aye aye, sir.'

Penn, at the age of 24, was one of the youngest submarine captains in the 'trade', which was how the Royal Navy had come to describe its submarine service. He was already blooded, having sunk a couple of smallish German transports trying to get up to Norway, and a small Type-UB inshore U-boat, off Texel. His main achievement so far, however, had been to survive. For there had been a lot of losses in the Submarine Service; an alarming number, given the war was still only months old. His boat had almost been one of them.

H57's dicky forward hydroplane wasn't some minor maintenance problem. Travelling underwater in an attempt to get into the German coastal shipping lanes, they had heard the tell-tale, sick-making scrape that could be made only by the anchor cable of a mine dragging along the outside of the hull. Penn had ordered all stop, intending to slowly turn away from the obstruction. But the massive tidal ebb running at the time was far greater than he'd calculated, and it not only took the forward way off them, but had sucked them back, sending the cable scraping back along the length of hull to jam behind the hydroplane mounting. They were barely a few miles off Heligoland, and the waters above were teeming with enemy patrol craft.

Surfacing and fending off the mine while the crew cut the cable was not an option. It had taken four hours of patient manoeuvring underwater to work *H57* free. But they were patched up now, and ready to go back out on the patrol line, hunting for U-boats trying to slip down into the Channel to wreak havoc in the supply lanes to the army in France.

Nursemaiding new recruits for the service was not Penn's main job, but it was a duty he didn't mind. Indeed, approved of. The Submarine Service had always been a tight, close-knit family since its inception in 1901, with a tremendous esprit d'corps. It took a certain type of man to prosper in its company. Also, it was by no means a favoured specialist branch for a career officer seeking to distinguish himself. Rear Admiral Arthur Wilson's words were not so far removed from official thought, which in many ways still considered the submarine to be 'the weapon of the weaker nation'.

But Penn had never any doubt where his career was going, right from the moment, at the age of 14, when he had walked through the gates of the Royal Navy's most renowned officer-training establishment, HMS *Britannia*, the Royal Naval College, Dartmouth. And that was to command a submarine. He couldn't imagine taking possession of a greater toy. Now, in time of war once again, the navy was coming round to his way of thinking; having to put aside its sniffy reserve and building up its submarine force.

The only thing was, you had to get the right type of chap. In peacetime the service was manned by volunteers. In war, that might prove a luxury, which was why the net had been cast wide so that the right types could be hauled in while there was still time. A right and proper submariner was a special breed, and you couldn't let any old Tom, Dick or, indeed, Harry, in. And being regular RN was no guarantee that you'd fit. Penn knew a few RNVR officers had already made the grade. This Gilmour fellow, however, was the first one he had encountered personally, and he seemed to be all right. You could tell. At least, Penn could tell. He and Andy Trumble had been watching him all through the exercise. You couldn't pin it down. He just had it. Fitted in.

The other two were a waste of space. Brown was too far up his own arse, and Hardesty was too frightened of offending anyone and everything. And, in the end, as a serving Skipper, it was Penn's call. For, every now and again, the Admiralty still had it in itself to make the right decision. In this case, it was the final decision about who got in, and who didn't. And that, the Admiralty had decided, would be left to the submariners themselves.

Candidates for submarine officer training could be put forward by anyone, including the candidate themselves. And indeed, such was the scramble to push as many through as was sanely possible, many got through every selection criteria on the nod. Until the last one. They were told they were going to sea in a submarine to decide whether they'd be comfortable going beneath the waves in an iron coffin as part of their job. But really it was for an experienced Skipper to judge whether a submarine crew would want them in the first place.

Penn wrote up his report that night. The next day Harry got his place on the next six-week course. Brown and Hardesty he never heard of again.

Chapter Five

There was two weeks to go until the next submarine officer course commenced at HMS *Dolphin*, so the office of the shore establishment's CO co-opted Harry to command, of all things, the damage-control parties for the base. It was not an onerous task, however, as the various fire-and-rescue teams on stand-by in the event of air raid or sabotage were ably run by a taut cadre of Petty Officers. For the first few days Harry rarely issued an order more complex than, 'Carry on, chief', and did not have his sleep disturbed once. The interlude was a godsend, allowing him to attend to the build-up of personal tasks, neglected for some time for a variety of reasons, not least his own youthful sloth.

Most pressing on the agenda was the matter of his uniform. He had been competently fitted-out by Hector Powe's on the front opposite HMS *King Alfred* during training. The rig did him well enough right through his posting to *Redoubtable*. Two regulation monkey jackets, eight gold buttons, set four aside down the front, two pairs of regulation trousers of similar colour and cloth, and a serviceable collection of grey flannels. There were enough white shirts with changeable collars to get him through from one laundry run to the next. A very smart cap and a slightly more functional watch cap. Two jet-black pairs of Oxford shoes and a pair of sea boots for boat work. The idea was to wear one's less presentable monkey jacket and flannels on duty, choice of footwear optional depending on duties for the day. Ditto the cap. But Harry had barely stepped aboard *H57* before his number two monkey jacket was smeared with several types of oil, and snagged by any number of brackets. Thus the reason for the entire crew's non-existent dress code quickly became all too apparent. 'No one wears a good uniform on board a submarine,' he'd been told by Andy Trumble. 'We don't do "at-homes" or drinks parties in the trade. So there's no call.'

So Harry took himself up to Southampton and an old Merchant Navy chandlery, and bought himself a reefer jacket with at least a passing semblance to the cut of the navy's monkey job. Except this one looked like it had been round the Horn a few times. He did a deal with the old salt behind the counter and got the jacket and a dozen second-hand RN buttons – extra in case of losses – and braid for his single stripe, and the old man to sew them all on, for just a few bob. He also invested in a comprehensive set of oilskins, leather gauntlets and a pair of ex-RAF flying boots, as his first impression of a bridge on a submarine was that it looked like it could get very cold, very easily. And he treated himself to a new switch-knife. A knife was the first thing he'd been told to buy when he started hanging round yachts.

'What will I need it for?' he'd asked.

'You'll hardly ever need it,' came the enigmatic reply, '. . . until you do. Then you'll *really* need it.'

That done, there was his personal correspondence to catch up on. No mean task. He began by writing to his parents. Then to his chums from his HMS *King Alfred* days, to his old headmaster, two of his tutors and Sir Alexander Scrimgeour, whose yacht, *Tangle*, he'd crewed on since he was fifteen, and a few school friends he promised to stay in touch with. Then there was Janis. The girlfriend, apparently; at least that's what she told him.

Janis Crumley was from back home, a precocious, gaudily glamorous young woman a year or two younger than Harry, who seemed to have designs on him for reasons he could not fathom. But there would be plenty of time to worry about that later. More immediately, after much deliberation, he wrote to Peter Dumaresq, to tell him his counsel had not been in vain, and to thank him.

Trumble also gave him a stack of his briefing notes from his time on the submarine course and Harry spent every available moment with his nose in their complexities. In the evenings, however, there was the ritual gathering around the wardroom's wireless to listen to the BBC's *Nine O'Clock News*. The collapse of the Norwegian campaign dominated.

On 10 May the news changed, but it wasn't the BBC who told Harry first. While having his morning tea in the wardroom, another officer burst in yelling, 'Jerry's on the move!'

All through that lovely, fresh spring morning, with the sun warm and slanting through the office windows on a diligent Harry attending to paperwork, the Germans had been sweeping through Holland and Luxembourg towards the Belgian frontier. Suddenly the war was no longer a distant inconvenience. The tempo changed, and the speed of events overtook even rumour. Before the day was over, Prime Minister Neville Chamberlain had resigned. Then they learned of his replacement: it was that man so detested by Harry's father. 'He'd have us in a police state!' was Mr Gilmour's mantra every time the vile name came from the enormous walnut and maple radiogram that presided over the living room. But that man had become Harry's civilian boss: First Lord of the Admiralty, Winston Churchill. And now he was prime minister.

The older officers looked grimly satisfied. 'Now you'll see,' was the sage muttering. But exactly what they were about to see was not made clear. As for Harry, in the eye of all this, it was as if a void were opening up under his youthful confidence. It was like watching the scenery change at the theatre. The narrative was breaking up. The Germans were moving fast. Events were not meant to unfold like this, and he was still young enough to fret about why the grown-ups weren't doing something.

Thankfully, opportunities to fret were limited as Harry spent the following days drilling intensively with his damage-control teams, and after 14 May, when the Luftwaffe razed Rotterdam to the ground, he was up most nights watching the skies.

The news was relentlessly grim. German armour had traversed the 'impenetrable' Ardennes forest and crossed the Meuse. The French army was beginning to collapse, and barely a week after Rotterdam, the British Expeditionary Force was in retreat to the Channel ports. The sailors crowded around the Mess radios every night to listen to the BBC newsreader itemise each incident of defeat and rout. By the third week in May, the port of Dunkirk was being mentioned with increasing frequency. Then one evening, the officers and Petty Officers were summoned to a meeting in the gym.

'Does anyone have small-boat experience, especially in running and maintaining small-boat engines?' a ruddy-faced and very harassed captain wanted to know. He didn't say why, and the grim-faced sailors knew better than to ask.

A number of Engine Room Artificers and some younger officers stepped forward. Harry had worked on yacht engines, he reckoned he knew enough. He started to shuffle out of the mob to go and stand with the growing number of volunteers, when a broad arm blocked his way. Harry had seen him about the base. It was another of those ubiquitous middle-aged Lieutenant Commanders wheeled out of retirement as trainers.

'There'll be plenty of time for volunteering, young man, before this lot is over,' he said paternally. 'You are about to begin a very important training course which will result in your contribution to this war being far, far greater than anything you could achieve stooging around small-boat engines.'

Harry had no option but to comply. 'Aye aye, sir,' he said and stepped back.

Over the next few days rumours started filtering through of an epic action off Dunkirk. The newspapers were silent, but the word was that the entire British Expeditionary Force had been plucked off the beaches round the port by a Royal Navy scratch force of destroyers and requisitioned pleasure craft, all of it carried out under the most sustained and heavy air attack.

Belgium surrendered on 27 May, a Monday. Harry's course began the same day.

It was relentless. All the principles of submarine propulsion, submarine electrical systems, batteries, pumps, motors, optics, supply, torpedo maintenance and firing procedures. And squeezed into all this was his celestial navigation class, as well as in-shore boat handling, basic first aid, and signals and ciphers.

Harry neither excelled nor flopped. The cribs Andy Trumble had provided helped him – just – to bluff through much of the technical part of the course, and he did show a certain flair in handling a submarine, navigation and even first aid. He worked and he slept; and nothing else. That is not to say the course was without its amusing moments.

The class, in little huddles of three and four, was regularly shipped out on to the training sub, to apply their classroom learning to the real world . . . and to be publicly humiliated by its unimpressed crew. The sub was another antiquated and flimsy

H-class, and it was on one of these early trips that Harry was 'blooded' in the use of a submarine's 'heads'.

He had asked where one went to 'spend a penny'. There was a pause.

'You're lucky,' he was told by a rather short Petty Officer in a misshapen white roll-neck pullover. 'H-class normally have the jawbox jammed in the open between the diesels. But we've been modified, sir, to 'ave all the comforts of a liner, sir.'

Harry waited to be told where to go but the Petty Officer just stared back at him. Reluctant to ask, Harry eventually said, 'If you wouldn't mind pointing me in the right direction, Petty Officer?'

A slow shake of the Petty Officer's head was the response.

Harry, being in increasing need, drew himself up. He had quickly learned that a certain amount of joshing was part and parcel of the navy at every level, and junior officers, especially those under training, were prime targets. And being a particularly sharp young man in many ways, he was equally quick to realise that how you reacted was very important in terms of the reputation and the respect – or lack of it – you earned among the lower deck. As the old adage went, if you can't take a joke, you shouldn't have joined. But there were times when even his genial patience could be tried. On the one hand there was the wisdom in knowing when to acquiesce in being the butt of a little sport, and on the other, there was impending disaster in the trouser department.

Before Harry could raise his voice in righteous remonstration, the Petty Officer began to explain with a solemn gravity: 'You can't just wander about doing your business on a submarine whenever you feel like it, sir. There's procedures, sir. You 'ave to ask the Capting for permission, sir. Or the officer of the watch, if the Capting is being by some ways indisposed.'

This was too much. Harry leant in to hiss in the little man's ear: 'Now this has gone far enough . . .'

The Petty Officer recoiled with a look of pained affront on his face. 'Sir,' he said firmly, 'the 'eads on a submarine is a very complex and sensitive piece of equipment, seeing as it is a device not just for your personal convenience, but for blowin' the stuff overboard, through the pressure hull, as and when, at whateffer depth . . . the crew's doings being an unnecessary impediment to the smooth running of the boat and not being wanted. That's why, like you and me, sir, a submarine cannot be goin' about discharging over the side whenever it feels like it. There could be people watchin'. Or listenin'. Which is why, since he is the bloke what knows what the submarine is about at any particular moment, we must ask the Capting when we want to go,' – a pause for emphasis – 'sir.'

Harry retreated. Immediately behind him in the tight space of the control room he was aware of an instructor going through the steps of an attack with one of his fellow students. He could see the Skipper's folded arms protruding from the corner of the chart table. Harry turned away from the Petty Officer and made to squeeze his way into the control room, preparing to choose a moment that promised least embarrassment. It was like being back in school.

The Skipper was leaning back against the chart table watching, amused, as the instructor shuffled behind the student officer, who in turn was crouched and draped over the periscope as if his eyes were glued to it, and was jerking back and forth as if trying to follow some target whose manoeuvres defied the laws of physics.

'Now the surface contact is up there, Mr Pettifer,' the instructor was intoning patiently, 'so just work back along the line of her track until you re-acquire.'

Harry, unable to shove his way in to the tight little compartment any further without disrupting proceedings, tensed himself for a wait. He needn't have bothered.

''Scuse me, sir!' came a voice from behind. It was the Petty Officer, in the strident tone he might use in a force 8 gale.

Over his shoulder the Skipper said, 'Petty Officer Sillitoe?'

'The young gentleman, sir. He wants to use the 'eads, sir.'

The Skipper turned to see Harry's face, inches from his own, now tinged crimson as to remove all doubt as to which young gentleman Petty Officer Sillitoe must be referring.

'You should have gone before you stepped on board,' was his terse response. Then to Sillitoe, 'Get one of the ratings to show him how to work it, Petty Officer. And try to keep him clean, please. He's on next.'

Harry was too distracted to puzzle over what the Skipper meant by, 'try to keep him clean'. He shuffled aft, following an Able Seaman who looked twice his age, and was certainly twice his size, through bulkheads which the AB in the ubiquitous white jumper moved with far greater ease than Harry, and finally into the engine spaces where the AB turned, and with a flourish, revealed a small cupboard with an extremely flimsy partition door that did not quite reach the deck.

'The seat of repose, sir,' he said, in a south London accent. 'Now before you go in, sir, there are fings 'ere you must bear in mind.'

And he opened the door. The space was two feet by two feet and not an inch more, and contained a tiny steel pan, an intimidating set of valves, gauges and an air bottle above it. By the side was what looked like a car handbrake, secured by a clip. The only object of familiarity was the Bakelite toilet lid – which Harry took to be quaintly superfluous, not yet being steeped enough in submarine lore to realise that nothing aboard a submarine is superfluous.

'Right, sir, 'ere's what we do . . . do your business as normal . . .'

'That's reassuring,' observed Harry, becoming increasingly impatient for all the obvious reasons.

The AB stopped to let him have his joke, then with great portent, said: 'The next bit, it is as well to pay close attention, sir . . . when you is finished, shut the lid. Open these here two valves. That opens the device to the sea. But don't worry cos the pan's still sealed at the bottom, and there is a non-return valve as well, what prevents the sea comin' in. Have you got it so far, sir?'

Harry was torn between desperation to be getting on with it, and a sudden and increasing unease that if he didn't overcome his distraction and listen, this device might do him serious injury. He nodded.

'Right, sir. Open that valve there to charge the bottle wif high pressure air. We're about thirty-five feet, and you'll need a coupla pounds per square inch above the outside water pressure . . . so what are we sayin'? About free atmospheres on that gauge is what you want. Now release the lever to position one to open the bottom of the pan. You will then be connected to the waste tank. Lever to position two now, sir. That lets in seawater which comes in and flushes your business back into the waste tank. Position free shuts the bottom of the pan sealing it from the waste tank. Position four vents the air from the bottle frough the waste tank and flushes the whole lot into the sea. It is vital, sir, for your shipmates, that you *leave* the lever in position four until *all* the air is vented. If not, if the next poor bleeder comin' in for 'is mornin' george tries to shift that lever to position one, he will experience what we in the trade call, "a return to sender" – in other words, the residual high pressure air what you have left in the tank, blows the stuff back at you. Which is also why, when *you* go to move the lever back to position one, you put the lid down and have your foot firmly on it, sir, just in case you haven't vented all the air, and you get a return to sender instead. Ready now, sir?'

Harry was transfixed. The only thing he could think to say was, 'I'm going in.'

The AB grinned suddenly: 'There's always a first time, sir. Best of luck.'

The AB waited outside, but Harry was too far gone to be shy. Once finished, he began the procedure. The AB monitored his progress, listening to all the clicks and hisses, so he understood what had happened even before Harry shouted, 'Jesus H fucking Christ!' And long before the smell. However, from the muffled nature of the blast, the AB was able to call reassuringly to Harry. 'At least you remembered to put your foot on the lid, sir.'

Harry's first true encounter with terror came one morning in the escape-training tank.

The course was almost over. At the end of one of the written finals, Harry was one of half a dozen officers under training to be called out and ordered to report to 'The Tank' for their DSEA orientation.

'DSEA stands for the Davis Submarine Escape Apparatus,' said a bare-headed, wiry Chief Petty Officer wearing nothing but blue denim overalls and black plimsolls. He was a very poised, precise man of indeterminate age; neat, clean-shaven with a warm smile and receding mouse-brown hair, he seemed to Harry rather like a concerned older brother. He held aloft a brownish rubber sack, the size of a shopping bag, with a corrugated tube coming from it; then he embarked on a complicated technical description of how it worked.

They were in a windowless warehouse with steel rafters. It was a bright day outside, but only a murky light came through huge frosted ball-shaped lamps suspended from a row of conduit tubes. Although summer was almost here, the space felt chill and draughty, which was why the officers under training – each wearing nothing but swimming trunks and a set of goggles on their heads – stood around the chief shivering, and looking like so many pale skittles.

Behind the chief loomed a forty-foot steel cylinder with a door bolted on to the side; and way up there, in the dim ceiling of the brick tower that surrounded it, was a platform bolted around the top, upon which perched three distant figures. Even at that height you could tell they were burly sailors, rank unknown, as they too were in trunks and goggles. They peered down and Harry could imagine the amused grins of men who knew what was about to happen and were looking forward to much laughter at the expense of others. This was 'The Tank' and, as lore had it, the sailors on top were there to clear it of bodies once the training was over.

As so often in the past, the technical briefing went in one of Harry's ears and out the other. He looked attentive enough, staring fixedly at the kit, but really he was in trance, trying to force himself to imagine having to actually use the DSEA device to save his own life. The reverie ended when the CPO called his name. Harry was to be first into the tank.

The rubber felt obscenely clammy against his chest as the chief hefted the set over his head. And it was surprisingly heavy, weighed by an oxygen bottle attached to the bottom. The chief guided him as he tightened the webbing straps and then handed him a set of nose clips. Then the dreaded door of the device was opened before him. With the set disgustingly clingy on his chest, he had to squeeze through the gap. The door clanged shut and he could hear it being secured – almost at the same time as he could hear, and feel, the water start to pump in.

Harry had never before experienced the fear of drowning. He had been out on the sea all his formative years, he was aware of the mariner's appreciation of his element: that if you did absolutely everything, exactly right, the sea might let you live. But trapped, sealed, and facing a watery tomb, was something he'd never contemplated. Death. Drowning. In a sealed metal container. It was at this moment he first discovered the taste of fear. It was metallic. He would taste it again and again before this war was over, though with never the same intensity as he did then in that bloody chamber.

Water. Water rising to engulf him and water into which his insides were turning. Panic was overwhelming Harry, apart from a tiny glimmer at the edge of his consciousness he recognised as shame. The water rose and covered his head. The goggles started to mist. He became aware he was still holding his breath, so he breathed. But nothing happened. The panic made his throat constrict; his whole body began to jerk involuntarily, and the walls and pipework in the tank lifted the skin off his elbows and knees. From somewhere outside the silent screaming in his head came the memory of a valve, and a bottle attached to the set. He fumbled, found it, and began to twitch it open. He heard the oxygen go in to his rubber bag, and his body suddenly lurched up against the hatch wheel above him. Just in time he remembered to turn off the bottle. The inflated bag pushed against him with an intimacy that momentarily replaced the panic with revulsion, and in that brief lucid flash he remembered to breathe again. He took a gulp, and oxygen flooded his lungs.

It was as if the inrush had freed his brain. He remembered to unclip the hatch above him. When the last clip came off, Harry, still stupefied by his panic, shot out like a bullet, slamming into every protruding edge of the tank with his cramped body on the way, and knocking off his goggles. Right at this juncture, he entered a peculiar frame of mind in which he abandoned all care; the panic departed and a superior kind of phlegmatic consideration ruled him. That was when he remembered that he was not supposed to be going up so fast. There had been something about pressure that had been mentioned in the lecture. Pressure and your ears, and something called embolisms to worry about. From somewhere, Harry remembered the set was fitted with a sort of folded apron, designed to be pulled out and used as a crude brake. The details of the lecture bubbled up: all the stuff about nitrogen dissolving in your blood under pressure, and how you had to come up slow from depths, otherwise, as the pressure came off, the nitrogen would begin to 'un-dissolve' and turn to bubbles in your bloodstream, and that the bubbles would then shoot straight to the places you didn't want them to, like your heart or your brain, and earn your next of kin the telegram.

He pulled the apron and immediately performed an immaculate underwater somersault before hitting the surface in a wallowing thrash.

Afterwards, the Petty Officer told Harry that he'd 'done all right' for the purposes of the exercise, despite the hilarity from the tank team. And, the PO added, it was unlikely he would ever have to do it in real life anyway – in submarines, either the boat returned from patrol, with you in it, or it didn't, and neither did you.

And then it was all over, and he was through the course. There had been beers in the wardroom after the last test had been handed in, but everyone was too knackered for revelry.

After breakfast the next day, he gravitated back there. Just hanging around waiting to see who had passed and what would happen next. Most of the class were there already. A few were conspicuous by their absence. Then chaps started getting the call: 'Captain (S) wants to see you.' Captain, Submarines, the base CO.

When Harry was called, he trouped out, still tired but tensed up. Gripped by one of those emotional tug-of-wars where you try and force yourself to believe failure doesn't really matter; that getting bumped back to the General List, on to a minesweeper or some old rattling conversion of an armed merchant cruiser or a Flower-class corvette and the life of an Atlantic convoy escort, will just be another twist of fate to take in one's stride. But knowing all the time, wishing, pleading to any higher power alert and on receive, to let you through; to pass you as a submarine officer, and at the same time, not really knowing why. Knowing it to be dangerous, yet still wanting it.

So with stomach knotted and shallow of breath, he headed off down the bland institution-coloured corridor to hear the verdict from Captain, Submarines. When he got to the office, he discovered the call wasn't strictly true. Captain (S) didn't want to see him. There was no avuncular figure in gold braid and four rings. No handshake, congratulations or ceremony awaited him. Just a Petty Officer Writer.

'You're appointed fourth in HMS submarine *Pelorus*, sir,' he'd said, handing him his sealed orders and travel dockets. 'Welcome to the trade.'

'You've got *Pelorus*?' One of the training officers said, impressed, after bumping into Harry on his way to pack: 'She's a Parthian-class boat, big by current navy standards. Commanded by a bit of a legend in the service. Commander Charlie Bonnalleck, otherwise known as "the Bonny Boy". You'll be in for an interesting time of it, Mr Gilmour.'

Harry was going to be the fourth officer, by seniority, in a submarine wardroom. And since he was at the age when the word 'interesting' still meant something to be looked forward to, his overall mood was excitement rather than trepidation as he went off to catch a train to Chatham. It should have been the other way round.

Chapter Six

At least twenty minutes had passed since the masthead had been sighted and His Majesty's Submarine *Pelorus* had gone to Diving Stations. Diving Stations – in the Submarine Service it also passed as the equivalent to Action Stations on a surface ship. Because on a submarine the everyday act of submerging was far more fraught with risk than mere contact with the enemy, and that was why Diving Stations was a call to cover every emergency eventuality.

Everyone who should be was in the control room and the entire crew were closed up and cleared for action. Lieutenant 'Sandy' Sandeman, *Pelorus*'s Jimmy, was at the trim board concentrating on his pumping and flooding, keeping the boat nailed to its periscope depth, delivering to the Skipper a perfect platform to calculate the target's bearing, range and speed, all the while compensating for the crew running to and fro, and the boat sprinting, then slowing as it manoeuvred into a firing position, with everything in movement acting to shift the load on board and affect the boat's buoyancy. Compensating was Sandy's job: ensuring the water was pumped and blown between the trim tanks, keeping the boat in balance as it hung there between the surface and the deep.

And then when the time came to fire each torpedo – each weighing more than one and half tons – he had to be there, flooding the forward trim tanks to prevent the submarine from reeling with every torpedo loosed, from breaking the surface, too light and out of control, right under the enemy's guns. Except time was passing and so far there hadn't been much trim to adjust.

For an attack, this lack of urgency was bewildering even to a new boy like Harry. He allowed himself the licence to risk a glance around the control room. The Skipper, the Bonny Boy, was at the periscope; behind him, the bulk of his favourite chief, Jimmy Gault, there to read off the bearings from the steel bezel engraved in degrees and minutes which sat fixed around the periscope casing above the Skipper's head.

Whatever direction the Skipper was looking in, when he shouted, 'The bearing is . . . that!' Gault had to call out the number on the bezel giving the bearing to the target. The new boy, Harry, was then supposed to crank it into the 'fruit machine', an electro-mechanical gizmo in the corner of the control room that, when fed all the right numbers, would deliver up the all-important 'target solution'. With the help of whoever was manning the plot and the fruit machine, the Skipper could then work out the periscope angle; in other words, the relative bearing on which he needed to fix his periscope crosswire so that when the target appeared he'd know when to fire.

The fruit machine was the new boy's action station, and there was Harry, glued to it.

Sandeman was watching the Skipper, too, and getting that awful sinking feeling, one he was becoming all too familiar with in recent weeks. For some time he had excused the Skipper's frequently erratic behaviour as the eccentricities of an old-fashioned war hero, but the truth had begun inexorably to make itself all too plain. Sandeman wondered if anyone else among the crew knew what was happening, especially the ones who had sailed with the Bonny Boy since the start of this commission.

The bloody Bonny Boy. Submarine legend, twice breaking into the Baltic in the last lot; an ace wreaking havoc among German shipping from the Gulf of Bothnia to Kiel Roads, blue-eyed boy to the Tsar's Admirals, a brass band every time he cruised in and out of Kronstadt or Reval or Riga, and a brass band and a VC when he returned home to Haslar Creek. Out of the navy in the twenties and then back in; seen as the sage of submarine operations, and a Commander now, and far too bloody senior to be commanding a submarine. Flotilla leader was a Commander's billet, so what was he doing here? Sandeman knew the literal answer to that: the Skipper was arsing about, risking the lives of his crew and the safety of the boat. And over the past few weeks he'd come to know why. Except that to ever utter it, to say out loud what he knew inside, especially to someone up the chain of command – who would know Bonalleck of old, and who would remember the veteran and not the man at the periscope over there – that would be a career killer.

Sandeman was regular RN, and a conscientious and ambitious officer, and a first Lieutenant at twenty-two. The way things were going he could have a good shot at 'the Perisher' – the commanding officers' qualifying course – in six to nine months at the latest, and if he passed, his own boat within a year if the war lasted that long – and it would.

'Up periscope!'

The sage speaks, thought Sandeman, as through the muted whirr the brass tube rose, and Commander Bonalleck stooped to pull down the grips.

Sandeman turned again to his trim board and waited. They had performed one sprint since the navigator, McVeigh, a surly Northern Irish RNR Lieutenant on duty-diving watch, had spotted that mast creep above the horizon from the direction of the Texel-Den Helder cut which lay about a score or more miles away to the north-east of their current position. The rest of the time they had been crawling. No urgency, just a gentle puttering along with barely an amp out of the batteries.

'I think you'll find there are two masts, Mr McVeigh,' said Bonalleck, once he'd finally made it to the control room and fastened his unusually bright, watery eyes to the periscope's viewfinder.

Sandeman didn't need to see the Ulsterman to know the look of seething contempt on his face. Two masts indeed, when it had taken the Skipper three calls of: 'Captain to the control room!' to get here. The entire Kriegsmarine could have been coming over the horizon by then, which was why McVeigh, who knew it, did not deign to respond to the Skipper's smug commentary even though an 'Aye aye, sir' was called for.

'Target bearing . . . that!' Bonalleck had intoned. 'Range . . .' and Gault had reeled off the figures. 'Down periscope,' Bonalleck had continued. 'Helmsman, steer zero-five-zero . . . engine room, group up, full ahead together for a three-minute run.'

He moves! thought Sandeman. The 'group up' order shifted the two electric motors up from 'series' to 'parallel' to give the necessary burst of speed. The engine room telegraphs rang, the Planesmen adjusted their angles of approach to compensate for the 'lift' the speeding propellers or 'screws' would give the hydroplanes, and as Sandeman watched his trim with one eye, with the other he watched young Gilmour diligently programme the fruit machine with Bonalleck's target data.

The control room was crowded, and the atmosphere alert. *Pelorus* had a good crew, together a long time by submarine standards these days. All older men: regulars, allowed to stay together because of the pull of the Bonny Boy; a crew as yet unraided to make up cadres for new crews pouring out of the training establishments to man the new submarines coming off the slips. But this was Gilmour's first war patrol, and Sandeman, like the good Jimmy he was, was looking out for his new man.

They were on their fourth day out from Chatham, and this was their first contact since reaching their patrol billet. Gilmour had performed adequately for an RNVR at any rate: always a minute or so early for his watch, competent in his use of the periscope, and when on diving watch there had been no fancy stuff or sudden manoeuvres to confound the Planesmen or the rating on the trim valves. He listened when you told him things, and remembered them. A bit shy, and obviously tense, but it was his first patrol and tense was what Sandeman wanted to see. Tense meant he was paying attention, blasé got people killed; and now, heading to engage the enemy, he was doing his duty, calm despite the atmosphere that gripped the tiny compartment tighter than an armature. And even if, like Sandeman on his first torpedo attack, Gilmour's heart was beating fit to burst out of his chest, he was displaying a cool head. We like cool heads, Sandeman noted to himself, by way of taking comfort; for there was no comfort to be taken anywhere else.

For the minutes since the sighting had passed in silence. No running commentary from the Skipper, no clue as to what the target was or what it was doing, whether they were going to attack, and if so, the torpedo tubes he intended to use. The Bonny Boy was saying nothing. On surface ships, silence was the captain's prerogative. Indeed, justifying his actions to his crew would have been seen as 'rather off'. But on a submarine, it was part of the contract. The Skipper was the eyes of the boat. But the Bonny Boy was saying nothing about what those eyes were seeing. Just, 'up periscope . . . down periscope'; a course change to the helmsman. Now this short sprint, and then nothing.

In the meantime, from what exchanges with the helmsman there had been, Sandeman had been constructing a mental picture of the Skipper's course relative to the target, which appeared to be running south-south-west at probably no more than nine knots. By his reckoning, the Bonny Boy had swung *Pelorus* on a parallel track most likely a mile or so ahead, but it was most assuredly not his place to pass on those surmises to the crew – that would have been a serious breach of naval discipline.

Sandeman didn't need to look round the control room to sense the deep unease. The Skipper leant back from the rubber eyepieces and began 'walking' the periscope round again for another 360-degree look; a check to make sure nothing was coming up from another quarter while his attention had been elsewhere. Sandeman watched the two pale rings of light shining on the Skipper's eyes, sunlight reflected down the scope through its maze of mirrors, from a clear, bright North Sea afternoon.

'Afternoon' explained the fug in the boat. They had dived just before dawn, not long after 04.00, and it was now 18:17 hours – more than fourteen hours underwater, and the air was getting a little thick. That was the trouble with submarine operations in northern waters in summer: there was always too much daylight keeping you down, and the shorter nights meant you never got enough time on the surface to charge the batteries properly either. This was about to become *Pelorus's* next problem: if the Skipper wanted to execute any more short, fast runs he would really start eating up the battery amps. If you kept the speed down on a boat as big as *Pelorus,* you could easily chug along under battery power for a good fifteen or sixteen hours, but the minute you started sprinting, the batteries drained like you'd pulled the plug on a bath.

'Down periscope!' ordered the Bonny Boy, as he snapped the grips shut and stood back from the scope in time to watch it hiss into the bowels of the boat. The navigator had to hurriedly move aside as his Skipper stepped back without looking, to lean against the chart table.

There was a momentary shuffling as each of those crammed into the control room's confining space repositioned themselves; their sudden movements rippled through, like a human wash, raising another wave of human stink from men gone four days without a wash. *Pelorus*, like all subs, carried only a finite amount of fresh water, and when you could be out as long as three weeks, you reserved what there was for drinking and cooking. A saltwater wash was only for when it was a case of needs must and you'd steeled yourself for the abrading rasp of saltwater soap.

They waited for the next order, but the Bonny Boy said nothing. No course change or 'group up' for another sprint. Each crewman, taut over his own lever, dial or valve, awaiting orders, held the tension for a too-long moment, before easing back enough to risk a look over their shoulder. The Bonny Boy, at rest against the wooden table, sported a sanguine look, meeting no one's gaze. Then at last he spoke, matter-of-factly: 'Take her down, number one. Eighty feet. Make your course two-six-five.'

They were disengaging. There was a terrible pause before his orders were bellowed back to him and executed without question. The pause was terrible, not because it was long – anyone not attuned to submarine life would never even have registered it. Nor had the delay been long enough for the Bonny Boy to be forced to recall his crew to their duty. It was terrible because it had happened at all, and it was just long enough for even the Bonny Boy to notice. Much import can be conveyed in such a pause, and no one in that control room, in that very moment, was in any doubt that everyone was sharing the same terrible suspicion that *Pelorus* was running away.

Oh god! thought Harry, concentrating on his mechanical box, which right at this moment looked particularly Heath Robinson, and stupid. What is going on now? Why can't we just get on and fight this bloody war? Please, please don't let me be aboard another floating lunatic asylum!

Harry looked around for reassurance but all he saw were the slab faces of the control room crew, reflecting absolutely nothing.

Sandeman went about his business, taking the boat down, making sure the helmsman put her on the right course, and tweaking the trim to make her just so. Then he straightened up and regarded the Skipper. Commander Bonalleck jutted his chin in a few random directions, before clearing his throat, and with an arch indifference said to no one in particular: 'A couple of minesweepers. Not worth alerting Jerry to the fact there's a submarine about. I'm minded to keep our torpedoes for more telling targets,' and then a sharp look directly at Sandeman, challenging his gaze. 'I'm sure you agree Sandy, eh?'

'Aye aye, sir.' There was nothing else Sandeman could say.

⌣

Harry had the middle watch, midnight to 04.00, and was on the bridge with two ratings acting as his lookouts. The night was a calm spring beauty with barely a swell, and an indigo sky exploded with stars as *Pelorus* continued to slice her way up the North Sea to the steady thrum of her two big diesels powering her progress and pumping amps into her ranks of battery cells against the coming daylight when she would run submerged. Thirty-odd miles over the dark eastern horizon was the coast of German-occupied Denmark, and just over a hundred miles away, directly on *Pelorus*'s bow, was

German-occupied Norway and the waters of the Skagerrak. This was the ascendant Third Reich's front doorstep, but Harry found it difficult to focus on his watch-keeping duties after what had occurred earlier in the evening. He forced himself into another sweep of the horizon trying to open his night vision to the slightest nuance in the shade of night that might betray the presence of an approaching prey, predator, or even friend, for *Pelorus* was now well north of her last assigned patrol billet, and other Allied submarines could be out there, perhaps unaware that a British submarine was straying into their hunting ground.

That last consideration Harry had picked up from one of the several hissed whispers passing between Sandeman and McVeigh since *Pelorus* had turned and run from the two German mine-sweepers. They had been discussing the drill for submarine operations in enemy waters. McVeigh had been saying: '. . . and a time off station, and then a rendezvous time with the trawler off Sheerness. You need to know all that. He should have told you as his first Lieutenant' – this last with a sotto-voce vehemence that Harry had last heard between grown-ups unwilling to alarm the children with their squabbling. And that was how all this was making him feel – like a child among grown-ups. He shut his racing mind and conducted another all-round sweep of the horizon, then checked the lookouts were continuing to make their regular ninety-degree pans back and forth, a pause, forth and back.

The sea was empty, just a vast obsidian plain beneath endless starlight where the diesel thump seemed like silence. Yet Harry knew that, down the hatch behind him, the boat was in silent ferment since the minesweepers had been allowed to get away. The old crew, the ones who had been with the Bonny Boy forever, were quiet, grim and battened down; the rest, nervous; and him and Swann, the other watch officer, left in a limbo-land between. Not that Swann bothered much: he was all noise and self-assertion, any sensitivity to nuance or feeling long battered out of him in some middle-ranked public school.

The whole atmosphere was making Harry angrier by the minute; it was *Redoubtable* all over again. He'd put up with the patronising all through his time aboard her, enduring it because he believed it was expected of him; ever the diligent student. Stay in your place and do not annoy the grown-ups while they conduct grown-up business; like a child, without say.

But out there, in the dark of this beautiful spring night, might be German warships, conducting anti-submarine patrols; German crews actively seeking out intruders in their own waters; intruders exactly like this submarine that Harry, as watch officer, was in temporary charge of. Harry, responsible for HMS *Pelorus* and all who sailed in her, by order of her captain through His Majesty's commission.

Harry had looked her up in HMS *Dolphin*'s wardroom copy of *Jane's Fighting Ships* before setting off to join her. And now he was aboard; part of ship's company. *Pelorus*: 1,500 tons, surfaced, just over 2,000 tons submerged, and not far off 300 feet long, with a beam of thirty feet. Her twin propellors or 'screws' were driven by two 5,000 horsepower diesels on the surface, and two 1,600 horsepower electric motors, dived. It gave her a top speed of about eighteen knots surfaced, and little less than nine knots underwater. She also packed quite a punch, with six 21-inch torpedo tubes forward, plus space to carry fourteen re-loads, and two tubes aft. And in an open turret, just below him, mounted on a sponson just forward of the bridge, she carried a quick-firing 4-inch gun. A big boat by current Royal Navy submarine standards indeed, with a crew of fifty-eight; and right now, Harry was in charge.

Harry was a long way from the second-year Glasgow university student who had walked into the recruiting office ten months ago. This time, a year ago, he'd been celebrating passing his first-year exams with a pub crawl down Byres Road, in a mob of young men decorously tipsy on weak beer, all tweed jackets and flowing university scarves despite the mildness of the spring evening. Now, tonight, he had the watch aboard one of His Majesty's submarines, thirty miles off an enemy-occupied coast, and he was buggered if he was going to be treated like a child any more. He raised his binoculars again, another sweep, another check of the lookouts, another hour and a half before Swann was due to relieve him.

Chapter Seven

McVeigh, the navigator, watched Swann peering over the chart table like some comic bug in his red goggles. Swann was noting the course and speed and standing orders before going up to relieve Gilmour for the morning watch. Despite the hour, it was still dark enough for him to need the goggles; even though the control room was red-lit and in semi-darkness, anyone going on watch wore them while they waited for the watch change. The red light helped acclimatise your eyes to the night above; the quicker your night vision was acquired, the better. Red light because no one wanted a target to escape or an enemy warship to appear in the minutes it took a watchkeeper's eyes to fully adjust to complete darkness. Swann, swaddled in an over-size fawn duffel coat, over the ubiquitous white pullover, crammed his not-yet-battered watch cap on his head and slung his binoculars strap round his neck before shooting up through the hatch without a word or a look McVeigh's way. Insubordinate little bastard, thought McVeigh. But he said nothing, his mind being on other things.

McVeigh's thoughts were the boat's course: zero-one-five degrees, steady. An invisible line projecting out across the sea, pulling them towards that x, scribbled by the Bonny Boy on the ocean blankness of the chart; a spot slap-bang in the middle of the entrance to the Skagerrak, scribbled before the Bonny Boy had retired to his curtained cubicle, not to be seen since.

McVeigh had been with Bonalleck since *Pelorus* commissioned. Before that he'd sailed as a junior watch officer on a T-class boat. But he'd learned his trade as a seafarer before the war with Alfred Holt & Co., The Blue Funnel Line as it was known across the globe. With them he had sailed every sea lane between Liverpool and South-east Asia. He had his first mate's ticket and was sailing as a second officer when war broke out; an experienced and highly competent mariner. That was how, in Bonalleck, McVeigh had recognised a kindred spirit, and that was why he was finding all this recent bloody nonsense so intolerable.

The Petty Officer and two senior rates on Swann's watch came shambling aft into the control room in their motley array of warm gear, and similarly bug-eyed in goggles. They acknowledged McVeigh, passed a few pleasantries about the day ahead, and after their own brief glance at course and standing orders, followed each other up into the pre-dawn darkness. McVeigh didn't wait for the relieved watch to come tumbling down. Instead, he gave a quick check over the helmsman's shoulder, nodded to the Planesmen and the outside ERA on the diving panel, and announced generally, 'I'll be with Mr Sandeman in the wardroom if anything comes up.' And with that he was gone aft.

The first Lieutenant was sitting hunched over the table in the tiny wardroom, little more than an alcove off the main companionway that ran fore and aft the length of the boat. The table was surrounded on three sides by banquettes, above them storage space for the crockery, the tiny but eclectic library, and the officers' personal stores. A portrait of the king presided over the space. Sandeman had a mug of coffee steaming before him, and was lost in thought when McVeigh swept back the curtain that served as privacy for

Pelorus's wardroom. The look on McVeigh's face told Sandeman all he needed to know about the conversation they were about to have.

———⌣———

As he slid down the hatch into the control room after hours in the fresh sea air, Harry was hit by the familiar smell of diesel oil and men's sweat. The rest of his watch had preceded him, and the control room watch change had already taken place by the time Harry's feet hit the deckplates. He put his binoculars by the chart table and proceeded to mark up his star sightings and times on the log. These would assist McVeigh when he next came to plot their position on the chart. He then slid through the after hatch heading for the wardroom and food.

Scanlon, the young Able Seaman to whom the role of 'cook' had fallen – or been thrust upon – was hunched over in the galley space. There was a savoury smell emanating from within that was powerful enough to master the permanent diesel fug: enough to know that Scanlon was re-heating a large mess of 'train smash' for the watch coming off duty. This powdered egg dish with canned bacon and tomatoes thrown in was the traditional early breakfast, and the first sitting had probably gone to the lads who had come up to relieve Harry. It was a submariner's favourite but right now did nothing for Harry's appetite, because Harry, standing on the other side of the wardroom curtain, had just lost it. They were at it again, the subdued voices of the 'grown ups' in muted discussion. Harry seethed. He was one of *Pelorus*'s officers and he was damned if he was going to be excluded any longer.

'I say, Scanlon,' said Harry, sufficiently sotto voce to rise above the thump of the main engines, but not to be heard in the wardroom or behind the captain's curtains, 'pour me a nice strong cuppa, please, then take the watch crew's breakfast to them for'ard, they're just getting out of their gear now.'

'Aye aye, sir,' said Scanlon.

You would never have been able to tell it from the young rating's face, but he quite approved of Mr Gilmour's order. Mr Gilmour hadn't been aboard long, but the general consensus was he was 'all right', and most definitely not like that arse, Swann. Swann, who would never, until hell froze over, have thought of sending the watch crew's breakfast to their mess, so that all they had to do after struggling out of their watch gear was to stuff their faces before turning in, knackered, and ready for a serious sesh of Egyptian PT.

McVeigh was silenced by the curtain swishing open. Both he and Sandeman jerked like puppets at Harry's sudden arrival. If Harry hadn't been concentrating so much on his mission, he might have laughed at the comic, caught-in-the-act look that had startled these grown men's faces, but it was come and gone in a flash. Harry sat, placing his cup before him, and looked from Sandeman to McVeigh, determined not to let any little silence deflect him from forcing his way in to their cabal.

'I've marked up the log,' said Harry neutrally.

The two men recovered, waited for the other to say something.

'Anything new on what happens after we reach the waypoint?' Harry asked, referring to the x in the middle of the Skaggerak.

'The Skipper hasn't said,' replied Sandeman, non-committally.

'In case it leaks out to the enemy, I suppose,' said Harry. He knew he was being insubordinate, but it was part of his plan.

'You're skating on thin ice, sonny,' said McVeigh.

Harry ignored him. 'Is it because the Skipper is drunk?' He was looking at Sandeman, however, not McVeigh. But he could see enough of McVeigh to see a brief turmoil of amusement and outrage work over his face.

In the event, Sandeman pre-empted any comment. 'What do you mean by "drunk", Mr Gilmour?' he said.

'I used to crew on rich men's yachts, I know how a gentleman holds his drink. I've seen it close enough and often enough. The glassy eyes and precision of speech, and the long lie-ins. Haven't you noticed, sir?'

Finishing with such a question was the final insult, and Harry had calculated it so. When you want something, and are determined to get it, be forthright. Don't shilly-shally. That was another of his mother's observations.

Sandeman's eyes arched menacingly, but McVeigh loved it. The barked laugh told Harry so.

'Of course we know he's drunk, we talk of little else, Mr Gilmour,' he said.

But it was Sandeman who took up the narrative: 'Why do you ask? Is there something you think we should be doing about it?'

And with these words, Sandeman made Harry feel as if he'd once again walked right into everything hidebound and stolidly 'naval' and unmoving and rigid and bloody stupid that this whole bloody racket was built on. Naval discipline and nowhere to go. Just like the wardroom of *Redoubtable*. It must have showed on his face, because McVeigh was smiling that removed, bemused smile he had. It served only to make Harry feel more forlorn and impotent. It also made him feel irresolute. Harry was trying to assert himself as an officer of this submarine, and he was feeling like a thwarted, wilful child. How did they get to do that?

McVeigh's expression didn't waver. Sandeman had retreated to contemplating his coffee.

'Mr Gilmour,' McVeigh said eventually. 'This. All of this: the armed forces, the Royal Navy; it only works because no one is in any doubt about anything. If you're looking for rationality, flexibility, willingness to adapt, even just plain common sense, you've come to the wrong shop. There are the Articles of War and the Naval Discipline Act. And that's it. Finish.'

McVeigh nodded aft in the direction of the Skipper's cubby. 'He's the Captain. And that makes him the sole, omniscient, in *loco parentis* representative on board of the entire might of the British Empire, the legacy of Nelson, the divine right of kings, will of parliament, and the blessing of the C of E. You might disagree. Have an argument – and quite possibly a very good argument – against the wisdom of his decisions. You might wish to point out the wisdom of your point of view, and the error of his. And in a sane world, a world ashore, there would be bodies you could appeal to, to press your case. Here, however, in the good old Andrew, such notions of democracy are liable to get in the way. We do as he says and if we don't they have a name for it: mutiny. And we all know the consequences of that, don't we?'

Harry kept his mouth shut, which was the best thing to do right then. It sent the right message to the two men before him, men who were already wrestling with a very dangerous and seemingly intractable problem. Sandeman looked up and said: 'Harry.'

The use of his first name sent an involuntary charge through Harry, and he leant imperceptibly in closer.

'Let me tell you why Mr McVeigh and I are worried,' said Sandeman, speaking softly and with calm emphasis. 'Submarines aren't quite the same as the rest of the navy. We're different, a navy within the navy. Because on a submarine, when we dive or go into action, the only bloke who knows what is going on is the Skipper, because he's the only one looking through the periscope. Everything, the boat, the crew, they depend on the Skipper doing it right every time. On a submarine submerged, there are no lookouts to shout "look out". Just the Skipper's eyes and judgement. That is a lot of trust being demanded of a crew going into action, much more than aboard one of those surface skimmers. And it's trust that has to be earned.'

McVeigh interrupted, 'And as you seem to have noticed, Mr Gilmour, our Skipper has not been playing the game in that department. He's not talking to us.'

He turned to Sandeman. 'We might as well lay it out. If young Lochinvar here is smart enough to sense it, he deserves to know what's happening, or at least what we think is happening.'

Sandeman stretched back on the banquette in a strangely expansive gesture given their conspiratorial huddle until now. He clasped his hands over his white pullover and waved for McVeigh to speak.

'We don't know what our orders are for the patrol,' said McVeigh.

This might be Harry's first war patrol on a submarine but he'd been diligent enough in his naval studies to bone up on what is supposed to happen when you put to sea to engage the enemy. And that was why he appreciated the full significance of McVeigh's words.

Harry was well aware that before a submarine sailed she was assigned her own patrol billet, so that two boats didn't end up in the same square of ocean taking shots at each other. Patrol orders included pre-arranged radio-reporting times, intelligence on expected enemy shipping movements, and whose boats are in the adjoining boxes. There was the duration of patrol, time off the billet, transit course back to home waters, the rendezvous time and position to meet the armed trawler or motor gunboat they sent out to escort her back home.

'Since we sailed, the Skipper has dealt directly with Sparks regarding the radio traffic,' said McVeigh, with a distraction that said he found the fact barely credible. 'Done his own encoding and deciphering – which by all rights should've been yours and Swann's job. Not that he's troubled the airwaves at all since we came off the

Texel billet. Nor has there been any incoming traffic. Obviously none of this has been missed by the wireless boys, so the whole crew knows. And that means they're thinking about it instead of thinking about being on a war patrol. And I am assuming even a submarine virgin such as you, knows that is not good.'

'Yes, sir,' said Harry nodding.

'Yes, sir, indeed,' said Sandeman.

'X marks the spot,' continued McVeigh, referring to the notional point on the chart, in the middle of the Skaggerak.

'What about it?' asked Harry.

'We think he has been given intelligence of Jerry shipping movements there. Secret stuff . . . something that has rattled him. Something so big he's hoarding his torpedoes. We think that's why we let the Jerry minesweepers go.'

'If that's the case,' said Harry, looking from McVeigh to Sandeman, 'then it's even more important he tells you what's happening.'

'He's after your job, Sandy,' said McVeigh, smiling.

But all Sandeman said was, 'I know exactly what you mean, Mr Gilmour.'

Harry retired to his bunk and was asleep when *Pelorus* dived for the day. By the time Harry was due back on watch above, it was another lovely cloudless spring afternoon. The submarine slipped relentlessly through the North Sea at a depth of fifty feet, moving at a steady four knots on her electric motors, course unchanged: a dark, monstrous, lethal shadow suspended between the surface and the not-so-deep, which extended now just a mere twenty-odd fathoms beneath the keel.

They had been running some twenty hours now, heading for their new rendezvous. Above them, at one point, there was a distant sighting of fishing boats away to starboard, and then gone, but no target broke their limited horizon, nor enemy warship hunting her. Unseen and unmarked from above while within her steel hull the men who tended *Pelorus*'s progress went about their duties with the same precision as the pumps, gears and motors that propelled her. Their mood, however, was quite a different thing. Unspoken, uncertain, the crew fell to their work, driven now only by duty rather than any sense of eager mission. They only knew one thing right then: their Skipper didn't trust them and that made it hard to trust him.

Harry slipped into the control room to relieve McVeigh, and waited by the Able Seaman messenger at the chart table as the shuffling gavotte of watch handover got underway: the two Planesmen were relieved, then the 'outside' Engine Room Artificer handed over to another Petty Officer Engineer on the dive panel. McVeigh briefed the new helmsman on the course, unchanged. Behind Harry the Asdic watch was relieved, and so was the Telegraphist's Mate in the radio cubby. McVeigh did the routine handover to Harry and waited as he toggled the little handset mic to confirm that two of *Pelorus*'s Torpedomen – the broad designation the navy gave to its electricians (for reasons known only to fleet lore) – had taken over the watch on the two humming electric motors. Forward, the watch in the torpedo room confirmed their handover, and with that *Pelorus* was Harry's. McVeigh vanished back down the companionway, too narrow for him to walk along shoulder-wide.

Not yet four days on board, Harry still couldn't remember names so didn't have the comfort of feeling immediately immersed in the body of the crew. Yet he was grateful to be back on watch. He might still feel them watching him, monitoring his performance, measuring him against their own exacting standards, but that was fine by Harry. At least they were taking him seriously now. And the concentration necessary for standing a periscope watch stopped him from constantly watching himself as if he might unravel at any moment, unpicked by a world changed in recent months from his peacetime everyday to the turmoil of war; stop him constantly wondering at his own passage through it, from feckless student to fighting sailor.

But right now it was, 'check you are still grouped down', and 'steady on dead slow ahead both', the engine-room telegraph ready to communicate any other order aft. The electric motors slowed to a speed that would not generate a 'feather' when the periscope went up, that tell-tale little white wake that said 'submarine' to a lookout on a surface ship. You checked with the Asdic cubby that there were no propeller noises in the water, then ordered 'up periscope!' A very quick 360-degree scan, searching for an enemy that might be close at hand and bearing down on you, or far away; and then down periscope, wait, then up again and another all-round check, this time of the sky, for some Dornier seaplane coming out of nowhere, hunting submarines just like his . . . All clear, so you turned the knob back to the horizon and began the slow ninety-degree sweep, west to north, eyes screwed to detect the first sign of a smudge of smoke, or the tip of a tiny hard vertical line: the masthead of a ship. If you missed it, by the time you came round again to that point on the compass a possible target might have escaped, or could be upon you, too close for the Skipper to set up an attack. Or if it was an enemy destroyer, too close to avoid its depth charges. Then down periscope, and wait, then up again, do the next ninety degrees, north to east, then down periscope. Never have the damn thing above the waves longer than you have to. Never give a competent lookout a chance to spot you; and wait; then the same drill again, working round the compass.

And when you were finished, you rang the telegraph for more speed, marked your progress on the chart and waited, running a little faster for quarter of an hour, maybe twenty minutes; not enough to drain the battery too much; then you began it all again. Hour in and hour out, slipping through the dark waters, moving inexorably, always unseen, towards that x marked on a chart. And as long as everybody kept paying attention and doing their job exactly right, then you all might live; because it took only one not to. Just one. That was what had been drilled into Harry at *Dolphin*. That was what the Bonny Boy had told him during their one and only conversation since he'd stepped aboard. That was life on patrol in the trade.

Chapter Eight

Harry was lying squirrelled in his bunk, eyes fixed on the ageing, caked white paint covering the steel deckhead mere inches above his nose, slathered on during how many refits he'd no idea. His curtain was closed, creating the illusion of separation between him and the narrow companionway immediately beyond its flimsy weft. There was the clamour in his head, while outside the crew passed like goods' trains between the engine spaces and the control room, then there was the too- and fro-ing to the radio cubby, and the chatter and the clash of pans in the galley as Scanlon repaired the devastation from his previous meal; all of it leaving Harry nowhere near sleep, which was not good, as he was due back on watch in less than two hours. The only thing missing was the all-pervading guttural thump of the diesels. It was still daylight and *Pelorus* was dived, running on her electric motors, whose hum did not extend this far forward. Another goods' train came past, except this time it did not lumber on through.

The curtain unceremoniously swished aside and the face of a control room rating he recognised but could not put a name to, even after six days of confinement, was inches from his face. The expression was shut-down and determined to such a degree that Harry didn't at first register that the boy was even younger than he was.

'Sir!' This was hissed, emphatic and low. 'Jimmy says control room pronto, sir!'

Harry was out of his bunk and airborne, feeling as if his feet weren't actually touching the deck until at least halfway down the passageway. He burst through the control room hatch to see the crew complete their hectic bundling into Diving Stations. Sandeman, eyes hidden, was at the handlebars of the main search periscope. Commander Bonalleck's 'mascot' chief, Jimmy Gault, was behind him, leaning forward over Sandeman's crouched figure. Gault, a big, jowly man with grizzled grey hair and a pair of totally incongruous, dainty pince-nez on his nose, was squinting at the bearing bezel above Sandeman's head. He was in the process of reading off the bearing, saying 'Red-six-five.' It could mean only one thing, a target.

McVeigh was already clearing the chart table to begin opening a plot for an attack.

'We have a warship coming out of the Baltic on our bows,' announced Sandeman to the control room, still glued to the periscope. 'And a big one at that. Bigger than a destroyer, anyway. Down periscope,' he said, and stepped back. 'Mr McVeigh, tell Mr Swann in the for'ard torpedo room to open the bow doors on tubes one to six for a snap attack. I got a bit of a look,' he added, and swept his hand through his blond waves in the absent way he had, not addressing anyone in particular. 'She's got some kind of control tower forward . . . not sure who she is, but she's a Jerry all right. It is my intention to attack her.'

Harry stepped forward to face him and said, 'Can I have a look?'

McVeigh shot him a look. It could not have held more shock and menace than if Harry had just dropped his trousers in front of the Princesses Elizabeth and Margaret. Harry, the new boy, could not conceive of the sheer scale of the breach of control room etiquette he had just committed. Sandeman turned his head slowly with that level expression on his face that could be as encouraging as it was scary. It was definitely the latter now. Everyone else assumed expressions of stone.

Harry hurriedly added, 'Apologies, sir. My ship recognition is excellent.'

That wasn't doing it, but Harry was not to be deflected. He had something to say and it was his duty to speak up. He wasn't a student any more, to be ignored. Bloody right he wasn't.

'*Jane's Fighting Ships* was bedtime reading, sir,' he added.

Sandeman frowned, then as if on impulse, suddenly sidestepped with a slightly theatrical gesture that said 'rise and approach'. He ordered: 'Up attack periscope! You already have the angle on the bow, Mr Gilmour. Who is she? And be quick, I don't want us scaring her off.'

Harry stepped forward. As the smaller of the two scopes came up, he flicked the skip of his cap aside, checked the bearing bezel was on red-four-five as the handles came up, and took a look. The slight chop leaped at him, splashing as if right in front of his eyes, a few droplets clinging for an instant, distracting his focus from the beyond, where in the middle distance, was the target; her starboard bows, three quarters on with a 'white bone in her teeth'. He flicked the scope briefly to either side, and he had her escorts, too. Then he flicked back to the target again, dwelling but an instant to confirm. It was but three blinks of his eyes, but he'd seen enough. He stepped back, his throat practically closing with excitement.

'Down scope!' said Harry.

The periscope slid away. Bloody Norah! he thought. The Bonny Boy has indeed been passed intelligence on Jerry shipping, for this bastard is it!

'Sir,' he said, struggling to keep calm in his voice, 'she's a Hipper-class heavy cruiser! With two Loewe-class torpedo boats . . . small destroyers, really. But, sir. She's coming about. Turning, sir.'

'Well I'll be damned. *Hipper*?' breathed Sandeman, his eyes lighting with a vivid intensity. 'You're sure?'

Harry grinned, the implications dawning on him too. 'Not *Hipper* herself, sir. Either *Prinz Eugen*, or *Graf von Zeithen*. Must be either. *Hipper*'s in drydock after *Glowworm* rammed a hole in her back in April . . . and the Norskies blew the bottom out of *Blücher* in Oslofjord during the invasion!'

A frisson ran round their tight little space, the men grinning that Harry couldn't stop blabbing: 'It's one of their heavy cruisers, sir, 18,000 tons if she's an ounce! Four 8-inch guns, six 4-inch. Capable of thirty-three knots . . . oh and a draught of over thirty feet.'

'We get the picture, Mr Gilmour,' said Sandeman, smiling. He stepped forward, creating a little eddy of confidence in the tense confines of the control room, and patted Harry's shoulder. 'Well done, Mr Gilmour. Excellent,' he announced, half to himself, then to the crew: 'We have identified our target, gentlemen, now let us sink her. Mr McVeigh, tell Mr Swann in the torpedo room to set the torpedo running depth for twenty feet, just to be on the safe side, Mr Gilmour, in case they've guzzled all their lager ration and are running light. Now, to your position, Mr Gilmour.' He paused, then, 'Oh, and I know you sailing chaps like to say "coming about", but in the navy we say, "she's under helm".'

Harry beamed at him. 'Aye aye, sir!' he said and shoved his way to his position at the fruit machine to begin setting it up.

If he'd been cocky one instant, he wasn't now: his throat was constricting again, but it was a cold fear that washed over him. *Pelorus,* his boat, was being set up to attack a major German warship, and his role in that attack was going to be critical. Him. Wee

Harry Gilmour, from Dunoon. All the dreaming, all the fantasy, all the training, leading to the right here and now. He swallowed, clamped his jaw and set to work.

Pelorus's true course and speed was already being automatically fed into the fruit machine through feeds from the gyro compass and log, and Harry looked over to the helmsman's position, to confirm. He couldn't see.

Then a hand with a slip of notepaper appeared in Harry's face. The hand belonged to the 'Wrecker', a slight, skelf-like, shrewd-looking Londoner who'd developed an easy cocksure way of appraising Harry's every move when he was on watch. Although the 'outside' ERA had seldom actually addressed him person-ally, Harry didn't like the familiarity of the man. Sandeman and McVeigh always appeared to hold him in great respect however, must have done, as he was now obviously in charge of the trim, with Sandeman on the periscope. Harry knew the ERA's name all right. Frank Lansley. But before he could consider Lansley further, some-thing interrupted Harry's train of thought.

Commander Bonalleck was nowhere to be seen. And no klaxon had sounded for Diving Stations, yet at Diving Stations they were. This was wrong.

Harry looked at the slip of paper Lansley had handed him, seeking enlightenment. On it was a scribble confirming *Pelorus*'s true course and speed. Lansley, a picture of calm benevolence, gave Harry a wink and turned away. Harry automatically checked the figures. Lansley, the man he'd decided to dislike, had just done him a favour of such immensity that even a wet-behind-the-ears Sub-Lieutenant could comprehend its import. It meant Harry did not have to start calling out for information, interrupting what was turn-ing into a fast-moving attack, sounding like an irritating schoolboy unable to keep up with the rest of the class, late on parade and looking like a prat. Harry's dislike for Lansley evaporated in a flash of comprehension. This was the actual arcane ritual at work, the one he had always wondered how it happened: he was becoming 'ship's company'.

Sandeman called up the periscope, and spoke again, the voice low and forceful, yes, but not the full-volume quarterdeck bellow which the tension of the moment might have merited. He looked at his watch, then over at the chronometer above the chart table.

'It is 13.02. I am commencing the attack, mark the time, Mr McVeigh,' he said. Then there was a pause as the periscope rose, and he gripped it for a quick 360-degree sweep before swinging back to the target. Then: 'The bearing is . . . that!'

Gault, squinting, read off the bezel: 'Red-five-zero.'

Sandeman began working a dial on the periscope, using its horizontal split-image device. Harry knew what he was doing; he was looking at two images of the target, one on top of the other, and he was bringing the waterline of the top image to sit on the superstructure of the bottom image. With the two together, it would give the range. Sandeman called again: 'Range is . . . that!'

And as fast as Gault read it off: 'Twenty minutes!' on the readout, McVeigh with his slide rule announced: 'Range 6,000 yards!'

Sandeman ordered, 'Down periscope!' and Harry cranked in the target's numbers. His machine had been storing and updating what *Pelorus* was doing, now it had to store and update the target.

Two minutes elapsed before Sandeman ordered the periscope back up. The bearing and the range were called again. The range was now a little over 5,000 yards. McVeigh estimated the target's speed at twenty knots.

Sandeman ordered the periscope down and observed: 'Right. She's been zigzagging and she's just completed a zig. If she stays on this course, and doesn't zag, for another seven minutes . . .' He trailed off, then said to Harry, still cranking in the readings: 'Mr Gilmour, what is the target doing?'

You're on, thought Harry. If you've paid attention, and dialled it all in correctly . . .

He kept his voice matter-of-fact, even though he certainly didn't feel it. This was battle now. 'Target on course two-three-four! Range now five-thousand two-hundred! Bearing red-four five!' he said.

And Sandeman replied: 'Give me a heading for a track angle of zero-nine-five degrees, Mr Gilmour.'

Harry made the regulation call-back, and began cranking figures into the fruit machine. Christ, he thought, anyone would think I know what I'm doing! The solution rolled up. 'Steer one-eight-zero, sir!' he said through a dry mouth.

Sandeman confirmed to the helmsman, 'Put me on one-eight-zero. Half ahead together.'

He waited until his orders were being executed, leaning against the chart table, his back to McVeigh. Without turning, looking into some far distance he spoke again: 'Mr Gilmour. What is my periscope angle?'

Harry read off the data with a certain precision and formality he didn't recognise as his own: 'Red-three-four, sir.'

The thought flashed into Harry's head again: a head going full pelt it hadn't had time to re-occur to him until now. Where *was* the Skipper?

There was an unknown target up there and Sandeman had brought the boat to Diving Stations . . . without informing the Skipper. Harry could only guess at the state Bonalleck might be in, but even so, this was wrong. He didn't dare look at Sandeman, yet the atmosphere in the control room was calm – taut yes, but business-like, as if the crew had no quibble with the first Lieutenant's conduct and were awaiting his orders.

Sandeman leant back into the passageway and called aft: 'Asdic. Any HE?'

This was to the wireless rating sitting in the Asdic cubby, right now manning the boat's other underwater listening device – the hydrophones, capable of passively picking up a target's propeller noises miles off. HE was 'hydrophone effects', and yes, there was.

From the cubby just beyond the control room door, the rating announced, 'Yes, sir, multiple . . . at least one set of heavy returns, and . . . one, maybe two light . . . all high speed. Moving quite fast, coming down our throat, sir, maybe twenty knots, still away off, but closing fast.'

'Very good,' said Sandeman.

No matter how many times Harry had thought he was preparing for this moment, he knew now that nothing could have prepared him. It would not have been true to say he was frightened. He sat at his position, not rigid but relaxed, a sense of cool, clear-headed anticipation suffusing his senses. Here was the moment he had conjured up countless times before. Now it was happening. He told himself this was an ancient moment, timeless among men: the approach to battle. Except this was nothing like that far-away fantasy that had happened to him at Narvik. That had been bangs and thuds directed from beyond steel doors to a place somewhere else, with consequences that took place beyond a mountain, and the fact it was happening only known about through a crackling radio he could not hear, broadcast to people he couldn't see.

Not this time, however. This was here, now, with the enemy 'coming down our throat'. He did not have a weapon in his hand, a gun, or a cutlass, but this clunky metal box he sat before would just as surely kill the enemy if he wielded it properly. He felt the control room crew around him, rather than saw them; like him, they were utterly immersed, bent together on putting their boat in the enemy's way.

He had only one concern: that he would not rise to the conduct expected of him; that he would in some way be found wanting by these grave and capable men; but he would not let that happen. He knew that. He would not allow himself to be found wanting.

'Up periscope!' Sandeman ordered again. The swift 360-degree scan, then on to the target. 'Bearing is . . . that!' Then the range was called. Harry cranked it in. McVeigh, over the plot, made his notations. Sandeman said: 'Down periscope!' The scope slid away, and he turned to the plot where McVeigh stood with undisguised blood-lust in his eyes, grinning evilly; in the tight space of the control room, Sandeman only had to lean to see their relative positions marked on the chart.

'We're not closing fast enough, Bill, not if we're still on for a ninety-five degree track angle,' Sandeman announced – 'track angle' was the difference between the course the target was steering and the torpedoes' course when they intercepted.

Sandeman unclipped a mic: 'Motor room? Control room. How are our batteries for a two-minute sprint?'

An excruciating silence, then: 'Full ahead together for two minutes,' said Sandeman. Almost immediately they all felt a surge. Sandeman waited, and as the surge came off he called, 'Up periscope.'

Bearing and range were called. Harry updated the machine, McVeigh his slide rule. Sandeman ordered the periscope down.

'We're there. If she stays on this course for another three, she'll be within two-thousand yards when we fire, and we'll hit her with a full salvo, beam on, on the stopwatch.' He turned: 'Harry, what's a Hipper's length?'

'About seven-hundred feet, sir.'

Before even Sandeman could ask, McVeigh had his slide rule up, muttering through gritted teeth, '. . . speed about twenty knots, length seven-hundred feet . . . give it five-second intervals between launches, Skipper, that'll hose the bastard from paint locker to steering flat.'

Sandeman nodded. 'Up periscope!' The scope slid up once more.

Each of those German warships would be bristling with lookouts whose only job was to spot the tell-tale 'feather' of a periscope. There would be no slackers; a dry bunk to sleep in that night depended on them keeping their eyes peeled. Their very lives depended on it!

Sandeman called the range and bearing again. The target was closing fast, maintaining course. The time was 13.09. A further three minutes had elapsed: Sandeman had had the periscope up for less than seven seconds.

If this happened, it would make the newspapers. It would be gazetted. HMS *Pelorus* would take her place in submarine lore. The boat that sank the Royal Navy's first German heavy cruiser of the war; and may there be many more of them! It would go down in the history books! And Harry was here, on his first war patrol. He could feel his chest tighten with the sheer epic intensity of it. Harry Gilmour, the boy who used to crew on *Tangle* and get his hair mussed by those grandee yachtsmen; young Harry, grand lad, always keen to lend a hand, fetch and carry and be taken for granted in a kindly, patronising, jollied-along sort of way, was about to sink a bloody great German cruiser.

'Up periscope!'

Harry jumped. He hadn't been paying attention. He snapped back from the runaway reverie, shamed by the horror of what he had allowed. His mind went back to the task in hand. The range was now 3,200 yards, target course steady, time 13.11.

Would Jerry zig again? Would she turn inside their attack, steaming so fast they no longer had battery reserves for another sprint to get in position for another shot? The seconds dripped away.

Or, what if instead of crossing her bows she would pass too close down their starboard side, too close for *Pelorus* to turn and fire? Was Harry's tender, now exultant thrill of impending glory to be snatched away in the spin of a bloody Jerry helmsman's wheel?

Sandeman was impossibly still, poised over the periscope well. Still no one breathed; chests hurt; then Sandeman, as if the words were almost being wrung from him, said in a level, conversational tone, 'Up periscope'. He looked, and Gault called the bearing. Still no course change on the target. Sandeman stepped back, 'Time?'

'13.12,' said McVeigh. And then it all happened very quickly. Sandeman and McVeigh were looking at their watches as Sandeman matter of factly requested, 'Confirm periscope angle for a nine-five degree track?'

Harry had already done his job. He'd cranked in all the data, Sandeman should have all the figures he needed to calculate that all-important angle. The angle between *Pelorus*'s course and the German cruiser which would draw the first line in a deadly triangle, marked in time and trigonometry, that when crossed would tell Sandeman when to fire; which would leave the German cruiser speeding, unknowing, to arrive at a spot on the ocean at exactly the same time as *Pelorus*'s torpedoes.

Harry read it off: 'Red-two-nine.'

If Harry had worked the machine correctly, when Jerry crossed that invisible line running from *Pelorus*, Sandeman would order, 'fire one', and the first of the steel monsters would launch into the sunlight-dappled sea to tear away at over forty knots, heading for a pre-determined rendezvous. If he had done his job, the cruiser would reach that spot in less than two minutes' time. No going back now to correct. Harry turned to watch the show.

No one was moving in the control room, save to execute an order. The helmsman had *Pelorus* steady on 180 degrees, his eyes never varying from the gyro repeater. On the fore and aft planes the two senior chiefs held her steady at periscope depth. Lansley's eyes never left the trim board; he stood poised to move whenever he would need to – fast – to adjust the trim as each torpedo left its tube and compressed air blew back into the boat, as *Pelorus* became lighter by one and a half tons, less the weight of the water flooding back into the empty tube. Little sheens of sweat began to mist around the temples of several of the control room crew.

Pelorus slid slowly towards her rendezvous, an unhurried killer moving silent and unseen, guided with an almost artistic deftness by her crew. In his mind's eye, Harry saw the forward torpedo room; Swann presiding over the preparations with a calmness born of his own utter lack of imagination. Harry might not like the bastard, and the bastard might regard him as beneath recognition, but Harry was in no doubt that Swann would do his job. He could almost imagine him ordering one of the young Torpedomen to remove the safety pins from the torpedo tubes' firing levers. Behind the boy would be standing a Leading Torpedoman ready to throw the number one tube lever on Sandeman's order. Next to him would be a chief with a stopwatch to tell him when to fire the remaining five; to be launched in a daisy chain, on timings that would spread the salvo over two-and-a-half ship lengths as the enemy ship thundered past.

Sandeman intended to fire the first torpedo just ahead of the target; and on the stopwatch, the last would be launched to pass just astern. It was a standard attack, Harry had read all about the simple lethal logic behind how it should work. At twenty knots, Jerry was going too fast to turn into the attack if he spotted the telltale torpedo tracks scything towards him. If he ordered full ahead in a bid to get out of their paths, he would plough into the first torpedo; if he ordered full astern in an attempt to let the torpedoes pass ahead of him, the last one would get him. If he did nothing, if he didn't see the bubble wakes streaking towards him, Jerry would take all remaining four kippers, right in his guts. Technically, Sandeman could not miss, Harry told himself, repeating it in his head like a mantra. Technically.

Sandeman once again ordered, 'Up periscope,' and stepped forward, asking Gault, almost politely, 'Put me on the periscope angle please, chief.'

As the periscope handles rose, Gault smiled. 'Aye aye, sir,' he said, and moved behind Sandeman as he crouched, released the handles and pressed his eyes to the rubber. This was the defining moment of Sandeman's entire naval career, thought Harry. If he pulls this off . . . but he could not complete the sentence in his head. His imagination did not reach that far. He could not imagine what glory would rain down on Sandeman if this day's work went well. He marvelled at the sangfroid, the cool, unhurried, detached professionalism of the man, and felt an unfamiliar pang of jealousy. He had forgotten all about the Bonny Boy, lying in god knows what state behind his tiny cabin's curtain; and he did not begin to consider what cataclysmic consequences must flow from Sandeman's courage.

The seconds dripped by. It had been barely six minutes since the target had been first sighted. Sandeman pulled down the periscope handles and as he focused, Gault placed his big maw hands over his, and squinting like a school master at the bezel, began to slowly walk him round. 'Red-two-nine . . . now!'

Sandeman acknowledged, 'Red-two-nine,' and there was a stomach-twisting beat, and then, '. . . and hee-re she comes . . . right on time . . . FIRE ONE! Down scope,' and he leapt back as the attack periscope slid away.

His command was instantly echoed by McVeigh, into his mic.

Suddenly there was a lurch, as if *Pelorus* had hit a bump in the road, and a sudden, subtle increase in pressure on the ears, as the compressed air used to launch the first torpedo vented back.

The control room galvanized as McVeigh was announcing, 'Range to target nineteen-hundred yards.'

Lansley was all over the trim board, adjusting stop cocks, squinting at dials; across the tiny space the senior Planesmen began edging their big wheels to hold *Pelorus* level. As they worked, the status calls came fast.

'One away and running!'

Sandeman called, 'Fire on the stopwatch!'

From the squawk box above Harry's head, a disembodied staticky voice began counting down, '. . . three, two, FIRE TWO! . . . four, three, two, FIRE THREE! . . .'

Pelorus started to buck as if she was passing over cobbles; and then, as if the speed of events had not been cranked high enough, two further shattering things happened at once.

A bellow from the hydrophones rating: 'HE effects on the starboard bow, high-speed propellors, approaching fast . . . going to pass ahead of us!'

Ahead. Between *Pelorus's* salvo, and the big fat cruiser!

Sandeman snapped round, his eyes on Harry, a huge question on his face. High-speed propellors . . . it could only be one of the escort ships . . . and she was in danger of shielding the primary target. Sandeman's fierce stare was asking, silently, agonisingly, Will she take the torpedoes meant for the cruiser?

Harry's mind froze, became a perfect blank, black void, until it suddenly filled with a page from *Janes's*, and a figure. 'Eighteen feet!' He hissed, 'Loewe-class TBs only draw eighteen feet. We set for twenty-plus!'

Sandeman threw his head back and seemed to suck in air. And then, before him, in the bulkhead doorway, stood Commander Bonalleck. Harry saw Sandeman's look, spun to follow its line, and there at his shoulder stood the wreck of his CO: dishevelled hair above a crumpled white officers' shirt, buttoned wrongly and nothing else; ivoried, lumpy sticks of legs extending beyond the shirt-tails, ending in feet in need of a wash. But it was the face and the expression; its porridgy mass, blobbed with red. The eyes rimmed with red too, like red wool woven round their bulging stare. And the mouth stretched into a rictus that seemed barely human. A foxy stink, rising from unwashed parts, eddied around him as the bug eyes crept round the tiny space, and wet lips drew back over yellowing teeth. Yet he seemed unable to speak. A hand reached out and he steadied himself on Harry's shoulder, but without seeing him. The other hand rose, sepulchral, reaching out from a grubby cuff to accuse Sandeman.

'You,' was all he managed to say, the word spoken not with a voice but with a breath.

Before he could develop his point, Sandeman, as if he was batting him aside, said with an imperative authority: 'You shouldn't have got out of your sickbed, sir!' And he was looking away before the words were out of his mouth, turning back to his fast-moving attack, not yet complete, still needing to be managed.

Another call from the Asdic cubby: 'High-speed propeller sounds, revs increasing, she's turning fast, coming directly at us, she's coming on fast, very fast.'

Over the hydrophones operator delivering his commentary, the squawk box announced, 'Four, three, two, fire SIX!'

Another bump, as the last torpedo left its tube, and a flash of movement across the control room, the trim crew and Planesmen's deft touch settling the *Pelorus*, calming her bucking. And Sandeman's voice above it all, no longer directed at the crazed figure in front of the aft bulkhead; staccato now, issuing precise orders, executing *Pelorus's* escape: 'Port thirty, helmsman, make your course zero-six-five. Flood Q! Mr Lansley. Make your depth one-eight-zero feet. Twenty degrees down angle. Group up, full ahead together.'

The deckplates began to fall away beneath Harry as he took in the brief intense activity and became aware of a growing sound, like a food mixer echoing through the hull, soft at first, but insistent. The Jerry torpedo boat.

To Bonalleck's side, ignoring him, stood McVeigh, grim, gripping a stopwatch, fit to crush it. And Bonalleck, just staring now, no longer seeing anything anymore, unaware; his eyes fixed on a point either inches beyond his nose or 1,000 miles away, Harry could not tell.

'Two minutes gone,' announced McVeigh, like a toll of doom, his and Sandeman's eyes locked. Too many seconds had elapsed. The silence said it all.

The first torpedo had crossed the cruiser's course, and the cruiser had not been there. The seconds again began to drip. Harry focused on a tiny oil leak down one of the runners on the main periscope. Counting.

One . . . two . . . three . . . four . . . And then the whole hull echoed as if hit by some vast steel hammer, reverberating away to a terrible silence.

One . . . two . . . three . . . four . . .

And another.

And another.

Sandeman, almost leisurely, picked the mic off its bulkhead catch and clicked it on.

'This is the first Lieutenant here,' he said to the crew, with a showman's ice-cool control. 'We have just scored three torpedo hits on a German Hipper-class heavy cruiser.' A pause. 'Shut off for depth charging. Prepare for depth charging.' And then he clipped back the mic, turned and treated the entire control room to one of his very boyish and rather fetching grins.

Chapter Nine

HMS *Pelorus* was a little over two hours away from her pre-arranged rendezvous with a Royal Navy motor gunboat scheduled to be waiting for her at 06:30 hours two miles east-north-east of the Bass Rock. She was running at a steady fourteen knots, on the surface on a pitch-black night, with a force 4 wind and a short stubby sea hitting her from the south-west. She had taken almost three days to weave her way through the North Sea minefields – German and British – and was now heading for the Rosyth Naval Base on the Firth of Forth.

The journey from the mouth of Skagerrak had been fraught, the crew cowed by Commander Bonalleck's unspoken recriminations, and a poisonous atmosphere that seemed to smother any celebration of their successful action against the German cruiser. Bonalleck had not slept in the sixty-odd hours since they managed to escape the attentions of the two German escorts accompanying the cruiser, such as they'd been. The first torpedo boat, obviously having spotted *Pelorus's* torpedo tracks, had turned towards them, opening her throttles and charging in at over thirty knots. But by the time the Jerry had reached the spot where *Pelorus* had fired, *Pelorus* was long gone, in a diving turn heading away at ninety degrees.

The Asdic cubby had reported a series of splashes as depth charges entered the water, and Harry had remembered a vague clenching of the guts. Over the next fifteen minutes there had been six boat-rattling bangs which had initially caused him some considerable alarm. But as no one else aboard appeared remotely concerned, and each succeeding bang had appeared to be getting farther away, Harry began to wonder what all the fuss was about; this depth-charging business hadn't been so bad. He certainly hadn't been impressed by the much-lauded Kriegsmarine's anti-submarine tactics.

Of the other escort there was no report. Sandeman, musing aloud, concluded she had probably stayed back to rescue survivors. Harry also remembered the very distant rumbles which followed the attack, echoing through their hull from the depths, and the creaking sound of tearing metal.

'That's bulkheads going,' a disembodied voice had said. A little later the voice reported HE effects for internal explosions. By then Bonalleck had vanished from the control room, missing all the grim smiles of satisfaction and relief. There had been no cheers or yells among the crew. Indeed the aftermath of the attack had felt something of an anti-climax to Harry who was already pinching himself to ram home the immensity of what they had done; the scale of their victory.

This was the biggest enemy warship so far to be lost to direct hits from Royal Navy ordnance. *Graf Spee* had been lost, but she'd scuttled herself. This one was a different matter altogether and he had expected a little more demonstrable triumph to accompany their achievement. But Harry was still a boy really, and his only experience until now of war at sea was the abstract news heard in *Redoubtable's* wardroom of the demise of a handful of German 'puddle-jumpers' picked off close to shore, in a bombardment whose effects had all taken place on the other side of a bloody great mountain. He wasn't thinking about what it must be like to be sunk at sea; to have your ship blown apart and disappear beneath you, throwing you into the cold, numbing water among the debris and the bodies and the spreading slick of bunker fuel. Nor could he know then that fate was already on the way, bent on his enlightenment.

Bonalleck had not returned to the control room until Sandeman was bringing *Pelorus* up to periscope depth again for a look back to make sure they had made good their escape. When he did, he was the CO once more: immaculately dressed and grim of countenance, scrutinising any gesture or word spoken in his presence as if sniffing for conspiracies.

He individually summoned Sandeman and McVeigh to his cabin where what was said could not be deciphered, even by the curious Scanlon, who, being in charge of the galley directly across the shoulder-wide passageway, was the only member of crew with any justification for lurking nearby. Both officers emerged separately to inform the control room crew that they had been relieved of their watch-keeping duties and would now only 'assist' in the operation of the boat. After that, the Bonny Boy's presence was ubiquitous in the control room and on the bridge. And he kept the crew busy. Pointless tasks, meticulous housekeeping and checks, all to be completed with utmost urgency and written up immediately on completion with the report presented to him personally; only for him to then ostentatiously file each one away, unread.

Harry, with Chief Petty Officer Gault in tow, was now involved in one such infuriating, petty little exercise as *Pelorus* sped towards her rendezvous: a spares inventory in the engine room, matching up stock with requisition forms. The deeply offensive suggestion being that *Pelorus*'s Chief Engineer, a warrant officer with 20 years service called Ted Padgett, was flogging off Admiralty stores. Ted was a short, paunchy man with a round Toby-Jug face that was usually plastered with oil and a smile. Now the fleshy jaw was set like a stone escarpment as he stood in his usual set of disreputable overalls, smeared and sweat-caked, with heavy gauntlets stuffed in one pocket and a rag in the other, peering over one of his senior ERA's shoulders as he counted the paper returns for securing bolts, marked 'used' or 'holding'.

Being in the engine room was like being inside the ribcage of some modernist replica dinosaur cast in steel and brass, with the rising flanks of the diesels pressing in on the steel-decked companionway, not dead, but moving, with rank upon rank of tappets dancing their perpetual dance, generating a din in the confined space that was extreme, especially with both diesels going flat out now, all their power driving the boat, since there was no need for a battery charge tonight. *Pelorus* would be entering the safe waters of the Forth when the sun came up tomorrow, not diving.

Harry could feel his teeth rattling, and his vision at times seemed close to blurring in the vibration. From where he stood aft by a tall desk for spreading plans and engine schematics, he could see the two Stokers on watch patrolling their engines, applying a little oil here and there from cans like a genie's bottle, or polishing a smeared part or pipe. The cramped cylinder in which the two throbbing diesels rested was gleaming, as were the diesels themselves, lovingly pampered by the two Stokers in their oily overalls, caps perched jauntily on the backs of their heads. Harry always felt he was entering a parallel universe every time he came aft to the engine spaces, especially when the boat was at sea and underway. A universe of noise and the reek of oil and diesel fuel, and these complex, moving engines, like beasts themselves, always seemingly on the verge of tearing free, the thrum of them rising in every steel plate and pipe surface. That was when, looking down the for'ard end of the engine room, Harry saw McVeigh appear, like a messenger from the other universe he'd left behind.

The men rose from their paperwork, and McVeigh, gesturing to his ears, pointed for Harry to go aft into the motor room. Harry pushed through the spring-loaded doors to be greeted by two Leading Torpedomen bent over a stripped-down rheostat. McVeigh pushed through behind him, and, still having to yell, told the LTs, 'Go to the galley. Scanlon's got a brew on.'

The two men tidied up their tools and slipped past, heading for'ard with a brief, 'Aye aye, sir,' and a salute. The doors were soundproofed and so rendered the noise level manageable.

'The Skipper's still on the bridge,' said McVeigh, without preamble. 'We should be picking up the gunboat in a couple of hours, then it's straight up to Rosyth. Whether it's to be met by a brass band or a firing squad remains to be seen. How are you?'

'All right, sir,' said Harry.

McVeigh nodded, then said: 'I don't know what the Skipper's intentions are ashore. I don't know what he's been sending under his "captain's only" code, or what has been signalled back to him. Just that he's said we sank a Jerry cruiser,' and then he paused, with a quick smile. 'We had a signal not long after we surfaced tonight, confirmation of the sinking from the Admiralty. You were right. It was the *Graf von Zeithen*.'

Harry just smiled. He was getting better at keeping his mouth shut when there was nothing useful to say.

McVeigh continued: 'Well, where do we stand.' It was a statement. 'At the very least, Mr Sandeman is guilty of disobeying submarine Commanders' standing operational orders by not immediately summoning the Skipper to the control room on sighting Jerry. It could be argued that I should've questioned the first Lieutenant's decision. It could be argued that we conspired together. I don't know whether the Skipper might want to take it that far though. Commander Bonalleck's own self-interest might not be best served if he were to seek to over-dramatise events, if you get my drift.

Obviously I can't tell you what to say if there are any . . . repercussions, but neither the first Lieutenant nor I think there will be. Anyway, what I do want to make clear is that we, Sandy and I, whoever asks, we are going to tell it straight, except we're not going to mention the booze. Lieutenant Sandeman's position is that he believed the Skipper was ill. That it was plain to him on sighting the Jerry that it would need to be a snap attack and that speed was of the essence, and that was why he decided to execute the attack without delay. The log confirms the actual action lasted barely six minutes from start to finish, so we have that behind us.' McVeigh paused to look away at something only he could see. 'A lot can happen in six minutes . . . on a submarine.' Then he looked back at Harry and smiled. 'Thought I'd better tell you all that before we go ashore, we thought it best for you to know what we are going to say, just in case.'

'Have you had this conversation with Mr Swann, sir?' Harry asked.

McVeigh gave him a long, level look. 'Don't be bloody foolish. Anyway, he wasn't in the control room. Didn't see anything or hear anything. Sub-Lieutenant Swann will say what he's going to say, and I very much doubt anyone will be any the wiser for it.'

Harry smiled. 'Thank you for letting me know, sir. I don't think I'll have much to add, except to say that the Skipper had been looking rather off for a few days.'

McVeigh snorted and gave a little rock of laughter. 'Off!' A pause, and another one of his appraising sideways looks. 'You did all right back there, young Gilmour. For a first war patrol. Not many snotty little oiks just out of *King Alfred* get to blow the arse out of a German heavy cruiser on their first day out in long trousers. You should think about taking this lark up professionally.'

'Thank you very much, sir,' replied Harry, grinning.

'Bill,' said McVeigh, 'but only when we're among consenting adults. See you in the bar.' As he got up, he gave Harry a punch on the shoulder. 'I'll get Scanlon to bring you lot back some java,' he added as he unlatched the bulkhead door and let the deafening din back in. Then McVeigh's hunched back lurched its way into the engine room.

Harry never saw him again.

The events of the minutes that followed would etch themselves on to Harry's mind forever, super-real in their intensity; the moments before, by their banal normality, and the moments after by their harsh, intruding violence.

After McVeigh had gone, Gault and Ted Padgett swung their way in through the motor room doors, clutching their paperwork. They were back here to agree the tallies and have Harry, as the officer, sign them off. The two LTs came back, too, to finish working on the rheostat. The swing doors, with their passably effectual soundproofing, were again swung shut and the noise diminished.

As well as being quieter, the motor room was an altogether more spacious place than where the diesels lived, the only direct noise really from the machine whine of the propeller shafts for the most part enclosed by the electric motor housings, and the control armatures for turning the batteries' electricity into shaft torque on the propellors.

The paperwork was spread out and Gault's dinky little pince-nez were placed delicately back on his nose so he could peer at the columns scribbled out on one of engine room's cardboard bound ledgers.

Ted Padgett, clutching the forms, said: 'Shall we get this out the way?'

'I'm sorry about this, Mr Padgett,' said Harry. 'It's all very . . .' But Harry was grinding to a halt under the warrant officer's baleful stare.

Gault, peering over his little spectacles, sighed audibly: 'He's new, Ted. The boy's new.'

Then turning to Harry, addressing him as if Padgett wasn't there, Gault said: 'Mr Padgett is old Andrew, Mr Gilmour. Once you've been in a blue suit long enough, you'll understand what that means. There's no need to apologise for bollocks like this to the likes of him. He knows the score, don't you, Ted?'

Padgett nodded. 'Oh, you and me both, Mr Gault. It's the navy. If you can't take a joke you shouldn't have joined, right?'

'What joke would that be, gentlemen?' Harry said, bridling. Ever since *Redoubtable*, Harry had sworn to himself that he wasn't going to take these verbal smokescreens everyone in this bloody navy kept throwing up, making sure he knew exactly where he stood – on the outside.

Gault sighed, sensing Harry's mood. 'Mr Gilmour, I think it's time some things should be explained to you, if you will allow. Sir?'

'From the beginning, if you please, Mr Gault,' said Harry. 'I'm on this boat, too.'

'Indeed you are, sir. From the beginning. It will not have escaped your notice, sir, that in the Andrew, the Royal Navy, that is, we're a very traditional bunch. Traditions within traditions even. And of course this lot, the trade, even though we're a new branch to the service, real johnny-cum-latelys by naval standards, we've still had time enough to come up with our own. Different from the surface skimmers up there. Different because to start with, there's a bit less of the "b-to-the-three" if you get my drift . . .'

Harry looked puzzled.

'"Bullshit baffles brains",' interjected Ted to be helpful.

'And of course there's a reason for that,' continued Gault, still in reverie mode. 'It's all about discipline really. Us lot, the trade, the way things are. On submarines there isn't any room for POs with nothing more to do but make sure able seamen aren't doing nothing. We all have proper jobs on a boat and we all have to know how to do them. That means we have to bring our own discipline. It don't work in the trade if you just look at life as a sort of search for opportunities to swing the lead, take it easy, bunk off. I'n't that right, Ted?'

'Aye,' said Padgett with a nod. 'Thing about the trade is, Mr Gilmour, unlike that lot upstairs, with us, if every man knows his job and does his duty exactly right, then there's a good chance we'll all live. If he don't, then we don't. It's simple as that. You can't arse about on a submarine, Mr Gilmour. Even a simple sin like tripping over yer own feet, something you havin' been to officers' school, sir, you'll know all about,' Ted Padgett and Jim Gault were grinning at each other so much so that Harry couldn't hold back a sardonic nod of recognition. 'Some halfwit fallin' over his own feet and the next thing, the halfwit has grabbed a vent valve or dropped his wrench into the battery space, and before you can say "any more for Winnie More, before she pulls her drawers up", we're all sharing our tot with Davy Jones.'

'We don't like gormless people in a boat,' added Gault.

'Right, Jim. On a boat yer first job is to keep yer "gorm" about yer at all times.' Padgett was laughing now, his sour countenance vanished.

'And the officers are supposed to know that,' added Gault. 'That's why the trade has a reputation for being a bit more easygoing than the proper navy. You'll have heard it and you'll hear it again. But only from those that don't understand. There isn't less discipline in the trade, Mr Gilmour. If anything, the discipline here is the hardest of all. Self-discipline. You look after yourself, your mates and your boat. At all times. And that's why when Skippers come on all hard-horse like Commander Bonalleck just now, it doesn't go down well, because it's not necessary. Because when Commander Bonalleck and all officers like him, when they sees

Ted here in his number ones, with that red picket fence of stripes up his arm,' said Gault, referring to Warrant Officer Engineer Ted Padgett's full dress uniform and the row of stripes that would be there on his left sleeve, denoting long service and good conduct, 'that should tell them something . . .'

'Twenty years of undetected crime,' interjected a sombre Padgett.

'Apart from that, Ted,' said Gault with mock patience, but before he could go on Harry made his sally into the ongoing badinage.

'I understand,' was all he managed, but inside his head it was a different story.

The message was simple . . . officers, even captains – especially captains – shouldn't piss off their senior rates. And junior officers shouldn't patronise those senior rates by apologising for it. He got that. But for Harry, the moment meant a lot more. It was one of those coming-of-age moments of the kind which engulfs every young tyro of adventurous spirit, who at last realises he is accepted into the company of men. And now it was Harry's turn to feel the timeless visceral burn as he looked back into the faces of these two old sea dogs: Gault, old enough to be his father, and Ted Padgett even older; men who were now candidly regarding him as one of their number. In the trade.

And McVeigh, not so much his words just now, but the fact that he'd spoken them at all. 'Just so as you know . . .', that was what he'd said. Including Harry in the affairs of the boat. One of the crew. Ship's company, HMS *Pelorus*. At last.

Harry felt so good that he even managed to stop himself from running off at the mouth in his gratitude and pride, but he was powerless to hold out against the grin trying to split his face. The spectre of *Redoubtable* was gone, along with all the impotence and humiliation of being a youth adrift in a man's world. He had been in battle with these men and together they had prevailed. The welling of emotion that rose in Harry's breast was such that right then he would have laid down his life for them, with a smile on his face.

'He thinks we're havin' a laugh, Jim,' said Padgett.

'Nah he doesn't. He understands, don't you, Mr Gilmour?'

'Understands what, Jim? If you can't take a joke, you shouldn't have joined?' asked Padgett, his mouth twitching with gleeful devilment.

'Yeah, Ted. Isn't that right, Mr Gilmour?'

But Harry started laughing and couldn't stop.

There was a thumping on the swing doors, and when Harry scrambled over to pull them open, Able Seaman Scanlon was demanding entry with a can of tea, some biscuits and three mugs. He was laying out the fare, about to play mother, when they all felt the submarine heel to starboard, and their grins vanished.

There was a yawning pause through which the heel increased, but no explanation filtered back to them from the control room or bridge. The engine room telegraph bell ripped through the diesel din. They looked up, all of them seeing the bridge ringing for 'full astern' on the port engine.

Padgett jumped to his feet and immediately shot into the main engine room, Gault and Scanlon reached out to save the impromptu tea party set out on one of the electric motor casings. The heel increased rapidly. Whatever was happening on the bridge, Bonalleck was executing a sharp turn to port.

Harry looked into Gault's worried eyes for some explanation as the engine room telegraph rang again, full astern on both engines. The next thing they were all sprawled and rolling on the deckplates, in pitch black, and even the noise of the diesels was being drowned by terrible ripping, interrupted only by an explosion forward and then a blue flash, like an arc of lightning, going off in the room next door.

'The fucking batteries!' yelled Gault, as the hull lurched and bounced, and the tearing noise was replaced by a long metallic scraping that seemed to drag its way down the length of the starboard hull.

The lurching threw Harry against steel; exactly what he couldn't tell in the darkness. It dead-armed him on his right side and then it smashed into his left ribs, winding him and leaving him flat on his back on a deckplate several feet aft down the motor room from where he'd been sitting. Then, just as suddenly as it had started, it stopped, so that *Pelorus* was left wallowing slightly, skewed and listing by the starboard bow.

A light came on. One of the LTs had clambered to his feet and was fixing a small emergency lamp to the forward bulkhead. Gault had another, its light dancing through the gloom a swirling mist which fugged the air with burnt rubber and the terrible reek of burnt steel.

Chapter Ten

'Shut all watertight doors!' Harry heard someone shout from way down forward.

He eased himself up on his good arm and peered into the swirling gloom. The doors into the main engine room were open and he could see that Gault had gone through. Scanlon was sitting propped up against one of the motors, and the two Leading Torpedomen were scrabbling about, opening storage spaces, looking for god knows what. He could hear shouts from deep in the boat, and another sound that chilled him, barely discernable above the engines, but there. The sound of rushing water.

Pelorus lurched again and he felt her beginning to fall away from him, the bows going down. Harry pushed himself up and as he rose he could see Gault hurrying away forward. Behind him, several half-dressed figures appeared, Stokers coming from the engine room crew's accommodation space. What the hell was happening? He turned again to see other men hurrying from for'ard, running up the slope of the deck past the imposing, confining flanks of the main diesels towards him, fear in the leading man's eyes; and behind him, the rest pushing and bundling each other in their rush to get away.

'Shut that bloody door!'

A violent shout, was it Gault's?

The sound of rushing water was audible above the diesel thump now. And then, dimly, all the way through to the for'ard bulkhead door, behind the scrambling body of sailors, suddenly – my god! Harry could see it! Water bubbling over the combing.

They were sinking. HMS *Pelorus* was sinking.

For no reason he could fathom, Harry shot through the door between the motor room and the main engine room before the buffeting daisy chain of men reached and blocked it in their frenzy to get away. What did he intend to do? What could he do? The realisation that *Pelorus* was going down, with him in it, had stunned him beyond coherent thought. Maybe he was going to help Gault, but help him to do what?

That's when he saw Ted Padgett, wedged between the port main diesel and what looked like some kind of pump. One side of his face was bloody and something dark had caked the front of his overalls. The rest of Padgett's face, normally pale, was sepulchre white, and his eyes, still partially open, had rolled back in his head. Harry dodged the leading sailor running up the deck, as he bent to shoot through the door. He yelled at the one following: 'You! Give me a hand with Mr Padgett!'

The young Able Seaman ignored him – a mistake. Harry's hand shot out and grabbed the man as he, too, reached for the door to pull himself through. Harry dragged him back into the man behind and the whole train derailed and thudded into the still-revving diesels.

'That wasn't a request, son!' This despite the fact that the AB probably had several years on Harry.

But Harry was cut short by a leading stoker charging through the door the other way: 'Out the fucking way! Out the fucking way!'

The deck around the door instantly transformed into a scrum, with the Stoker and several of his chums, older and bigger, and obviously on a mission, not simply in flight. Harry, still gripping the AB, was brushed aside, almost falling on to the stricken Padgett.

The leading stoker started yelling orders and gesticulating to a forest of levers. It took mere seconds for Harry to realise the Stoker was frantically trying to shut down the engines. Why was obvious to him now. *Pelorus*, her hull obviously ruptured somewhere for'ard, was going down. Until now, all the air the engines needed for combustion was coming down the conning tower. If that got cut off, the diesels would suck the air out of the boat and they'd all suffocate in seconds.

The Stokers went into a frenetic choreography, the background of metallic bedlam, its quality of noise changing as the engines were first disengaged from the spinning prop shafts, ran free and then ran down, so the rushing water sounded like silence in the dark swirling chaos.

The absence of noise seemed to create a breathing space for the tumbled mass of sailors, crushed together, vying for room among the now quiet, dwarfing machinery, a tiny eye in a storm where each man could take stock. The emergency lighting picked them out in silhouette; mythic, elemental creatures, moving dazed in the murk. Harry let go of the AB.

'Here, help lift Mr Padgett,' he said, his voice quiet and under control. The sailor mutely obeyed, and they gently lifted Padgett's bloodied, inert body out on to the deck. Harry looped the collar of the older man's overalls into the head of one of the diesel casing bolts, to stop his stricken body sliding away down the engine-room deck. That was when Harry saw the side of Padgett's head, where the blood had clotted around a crumpled dent in his skull, the bone impacted and lightly crazed like the first blow to the top of a boiled egg, so that there were little glitters of white bone through the dark goo and grey, matted hairs. Harry felt an involuntary sob release itself from his chest.

'Aw, Ted,' he breathed, as he felt his eyes fill.

But he wasn't allowed the luxury of dwelling on the wounded Engineer. Gault had returned, barrelling through the bulkhead door leading into the for'ard end of the engine room. He was climbing now, rather than running, because the deck was still slipping away in an irresistible gradient. He was bellowing, too: 'You two, get down here now! Move it! Help me shut this bloody door!'

Two sailors leapt from their perches on the starboard diesel's imposing flank, and dropped down in a series of handholds on the engine to where Gault bestrode the bulkhead's slope and the canted deck. The water, a friendly looking frothy emerald colour, was rising to lap over the doors combing beneath them. That was the moment when the noise returned, as stuff – heavy steel tools stuff, huge cast-steel engine parts and bolt trays – started to break free and hurtle down the engine room, ricocheting in clanging knells off the engine casings, ushering back the fear and the nagging tugs of panic.

Another figure slipped past Harry, urgency in his movements, oblivious to the falling debris. It was only as he passed in to the spill of light from an emergency lighting unit that Harry recognised Frank Lansley, the cockney 'Wrecker'.

Gault, peeking from behind the starboard diesel, yelled at Harry above the lessening din. 'Mr Gilmour, sir! Can you organise some of those blokes to get a pump going, and can you get the engine exhaust vents shut, before they start flooding us!'

Harry stared back, almost catatonic, stunned by the disaster unfolding around him. He heard the words, but was frozen to the spot. Lansley, perched in mid-descent, turned and shouted at the two LTs: 'Oi! Flannagan and Allen! Yer on! Help Mr Gilmour, now!'

The two Leading Torpedomen turned and pushed their way back into the electric motor room, heading to rig a pump. They both buffeted Harry on the way past, knocking not just the wind but the daze as well.

Harry, having returned to terrifying reality, demonstrated he was back in the game by nominating two equally dazed and fearful sailors with punches to their shoulders, shouting, 'You two, crank the vent valves shut now!'

The sailors snapped back, the chance to do something unfreezing them. They scuttled up on to their respective diesel casings, reaching out for the exhaust valves.

Movement was the thing: don't think, do. Harry bent down to the prone body of Ted Padgett at his feet, dropping to his knees, ordering two more sailors to come to Padgett's aid, and another to bring bandages and burn dressings from the first-aid locker in the motor room. Two of them required shoving to attend to their duty, but all responded to action rather than standing, idle witnesses, mantled by dread.

Down by the for'ard bulkhead Gault and Lansley were straining to push the watertight door closed against the seawater pouring over the combing. Two more sailors joined them, leaning into the maw of the hatchway, pushing against the door. Harry cradling Padgett, looked back, amazed at how so little water could fight back against their efforts. All the while he was feeling for Padgett's pulse, but not finding any.

He felt a flutter in his chest. He wasn't going to let this happen. Stupid old bastard! He had been talking to this man seconds ago – by right of the commission he held, one of *his* men. He wasn't going to allow the silly old bastard to fucking die on him. Not on his first patrol.

Gault and his crew were still leaning all their weight on the solid-steel door. All of them were straining, you could see the veins bulging on their necks.

Harry had the two sailors help him lift Padgett through the swing doors into the more spacious motor room, where the other rating was clutching a bundle of medical gauze. He offered it to

Harry, who turned around, asking no one in particular: 'Does anyone here know first aid?'

The faces stared back, blank.

There was suddenly another deep shudder, rippling up through the fabric of the hull, as if *Pelorus* had hit something solid. The deck beneath them wobbled and then settled at a slightly less crazy angle. They must be hanging bow down by well over twenty degrees. The sailors before him had reached out and were gripping to steady themselves. The fear was back in their faces. He had to think of something else to occupy them.

'Go and get as many Davis escape sets and pile them at the aft bulkhead,' said Harry. Then, to the bandage boy, he said, 'You stay with me.'

Now he had to do something about Padgett, but first he had to fight the urge to crawl under one of the diesels, curl up and hide and wallow in the bitter self-pity of life and everything being snatched away. But he couldn't do that. Because here was Ted and here was this terrified rating, both of them requiring him, needing him to do what that silly wavy gold ring on his sleeve said he should: be an officer.

This wasn't going to be pretty. He knew vaguely from his basic training that Padgett was almost certainly in shock and should be moved as little as possible; but leaving him on the deckplates by the door wasn't on. He was equally sure there were certain procedures for head wounds, but had no idea what they were. He had to get the wounds as clean as possible and protected against further damage. From the pile handed him he slathered on antiseptic jelly, careful not to press on the skull in case he disturbed some fragment of bone. Then over that he began gently laying pad after pad of burn gauze, which he held in place with loosely swathed bandage. When it was in position, he turned to the sailor cradling Padgett's head in his shaking hands. Harry looked at the boy; his eyes were bulging and he was yawning, again and again. He had read somewhere that yawning was a telltale sign of fear, and he had seen it for himself, in youths his own age queuing to be beaten by the headmaster for misdemeanors too grave to be dealt with by a lesser mortal. Thanking god it wasn't him.

But he was a long way from school now.

'Give me your cap, quick,' barked Harry. The boy obeyed, and Harry slid it under Ted's head, covering the confection of burn gauze. 'Right, hold it there while I wrap some more bandage.'

Again the boy obeyed, calming a little, certainly enough to venture a few words. 'I think he's dead, sir,' he whispered.

Harry, finishing his bandaging, fixed the boy with his eyes and what the boy saw made him flinch. Harry laid the back of his hand across Padgett's mouth and held it for a moment.

'He's still breathing,' he lied.

Gault came through the partition doors and crouched down beside them. He gave the lifeless body of his friend Ted Padgett a quick, resigned glance and then turned to Harry, but Harry spoke before he could.

'Where's Mr Sandeman, Mr McVeigh, the Skipper?'

Gault didn't waste time replying. 'We've been rammed by some bloody rust-bucket of a tramp steamer. The Skipper's sailed us right into the path of a southbound coastal convoy and some scow ploughed into us just for'ard of the control room.' A pause. 'What's the depth here, sir? When you last looked at the chart, what was the depth?'

From the look on Gault's face he wasn't going to brook any back chat, not even from an officer.

'The North Sea's all shallow around here, no more than a hundred, a hundred and fifty feet. Why?'

'We've got a chance, then. That bump we just had was the bows hitting the bottom. Up for'ard, the torpedo room, torpedo storage, the control room, they're all flooded. But we're still watertight here. It's keeping us buoyant – for now. Our nose might be in the mud, but our arse is in the air . . . well maybe not quite in the air, but we're two hundred and ninety feet long. Given where the aft escape hatch is, we might be less than thirty feet from the surface. If we can keep these compartments watertight it will keep our arse up and we can get out of here. Christ! We wouldn't need the Davis gear, we could free-swim it to the surface. And there're ships up there, they know they've hit us.'

But Harry wasn't listening. He was back in training in the submarine escape tank in Gosport, entombed in that steel cylinder with the water rising over his head, and only his terror for company, and the instructor telling him it was OK, because the chances of him ever having to do it in real life were so remote. Despair and hopelessness washed over him; he was going to drown, snagged, trapped in that escape hatch, in the dark, in a press of other drowning men, their struggling bodies and their screams sealed in by steel, the final sensations of his short imperfect life. Panic rose in his gorge like the sac of an egg without its shell, slopping, threatening to rupture.

He couldn't keep thinking like that! Thinking himself into a panic!

'What about everyone for'ard?' he asked. 'The first Lieutenant? Mr McVeigh?'

Gault looked at him, then realised what was happening and stopped to reply. 'They were going into the conning tower to get out,' he said, 'them and the boys on the planes and the helm. They were going to try and get out from there. The Skipper was on the bridge. Dunno what happened to him or the two lookouts.'

Then he was back to issuing brusque matter-of-fact orders, telling Lansley to hand out the Davis sets, telling the men to strap them on but not to use them to breathe, to keep their oxygen charge until the surface, and then use them as life jackets.

Harry took a deep breath and squeezed through the crush of men to reach for the remaining Davis sets. He grabbed two, one for him and one for Ted Padgett. Gault was already shoving everyone: 'Get aft, through the aft bulkhead door, into the Stokers' mess where the escape hatch is. Get going, now!'

He manhandled everyone through the bulkhead, even Harry and Padgett, and then turned and doggedly shut the bulkhead door, sealing off the engine room spaces. The Stokers' mess was a tight fit, lined by stacked bunks, piping and cable runs. In the middle dropped the escape hatch tube, surrounded by a rubberized canvas necklace – the tube trunking. When dropped, it formed a cylinder that reached halfway into the compartment and was tethered to the deck.

'Drop the trunking,' ordered Gault, and down it came, while he himself opened a valve and water began jetting into their space. There were sixteen of them crowded in there, barely the length of three men, their bare heads touching the deckhead pipe runs and the metal frames of the bunks jabbing at their sides. There was barely room for Harry to cradle Padgett, jammed in by the bulkhead door. Everyone was breathing hard, their bodies shaking with the chill of the water and fear. When the water reached the bottom of the trunk, Gault would open an air valve and begin letting high-pressure air into the compartment.

'When the water's up to our chests and the pressure in here is equal to the sea outside, it'll let us crack open the escape hatch and we'll be on our way, gentlemen.' The steady, monotonous tones of Gault briefed everyone. 'Frank,' he said to Lansley, 'you get ready to go first. You get to the surface and keep them together as they come up. The rest of you, feel your way nice and easy out the hatch then kick like mad for the surface. Thirty feet, no more. You'll be fine, and don't forget to breathe out a bit on the way, you don't want your lungs busting, you don't want an embolism, now do you?'

Harry recited the physics of how this should work in his head, to keep himself from thinking about how it wouldn't.

When the time came, Harry began fitting Ted's limp body into the Davis set, still reciting what must happen . . . Lansley would go into the trunking, swim up into the bubble of air between the water and the hatch, and he would open the hatch to the sea; the sea which logic said should then pour in, wouldn't; it would be kept at bay . . . initially . . . by the air bubble's pressure. But the pressure would leak, a tiny bubble, then the whole bubble would shoot out letting the sea in to fill the void it left behind, leaving a column of water held inside the trunking, trapped by the pressure in the compartment. One by one they'd duck down into the trunking entrance and themselves shoot up, out the hatch, and be kicking for the surface. That was the idea until . . .

Pelorus wallowed again. The movement seemed to trigger a terrible tearing of metal from the main engine room, followed by a resonating clang, and an explosive roar of jetting water. Everyone spun and peered through the dim glow spilled by the emergency lighting units towards the bulkhead door into the main engine spaces. Gault sloshed his way through and bent to peer through the door's small glass panel.

'Shite!' he said, under his breath, and withdrew his head. Everyone looked to him for reassurance. They didn't get any. What Gault had witnessed was a scene of utter mayhem. A giant geyser of water was bursting from underneath the deckplates, obviously shooting through the engine room for'ard bulkhead below deck level. The steel plates were flying, and walls of spray fanned out in every direction as the water jet cannoned off every solid surface. Gault realised immediately what had happened.

'It's the bulkhead valve on the battery vents,' he said. 'It's blown out. The engine room's open to the flooded compartment for'ard.

In a minute the engine room will be flooded too, and she'll start to sink proper. We've got to go now, Mr Gilmour!'

Gault turned to open a valve, letting loose a terrible scream of high-pressure air venting into the compartment.

'We're all going out fast, right up the trunking and out the hatch one after the other, no dilly-dallying. Got it?' yelled Gault.

Everyone nodded. Jerking, pallid faces in the spectral light. The water was already lapping around the trunking base. This is just like the escape tank in Portsmouth, thought Harry. The steel walls pressing and the rising water, except this time there were others in it with him. The staring faces, eyes bulging, short, sharp breaths, the hideous proximity of other men's fear. The water reached his waist, and he could see the detritus of the Stokers rise up with it on a thin scum of oil from the bilges: a tin mug, ditty boxes, pencils, the billow of blankets trapping air; a cap, floating. His ears and eyes began to hurt as the pressure built in the tiny space, and then another noise rose above the rushing water and screaming air. It was an animal sound, a sort of high keening. Not mechanical at all. Was it human? If it was, then it sounded like the tearing of a soul might.

Gault, by the trunking, squeezed his sopping bulk back down into the crush of bodies, reaching for a matted wet skull in the crush. The skull was turned away from Harry, but from the improbable ears, it must be Scanlon, and when Gault finally managed to insinuate himself into the press and take the boy into his embrace, the head turned and Harry could see that it was indeed the young AB. The impossible, inhuman noise was issuing from him, coming from some place deep behind the kettledrum tautness that passed for his face. The boy was coming apart, and as the water began slapping against their chests, Harry could see that the other faces in the press around him were quietly catching his disease.

It was going to end here, in a blind, mewing and clawing panic, with abattoir certainty; in a heaving mass of life expiring without dignity. Harry too, could feel the disease clench him; until he became aware of Gault's soft voice, barely audible above the other din, talking in Scanlon's ear, cooing almost, like a broody dove: 'Here, young Scanlon, what's all this then, all this faffing? Calm yerself lad, calm yerself and don't take on so. It's all right, everything is all right, see. It doesn't matter, see.'

Gault shut off the high-pressure air so that the calm, insistent rhythm of his voice washed over them, until they were all listening. Scanlon's keening stopped.

'What's the worst that can happen, eh?' asked Gault, all matter-of-fact now, in the seeming quiet. 'You die. And what good would all this takin' on have done yer then? Eh? Yer still gonna be dead. But if we make it out, and five minutes from now we're all tucked up in a bunk with a three-badge Stoker feeding us hot toddies and singing us lullabies, yer ain't half going to be feeling a right Herbert ain't cha? All this noise and nonsense.'

Scanlon, eyes still wide, was nodding silently to Gault's rhythm.

'You wouldn't be able to call for a pint for yourself in an orderly fashion ever again, would yer? No you wouldn't.' The water was high enough now, and Harry saw Lansley duck down, presumably to shut the water valve. A seeming silence, apart from the distant roar of the failed battery vent. Scanlon's breathing became more measured. 'There,' said Gault, in a tone that closed proceedings. 'Good on yer young Scanlon, you just stick with me, son. Now, Mr Lansley . . . get in the trunking and up' – a gurgle as the water slopped to a stop – 'unclip the hatch. The air that's left will blow you out so keep them elbows in. Then you next,' to one of the Torpedomen, 'the Tiffy will be waiting for you upstairs,' he said, referring to the ERA, Lansley, 'and we'll all be right behind you, eh, Mr Gilmour?'

'Aye aye, chief!' said Harry in a voice that was too loud. And right away there was the noise as Lansley popped the hatch and the trunking's air bubble exploded out.

After that, they started, one after the other, ducking down below the scummy surface and were gone, with only the canvas of the trunking shimmying like the throat of a whale disgorging Jonah whole, as each man struggled for the surface.

Harry gripped Padgett, holding him close like a teddy bear, watching the heads disappear. There were three, or was it four left, when above him, a cable tray sheered and sliced through the trunking just below the escape hatch, freeing the column of water, and Gault yelled, 'Everybody . . . grab everybody else, hold on!' And the sea came in.

It was the last thing Harry heard before the air he was breathing, the air that filled the Stokers' mess between the chest-high water and the deckhead, was gone. Vanished in a chest-sucking *whumpf* that he felt more than heard, and then everything was churning sea.

Harry had already fastened his and Padgett's nose-clips before the water, in a surge, had enveloped him in a maelstrom of bubbles and debris sucked up from beneath the deckplates, the great swirling commotion in the water almost making him fill his lungs with the stuff in fright. He felt he was inside a washing machine, being battered against steel machinery. Yet he did not let go, and other hands were grabbing him.

A subterranean greenish gloom, courtesy of the one remaining emergency light, began to coalesce and then it was as if hours passed. The ripped trunking had let all the air out and the water in. No orderly escape was possible now, and the lost buoyancy of that remaining air, vented through the escape hatch, made the submarine lurch deeper.

Gripping Padgett for all he was worth, chased by panic, he began chanting a little mantra to himself: that if he could just get

Padgett out of that hatch, to the surface, then maybe he too would be worthy of surviving. If he could just get him out of this bloody iron coffin and up in the fresh air.

There was a scrambling of bodies in front of him. One seemed lifeless, battered against the hatch by the force of the exiting air. Harry adjusted Padgett's set, bled a little oxygen into it for him to breathe, making sure the mouthpiece was snug as he shuffled himself to the shredded ends of the trunking. He was kicked by someone in front, Scanlon or Gault, he didn't know, and again, so that what was left in his lungs was fighting to burst out, and then he was at the hatch.

No one was in the way. He didn't push Padgett up, he dragged him up, then pressed him so as to squeeze them both through together, and then they were in the hatch, and Harry knew beyond all question that he could not hold on any longer, that the fight not to take one huge breath was lost; except that it wouldn't be air he would draw deep into his lungs. He was done. So close. Poor Ted, I tried, he said inside his head, as he banged it on something smooth and bevelled and steel, and his foot was on the hatch rim and he felt himself in open water, and above him like a liquid borealis was a light playing behind the ripples of the surface, and his legs were pumping and pumping and pumping.

Chapter Eleven

Harry, standing on the railway pier at Gourock. A bright summer's morning, the light scrubbed and the mountains across the Firth of Clyde picked out in lush velvety greens and dappled shadow from a random scatter of high, white fluffy clouds. And the waters of the Firth in-between, thick with dull grey shipping lying in steel clots on the deep-blue anchorage. Scores of them: cargo ships, a tanker or two, and warships; a new fleet carrier, cruisers, destroyers and smaller escorts. Here at the Tail o' the Bank, where the river meets the Firth, one of Britain's main convoy assembly areas, a terminus for the trans-Atlantic sea lanes, down which pass the country's lifeline to America and the Empire. It is an impressive tableau. Harry, the boy, would have been thrilled beyond words. Harry today, however, is altogether more sober.

He is going home for the first time since he caught the train for HMS *King Alfred* in September 1939. Survivors' leave. Two weeks of peace and quiet, your reward for staying afloat when your ship didn't. There hadn't been many others from *Pelorus* left afloat to collect that prize. McVeigh and Sandeman were gone, and that irritating little Torpedo Officer, whose name Harry couldn't quite recall now. Swann. That was it. And all the other sailors from the control room and torpedo rooms. All gone. Just Harry, and CPO Gault, and the outside ERA Frank Lansley and Scanlon, and the handful of Stokers and Leading Torpedomen who'd all got out of the escape hatch and had been picked up.

Oh, and then there were the two miracles. Ted Padgett was still alive. Even Harry couldn't quite believe it. And the Skipper, the Bonny Boy, thrown from the bridge on impact and the first to be picked up. He couldn't account for the two young ABs on watch with him. They were never seen again. Nobody pressed too hard on that one. Poor Commander Bonalleck, to have lost his boat and most of his crew, and to have survived. How must he feel?

Harry knew. Harry had had an interview with him, one of many seemingly endless interviews after he walked down the gangway of the armed trawler which had rescued him. It would be a long time before Harry would forget that interview. As usual, Bonalleck had been drunk.

Standing on the railway pier at Gourock, Harry watched a little paddle steamer churning and foaming as she came alongside the one remaining civilian berth on the pier. Her long, slim hull was yacht-like apart from the barn-sized box arrangement midships, beneath which her paddles beat to and fro, and out of which stabbed the natural-draught smokestack.

She was angling close to allow a grizzled old deckhand to throw his heaving line. A crush of passengers lined her side, nearly all men and women in uniform, their expressions glum, despite the sun, just like the little ship herself – no longer decked out in the elegant colours of the Caledonian Steam Packet Company that he remembered; instead, in the same drab grey as every other craft, great or small, on the Firth this morning. Like everything else that used to be familiar, that he'd seen between here and Rosyth, the little steamer too had been touched by the war. Still here, but different. Grimmer, like him.

The guilt at surviving was still gnawing Harry, and he wasn't helping himself by leaving it alone. He kept going back to the scab and picking it. He remembered every little thing that had happened, vividly. And his feelings. He kept going back to it all, telling himself he was resetting his soul, like you'd reset a bone; except this felt much more painful. But he was, after all, still not much more than an adolescent, and what he was dealing with was man's work.

Ted, lying tucked up in that pristine white hospital bed, still unconscious, intubated, drips attached, and looking so small and frail, his white hair now turned to cotton wool beneath the swathe of bandage. Harry had sat with him, holding his hand for god knows how long, still unable to let him go, just like on *Pelorus*. In his jumble of emotions was something like pride. Back in that compartment, when *Pelorus* was sinking, Sub-Lieutenant Gilmour had been the officer in charge, except it was Gault and Lansley who had got them out. Not him. But they would have left Ted. He didn't.

The old fellah had accepted him into ship's company with his twinkly grin and cheeky jibes, and then . . . in the blink of an eye . . . he'd been about to die. Did Harry actually make the decision that he wasn't going to let it happen? That he wasn't going to allow Ted Padgett, his new shipmate, to die? Or was it one of those melodramatic, lucky talisman things: that if he could just get this one man, this Ted fellow, whom he hardly knew out of the damn boat and to the surface, that only then would Harry deserve to live?

He remembered sailing into Rosyth, standing alone on his rescuers' deck; how when the sun came up he'd gone on deck and refused to go below again despite the drizzle, unable to tear his eyes from the passing shore, and the magnificent, preposterous loom of the Forth bridge; feeling the waft of the breeze on his wet cheeks, hearing the sound of the gulls above the engine thump in his ears; gripped by the sheer, tear-pricking joy of still being alive; brushing aside the offer of a stretcher, insisting on walking up the gangway off the trawler and on to the firm concrete of the dock just to feel the solid land beneath his feet.

There had been medicals, but there wasn't much wrong with him that lashings of sweet tea, a hot bath and fifteen hours sleep hadn't sorted. The sailors at Rosyth could not have been kinder. He wanted for nothing – a clean uniform, shirts, socks, new split dress oxfords, boots, even a hand-knitted muffler from someone's sister; and endless rounds of large ones at the wardroom bar. He'd sunk the *Graf von Zeithen* after all, and that was 'a bloody good show' in everyone's book. But he was also a shipwrecked mariner, and that made him different. The generosity and the solicitousness created a distance as well as a bond and Harry was sensitive enough to register the subtle diffidence with which even relatively senior officers treated him. He'd been sunk; he carried the mark that no one wanted. And he was coming to learn some of the ways of sailors, that they were, in general, an open-hearted lot, bound by the sea and all that meant. But Harry had been where they all dreaded, and returned as a living reminder that they were there but for the grace of God . . .

Then had come the official questions. McVeigh's words echoed. He told it straight, apart from the Bonny Boy's drinking. They'd kept him apart from other members of the crew until the interviews were over, and the evidence pending the inevitable Naval Court of Inquiry was gathered. Then on the afternoon of the third day, the Bonny Boy had invited him for a drink.

Harry shut his eyes briefly, so he could see the Bonny Boy again resplendent in a borrowed Commander's jacket, his luxuriant grey hair Brylcreemed, the flaccid jowls shaved waxy beneath the Martian canals of burst capillaries criss-crossing his cheeks, the wet eyes dancing with gin-fuelled light. He was posed Pharaoh-like in a rubbed relic of an easy chair, one of two that filled the sitting room part of the shore cabin he'd been assigned by the sympathetic base Flag Officer. On a card table by the Bonny Boy's elbow was a gin bottle, already damaged before Harry's arrival. Harry was invited to help himself, had been going to decline, but thought better of it. His Skipper had an edginess about him that Harry didn't like.

Listening to Bonalleck that afternoon had been like being forced against one's will to look into some Lewis Carroll landscape where the talker dwelled, and from which he returned only occasionally for appearance's sake. Bonalleck had maintained a reverent silence throughout the ritual pouring of Harry's gin, then from nowhere he'd begun with what seemed an irrelevance: 'I put six torpedoes into the flagship and the umpire said her effectiveness had been reduced by twenty per cent. Six torpedoes.'

Harry had no idea what he was talking about. Then, as if by way of belated explanation Bonalleck continued, his voice sounding almost as if he was reminiscing to a favoured nephew, his eyes staring as if watching a movie.

'A hundred miles south-west of the Fastnet Rock. Fleet exercises, 1926. You shouldn't ask submarines to take part in fleet exercises . . . not unless they're there to show how pathetic the A/S is . . . because you just sink everything . . . what's the point of being there otherwise?'

A sudden look up, directly into Harry's eyes. He was completely lucid, and then he looked away. 'I went off on my own and I set about "sinking" . . . that is what submarines are supposed to do . . . sink . . . so I did . . . everybody . . . they didn't think the Bonny Boy was so "bonny" that day . . . Mr Gilbert.'

Harry had realised he was hearing some tale from Bonalleck's past, but its relevance was beyond him. They should be talking about the sinking of *Pelorus*. Of *Von Zeithen*.

Another volume of gin disappeared down Bonalleck's throat. Harry watched its progress, mesmerised.

'I'm going to tell you something about your betters, Mr Gilbert,' Bonalleck continued, getting his name wrong again, leaning in, conspiratorial, so Harry could hear the alcohol wheeze in his breath. '. . . professional jealousy. Ever heard that expression, sir? Eh? Worming and twisting in their bellies . . . for years, decades. All the braid they put on only feeding it . . .'

And then he had sat upright, jolting Harry back in his seat, and it was as if his captain had retreated from him like a view suddenly going out of focus. It took a second to realise that Bonalleck had become quite mad, and that he had begun to address an audience Harry couldn't see . . . like the worst ham actor imaginable. Harry didn't think this an appropriate moment to correct him on his name.

'Oh, aren't you just the dashing chap, Bonny Boy?' Bonalleck declaimed, having suddenly become a third party in the room. 'More laurels for the Bonny Boy! Ribbons and gongs! And strike up the band! Knew the Tsar, you know! And the King! It's another war now, but what the hell! The Bonny Boy's not shy! He'd sail a Serpentine punt against the Jerry! Another plum for the Bonny Boy, here! Let him show us he's still Britannia's favoured son. We'll lay it on a plate for you . . . you just have to turn up and there's glory just for the picking!'

Bonalleck paused again, returning to himself, looking thoughtful. '. . . people like that don't appreciate you, especially when you're right. Professional jealousy. So they set you up to shoot you down.'

He swallowed another gulp and suddenly became surly and sarky-sounding. '. . . just change a few minutes on the co-ordinates . . . sloppy Morse . . . a decoding error . . . oh, they're quite capable . . .'

And then he reared up again, glaring at Harry. 'Of course they would know I'd have to tell you . . . got to tell the crew where we're going . . . what we're after. So that when I missed, you'd all be sharing in the joke, eh!? Bonny Boy missed her! . . . But I am wise to them, Mr Gilbert. Oh yes. I had my own plan. Oh yes. I wasn't going to go wandering over some "diversionary" patrol area, loosing torpedos at useless targets . . . they like to punish. Punish other people for being better than them . . . oh so we've got one of those VCs who loves glory more than the service, have we? Knows better than us, does he? Well it's time he was reminded of . . .'

He tailed off into another long long silence, then became quite lucid again: 'Our orders were specific. Go off on your scheduled patrol . . . don't attract attention . . . then when we signal you, head for the Skagerrak and wait for Jerry. She'll be a big one. Definitely worth the name of the Bonny Boy. Just tiptoe up there and he'll come right into our trap. How do they know these things, Mr Gilbert? Did they expect me to believe they've got some shifty chap in a trench coat hanging round Wilhelmshaven dockyard dropping a penny in the phone box and chatting to Whitehall every time Jerry slips to sea? I knew what they really wanted. They wanted to humiliate me. They wanted to send me to the scene of my past glory . . . *my* glory! Not theirs . . . so they could say behind my back: not so clever now, Bonny Boy . . .'

He was staring fixedly at Harry now. A cold, hard stare, almost unblinking. Harry felt forced to speak.

'What was your plan, sir?'

Bonalleck's eyes narrowed. 'What was my plan? . . . my plan? . . . hah! Wouldn't you like to know! . . . You were in it with them, weren't you? With Sandeman and McVeigh? . . . they were part of it . . .'

'We did sink her, sir,' Harry ventured, but was cut off by an explosion from Bonalleck.

'We? We?' Another belt of gin. 'We . . .?'

And then the third person, the ham actor, was suddenly back on stage. 'All very well taking snaps of our battleships through your periscope, Charles, way back then . . . but it's war now and it would appear when it comes to the real thing, you're not really up to it. Are you? . . . ruined your career of course, Charles, back then. All that messing about in stupid submarines. Young man's game, don't you think? *Silly* young man's game. Tsar thought you were a splendid chap, of course, but where's the tsar now, eh? Eh?'

And then his voice dropped again, to the growl.

'Shits. All of them. Utter, utter shits. I did all those things. I gave this service its name. I made this service what it is today! My deeds! My victories! It was my hand the tsar shook for blasting Jerry out the Eastern Baltic. While *they* shined the seats of their pants and buffed their braid. It was me that was earning the glory. I . . . made . . . them! And they can't stand that . . . got to bring me down . . . can't have any more laurels for the Bonny Boy . . . got to see he comes a cropper . . . so don't give me "we"!'

Then he had appeared to rally, and smiled at Harry.

'That was the Great War. The last lot. Stupid, stupid men, their *lordships,* back then. Of course they never liked submarines, the Admiralty. Said we should all be hanged as pirates,' a big smile from the man then, warm and confiding . . . and reasonable. 'Horton started flying the Jolly Roger when he heard. You know Horton. He's our *flag officer, submarines* now, is our Max. He was just another two-ringer Skipper in those days, like me. But their *lordships.* "We have spoken. Make it so." All our blokes who'd died. Sunk by Jerry submarines. Jerries who knew what they were doing. Our lot? They didn't learn a thing. Still haven't.'

Another pause, while Bonalleck gazed into the abyss.

'You were there . . . you saw . . .' his tone had totally changed again, become confiding: 'We could achieve great things in this coming war . . .'

But Harry 'saw' nothing: had no idea what this mad man was raving about. He fell back on his prepared speech.

'Sir, I have told the inquiry officers all I know,' Harry said. 'You'd been unwell during the patrol and were in your cabin when we encountered the *Von Zeithen*, and the first Lieutenant had been on watch and begun the attack in case she got away. Obviously any evidence I give to the inquiry will be guided by the good of the service.'

But it had been Bonalleck's ravaged face, suffused with drink and self-justification, which had done it. That had made Harry go on. That had stoked his young man's sense of injustice. He had bridled at the thought that the Bonny Boy was trying to suck him into some kind of conspiracy over the truth of what had happened. It stuck in his gullet that Bonalleck had steered them in the dark into the middle of a coastal convoy, who could not account for the two members of his crew on watch with him, who was likely going to escape unaccused. And even after all that, the fact that Bonalleck was more interested in pouring himself another gin. It pushed Harry over the edge.

'Sir,' said Harry. Bonalleck had looked up, as if surprised to see Harry still there. 'You are a shameless drunk, sir.'

Bonalleck squinted as if he was thinking, I can't be hearing this.

'You have lost your boat and you have killed half your crew. You are a disgrace to the uniform you wear. You're going to get away with this, I know that. But I want you to know, no matter whatever else happens, there is someone who knows the truth.'

'Really,' Bonalleck had said.

After that, what did Harry remember? Drizzly days by the Forth. And Lansley inviting him to the Rosyth Petty Officers' mess, along with Jim Gault. There had been warm bitter and a press of smiling faces, and loud, hollow rhetoric about how *Pelorus's* victory had delivered much-needed good news to offset the loss of the carriers *Glorious* and *Courageous* and the bad news from the North Atlantic convoys, and the fact that Jerry was massing on the Channel ports and an invasion was expected.

Harry had asked, 'What d'you think will happen to that bloody idiot of a Merchant Navy Skipper for ramming his tramp steamer into a Royal Navy submarine? Eh?'

'Nothing,' Gault had said.

'Don't they know how to stand a bloody watch?'

No one replied. Harry was too new to realise that in wartime, the navy was not in the habit of raking over its own coals in public. If you wondered whether retribution might be meted out for the death of so many sailors and a fine boat, you'd just upset yourself. He'd learn soon enough. No one mentioned that *Pelorus* was now at the bottom of the North Sea after that, or that most of her crew were too. It let the evening continue without anyone else getting upset. Nor did they mention the high chop rate that was remorselessly culling its way through the Submarine Service. And anyway, the air between Harry and Gault and Lansley was too full of stuff for anything other than a stiff parody of victors' bonhomie to pass.

Harry had found himself drinking with a grim intent, quickly noticing that he was not far behind the two Petty Officers.

The squeeze of passengers for Dunoon moving towards the gangway brought Harry back to the present for a moment, and he joined them filing aboard the paddle steamer, making his way to the ranks of wooden Carley rafts that doubled as seats up forward. He sat down and re-composed his blankest expression to conceal the confusion beneath.

Gault had actually thanked him in so many words for hauling Ted Padgett out of the *Pelorus*, and asked to shake his hand.

'Thank you, sir, for saving my friend,' he'd said with a solemn gravity that had left Harry swallowing hard, making him think of Sandeman and McVeigh. Especially McVeigh. The admirable McVeigh. The friend he would now never have. Bluff, self-assured, unruffable, master of that star quality of effortless professionalism. Harry had wanted to be his pupil, to measure himself by the older man, had looked forward to standing beside him and one day donning the mantle. And now he was gone. All that was left was the memory of his final words, and his back disappearing down the engine room companionway to where he would die beside Lieutenant Sandeman, trapped in a sunken submarine.

Sandeman, too. Gault had said, 'You remember that attack, Mr Gilmour. Remember and learn from it. Mr Sandeman – that wasn't just textbook, that was a work of fucking art. From the moment the Jerry cruiser's mast came over the horizon he never put a foot wrong.'

'Except best not tell the Skipper, eh?' Harry had said without meaning to.

Gault had replied without hesitation, 'Just what I said, sir. Mr Sandeman, he never put a foot wrong.'

The memory of those words brought Harry back again to just what he didn't want to think about. The meeting he'd had with the Bonny Boy in his cabin. The bottle of Plymouth gin on the table.

Harry looked round for distraction, and found it. The paddle steamer was just emerging from its weave through the crush of anchored shipping and ahead, coming through the anti-submarine boom that stretched from Dunoon pier across the Firth to the Cloch lighthouse, was a submarine. A Royal Navy T-class boat, heading into the Holy Loch, no doubt back from patrol, too, with a black Jolly Roger flying, announcing she had met the enemy somewhere and sunk him.

And that was the other thing he didn't want to think about . . . whether he was ever going to go back down in a submarine again, or whether he was going to put in a formal request to be returned to general service. He had been very afraid in those final minutes on *Pelorus*. Very afraid. A primal thing that had gone deep, so that it felt as if he would have to lean way out over a precipice in order to peer down to where the damage was. But the paddle steamer was coming into the pier; he was going home, and that was going to be another whole issue to deal with right here and now.

He slung his small canvas grip and slipped in with a press of naval ratings heading down the gangway. The wooden Victorian confection which housed the piermaster's offices and a tea room were part of his life, he had grown up with them, but coming back now they looked smaller than he remembered, and more frayed.

At the pier end, drawn up by the kerb, were two blue three-tonners, obviously waiting to take most of the sailors round to Sandbank where the depot ship HMS *Titania* was anchored, playing mother hen to the Third Submarine Flotilla. She was a sight he'd still to see. She hadn't been there when he left, but there hadn't been a proper shooting war back then either.

They dropped him off at the Queen's Hotel in Kirn. He walked up the hill, past the grey stone villas overlooking the Firth, to where his parents' house sat on the corner of the road leading up to the golf club, his mind not at all composed.

He couldn't say he was glad to be home, or was looking forward to seeing his mother and father. They would not be expecting him

– that was certain. *Pelorus's* sinking of the *Von Zeithen* had already hit the papers; only *Pelorus's* own losses had been kept quiet. He had written no letter to say he would be home, and although his parents did have a phone, calling up on an open line to say: 'Hello, Mum, Dad, my boat was sunk and I'm popping back for a few days lie down before they send me back out again' – it wasn't what one was supposed to do. You never knew who was listening, as the posters everywhere warned. 'Walls have ears.' 'Be like Dad – keep Mum!' Dad and Mum, indeed.

Dad wouldn't be there when he walked through the door, he'd still be teaching at the grammar school, but his mother would be in, preparing lunch; and Gordon the dog, the black Labrador named after Flash Gordon, he'd be there, pleased to see him anyway, come what may.

He walked up the drive and there was the two-storey grey stone house as it had always looked throughout his entire life. He wanted to feel like he was coming home, but the knowledge that another world owned him now weighed on him, suddenly heavy.

The little white wood porch and the imposing panelled door with its stained-glass windows filled him with something like poignancy. He knocked and the feeling wasn't helped by the familiar shadow of his mother bustling from the kitchen, laughing and saying something over her shoulder, indistinct, to some visitor, likely Auntie Eleanor, his father's sister.

Although Harry was too young to know it, he wasn't experiencing anything new. Returning warriors through the ages have all, at some point or other, been 'unmanned' by their first whiff of domesticity after battle.

And then the door opened and there she was: smart, slim, sparkly, wearing an apron that, on the occasions she did, always looked like it shouldn't be there. He didn't get a chance to say anything, she grabbed him so fast, reaching up and dragging his face down into the nape of her neck; holding on like he'd done with Ted when he was dragging him through the escape hatch.

'Who is it, Edith?' A voice from the kitchen; Aunt Eleanor right enough, and the domesticity at last overwhelmed him.

The women talked a lot and the dog barked, but only once, because Gordon was the strong, silent type, communicating mainly through tail-wagging and lots of licking and slobbering. There were of course questions. His answers were elliptical to say the least. God knows it wasn't because he wanted to be stand-offish or rude. He just didn't have the language to condense everything that had happened to him since he walked out the door almost ten months ago . . . was that all the time it was? But there was local news too to be communicated, which allowed the women to fill the silence; and anyway, a lot of the questions were of the simple domestic house-keeping kind. Like, when do you have to leave? Which his mother always asked him five minutes after he'd walked through the door. The specific, pin-you-down ones were the ones that left the silences.

Pans were clashed, lunch cooked and served, and conversation moved on to the draconian impact of the steep escalation in ration-ing. Bananas, apparently, were becoming 'creatures of myth and a dim memory!' But Eleanor had a recipe for boiling parsnips to a sludge, adding banana essence and 'whipping it all up into a gooey puree that makes a passably edible banana sandwich', if you liked that sort of thing. Of course, living in the country meant the ration-ing of some things didn't mean they were not available through friends and neighbours. And Dunoon was such a seafarers' town.

'Only last week Willy MacLeod, you remember, a Second Engineer with the Clan Line, he brought back a whole chest of bro-ken orange pekoe from Mombasa,' said his mother.

And then time was getting on, and Eleanor left because his father would be home soon, looking for his tea. So there were more hugs and kisses, and then mother and son were left alone.

They sat at the kitchen table in the big rustic kitchen with its range, stacked wood and neat, crockery-populated dressers; all white distemper and polished wood; bright from the unfashionably large windows that looked on to their woodland garden, and the meadow towards the golf course. More tea, courtesy of Willy MacLeod presumably, and his mother, apron dismissed, looking very chic in a tailored brown and green plaid skirt, crisp white blouse, and her hair in a very fashionable-for-her-age bob, fair, going rapidly grey without a trace of any effort to hide the evidence. Tell it like it is, was definitely Harry's mother. She reached over the table and gripped both his hands in both of hers, and fixed his soft brown eyes with her soft brown eyes in a way Harry knew presaged something of import.

'Welcome home, Harry, whoever you are now,' she said. So you've noticed, he thought. Well, you were always pretty sharp that way, can't keep much from Mum, eh? But he only smiled.

'Your father,' she continued. Harry picking up the sign, seamlessly, like she'd taught him to long ago, thought: Ah. Here it comes. 'You cannot have failed to remember what he is like. His very fixed ideas on killing people in general, and wars in particular.' And there they were back with the same elephant in the room, sitting there immovable, just the way he remembered it when he'd left. 'Try not to goad him,' she said.

Just after 4.30 his father had come home. Harry and his mother were still sitting at the kitchen table, Harry still in his uniform, when the kitchen door had flown open, and there stood the man himself in his tweed jacket and flannels, clutching his bulging leather briefcase, papers bursting out of its flap. He was a tall, angular man, with matinee-idol looks and thick, dark hair that swept back from his high forehead with an almost theatrical wave. The hair was greying, but that just made him more distinguished. His face was clean-shaven, with remarkable smooth, almost peachy skin which carried a light tan from many hours spent outside. The only sign that age was stalking him, apart from the silvering hair, was that he was a bit more stooped than Harry remembered. The eyes were a bit madder too, which didn't bode well.

His father was momentarily surprised; then gathering himself together, plonked the briefcase down by the dresser and hung his jacket on the back of the door. Only then did he address his son: 'Make an old man happy. Tell me you've deserted and you want us to hide you in the hills.'

'No, Dad. It's just leave. Two weeks.'

'Two weeks off from killing. We've heard all about your killing. How many of "those damn Fritzies" did you take from their families that day? A hundred? Five hundred? More?'

Harry knew better than to answer; to say anything. His father sat down, and his mother poured him tea.

'That Crumley girl will be glad to see you at any rate,' said his father, stirring in sugar. 'She's been mooning around here for months now, cluttering up the kitchen, and reeking the place out with that gauche scent she dips herself in. I think she's spraying her territory . . .'

'Don't be crude, Duncan,' said his mother.

'. . . Harry this and Harry that.'

Harry's mother gave him a 'we'll talk later' look.

'That Crumley girl' was Janis, the 'girl he'd left behind', although it was hard to think of her like that. Hard to think of her at all without a frown forming. She was the daughter of a local businessman, Hector Crumley, who owned the local bakery, except 'local' didn't quite cover it. He was a self-made man, as he was often fond of saying, and what he'd made was a mini-empire, covering most of Argyll from Oban to Campbeltown. He lived in a rather vulgar mansion overlooking Dunoon's west bay. He was self-made, new money, and Janis was his only child, so not surprisingly she wanted for nothing, and these days one of the things she appeared to want was Harry, which was rather flattering given what a looker she was.

Not that anything had actually happened between them: a few snogs up in the seclusion of the Bishop's Glen and some serial hand-holding at the local cinema. At Harry's first attempt at a straying hand, he'd been told in no uncertain terms she was not that kind of girl, and in such a scary fashion he'd never risked it again. Nonetheless, she'd soon started describing herself as his girlfriend, a development he'd only found out about through other people. However, her letters to him after he'd joined up confirmed it.

After a year as an undergraduate at Glasgow University, Harry had fancied himself a bit of a man of the world. You couldn't call him a womaniser, but there had been women in his life: girls met at the Saturday night dances in the city's St Andrew's Halls, or at the university union; office girls mostly, some of them just as keen to be seduced as he had been on seduction in the little garret room he rented off one of his father's academic friends in the smart part of Partick. The old bloke owned a hut at a place called Carbeth, along with a whole community of hut dwellers, out towards Loch Lomond, and had a car! He was never in town at weekends, out living the outdoors life among the midges and the rain, leaving Harry the run of the house for his trysts.

He'd almost become quite serious over one of the girls: Violet, a shorthand typist who worked at Weir's Pumps. But she turned out to be more sensible than the careless Harry, and dumped him. He'd been heartbroken for a good several days. Sometimes, when the fleshpots of Glasgow's west end bored him, he'd go back to Dunoon for a weekend.

It was a time when being an undergraduate carried some cachet, and even though he was still a bit young and gangly, there was definitely a promise that he had inherited his father's good looks. And you'd be blind not to see what a naval uniform might do for him. Janis, for one, could certainly see a young man on his way, so she was there with all her complacent assumptions resolutely undisturbed, demanding to be escorted to all the places a girl of her station should be seen.

'So what does Janis do when she comes here?' Harry asked his mother after a silent dinner and his father's retreat to his study.

'Oh not much.' Harry's mother never liked saying anything bad about folk, even irritating ones like Janis. She was washing the dishes. Harry wasn't drying: his father believed it was more hygienic to let them drip. And what his father believed ran as writ in their house.

'What?' asked Harry. 'She just sits there?' Actually, Harry could quite easily imagine Janis plonked impervious at the end of the table as if she belonged; making her presence felt, expecting to be entertained. His father hadn't been that far off the mark.

'Pretty much.' Mother being so uncommunicative meant she really must have been irritated; Mother liked talking. 'Well, sometimes she talks about you.'

'About me? What does she say about me?'

'It's not what she says about you; it's more about what she's got planned for you.' His mother finished the dishes, and sat down, fixing a wry smile on Harry: 'You're hardly going to recognise yourself.'

'I don't know what she sees in me,' said Harry, genuinely puzzled. For like all only children, Harry had never quite grasped the effect he had on other people. Because his life was his, he thought it ordinary, like everyone else's. He did not see that, unlike most of the other young men around him, he was not a procrastinator.

While others might say, 'I'd love to do that,' Harry tended to follow his mother's advice, and do it. And when it came to sailing, he was always hanging around toffs like Sir Alexander Scrimgeour.

His mother didn't actually tell him that this was one of the things an upwardly mobile girl like Janis might see in him: an opportunity to one day hang around the Sir Alexander Scrimgeours of this world.

'You're charming,' she said instead from behind her knowing smile, 'and are obviously going to be quite the man of the world.' Which wasn't actually a lie. But later she said right out of the blue, 'You know it will be important that you tell someone about all this.'

Harry knew she was talking about the war then, and not about Janis, but he couldn't think how to answer.

So she said: 'You are only through the door five minutes and I can tell. I don't know what has happened to you since you . . . sailed away . . . but I know that something has,' she said.

Harry managed a 'Yes.'

'You probably don't want to tell your mother. That's all right. I'd probably never sleep again if you did. But you should find someone. You need to tell someone . . . everything that happens . . . so that you'll know who you've become when it ends. It will be the only way to save yourself.'

Harry didn't telephone Janis until teatime the next day, mainly because he'd been asleep for most of it. As any survivor will tell you, getting sunk doesn't half take it out of a chap. If he'd been expecting a hero's welcome, he was to be disappointed.

'What do you want?' was the extent of Janis's response.

'I'm home on leave,' said Harry.

'So I've heard. From several people.'

She had a knack of making him feel guilty and lumpen so that he gibbered away while a punishing chill emanated down the phone. However, once he'd demonstrated a sufficient level of abnegation, it was arranged he should present himself at her place: Daddy was having people round. Be there by 7 p.m.

Harry obeyed. The door was answered by Mr Crumley, a dapper little fellow with pomaded hair and a moleskin waistcoat under his barathea blazer. Everything about him was expensive, which would have been impressive on a man who could carry it off. Hector Crumley couldn't; not that such a truth would ever occur to him.

'Ah. Why it's Harris Gilmour, back from the wars. Janis is expecting you.' All delivered in a polite accent that hadn't quite been mastered.

Hector Crumley stood aside to let Harry pass into a huge hall, all tartan wallpaper and antlers. He was pointed to an open door that led to the main reception room, too crowded to reveal the décor, a blessing as Harry had been in it when empty; even allowing for youth's insensitivity, the place had made him feel queasy with its sheer weight of fripperies and folderols.

Everyone who should have been there, was. Dunoon was a small town.

'Harry!' An excited screech from Janis as she appeared from a dense huddle of guests and wrapped him in an effusive, territory-marking embrace.

Christ! She looked stunning in a figure-hugging mauve dress, with a back split to reveal shapely calves, and her blonde tresses piled up and not too obviously dyed a rich golden colour. When she gave him a brief smacker he could taste the sweet perfume from that deep red gash that was her mouth.

Crumley thrust a drink into his hand, from which he took a swift slurp to steady himself; a gin with Indian tonic; and ice! Harry wondered where Crumley had got that; the Gilmours didn't own a refrigerator. Who did? Crumley, obviously. He led Harry to the big bay window overlooking the Firth, and began engaging him in one of those conversations that are just preambles to the main event. He began by talking about the war; not Harry's war, his own war.

'It's a very anxious time, Harris,' said Mr Crumley. 'You young chaps off doing your derring-do have no idea. Very anxious. We're just waiting for the Hun to come. No idea what is going to happen, what the future will hold. Now that Herr Hitler has all of France and Holland and Norway it's just a matter of time. Invasion! We all know it's coming! And of course, the Germans! Their reputation precedes them. Look at Poland, what they did to Rotterdam. A very anxious time, Harris. Especially if you have a daughter. I mean, just what will they be capable of? Tell me that, Harris, tell me that!'

Harry didn't know how to reply. All Winston had been saying was that it was going to be tough. Even he seemed to think a German invasion was imminent. Blood, sweat and toil, with the only consolation on offer that they were all in it together. Nobody doubted him, just as nobody doubted Jerry was going to come, and they were going to fight. As for what the future held after that; Harry didn't want to think about it.

'You chaps in the navy, you've got options,' said Mr Crumley.

Harry squinted at the little man whose jowls were working with emotion: 'I'm sorry, Mr Crumley, I don't follow. What kind of options?'

Crumley's jowls stopped moving and he fixed Harry: 'I'm sure you'll all do your duty, fight them off as long as you can. But when they're marching up Argyle Street, you'll be sailing off to Canada with the King and all the nation's gold reserves. Everybody knows that.'

'I'm not sure I understand you, Mr Crumley,' was the absolute best Harry could do.

Crumley was silent, then, full of pent-up emotion and anxiety, he began, 'The Germans, Harry. They're coming. Everybody knows it.'

Well, indeed. His mother and Auntie Eleanor had thought so too. But they didn't seem to be quite as terrorised by the prospect as Mr Crumley. Invasion did seem almost an inevitability. But Harry had been too busy lately to think about that, and anyway, everyone else he'd been around seemed to treat the idea with a sort of decorous sangfroid. Harry didn't know what to say.

He didn't have to. Crumley turned square on to Harry, all emollient smiles.

'You made the right choice, Harris,' he said, still using his full name. 'The navy looks after its own. I'm sure all the plans are made for the evacuation. It won't just be the ships, will it? All the equipment and the stores and the paperwork it takes to run an enterprise like the navy . . . it'll all have to go with you . . . you don't have to tell me about it . . . you don't build a business from nothing without learning a thing or two. You university men . . . you don't know everything, you know. And of course I imagine all that . . . stuff . . . will include the officers' wives. Can't leave the ladies behind . . . can't expect you chaps to fight on if you've been forced to leave the ladies, or the children. Isn't that right, Harris?'

'I've no idea, Mr Crumley, what the plans are.'

But Hector Crumley wasn't listening: 'Right indeed. That's why now is the time young men should be thinking of their sweethearts, of what's best for them. With this war going the way it is, they won't get another chance. It's time for young men to make their minds up, and act! Or forever more regret what they will have left behind. You think on that, Harris. How would you feel sailing off to Canada, knowing you'd left your sweetheart behind . . . at the mercy of the Germans!'

Harry's mother was still up when he got home, in the kitchen with a pot of tea, knitting in candlelight.

'He practically told me to marry Janis,' said Harry, taking a seat at the table. 'Father's right about old man Crumley. He's frightful.'

'He's just worried,' said his mother, 'about his only child. He wants you to snatch her away, out of the path of the approaching German juggernaut. He imagines all the unspeakable things the Hun might do to his little girl. Are you thinking about it?'

Harry was back in the Crumleys' garden, strolling with Janis; remembering their brief disappearance behind the rhododendrons when she had expertly spun herself into his arms and kissed him. Thinking: If Janis is totally gorgeous in that mauve dress, what would she be like without it?

'I dunno . . .' he said, thinking about it.

'Oh Harry. Please don't tell your father. At least, not just now.'

Harry knew exactly what she meant; what she was thinking: Am I going to have to sit opposite that complacent, self-obsessed, etc. etc. at my kitchen table for the rest of my life?

'Can I tell him about all the electric lights Crumley's got burning behind the blackout curtains?' he said.

There was no mains electricity on the Cowal peninsula, so old man Crumley must have had a bloody great generator somewhere churning out the amps. Begging the question: how did old man Crumley manage to swing enough petrol to power that generator, to generate all that bloody light?

'No. Don't tell him that either,' said his mother.

Chapter Twelve

Growing up, one thing Harry had cottoned on to pretty quick was that the Gilmours were a popular family, probably down to the fact that there was indeed a whiff of the exotic about them.

Duncan, his father, was head of modern languages at the grammar school where he was known as Dr Gilmour, for Duncan was also a PhD in French literature. A mystique compounded by the fact that in his spare time he wrote books and pamphlets on French literature and philosophy. Books that were actually published. Also he wasn't a local boy, but a child of empire.

Duncan's father, Harry's grandfather, had been someone senior in the Indian Civil Service, and died of a fever in Calcutta. Duncan's mother, in her bereavement, had returned to live in Dunoon in genteel poverty, managing to support him and his sister, Eleanor, on her late husband's pension with a Calvinistic stoicism that had never failed to be admired. That admiration meant that Mrs Gilmour's position had never been what one might call arduous: she and her delightful children were seen as fitting people, readily accepted into society and most deserving of whatever one might do to lend a hand. Duncan had been such a clever boy, sitting scholarship exams the same way ordinary people filled in forms, accumulating the funds and then the learning with seamless ease.

Then there was Duncan's war, which infuriatingly he never talked about; his two years on the Western Front and his Military Medal remained a mystery, never discussed; no clue as to how Harry's father had won it. No one else ever talked about it either. In fact, Duncan Gilmour's 'Great War' was something studiously avoided, almost as if some whiff of disgrace lurked there, somewhere. Despite the medal. The only fact the medal confirmed was that Harry's father hadn't been an officer. The MM was strictly an 'other ranks' gong.

Harry's mother, Edith, was a few years younger, a little less bright but only just, and certainly no less attractive. One of four daughters of the County Engineer, she'd trained as a primary school teacher, and was a joiner-in at everything from amateur dramatics to licking envelopes for the local Liberal constituency party. Where she was dazzling and gay, Duncan was solid and considered, and they made a perfect couple, a golden couple, as they cut the rug together through polite Argyll society. Growing up, Harry had heard all the stories. For apparently, the man who had returned from France had not been the man who left. Beneath all the sangfroid, Duncan had come back a chaos of contradictions. He'd been a man anointed with charm, who now never used it; a writer on French literature and philosophy who refused to return to France. And of course, Harry's father was a war hero; or was he? A war hero who refused point-blank to speak of his glory.

Duncan intruded very little on Harry's upbringing and was never a very tactile or playful father. He would politely listen to the 5-year-old Harry recite poetry he'd learned for school, and clap where expected, but he would look puzzled rather than angry when the 8-year-old Harry misbehaved, as if he was watching a creature that had just arrived from another planet and was unsure how to communicate with it. Only Edith was aware of the tumult of emotions Duncan's son evoked in him, and the fear he felt for the little mite's existence; and she loved him for it.

It wasn't that life in the Gilmour house was dour and joyless. Far from it. There was always a lot of laughter. Duncan would hold impromptu French nights in which everyone had to speak French around the dinner table, and failure to do so would incur a forfeit. Duncan also loved to discuss history and its parallels with life today. Everyone had to have an opinion, and when the discussion was over, it would be rounded off with Duncan conducting a finale in which everyone had to recite – everyone being wife, son, Auntie Eleanor, and every fortunate guest invited into the Gilmours' rambunctious celebrations of man's history and philosophy, '. . . for as George Santayana wrote in 1905,' Duncan would intone, 'those who cannot remember the past are condemned to repeat it!' He loved to discuss Voltaire, Rousseau, Descartes, Hugo, de Tocqueville and most of all, the works of Napoleon. He was passionate about Napoleon, admiring his social reforms, contemptuous of his conquests.

'Discuss!' he would bark with manic glee. 'How can a man who could save his nation's revolution from tyranny, create an entirely new system of justice in the Napoleonic Code, then sink into such utter self-aggrandizing melodrama? . . . "I did not usurp the crown of France, I found it lying in the gutter and raised it up with the tip of my sword!" What a silly, preposterous, preening little man! I ask you! Idiot! History's full of 'em. Great men with feet of clay. And we haven't even begun to discuss the millions they end up killing.'

And Duncan was capricious, in a devilish sort of way. During a 'French night' he'd once suddenly asked Harry something in Italian, and Harry, not thinking, had replied in Italian.

'Forfeit!' Duncan shouted. 'You spoke in Italian.'

'But you spoke Italian first!' an outraged Harry yelled back.

And with a wave of his hand and an insouciant smirk, his father had replied, 'In this house, my power is absolute, like Napoléon's . . . and my character, flawed!'

All this to much eye-rolling from all around.

Then in 1936 came the Spanish Civil War and things began to change in the Gilmour household. Duncan seemed to discover anger. He espoused neither the republican nor fascist cause; it was the war itself he railed against. Incessantly. He could become embarrassing in his intensity, butting into people's conversation in shops and on the street. Ranting about the sheer barbaric, wanton stupidity and pernicious evil of organising sentient beings together for the indefensible purpose of killing each other . . . for a cause, for Christ's sake! A cause! Were these people mad? It was their one and only life they were dicing with.

Any attempt to reason with him, or calm him, or god forbid, take a side, incensed him all the more. At the grammar school, the rector even had to have words with Duncan about him hectoring the pupils. It was a small town, and people began to talk; and that was when Harry first began to pick up the first odd asides, eyes looking away, conversations ceasing, and it all seemed to turn around Duncan Gilmour's war. So Harry had asked his mum.

'Your father has never discussed his war with me, and I have never asked,' Edith had told the 16-year-old Harry, but only after a long and considered moment. When Harry's level gaze failed to shift from her, she was forced to say more. 'Your father is a very complex and intense man,' she said, choosing her words as a surgeon might choose instruments. 'I don't think it's any secret what he thinks about war and governments – he abhors them. Doesn't get the arguments, doesn't see the glory; only the death and hurt and waste, and for those left behind, the unbearable loss,' she said, but they both knew that was just part of the story. 'In itself, not approving of people killing each other isn't exactly irrational, is it?

That isn't the point though, is it? It's whether he's ever explained to me why war and killing with him is more personal. That's what you want to know. Well, it is none of your business. If he wants you to know, one day he'll tell you.'

And that was it. It hadn't really surprised Harry, for the other thing he had learned growing up was that although he was never in any doubt his parents doted on him, they doted on each other more. This had always been made plain to him by Edith, who told him the truth about everything. And that had been OK with him; not being the centre of attention all the time isn't the worst way for a child to grow up.

Harry had a lot of freedom in his upbringing, more than most of his peers, which allowed him the option of being able to step back from things; made him realise that he didn't always have to be on parade, and could get on with things for himself, and that had made him quite a sensitive, intuitive sort of chap. An adventurous one, too; something his mother always encouraged in him. She used to sit up after his father had gone to bed and talk to him long and often as he grew older, sometimes well into the candle-lit night over endless cups of Earl Grey tea, as if he was an adult, not a child. 'To dream and not to act, Harry,' she used to tell him. 'That's the greatest tragedy.'

Which was why he'd ended up hanging round the yacht builders in Sandbank where the members of the Royal Northern Yacht Squadron maintained their vessels. Because if you love the sea and sailing, there's no point mooning about on the beach being jealous because you can't afford a yacht. You make yourself useful to someone who can, and get him to let you sail his.

Then 3 September, 1939, had come. Harry had come home from his digs in Glasgow for Sunday lunch. Chamberlain was on the radio in the morning, and they'd all sat round the set, glum. After a lunch made all but impossible by his father's anti-war ranting, Harry went for a walk. He called into see Janis, only to find her house in equal turmoil; but the rants there had been more about the cost of flour and where Daddy would get his labour if all the men were called up.

When Harry returned, he went upstairs first, only later coming back down into the kitchen where his father was reading the Sunday papers and his mother was going through the domestic accounts as the late-afternoon sunshine flickered on the big oak table strewn with bills. He would remember the scene often in the years to come: his parents; peacetime. For no one would have guessed that the prime minister had been on the radio mere hours before, announcing the country was now in a state of war.

Harry hadn't known whether to sit down or stay standing. His travel grip, packed and with his tweed sports jacket thrown across it, was in the hall; a voice inside his head said he'd be better turning right around, grabbing his stuff and heading out without more ado. But it didn't seem good manners to go off to war without saying. So he stayed, rooted to the spot, until his mother looked up and asked, 'What is it, darling?' And the minute she did, Harry could tell she knew. His father stopped reading and lowered his paper, not because of Harry's sudden appearance, but because his wife was the only creature on earth whose moods he was sensitive to. He frowned to mark his irritation that his own son had had the impertinence to interrupt his wife's Sunday afternoon routine; and that was when Harry had told them what he was about to do.

His father had stared at his paper for a long time, his breathing heavy through his nose. Harry couldn't look at him. And then suddenly his father had leapt out of his chair and stormed out of the kitchen, and then the house. As Harry had followed him into the hall and his father was disappearing out of the front door, Harry heard a sound from him that would haunt him for a long time to come. He did not want to admit that it sounded like a sob.

Chapter Thirteen

The day after the Crumleys' party a letter arrived from Peter Dumaresq. He had replied to all Harry's letters from training, and Harry had thanked him for the wise words that had put him there. From those letters Harry had learned Dumaresq was now promoted to Lieutenant Commander and executive officer of the light cruiser, HMS *Wolverhampton*. This letter congratulated Harry on the sinking of the *Von Zeithen*, and commiserated with him on his 'little spot of bother' – which meant he also knew *Pelorus* had been sunk but wasn't saying, since like everyone else in the country he was keeping mum. It also explained why he knew where to send the letter – Harry would be on survivors' leave, so he would likely be at home. And Dumaresq, it transpired, was close at hand; his ship in a yard on the Clyde, just completing a refit. The letter concluded: '. . . so why not pop over for some lunch in the wardroom? Bring a tin hat, Jerry's been known to call too!'

Harry didn't have a tin hat; they hadn't issued him with one at Rosyth, so it was only an inherited watch cap and his gas mask bag that he grabbed before he headed for the steamer. This time the sailing was from Kirn Pier, a hundred yards down the hill from his front door, from where the little paddle steamer would go all the way up the Clyde to the Broomielaw in Glasgow's city centre. It was a greyish day, with thin, high cloud blocking the sun and making the air close.

The pier was jammed with sailors, some burdened down with giant white slugs of kitbags, others just heading for the city on passes, to the pubs and the dance halls. Despite the early hour the lads were raucous, full of it. Many of them sported 'HM Submarines' cap bands, begging the question: was Harry still one of them? He shut his eyes and conjured up *Pelorus's* bridge, the gaping 'O' of the hatchway that led down through the conning tower to the control room, and every time he closed his eyes he would see its black hole; tried to imagine going through another just like it on another submarine, and his stomach would churn. A settled and terrible conviction seemed to be forming in him, that somehow if he were ever to shut that steel hatch on the good, fresh air, he would never see the sky again. The little paddler chuffed and beat its way through the flock of anchored ships cluttering the Firth, and he leant on the rail and let the conviction fill him with despair.

As the Clyde's banks narrowed towards the city the paddle steamer began passing docks, and then shipyards bristling with cranes disgorging cargo, or lifting plates and giant hull frames; serried ranks of freighters, the slab sides of a *King George V*-class battleship in the fitting-out basin at the John Brown yard, an aircraft carrier taking shape on the slips; other lesser warships, dwarfed by the giant structures, all seething with workers. And still audible above the belly rumbling of the paddler's reciprocating steam engine was the all-pervasive background din drifting out across the river of caulkers' hammers forming hulls; and the sparkly guttering flashes of welding torches, and every now and then the unmistakable smell of burning steel wafting on air that looked and smelled greyer than air should, too thick to carry away the stink and fug of heavy industry going full-pelt. The sky became high and narrow as the ranks of hulls began to bunch, each ship perched on a slipway, angled into the curve of the river, towering over the turbid water, all self-contained and huge and swarming with blackened gangs of men. Another *King George V*-class sat like a vast, propped-up, bath-time toy on the slips at Fairfield's yard, and then tucked behind in the next door Stephens' yard, just where the letter had told him, was HMS *Wolverhampton*: dazzle camouflage paint almost complete, ship's stores going aboard, almost ready for sea. Harry couldn't help a little thrill at how poised and capable she looked amid all the clanging, banging chaos around her.

He took a tram from the Broomielaw along the streets of Govan that backed on to the yards and the river; streets of grimy tenements, one collapsed like a rotten tooth: German bombs falling short of the shipyard, a failed one-off attempt to keep *Wolverhampton* in port. It was a shocking sight, mainly because the destruction was specific and local, a little atrocity in the middle of the mundane and the everyday. If Poland and the Low Countries were anything to go by, apparently the Germans were capable of much, much worse; but so far, this country had not been Rotterdam-ed. No one, however, appeared in any doubt the Luftwaffe were only staying their hand in order to stockpile and prepare. Maybe Crumley was right. Maybe with the coming of the Hun, humanity really was going to reprise some blackly medieval past.

Harry was at the gangway before he snapped out of his gloomy reverie. He was going to see the flamboyant Peter Dumaresq, the man who'd saved him from *Redoubtable*'s wardroom; to toast Peter's new half ring and swap war stories.

'Sub-Lieutenant Gilmour, for Lieutenant Commander Dumaresq,' said Harry to the officer of the deck, as he snapped off a salute to the quarter deck.

'Mr Gilmour. The yeoman will take you to the wardroom,' said a fellow Sub with a friendly smile. Not like *Redoubtable* at all, even though he was RN. A 'welcome aboard' followed. Down through the labyrinth of passages to the officers' flat.

'We've been ordered to look out our tropic kit, so we're probably headed for the Arctic,' said Dumaresq, after shaking his hand, after Harry asked where they were bound. 'The Captain's ashore in deep pow-wow as we speak, so I suppose the rest of us will find out as we steam past Arran.'

Then into lunch: a gaggle of officers, draped in various shirt-sleeved poses, sat around the main wardroom table in a half gloom from the limited light the open scuttles allowed in. The crisp white tablecloth was covered in remove after remove until only the detritus from their dessert was left and clean ashtrays were being slid along the table. They were mostly young men, a dozen or so spared last-minute pre-sailing duties, all in their late twenties and early thirties.

All the department heads were there: 'Guns', the navigator, the Chief Engineer, career officers letting their hair down just a little, all having drunk their share of claret, and zeroing in on the port; drunk, but only a little. After all they'd be sailing on the dawn tide, heading back to sea, and the war.

This wasn't *Redoubtable*. Not at all. Not a whiff of the upper-sixth common room here. These were hard, serious, professional men, many with experience won in battle, and right now they were getting ready to listen to Harry's tale. The steward had been summoned, told to bring more port and clear the table – but leave the condiment dishes, mind you! They didn't just want to hear how Harry had sunk the *Von Zeithen*, they wanted to see it as well.

Their eagerness, and what it meant, was not lost on Harry, despite his feeling a bit droopy from the wine and the magnificent and eminently tasty concoction the wardroom chef had miracled out of mounds of corned beef, instant potatoes and carrots. He looked at the faces around the table, feeling a long way from the wretchedness of being on *Redoubtable*. The faces here didn't make him feel like an outsider anymore, a butt for bored bullies; wavy stripes and all, he was being treated as one of them now. A fighting sailor, part of a crew who'd met Jerry on the high seas in a straight fight, and sunk him; credentials didn't come much more credible than that. He'd dreamed of this; this was exactly how he'd dressed it up as he scrawled his signature that Tuesday afternoon after war had been declared in the recruiting office in this very city. But it had taken a lot of growing up to get here.

Harry, before all this the easy-going, charming, diffident owner of a poseur's pipe he actually couldn't bear to smoke, was much given to leaning raffishly against a students' bar on Byre's Road, waiting to be admired. That Harry would never have recognised the bloke who'd called out the readings from a 'fruit machine', sitting in a steel tube with fifty-odd other tensed-up, sweating matelots, forty feet under the North Sea, stalking an enemy cruiser, with the murderous intention of shooting several tons of high explosives into her guts.

There was a toast: 'To the next port! Wherever it may be!'

'Is it true we're all going to Canada?' Harry asked, made bold by the booze.

'Canada?' said 'Guns', a chubby, cheery two-ringer with tow hair and a distant, half surprised look at him.

'It's the rumour,' added an older officer, the oldest at the table, another Lieutenant Commander with a centre parting and the vaguest hint of posh Scots in his accent and with red piping between his stripes – the ship's surgeon. 'When the invasion comes we're all supposed to bugger off across the Atlantic with the Crown Jewels, "to carry on the fight", at least, that's the talk of the steamie,' he said.

'What are you talking about, Doc? What do you mean "all"?' said Dumaresq.

'All,' said the Doc. 'The lot of us. The entire home fleet and all who sail in her.'

'Bollocks!' said Dumaresq. 'Who's saying that?' He paused to put more menace into his scowl. 'It's propaganda to lull the bastard Jerries into a false sense of security.' Another pause, then: 'If Jerry is stupid enough to attempt a landing he'll find *Nelson*, *Rodney* and every other battleship in the bloody navy steaming down the Channel line abreast, firing their 16-inchers over open sights right into their bloody hammocks. And bugger the Luftwaffe!' Dumaresq paused again as if to reflect, then carried on: 'If he tries it'll be a bloodbath, probably for both of us, but that doesn't matter. All that matters is it means Jerry can't win. He might sink the whole bloody fleet in the process, but as the last destroyer goes down, there'll be "Jack", balancing on her main truck with a Lewis gun stuck to his hip, still firing till his hat floats. Even if a few Jerries do get ashore, they'll have paid too dearly for the entrance fee to have anything left to pay for the rides.'

While he was talking, Dumaresq had absently drawn a pad of bar chitties towards him and was scribbling on it. 'That is what we are here for, not as a lifeboat for the Crown Jewels. We've seen off the Armada, the Dutch and the French. And Jerry will be no different. I refer you to Old Jarvie, a man not known for prevarication – you know who Old Jarvie was, Mr Gilmour? Don't you?'

Harry didn't get a chance to answer.

'Sir John Jervis, Earl St Vincent, First Sea Lord,' said 'Guns', butting in, 'Took his title from the drubbing he gave the French off Cape St Vincent in 1797.'

'I think you'll find it was the Dons that time, but you're on the right track,' said Dumaresq with a smug grin. 'In 1801, when Parliament was in a funk over Bonaparte threatening to invade, he told them . . .'

Another Lieutenant farther down the table decided he too was going to butt in. Grinning, he interrupted with a sombre archness: '"I do not say, my lords, that the French cannot come . . ."'

Dumaresq butted back, '. . . "I say only that they cannot come by sea." Quite right, Mr Chapman. So I don't want to hear any more of this talk. For the pure and simple reason – and I guarantee you this, gentlemen – the Germans are not going to invade these islands. Because the Royal Navy isn't going to let them.'

All said in a tone that brooked no contradiction, at least not from one of his junior officers. But the Doc wasn't junior.

'So you don't subscribe to the old "fleet-in-being" concept, Peter?' he said, smirking away in the corner. 'Remain intact, maintain the threat. Very popular in the Italian navy one hears.'

'We don't have a concept of "fleet-in-being" in the Royal Navy, Doc,' said Dumaresq, calmer now as he slid the bar chitty tablet he'd been scribbling on down the table towards *Wolverhampton*'s Surgeon Commander. As it passed Harry, he could see his friend had been sketching a series of signal flags.

'We have that instead, and I'm assuming you know what it is?' asked Dumaresq, leaning back.

The Doc peered at it. 'A signal hoist . . . ,' he said, recognising it immediately and beaming as befits a gentleman who acknowledges he's been bested.

'. . . and you know what it says?'

'"Engage The Enemy More Closely",' said the Doc, much to the amusement of the assembled young men, all now sporting expressions of naked aggression.

Into the middle of this leant 'Guns', slamming down the salt with a thump on the table: 'Right, Gilmour, let's get down to it now we've got Henry the Fifth Part Two out the way. There's *Pelorus*, in the Skagerrak, sun's up; what's your exact position, course and speed . . .?'

Later, after the action had been played out across the cloth, Harry was sat in Peter Dumaresq's linen-cupboard-sized cabin, a palatial space by naval standards. Harry was sat on the desk's chair, with the desk's top folded up behind him, and flush with a shelf crammed with the cabin's only fripperies – photographs of an eighteenth-century vine-encrusted English farmhouse and a stout tweedy man, one of a young woman of stunning elegance, in a light print dress, smoking a cigarette and cupping a wine glass, sitting against a bright, Mediterranean backdrop, with bougainvillea everywhere. A girlfriend? Fiancée?

Dumaresq was leaning across to tip a few drops of angostura into Harry's tumbler of gin.

'I didn't do anything,' said Harry suddenly, staring at the bulkhead, waiting to be censured. 'In the engine room, after we were rammed. I didn't take command. I didn't lead. I was the only officer in the compartment and I didn't do anything.'

He'd decided to come clean right away. Confess to the doubt and shame that had been eating him since.

Dumaresq, perched on the edge of his bunk, was paying more attention to doctoring his own gin, slowly swirling the spirals of bitters until the clear gin assumed the proper hue, then he raised the tumbler for a toast, looking at Harry, who responded with his glass, and Dumaresq said simply: 'To Ted Padgett. Who will live to tell it all to his grandchildren, thanks to you.' He took a hefty belt, then considered his glass: 'Everybody wonders how they will stand up the first time. Now you know.'

'Indeed I do,' said Harry, dripping wretchedness.

'You kept your head,' said the older man, as if discussing something entirely different. 'You let the chiefs get on with their jobs, and you saved the life of one of your wounded crew . . .' a pause . . . 'I hope you're not going to start getting all soppy now, like a girl.'

And with that, he looked up with the broadest, friendliest smile. Harry didn't know even what expression to wear. But he got the point, and stepped back from the precipice of self-indulgence just in time. A voice in his head even said, Oh, do shut up! And then as he remembered his mother's entreaty to 'tell someone', he started to laugh. Whoever that someone might one day be, it certainly wasn't going to be Peter Dumaresq; or indeed any of them from among the wardroom of HMS *Wolverhampton*. These men hadn't wanted to know how he'd 'felt', or what he was 'going through', they had only wanted to know what he'd done. And the relief that washed over him right then 'felt' pretty good. He'd just been judged by his deeds, and so far had not been found wanting. Everything else was flummery. The message was simple – get on with it!

From that moment on he knew that if he was to turn in his papers as a submarine officer he would never again feel he had the right to sit in the company of men like Peter Dumaresq, or indeed any of the other officers of *Wolverhampton*'s wardroom. But more than that, he knew he would never be able to face himself. The dilemma had been resolved. He could not back out now. That it meant he was going to be very afraid again, very soon, was no longer the issue. He had got his wish, he had become like the men he had just dined with. And with that little matter of housekeeping out of the way, he proffered his glass to Dumaresq to be charged with more gin. The conversation, naval fashion, immediately cut to the real reason Dumaresq had called Harry back into his cabin: what had really happened aboard *Pelorus*?

The story of the patrol up to and including the sinking of the *Graf Von Zeithen* had been easy to tell, what Harry knew of it. Then there was the loss of *Pelorus*; but what did Dumaresq want to know about the scramble for life in an oily sunken steel tube, just another mortal vignette from their particular house in the human zoo; there were endless others being played out on stricken ships from Halifax to Cape Town. Men dying in warships wasn't news these days. But what had happened in the interview with the Bonny Boy back in Rosyth was different. Dumaresq wanted to take Harry back to *that* place; the place Harry hadn't gone back to since.

It wasn't out of prurient interest either. Dumaresq was such an affable chap it was easy to forget how connected, just how 'old navy' he was. What did Harry remember that made sense, which he could succinctly communicate, naval-fashion, to Dumaresq? Pared back to the language of an Admiralty dispatch, bald precision would not address the deep unease he'd felt.

'He described the patrol, from his point of view,' began Harry, 'although there wasn't much of his version I recognised.'

'Go on.'

Harry looked at Dumaresq, at loss as to how he could communicate what had gone on in Bonalleck's tatty naval quarters. How do you explain the abyss to someone normal, who has never had an occasion to look into it? How do you explain it to yourself, when for the first time in your life you are confronted with madness? When it only comes at you in flashes? Against everything else that seems so normal?

Harry couldn't think how to excuse himself, or indeed if an excuse was necessary. All he could think of was the black hole he'd seen opening up beneath him if he tried to make an issue of Bonalleck's conduct; the hole he was going to fall into if he announced he was actually going to tell what had happened to a court of inquiry.

'I just told him that as far as I was concerned, he'd been unwell during the patrol and was in his cabin when we encountered the *Von Zeithen*, and the First Lieutenant had been on watch and begun the attack in case she got away. And then I added that any evidence I gave to the inquiry would be guided by what's best for the good of the service.'

Dumaresq smiled a very knowing smile. 'Did you now? What a very clever young man you are. That was the correct answer . . .'

'I didn't leave it there, though,' Harry added.

'Ah.'

Harry spoke with his eyes closed: 'I told him he was a shameless drunk who had killed half his crew.'

Dumaresq sat back, steepled his fingers on his chest and studied them closely.

Harry continued, 'There had been two lookouts on the bridge with him, I don't know who they were. A couple of young ABs. He survived. They didn't. But he never even bothered to mention them. His crew. Two of his crew. And he just turned his back. Didn't care. Probably like he did that night. I just couldn't let him get away with it. So I opened my big gob. I told him I knew who he was, what he had done.'

Dumaresq very quietly asked, without looking up: 'What did the Bonny Boy say?'

Harry remembered the chill that had swept over him as the Bonny Boy had slowly reassembled himself in the silence that had followed his harangue, from drunken rambling wreck to the very picture of a senior naval officer, without a wash of his face, trim of whisker or adjustment to uniform. Bonalleck's smile had been almost avuncular, but it was a smile that only extended as far as his lips. Harry would never forget the way his former Skipper had looked at him from pools of bottomless malevolence.

'He didn't like it,' Harry told Dumaresq.

'You don't say,' Dumaresq replied.

Chapter Fourteen

Harry woke up with a hangover, the sun streaming through his bedroom window, slowly ungluing his gummy eyes, and heating up a sloppy nausea that rode in waves from head to guts. He had to make several attempts to sit upright. The effort to wash and clean his teeth meant he had to go and lie down again. He tried gulping down ice-cool water from the tap, but it merely rushed over the now desiccated tissue of his mouth and throat.

So he lay down again, eyes closed, and remembered what Peter Dumaresq had said about the Bonny Boy: 'He's far too old and far too senior to be given command of another boat. You'll more than likely never cross his path again. Stick to your story before the court of inquiry, and don't try to tell them anything they don't ask for, and then forget about it.'

As he saw Harry down *Wolverhampton*'s gangway, he'd said it was important that Harry had told him what had happened; important that certain people be made aware, but that done, it was none of Harry's business any more.

Harry managed finally to rise and go downstairs. It was mid-morning and the house was empty. He put the kettle on and sat, head buried in hands, as it boiled. He was on his second cup when he saw the head and shoulders of a figure purposefully stride past the kitchen window. A girl, he was sure.

Seconds later the door knocker split his skull ear to ear and sent nausea sloshing through him again. He placed his cup on the table and forced himself to stand and move to the back door. He opened it to be confronted by a young woman with an exquisitely pale skin drawn over high cheekbones, a big, wide smile and a pre-Raphaelite explosion of chestnut hair.

'Hallo, Harry Gilmour, still sea sick?' she said. The voice had none of the local west coast brogue; it was received pronunciation at perfect pitch, but with too much fun in it to be clipped or glass.

Harry managed a 'Huh?'

'You look dreadful, Harry, are you OK?'

Then he placed her. Shirley. Three years below him at school. The daughter of the peninsula's very own flat-broke aristocratic family. Daft as a brush apparently, not that he'd known that personally, seeing as this was the first time he'd actually spoken to her; actually found himself in conversation.

'It's what we in the navy call a self-inflicted wound,' he said, wanting to affect a worldly sangfroid. 'Can I help you?'

'No. Not really. Is Edith in?'

Harry bridled at her familiarity, and decided he too could be just as impertinent. 'Might I ask who's asking?'

'Me.'

Harry scowled, and the effort made him wobble a little.

'Oh come on, Harry, it's me, Shirley Lamont. You know who I am, everybody does. I've got a load more plant cuttings for Edith – your *mother* – and I should put them in the shed if she's not here,' and with that she slid past Harry clutching a little box full of twigs and dirt, and vanished into the pantry, only to reappear a moment later with the potting shed key. Nobody locked anything in Dunoon normally, but their small petrol generator and the half a dozen battery cells they charged, were out there; and his mother was always worried next door's children would get in and play havoc with the family's only access to domestic electricity.

As Shirley swept past she saw the teapot on the table. 'Oh tea!' she said. 'I'd love a cup. You wouldn't make me pedal all the way back without one? Please? Pretty, please?' Then she was gone round the corner and out to the shed with her cuttings.

Harry popped his head round the door after her and saw her battered bicycle leaning against the wall, shook his head, and went inside to pour her a cup of tea.

And that was how Harry got to know Shirley Lamont, someone he remembered only as a figure from the grammar school mainly because of her hair, its wild tresses flashing down corridors or across the playground, always in a tearing hurry and trailing bohemian chaos. She was the only daughter and youngest child of the Viscount and Lady Cowal, of Castle Cowal, sibling to two older brothers whom he did know in passing, and certainly not from the grammar school. The old man, their father, was long dead: a car accident on the North West Frontier while with the horsey regiment the family had served as breeding stock, from a time dating back to the Covenanters.

With her husband dead, Shirley's mother had soldiered on into accelerated dotage, raising enough money on the way to send her two sons through public school in Edinburgh, and onward without any distinction, into the regiment; and that was where they were now, with the Colours, somewhere on some foreign field. Cameron, the new lord, and Hamish, who was the same age as Harry. Cammy and Hammy. What a pair. Still it wasn't her fault she was family to Cammy and Hammy, thought Harry, as one cuppa extended to three, and a scone.

Shirley really was rather a refreshing girl, Harry thought, in her shapeless blue sweater and green, mud-spattered knee-length skirt and plimsolls. And that pre-Raphaelite explosion of chestnut hair. And her hazel eyes.

'So you asked her out?' said his mother, having arrived home long after a grinning, waving Shirley had bicycled out of the front gate. 'She is only sixteen, Harry.'

'Seventeen, actually. You didn't tell me you've been forcing a destitute girl into stealing plants for you. And then not even paying her!'

His mother scowled at him.

'I did not ask her out, as such,' Harry finally said to break the silence. 'She wanted to know how I was spending my leave. I said long walks, and then enquired if she might like to join me one day. Just to be polite. And she said yes . . . tomorrow, since you ask.'

'I didn't ask,' said his mother.

———

It wasn't that long a walk. They climbed the Camel's Hump behind the town and sat looking out over the majesty of the Firth with its shipping, and beyond to the velvety smoothness of the Bens and the toy-like barrage balloons above the Greenock shipyards, and then south over the Ayrshire hills down to the steel-blue waters beyond the anti-submarine boom, to Paddy's Milestone and the Irish Sea. They had brought a flask and sandwiches, or rather Shirley had, stuffed into her gas mask bag instead of the gas mask.

'Who's going to gas Argyll? The wind would blow it away before it could even make a sparrow sick,' was her last word on the matter. Then they talked about the war.

Shirley thought Harry was doing the right thing, and was so proud of him when she'd heard he'd dropped out of university to volunteer. She had set her sights on going to art school, but she wanted to do her bit too and was going to volunteer as an ambulance driver in Glasgow to free up a man for the fighting forces.

The Germans had to be stopped. How dare they march into other people's countries and wreck their homes and tell them what they couldn't think or say? Harry found little to disagree with.

'They weren't even a proper country seventy years ago,' said Shirley, 'and now look at them . . . and that Hitler . . . preposterous little man.'

'Dangerous, preposterous little man,' corrected Harry.

'Exactly,' she said, then let it hang for a while as they munched through the fish-paste sandwiches, drank their tea and gazed out upon the vista. Then she spoke, as if there had been no interval at all. 'Are you frightened?'

Harry rolled on to his back and ceremoniously stuck a stem of grass in his mouth. It wasn't that she had caught him unawares; the exact opposite in fact. His thoughts had been running along remarkably similar lines. The war, with him in it; what had happened so far, and the story his mother had said he would have to tell.

He stared up into the big blue, and reached a decision. Young Harry, just turned twenty. Not a bad chap, or malicious, just the carelessness of youth driving him. He'd not a notion of the way truth can bind you to another; the effect it can have on a young woman, to have a young man open his heart to her. And we're not talking romantic declarations here – the heartfelt pledges of undying love and other such guff that gets kicked up like debris by every blindly charging cavalier – but the opening of the door to his intimate workings, to the stuff that was in the process of making him, forming him, turning him into the man he would one day become.

Harry was some way into his wistful soliloquy when Shirley reached across and took his hand, and Harry, god forgive him, had the overweening arrogance to feel smugly mature at such a 'girlish' gesture. Nonetheless, he thought it was quite nice.

She held his hand all the way down the hill, to where she'd left her bicycle at the back of Dunloskin Farm. The dairy cows studied them gravely as Harry held her bike upright by the saddle and they strolled slowly to the metalled road.

'When you push off again, you'll write?' she said.

Harry, surprised at his own conviction, said: 'Yes. I'd like that. If you didn't mind.'

'I shan't think much of you if you don't.'

And that was that.

The next day, in a stuffy grey little cubby, with the familiar racket of workshops and extractor fans drowning out the closer rattle of type-writers, Harry sat once again in the midst of naval activity, aboard the submarine depot ship HMS *Titania*. He was barely three miles as the seagull flies from his own back door, serenely afloat on the placid waters of the Holy Loch. Having cadged a lift out first thing on the early picket boat he'd even managed a second breakfast from the wardroom galley before settling down to begin his vigil.

Last night, after waving Shirley goodbye, and after a stiltedly silent tea at home in the presence of his father, he'd sat out in the garden with a glass of whisky and the late-evening sun for company and made up his mind about many things, not least that if he was going back into submarines, the sooner the better. And so here he was aboard *Titania*, waiting for the Paymaster Commander, or whoever cut rail passes, for a trip back to Portsmouth.

'Is there still no bugger in yet from your lot?' The voice of the senior rating Writer he'd been fobbed off on echoed from the next compartment. Mutterings, then the booming reply from the Writer: ''Cos we've got this single-ringer in next door waiting for a chitty back to *Dolphin*, and at this rate by the time any of your lot get him fixed up, he'll be a bleeding admiral.'

This was followed by a bit of a kerfuffle, a few more mutters and a silence, broken by the Writer who could now be heard saying most respectfully: 'I dunno, sir. I never asked him his name, sir.'

Harry looked up from his reverie as a sandy head poked round the doorway and eyed him curiously. 'And you are . . . ?'

The mention of the word 'sir' and the age of the face before him advised Harry to stand and come to attention: 'Sub-Lieutenant Gilmour, sir.'

The head's body followed it into the cubby, revealing a watch jacket with three Commander's rings on the sleeve; the face squinted. '*Pelorus* Gilmour?'

'Yes, sir.'

'Dear boy! Dear boy!' A hand shot out to be shaken. 'The very fellow who snatched that rogue Ted Padgett from Davy Jones' clutches. Allow me to shake your hand. Jack Twentyman. Commander (S), Seventh Flotilla, but no need to kneel. Come this way, my dear boy, and let's get you sorted. Tea for this young man. And me. In my day cabin.'

A flotilla Commander no less, thought Harry. Well if he can't get me squared away, who can?

'So you're looking for another berth are you?' asked Twentyman, seated now on a tiny easy chair, with Harry, his bum on its twin. 'Didn't give you cold feet then?'

'What, sir?'

'Being sunk on your first war patrol. You're not exactly long in the trade are you? If you applied to go back and join the "surface skimmers", you'd probably get it.'

'I volunteered for submarines, sir. I think I should see it through.'

The story of the sinking of *Graf von Zeithen* and then the loss of *Pelorus* herself had obviously zipped through the fleet – the headlines anyway. Even Harry, and the rescue of the notorious Padgett, was out there. But that didn't appear to be everything on the Commander's mind. Harry felt Twentyman's gaze and could almost feel the question mark hanging above his head like some halo of doubt.

Harry had no real idea how he would react the first time he stepped aboard a submarine again, and had to drop down through the conning tower hatch and back into the exact same type of steel tube which had so nearly become his tomb. But sitting here under the evaluating eye of this senior submariner, the necessity of his earlier decision was rammed home. If he shied away, everyone would know. Everyone was afraid, sure; it was war. But everyone would know that he, Harry Gilmour, couldn't face his fear; and how would that feel? The knowledge that every other bloke was capable of accepting the same risk when it came to sliding down that ladder, except that on the day, they would do it and he wouldn't? What would it be like to carry that around for the rest of his life?

'When's your leave up, Mr Gilmour?'

'Not until the end of next week, sir, but I thought I might as well get back and get going again, sir?'

'Really. That keen are we? Well, if you don't fancy numbing your bum on a train for two days, I might be able to help you. Depending on how keen, and how nippy you can be?'

'Very keen, sir.'

'I'm losing an N-class boat to another flotilla, and she'll be passing through *Dolphin* on her way. But she slips in,' he squinted at his watch, 'just over five hours. I'm sure Bobby Whitlock, her Skipper, would be pleased to give you a lift if you can shift quickly enough.'

＊　＊　＊

There was no one at home when he dashed back in so it was just a matter of throwing his kit together. He scribbled a quick note, explaining, and felt a pang of guilt that he preferred it this way.

Harry wasn't a fan of goodbyes. For a moment he hesitated, before adding 'Dad' to the envelope too. Then it was out of the door.

Despite being barely three miles to the *Titania* over the back roads from his house, Harry took the long way round so that he could call in at the Royal Northern Yacht Squadron clubhouse, a huge mock-Tudor mansion sitting behind the slips at Hunter's Quay. Sir Alexander Scrimgeour, the Edinburgh financier and member, wouldn't be there, not on a day set aside for sitting in his counting house in the city's St Andrew Square, but Harry was going to leave a note for him, the patronising old fart. Old Lexie. Harry's mentor; his role model for better days to come; his guide in matters nautical and social.

As a youth, Harry had crewed for him on his exquisite twelve-metre yacht, *Tangle,* as in tangle o' the isles. Hauling on ropes for him, polishing and scrubbing, boiling kettles and filling teapots, and then donning a starched patrol jacket to serve tea, or gin, in the cockpit to Lexie's other 'crew' of guffawing *matelots manqués*.

Harry could never recall without a grin old Lexie's beatific countenance as he would regard his biddable young protégé on those sailing days. Smugness in a sea of complacency. That was how he would describe old Lexie to his giggling mother. Yet regardless of how much of a god that old man regarded himself – in love with his own enlightenment and benevolence – Harry couldn't help but like him, for he was kind, too, and not just to Harry. Waiters and bell-hops were always treated with scrupulous politeness when men of his status rarely did. Harry's mother and father were always inquired after too. Not out of nosiness, but in a way that told you he was making sure Harry's parents knew and approved of what Harry was doing, and who he was doing it with.

As for Harry? Who was only in it for the sea time, who tended to mock the old man and his conceits. What did Harry, the boy who always noticed the little things, really think? Well, for a start he knew the politeness meant that at heart old Lexie really must be a nice person. And he also recognised, that as a benefactor, Sir Alexander Scrimgeour wasn't just feeding a jumped-up ego; he really *was* generous and kind. And yes, Harry had to pander to all the puffed-up posturing to earn his crew berth on old Lexie's yacht; but what a yacht! And what sailing! That was why it never troubled Harry to take time to show his respect and gratitude, and if the odd line or two was all it took, he didn't mind taking the long way round.

His note delivered to the concierge, Harry continued round the coast road to the navy pier to wait for a space on a tender heading out to the depot ship.

When the tender arrived, it was a fight to get to the departing boat's gangway through the scrum of sailors humping supplies to stuff into her open hatches. They laboured away with preoccupied intensity in the mid-afternoon sunshine dressed only in shorts and singlets, or blue overalls folded down and tied at the waist with the sleeves, showing paint-white torsos untouched by sun for weeks on end. From behind a steady stream of them filing over a single plank to the submarine's casing, Harry was clutching to his chest the grip containing all the kit he currently owned.

'Sub-Lieutenant Gilmour, permission to come aboard,' he called out to a Petty Officer who had a clip board and a particularly foul line in entreaties to chivvy the men along.

There was a din of chains clanking and scrapping and much cursing forward as a gaggle of ratings wrestled an ungainly, dangling torpedo over the forward hatch, trying to fit it down the hole. The clipboard owner ignored Harry, scribbling as each box passed him and went up and over the bridge. Eventually the stream of loaders halted abruptly, and as a gathering queue of sailors waiting to come off was about to move, the Petty Officer held up his hand against the lead rating's chest, and without looking up, waved Harry on.

Harry stepped nimbly over the plank and on to the submarine's deck, stepping aside just in time to avoid the 'going ashore' line charging towards him.

She was a much smaller boat than *Pelorus*, about 200 feet long, and she didn't look much over 600 or 700 tons, newly painted a drab grey, with a small 3-inch pop gun mounted forward of the conning tower, flush on the casing instead of in its own raised mounting as on *Pelorus*. He could read her name plate fixed to the side of the conning tower, *N'galawa*. Bloody funny name for a warship, thought Harry. HMS *N'galawa* sounded like something Johnny Weissmuller would shout at the natives in one of those awful Tarzan films.

'Oi! 'arry!' yelled the clipboard man, right by Harry's ear.

Harry spun with an ingratiating smile, surprised at being recognized, but he hadn't been. The Petty Officer didn't even raise his eyes from his clipboard; not even when the Harry he was after stuck his bare, oil-smeared head above the bridge, obviously irritated at being dragged from some below-deck task, and bellowed back in a thick accent, 'Wot?'

'This here's our passenger, Mr Gilmour,' said Harry's welcomer, finally looking up with a narrow eye. 'Stow him in the wardroom and make sure he stays out the way.'

He turned to Harry with a suddenly sunny grin, disfigured by at least two gaping holes in a row of teeth the colour of stewed tea. 'We wouldn't want you getting belted by a packing case of tinned peaches, sir, now would we?'

And Harry was guided by the man's hand – actually, more like shoved – into the 'going aboard' line, and found himself being shuffled forward at a tripping rate up the ladder on to the bridge, pushed and buffeted, grunts, a curse, a big big hurry behind him. Through the rush and his own irritation, he realised that his feet had just hit the deckplates of *N'galawa*'s control room and he'd gone straight through the dread threshold he'd conjured and worried and fretted about; through and beyond the fear he'd had of that moment, of having to stand in the conning tower hatch and lower himself into its black gaping maw. Right through, without even noticing, propelled along by a good old-fashioned Royal Navy ''urry up!'

Out of the corner of his turning eye he was aware of the mechanical spaghetti of the control room, and then the other 'arry was roughly spinning his shoulders and peremptorily announcing 'Aft, sir' and he was in the tunnel of the passageway, stumbling on an unfamiliar deck of flat packs of tinned food laid out to make use of every conceivable storage space.

'Hard a'port, sir,' and he was through the curtains and into the wardroom, and the other 'arry had his grip off him and was cramming him into a tiny shoebox-size shelf above what looked like folded up bunks. 'Can't do ya no char or nuffin', sir – galley's closed.' The man, wearing only shorts, singlet and a lot of body hair, displayed no insignia of rank, leaving Harry at a loss as to how to address him. He was also too big for the space, and was bent too close to just turn and bugger off back to his duties, which he obviously wanted to do.

The two Harrys looked at each other for a moment.

And then it came to him at last, out of the all too familiar reek of oil, and sweat and bilge water, and the hemming-in steel-ness and the sense of the crush of human bodies – all too real, with the fast-paced daisy chain of ratings charging past eighteen inches away with their loads for stowing further aft. It was the first flutter of panic. Like something encroaching on where he lived, 'noises off' and threatening. Suddenly shaky, trying to drown it out, Harry said: '*N'galawa*? That's a bloody funny name.' Knowing immediately after speaking that to mock the name of another sailor's ship was beyond bad manners.

The other 'arry stopped the supply train passing outside by sticking his backside into it, and as he went to swish shut the ward-room curtains, fixed Harry with a cold, indifferent eye again. 'It's Swahili . . . for "I want my mum". Sir.'

Harry flopped bum first on to the banquette that lined the tiny space, and laughed a quiet, sardonic laugh. 'How did he know?' he said to the portrait of the King, hanging less than six inches from his ear on the wood-panelled bulkhead. The noise of the sailors going about the replenishment of their boat was now doing all the drowning out that Harry needed. A blue funk wasn't anything he couldn't handle, was it? After all, he'd handled funk before, hadn't he? He smiled at the King. He was back.

Harry was also left alone. He passed the time browsing *N'galawa's* meagre library – a couple of Somerset Maughams, a translation of Jules Verne's *Michael Strogoff*, some Margery Allinghams – all of them he'd read – and two obscure travel books. Eventually he heard and felt the boat slip her moorings, and the diesels power up; still no one came. Then a rating's face, and the offer: 'Skipper says do you fancy a last look at home, sir?'

They were rounding past Hunter's Quay when Harry scrambled up between the lookouts to stand beside *N'galawa's* Captain, Lieutenant Robert Whitlock RN. He wore a disreputable watch jacket and the usual white pullover, his thick black curls bared to the light breeze wafting like prairie grass. He had a good five or six years on Harry. A lot, when you're that age, even if you have already been through almost a year of war. The bridge was a tight squeeze and made introductory handshakes a bit of a fumble.

'I hear you think we have a funny name,' said Whitlock.

'Unforgivable, sir,' said Harry. 'Nerves. Trotted out the very thing I didn't mean to say.'

'First time back in a boat,' said Whitlock, 'since you got sunk?'

'Yes.'

'But you're back. No screaming hab-dabs?'

'Not that I've noticed, sir.'

'Good man.' Whitlock looked away and swept his arm the length of the shore, a mere few hundred yards off their starboard beam, 'Nice here, isn't it? Very pretty.'

And that was it. All said and done. The vital question settled. Harry was back in the trade. What was all the fuss about?

'Yes, sir,' he replied. 'Very pretty.'

And so it was. He studied his little town, nestled in a bowl of the Cowal hills, the clouds dappled in the evening sun, with the forlorn statue of Highland Mary on the little plug of rock above the pier, the church and castle behind it, the town's slate-grey facades redolent with all the beneficence that over 200 years of tranquillity can bestow. And now he was sailing away to defend it. An inchoate pressure of his mission and pride and grim resolve thumped away in his chest and in those passing minutes a serene certainty descended on him, a sense that all that was fine and decent in a world being ripped apart was vested here; and that he would give his life to defend it.

Chapter Fifteen

It is 01:47 hours, 16 August, 1940; there is a position marked on the chart in degrees and minutes north and degrees and minutes west, that places His Majesty's Submarine *Trebuchet* some thirty miles west-south-west of Les Sables-d'Olonne on the Bay of Biscay.

Sub-Lieutenant Harry Gilmour RNVR, on her bridge, is pretty confident of the figures, having just drawn down Jupiter to the horizon for the second time – just to check – using the sextant with the modified, more powerful lens that makes it easier to see the line between the dark of the sea and the dark of the sky; the one that old Lexie had presented to him like a school prize to a school boy, so long ago, when Harry had announced he was going into the navy.

It is a crystal-clear, moonless night with the long, slow swell of the Atlantic barely discernible beneath Harry's feet. Not a rumour of the tempest that normally rules this notorious pan of ocean. Only starlight illuminates the dimpled surface as *Trebuchet* noses at a steady six knots towards the dancing line of fairy lights that is the French fishing fleet, out for a night's work from the tiny ports that line La Roche-sur-Yon coastline between St Nazaire and La Rochelle. The German-occupied coastline.

On the bridge with Harry is *Trebuchet*'s Captain, Lieutenant Andy Trumble RN. He is the same tousled blond youth who had stuck his head over the bridge of that old H-boat all those months ago to welcome Harry aboard on his first dive in a submarine, although his hair is a lot shorter these days. Trumble had been the Jimmy back then. Now he is the Skipper and *Trebuchet* is his first command.

Also with them are two ratings: lookouts keeping an all-round eye while the Skipper studies the bobbing light show. A fifth man on the bridge, Leading Seaman Billy Wardell, mans a somewhat gimcrack twin Lewis gun mount, the wisdom of which the Skipper has often doubted, but for tonight's enterprise he has allowed it to be assembled.

They are here to make a rendezvous with a fishing boat, to meet a man called Gabriel, and to collect a package from him, then transport it back to Portsmouth. However, the fishing boat they are to rendezvous with is supposed to be alone, and the presence of these other boats bobbing between them and the shore is a most unwelcome development.

This is Harry's third war patrol aboard HMS *Trebuchet*, and given the mission it is the most likely to generate any excitement. Especially with the presence of this surprise Armada. Harry has already called down his estimated position to the control room. He packs his sextant back in its wooden box and passes it down the conning tower hatch to a rating for stowing behind the chart table. He resumes his scanning of the dark horizon to seaward, while Trumble and the other lookouts peer into the mob of fishing boats hoping to find *their* fishing boat among them.

Harry's job is to look out for any Jerry sneaking up behind them, for Jerry is here already, busily putting France's Atlantic ports to good use. Brest, Lorient, St Nazaire, Roscoff and La Rochelle, over the eastern horizon, are all being fortified to accommodate U-boats; preparing to get them farther out into the Atlantic in order to disrupt

Britain's convoy arteries to the New World just as they are starting to pump. There's not much of a Jerry naval presence in the Bay yet, just a few light craft; E-boats, and the slower but no less armed *Räumbooten.* Most of the Jerry light forces are in the Channel with the landing barges, waiting for the Luftwaffe to finish the job they started less than a week ago, pounding the RAF airfields across southern England, clearing the way for their invasion forces; but there is still a chance there are one or two out there tonight, eager to pounce on any Royal Navy submarine looking the wrong way.

Harry watches the Bay, his concentration complete, his daydreaming days knocked out of him by the early raids on Portsmouth. The dislocating, sobering, profound shock of seeing rows of mutilated terraced houses standing in landscapes of broken glass and smashed masonry, the intimacy of their patterned wallpaper, and naked bath-tubs on view to the world; the buses down holes deeper than their top decks; burning factories and workshops, the bodies in the streets; women's legs poking out from under muck-caked blankets, or worse, the children.

Jerry raids on Channel shipping and the big naval base began over a month ago; relentless, or so they had all thought, until the intensity of the current phase of the air battle. At this very hour, away to the north-east, on airfields in the hinterland behind the giant sweeping arc between the Baie de Seine and the Pas-de-Calais, hundreds and hundreds of German fighters and bombers are being armed and fuelled for yet another day in the skies over England. But Harry doesn't think about any of that; right now his own little bit of the war has his undivided attention.

Harry is dimly aware of Andy Trumble muttering away to himself about 'bloody' this and 'bloody' that, seriously disgruntled by the presence of these other fishing boats, and the nigh-on impossibility of him sighting *his* fishing boat and its convoluted light signal against a backdrop of a score of other lights. This, and his fretting over the fact that Johnnie Frenchman isn't all that well disposed towards the Royal Navy these days, not after Force H sunk half the French fleet at anchor in Mers-el-Kébir last month. God knows how many French sailors they'd killed – a thousand at least – all to keep the ships from falling into Jerry's hands. Which is why, if those fishing boats were to spot *Trebuchet*, the game would be as good as up. So the muttering continues apace, barely audible above the dull diesel thump of *Trebuchet*'s two engines – one pushing her through the limpid bay, and the other cramming her batteries full of amps for the coming day, submerged.

The first white light leapt into Harry's peripheral vision as he held his binoculars, the seals slightly away from his eye sockets, but he was focused on it in a second. 'Light on the port quarter!'

As he said it, he knew it was too close. A mile? Or three? It was too dark for a useful guess at range, but it hadn't just come over the horizon; so much closer than that. The light had sprung out of nowhere, out of the dark sea background, too dark to separate even the dimmest silhouette.

A second white light appeared as all binoculars on the bridge trained in unison, in plenty of time to see a green light rise up and then dip. But it was a stuttering, hurried hoist. Behind him Harry heard the Skipper hiss a series of orders down the open hatch to the control room, and immediately the boat's big diesels went silent. As they did so, Trumble's hiss became audible, insistent, '. . . group down, slow ahead, bring her on to two-nine-five.' They had gone on to electric motors.

Trumble's shadow was up and beside Harry. 'Our recognition signal, but back to front,' he said in his ear. 'What exactly did you see, Harry?'

'Nothing at all, sir. Then the white light just flashed on, and then . . .'

He was still speaking when the sound of shouts came over the silent water. Not close, but distinct. And then suddenly a fishing boat was all lit up. Not by her own blaze of lights, but a pool at the end of a stab of light, like a white pencil in the dark, and at its end a French drift-netter all picked out. Then the fishing boat's own lights came on in her wheel house, and a few deck lights, and in their wash could be seen, lolling off her beam, a dim shape that Harry recognised immediately from all the recognition silhouettes pasted up in *Dolphin*'s wardroom. It was a *Räumboote*, and she was probing the French boat with her bridge-wing searchlight.

'Bugger,' said Trumble, and everyone on the bridge was instantly on tiptoe ready to leap into action, but the Skipper did not shout, 'Diving Stations!' He said nothing. Then, after a long moment, he said, 'Bugger' again before sotto voce issuing a series of further commands down the bridge voice-pipes. He was conning the submarine out in a wide circle, taking them to seaward of the fishing boat and her *Räumboote* companion, moving silently on her motors to put them between *Trebuchet* and the gaggle of other French boats.

Harry kept his binoculars trained on the two light-spattered silhouettes. Here were his first live Germans, tiny mannequins jigging and bobbing on the *Räumboote*'s bridge. Others were moving, boarding the fishing boat, it all playing out barely a mile away across the black lead of the water. The angry shouting had died down, yet there were still exchanges taking place; even above the burbling of the German's idling diesels he could still make out the distinct sound of emphatic *nons*!

'That Jerry's obviously the sheep dog,' said the Skipper to *Trebuchet*'s First Lieutenant, who had just climbed up from the control room, 'padding about out there to seaward, making sure none of his flock tries to slip away to friendlier shores. He'll be giving our chaps in the drifter a right bollocking, so while he's occupied, I'm going round behind him. We'll not dive as long as he doesn't spot us, it'll waste too much time going down only to have to come up again.'

'Too right,' Harry heard the First Lieutenant whisper out of the darkness.

'Get Mike to get his pop gun party ready in the well,' Trumble whispered from behind his binoculars. 'I don't want them up yet in case we have to go down fast, but I want them ready for a gun action pronto if the need arises.'

The First Lieutenant's shadow slipped down the conning tower hatch and was gone.

Without taking his eyes off the two boats in the darkness, Harry had been hanging on every word. This was it: he was watching the movements of real enemy sailors, operating against an Allied vessel, and he was listening to his Skipper laying plans to engage it. His mouth was dry, his palms moist, and he could not imagine a life more extraordinary than the minutes he was living through now, out in the Bay of Biscay, stalking a German warship through the dead of night.

Two war patrols aboard *Trebuchet* had introduced Harry to the submariner's life proper, had at last allowed him to grow into being part of a crew. The 'voyage of the damned' that had been his patrol aboard *Pelorus* counted only inasmuch as it let him come to *Trebuchet* with a 'name', a certain cachet that allowed him to start not quite at the beginning, that offered quite considerable benefit of the doubt, especially as far as 'Jack' was concerned. He had done something they respected. It was nothing to do with his role in sending to the bottom a major German warship. It was everything to do with him saving Ted Padgett. And it wasn't just *Trebuchet*'s crew; he heard it everywhere he went in the trade. The fact that he had personally wrestled Davy Jones for the life of one of their most prodigious sinners – and won; that was something. No one was interested in the glory; and the more Harry thought about it, that was all right by him. Now here he was, part of an experienced submarine crew with more than 6,000 tons of enemy shipping sunk, under their belt.

He'd learned one other thing about HMS *Trebuchet* since joining. She wasn't ever called HMS *Trebuchet* – at least not by her crew. They had another name for her, and they'd started allowing Harry to call their boat by its 'real' name. HMS *Trebuchet*, pronounced *treb-oo-shay*, was named after a medieval French catapult – indeed that's what the boat's crest should have shown. But, as the Skipper had to explain to Harry, 'Jack' had never taken warmly to 'talking foreign'. If proof were needed, he need only go back to HMS *Bellerophon*, the 74-gun that fought with Nelson at the Nile, and on whose deck Napoleon would later surrender. 'Jack' could never get his gob around that one, so then and forever after every ship of that name became the *Billy Ruffian*; which was why HMS *Trebuchet*'s 'Jack's called their boat *The Bucket*. A concept reflected in her crest hanging in the wardroom. It might technically be a medieval catapult, but the perspective showed only a tiny array of struts protruding deep into the crest's plane, while what you saw was the bucket that held all the rocks.

The First Lieutenant was back on the bridge. Lieutenant Malcolm Carey was an Australian, and the complete antithesis of every Aussie archetype, for the most part.

'Mike's mob's in the well, Skip,' he whispered in Trumble's ear, and then he settled beside him in the darkness, a shadow in a conspiratorial hunch, so that right away Harry felt his guts clench, because Harry, being his mother's son, knew what was coming. 'Cobber' Carey was about to start discussing; and in the two patrols he'd completed so far, Harry had never seen any good come of that.

'Not sure it'd be a good one to get in a gunfight with this fellah, Skip. What d'you think?'

Harry could barely hear Carey's words, but could almost sense the stiffening of the shadow next to him. Here we go, he thought, willing Carey to shut up. But he didn't.

'Even if Mike's mob pots him with their first round, we'll still have lit up the coast. The Hun'll be all over us like a bad suit, and our mate Gabriel, he won't be sneaking back home unnoticed.'

Andy Trumble continued to fix the two boats out there in the darkness with his binoculars. Carey continued to blithely ignore his ominous silence: 'We've got fallback rendezvous over the next two nights, then the fallbacks next week. When you think about it, what'll be served in stirring Jerry up tonight, when we can come back tomorrow? I mean we ought to weigh it up, Skip.'

Whether Carey had a point or not was now academic, thought Harry, the watcher and weigher of men. No solid judge of character would ever deny Harry's assessment that the two officers were good men, but Harry was still too young himself to comprehend just how very young they were too. Andy Trumble and Malcolm Carey, both 24 years old; the latter, although as yet untested by real responsibility, was a man of calm certainty and like most Aussies, infallible confidence; the former was a harum-scarum boy brought suddenly to earth by command at sea in wartime, and still uncertain whether he was striking the right poses.

Without taking his eyes off the targets, Andy whispered back, 'If you enjoy debating so much, you should have gone to that university like your old man told you to.'

It was Carey's turn to stiffen. There we are, thought Harry; mission accomplished, and in front of crew, just as we are about to go into action; because we are going into action now, good idea or not. From the heights of his rarefied intellect Carey could not comprehend that you didn't advise the captain of a king's ship what to do on his own bridge, especially a newly hatched captain lacking in the necessary confidence to ignore you and leave the righteous bollocking you deserved until later. As a result, *The Bucket*'s two most senior officers were now sulking instead of concentrating on fighting Jerry. Brilliant, said Harry to himself, as the Skipper turned and hissed down into the control room, 'Gun crew, close up for action!'

Instantly Harry could hear the commotion as Mike, Sub-Lieutenant Michael Milner, the Torpedo and Gunnery Officer, led his 'mob' in a mad rush up out the hatch and on to the little raised platform just forward and below the bridge where *The Bucket*'s quick-firing 4-inch gun nestled.

From where Harry stood watching the *Räumboote* and their cornered French drifter, if he twitched to his right he could just make out the flurry of heads below the bridge and hear the opening *schaungs!* of precision steel being worked. He'd seen Mike drill his gun crew many times now. Last thing before diving at dawn he'd have them up and at it, and the same every evening immediately after surfacing. Up, gun cleared, loaded and laid, and, 'shoot!' – although the Skipper seldom permitted the waste of a live round. All against Mike's stopwatch. Apparently their times were the envy of many another boat, the interval between the order 'gun crew close up' and being ready to fire mere seconds. In time Harry would come to understand just how important those seconds were.

Things were moving out there across the water. Harry focused just as an improbable yell ripped the silence. It was Mike! Shouting, 'Gun crew closed up!' In full-throated excitement, like he didn't know or care how far a voice, a sound, could carry over water at night-time. Harry could almost see Andy Trumble's eyes rolling with exasperation, but any reprimand was lost in the equally full-throated explosion from Jerry's diesels as they revved back into life, drowning out Mike's exuberance.

'Jerry's pulling away, sir,' Harry whispered to the Skipper's back, 'and it looks like our Frenchy is hoisting his sails.'

Indeed he was not sure that they would see 'Frenchy' achieve any great velocity, thought Harry. The veteran of many a regatta, he knew what it took to eat every point out of a contrary breeze as the one blowing now, and on far, far more weatherly sailors than this fishing scow.

'Jerry's going to shove our chap back with the rest of them over there,' said Trumble to no one in particular.

All tonight there had been a breeze coming off a collapsing anti-cyclone, blowing out of the north-east, force 3 at most, barely enough to ruffle the surface. Harry took his eyes off the drifter and mentally drew his course. He turned to Trumble, facing him square, because this was going to be a delicate conversation after 'Cobber' Carey's helpful 'remarks', but this was stuff the Skipper needed to know, if he didn't already. So Harry said it straight.

'Obviously our girl isn't intending on wasting what petrol she's been rationed, sir, but the breeze is pretty foul for her getting back to the rest of the fishing fleet. She'll have to run inshore of them, and then tack to get back. Looking at the tub she is, I don't think she'll be able to sail closer on the run-in than one-three-zero.'

Trumble looked hard at Harry. Harry tensed for the put-down, but his words were met with only a brisk nod before Trumble turned and began issuing his commands into the control room voice-pipe: 'Steer port thirty, bring her on to two-zero-zero, then finish with motors, main engines on line, half ahead. Prepare for gun action.' The Skipper leant back and fixed Carey with a stare. 'Get below, number one. I want the rubber raft inflated and ready under the forward torpedo hatch, and two crew with oars. And make sure Mike's shells keep coming and the damage-control team's on their toes . . . and be ready to take over the con if anything happens to me.' He turned away abruptly, jamming his binoculars to his face and looking out to the French drifter, now all a-billow with flapping canvas.

For one heart-stopping moment Harry thought Carey was going to say something, but he must have thought the better of it and vanished down the hole.

Harry moved to the front of the bridge with Trumble as he felt *The Bucket* heel with her turn. Behind him the main engines started up with reports like rifles; loud, but not enough to be heard above the German's own rattling diesels. Looking over the lip of the bridge, Harry could see the dark shapes: Mike Milner and his crew working around the gun; a ready-use magazine, like a rack of post boxes behind them, was being filled with shells by the darkened shape of a rating, turning and bending between it and the open gun deck hatch where a head and shoulders was sticking up, passing up shell after shell.

'Right, Mike,' Trumble was saying over the lip of the bridge to the pale smudge of face below him. 'We're going to run inside the drifter so her sails will mask us from any Hun matelot with a carrot habit. Harry here reckons she'll run away on this course before she tries to tack but I think she'll wear instead . . .'

Harry bridled at this correction, but quickly agreed; the wind was nothing and the drifter was a big broad-beamed waddler; better to just fall off before the wind and paddle round on to a new course than try and win any points for elegance with a tack. Harry's respect for his Skipper ratcheted up another notch.

'. . . which means Frenchy will be turning towards the *Räumboote* like a pregnant duck. When he does, I'll bring *The Bucket* round inside her so that as she wears, she'll unmask Jerry for us, and we will be pointing straight at him, hopefully broad on his port bow. Then you start pouring them in. Go for his bridge and fo'c'sle first, he's got some scary stuff up there. Then go for the waterline aft, see if you can open up his engine room. Got it?'

'Aye aye, Skipper!' said Mike, the gleam in his eyes actually visible in the dark.

Mike, who to Harry's mild irritation had contrived to be younger than him by over a year, was a Dartmouth boy; regular RN, not overly bright, yet his innocent zeal for the service and the energy with which he fell to every task assigned him, continued to fill Harry with a sort of amazed humility. He was a short, broad-shouldered boy, keen to the point of parody, who made no attempt to conceal his undiluted glee at being allowed to work and control the array of lethal toys the navy had presented him with.

Off to starboard, the little bobbing Christmas tree that was now the French drifter was slowly sliding abaft their beam to seaward, plain to see. Jerry, who had obviously told her to keep her navigation lights on like all the other fishing boats lest she slip from view again, was now somewhere out there keeping a beady eye on his errant charge.

Harry was keeping an equally beady eye fore and aft of the drifter, peering into the darkness for any hint of a denser shadow that might reveal the Frenchman was no longer hiding them from the German gunboat. *The Bucket*, at slow ahead, was keeping pace with the spread of pale canvas labouring along a quarter of a mile or so away. Harry kept checking the relative position of the rest of the French fishing fleet, feeling the direction and strength of the wind on his cheek, watching the drifter's decks for any sign of activity.

The time wore on, and soon, as everyone on the bridge well knew, the first glimmers of dawn would be arriving over the port beam. The lookouts were starting to give Trumble the odd glance when they eased their binoculars to give their eyes a moment's break. But Trumble remained impassive. Harry kept checking him too, between watching the drifter and checking his watch against the hour of sunrise. It was as he was turning back to the drifter after one of those little 'divertimentos' that he saw the French crew already clambering over their deck.

'She's standing by to wear, sir!' said Harry. Trumble immediately flipped open the voice-pipe and start barking orders, and Harry felt *The Bucket* heel under his feet. She wasn't as big or heavy a boat as *Pelorus*, just over 270 feet long with a twenty-six-foot beam, and weighing in at about 1,300 tons, but she was a nimble beast on the surface for a submarine. It was nothing short of exhilarating for Harry to feel her bound away, rapidly closing the distance to the drifter as he fixed the Frenchman through his binoculars again. But the drifter seemed to be wallowing on the same course despite the activity on her deck, and for a long stomach-sinking moment it looked as if he had called it wrong.

How could it be? He knew these things. The distance she'd run, the position of the rest of the fishing fleet, their lights still dancing away astern just on the lip of the horizon, it should be now or never . . . and indeed, there she was, Harry could make her out now, the length of her hull's shadow shrinking as she fell away, the speed starting to come off her until her stern was coming round to present itself. Against the glimmer of her deck's working lights, there were the crew, seen quite clearly now, hauling on her fore and main sheets with all the gusto of bored laundry women bringing in the washing. But their antics went largely unnoticed.

All eyes on *The Bucket*'s bridge were now forward, screwed to that patch of opening water, straining for the first glimpse of the *Räumboote* as they heeled inside the fishing boat's turn. Harry didn't see her first, nor did Trumble, but Jerry was there all right. And it was Mike Milner who spotted her: 'Target coming clear, fine on the port bow, sir!' he said. Just where Trumble had said she'd be.

Harry felt a sudden rise of fierce pride, and that madness of battle which fills all warriors the first time they face the enemy, before they learn what war really is; that madness that had escaped him during the sinking of the *Von Zeithen*, where the only challenges he faced were cranking in numbers, and the humiliation if he cranked them in wrong; that madness came upon him at last.

'Commence firing!' yelled Trumble.

The words were still coming from his lips, when Milner's reedy pipe could be heard ordering, 'Traverse! . . . up! . . .' the numbers he was calling inaudible. The gun mount and barrel moved with sudden independent jerks and then the boy Milner's scream, so loud and sharp it sounded almost like a girl: 'Shoot!' And in that instant there was a crack, not so much a sound as a needle in the ear and whump of pressure.

'Action commenced at 03:42 hours!' yelled Harry, and scribbled the time in his notebook as the noises all around became denser and more confused.

The Bucket's gun had gone off without any flicker of telltale flame from the barrel, just a gout of all-but-invisible smoke, her shells using the latest flashless propellant. All remained dark, and Harry still couldn't see the *Räumboote*, but he saw the fall of shot; a sudden pale stalk of water appeared a bit less than a mile away, and then Harry could make out the denser shadow right behind it. He waited for the thud of the shell detonating to echo back over the water, his mind quiet and functioning just below the confusing din.

'Shoot!' Milner screamed, and the 4-incher went off again.

This time there was no fall of shot, but a commotion seemed to shiver the *Räumboote's* shadow. Harry was still waiting for the crack of the previous shell detonating. And then the Jerry's searchlights came on, two fierce stabs of white light swinging wildly across the backdrop of night, one waving in a huge skyward arc and the other sweeping away low across the water, but to seaward, away from them. The flashless shells: Jerry didn't know yet where the fire was coming from.

'Shoot!'

Just seconds had passed since the last, and the bang was still ringing in their ears, when everyone on the bridge saw it. A brief fountain of debris, a bit of plank, a lifebelt, other smaller lumps of stuff, pirouetting away in the darkness. But again, no sound of an explosion or the flash of igniting explosives.

Almost in the same instant Trumble shouted, 'Mike!' and Mike shouted 'Shoot!' again.

Trumble was at the bridge lip, but before he could say anything Jerry's searchlight was swinging back in their direction. He flipped the voice-pipe and yelled, 'Dive! Dive! Flood Q! Ahead full together, down angle twenty degrees for a hundred feet!' The pipe lid flipped shut as he hit the klaxon twice. 'Clear the bridge! Clear the gun deck! Dive! Dive!' As he did so Milner's last 4-inch shell hit the *Räumboote* – and like the others, it failed to explode.

There was the chaos of scrambling boots, muttered effing and blinding, and the peculiar, surrealist cameo of Milner and his gun layer-dancing on the gun platform . . . except they weren't really dancing. They were slinging shells from the ready-use magazine, out over the sides as far as they would go. Harry dropped to the hatch and vanished below, the Skipper giving his head an ungentlemanly shove.

In the control room Carey was giving orders and Harry was backing away from the ladder, giving space for the Skipper to jump down, him barking: 'One clip on! Two clips on!' as he secured the hatch and then landed on the deckplates crouched and ready.

There was a pause, everyone frozen in theatrical red light, as *The Bucket* plunged to her ordered depth. Carey called, 'One hundred feet', and the Skipper ordered 'Group up, port thirty.' At the words 'Dive, dive', the engine room shut down the diesels and their exhaust vents to prevent water rushing in as the submarine went down, and closed the breakers on *The Bucket*'s electric motors. The motors were now surging the boat into a hard turn, forcing everyone in the control room to brace themselves. Now they were swiftly moving under the wearing French fishing boat, putting it between them and the Jerry.

Andy Trumble looked around the control room, his face satanic in the red. He looked at his watch. 'Steer starboard thirty.'

They swung again.

'Midships, group down, slow ahead together . . . bring her to periscope depth.'

Another moment, then another. The depth was called.

'Up periscope,' said Andy, and as the brass cylinder shot up, he removed his watch cap and handed it to Harry with a tight smile – Harry's reward as the only innocent among a host of guilty. As he bent to fix his face to the eyepiece, he said, 'Would someone please like to tell me what just happened there?'

Carey was out of the control room, heading forward without being asked; Harry jumped to set up a plot, leaning over the chart table to sketch the changing positions of submarine, *Räumboote*, fishing boat and fishing fleet.

The minutes passed. Trumble conned the boat and called out headings; Harry scribbled; and in-between, Trumble gave an account of all the happenings upstairs, finishing with, 'And with all the bloody racket we'd've made going down, if he was in any doubt about a submarine being out here, he isn't now.'

The *Räumboote* had opened her throttles and shot off in a creamy cleave of foam. She was circling now at high speed, some four hundred yards off the fishing boat, searchlights wildly stabbing the surface of water in great probing sweeps, but aimed to seaward, instead of in close to the fishing boat, where *The Bucket*'s periscope was keeping a beady eye on its erratic progress.

One searchlight, however, was firmly trained on the fishing boat. Which was even better, said Trumble, because anyone following its glare would have no night vision to separate the dark pencil of *The Bucket*'s periscope against the dark of the water, as it followed twenty yards astern of the fishing boat's slow progress back to the fleet. The control room also learned that the fishing boat crew was lining her sides, peering uselessly into the night, also blinded by the *Räumboote*'s searchlight. Oh, and that the *Räumboote* had quite a collection of automatic weapons on her deck, but none larger than twenty millimetres. Still, in a surface action, that was enough to put a hole in *The Bucket's* pressure hull. And if Jerry did that, then *The Bucket* wouldn't be able to dive. And no diving was effectively a death sentence.

The *Räumboote* was also carrying depth charges. Trumble couldn't count them all, but he could see three down either side, astern, and on the flat deck aft there could be a rank of four, ready to roll off the stern. Certainly no more, and they weren't very big ones. But even Harry could work out that wasn't where the real threat lay. The *Räumboote* had a radio shack and its operator would be screaming blue murder, and god knows who would be responding. It wasn't long until dawn. And now that the balloon had gone up, if they didn't collect their package tonight they would be returning empty-handed, mission very definitely unaccomplished.

Carey swung back through the forward hatch into the control room. He was gripping a small pair of pliers as if they were exhibit A in a court case. 'The shells weren't fused,' he said.

Trumble withdrew his eyes. 'Down scope. What?'

Carey said: 'In a gun action, the crew go up, loader first, layer second. The loader already has the first shell out the ready-use magazine,' he twisted the pliers in mid air, 'and up the spout as the layer is traversing the gun for action. But the seal's gone on our ready-use magazine. Not good to try firing shells that've been underwater all day. So the shells were getting passed direct from the main magazine forward. A daisy chain, from the magazine, along the passage, and up the ladder to the loader, who grabbed them, one at a time, and as per procedure, twisted the fuse on the nose, one half turn to the right, to arm it, ready to fire. Except when he was twisting the fuse, one half turn to the right, he was disarming the fuse, because some stupid bastard in the magazine was arming them as he pulled them off the racks. A new addition to the crew . . . thought he was helping . . . helping by passing a live shell the length of the bloody boat, that if it had been dropped or banged would have gone off and blown a bloody great hole in us!'

Harry was watching the Skipper in profile, so that when he turned away from Carey it was obvious he was suppressing the beginnings of a smile. His face was composed when he turned back. 'Why have you got pliers?' the Skipper asked.

'To stop Milner ramming them up the rating's arse,' said Carey.

'Well, now that's sorted, I think we should have another go, what d'you say?'

Chapter Sixteen

Harry and Carey were alone in the wardroom. It was late afternoon on the day after their second attempt at a gun action with the *Räumboote*. HMS *Trebuchet*, safe in the embrace of routine, was heading out of the Bay of Biscay, her electric motors easing her north at a steady three knots, some forty feet beneath a flat calm sea, the surface ruffled only by light airs and dappled with sunlight.

Milner was on periscope watch, and the Skipper was aft with Mr Partridge, the boat's Warrant Officer Engineer and the man in charge of *The Bucket*'s hitherto trouble-free engines; the Skipper more than likely having to listen to Mr Partridge's endless complaining over potential threats to their continued smooth running.

Gabriel, the man they had come all this way to relieve of a 'package', was asleep a bare few inches above Harry and Carey in a slung-down bunk that hung over the tiny wardroom cubby like an extra deck. His package was now safe next door under the bunk in the Skipper's tiny six-foot cabin.

Harry and Carey were sitting, or rather perched, on the little banquettes that ran round two sides of their cubby and doubled for their sleeping accommodation, drinking French coffee from another package Gabriel had brought aboard. Carey was looking glum, and

Harry, being the sensitive chap he was, knew why; although up until now wild horses wouldn't have prompted him say so. Gabriel, a rumpled hump beneath his blankets, would now and then emit a delicate snore as if to remind the two young officers of the continuing silence between them.

'What I don't get, Harry,' said Carey eventually, without looking up, 'is what he found so funny.'

Harry stifled a grin of his own. He took a gulp of coffee, which, even with condensed milk, tasted damn good. 'Relief of tension I suppose.'

Carey shook his head: 'He was laughing at me. I know he was.'

The Skipper's reaction on learning they'd been firing dud shells at the *Räumboote* had indeed been a series of sniggers. The crew just thought this was one more manifestation of their Skipper's general madcap derangement, a talent he'd been known for in the trade for some time. But the Skipper's eyes had been fixed on Carey, and Harry had guessed why.

Jerry had a good name for it: *schadenfreude*. Mr Smart-alec-clever-clogs Carey had got his comeuppance. But what do you say to your first Lieutenant when you realize the joke is on him, and he doesn't? In the real navy, the answer would have been simple: nothing. Keep your mouth shut and obey the last order. Even in Harry's short time in a blue suit he was becoming all too aware of what the navy demanded of you. But then there was also what the trade demanded of you, which, he was coming to learn, wasn't always the same thing.

Life in a submarine was a unique experience. On a big ship, hierarchy prevailed. On a submarine, it was different. You had to rub along, mainly because it wasn't safe to do otherwise. Resentments couldn't be allowed to fester; you let that happen and it stopped people from covering each other's backs. You had to know that the other bloke knew his job and was doing it, and not going off in a huff. That was how valves got left open and the sea poured in, or new ratings in the magazine decided to help out by arming the bloody shells in the racks instead of leaving it to the gun crew. Or Skippers stopped listening to their number ones, because the number ones kept trying to tell them how to do their jobs. So that was why Harry decided, since Carey had raised the subject, that he would say something.

'It's because you told the Skipper he shouldn't attack,' he said.

'What?'

Harry repeated himself.

'Given the complete bloody shambles that resulted, *he* should be hanging his head in shame for not listening to *me*,' said Carey through gritted teeth.

'He's the Skipper. Even when he's wrong, he's right. According to the Articles of War, disagreeing with him is mutiny.' Harry, back on *Pelorus* . . . he decided to moderate his case a little . . . things weren't that bad, yet. 'Well, insubordination at least.' He paused, then decided to make his point. 'When you, Mr Know-it-all, falls on his arse, the Skipper's first reaction is to laugh.'

'Don't you swear at me, Mr Gilmour. Remember who you are – and who I am,' said Carey. His face began working overtime – a totally unprecedented sight for *The Bucket*'s scion of sangfroid. Then he calmed himself, before saying: 'What do you mean, fall on my arse?'

'His job as Skipper is to command and to fight the boat. Your job as "Jimmy" is to deliver to him a fully worked up and efficient boat with *which* to fight. Allowing new ratings to dick around with pliers, leaving the gun crew to play pass the parcel with live shells up and down the companionway, in his eyes counts as failing in that duty, sir. With all due respect.'

The atmosphere in the wardroom on the passage back to Portsmouth improved remarkably after that exchange. Carey was aware enough to know when to curb his innate superiority, and how to do it with a certain amount of subtlety; and Andy Trumble was not so lumpen as to miss the new attention to duty on the part of his number one, and the grace with which it was offered up. There were no recriminations, because they were not necessary. Everyone just held their noses and let that one pass downstream. Apart from the new rating, who got a right royal bollocking from the gunner's mate.

Much as it stuck in Andy Trumble's gullet to return from any patrol with torpedoes left, let alone a full complement of them, *The Bucket* had been ordered back to Portsmouth on completion of her mission. No swanning around looking for targets – straight back to her berth and deliver her package. So the boat was proceeding under regular watch routine: one watch on duty, one asleep and the other attending to the little rituals of submarine life – darning socks, writing letters, polishing and cleaning, and on this occasion, making sure the boat's battle honours were up to date.

It was the Torpedo Gunner's Mate who took charge of sewing up *The Bucket*'s Jolly Roger for her arrival back at Fort Blockhouse. A patch representing crossed guns designated the gun action, two stars beneath for the *Räumboote* and the French fishing boat, sunk. And since it was the collective opinion of all aboard that plucking Gabriel off the fishing boat qualified as 'cloak-and-dagger' work by anyone's standards – and the crew were never ones for false modesty, especially since the action had been a bit of a Boys' Own epic – there was a dagger patch for Gabriel.

The action had indeed been brisk. The Skipper hadn't hung about to digest the ramifications of Carey's news that the dud shells were not dud after all. He had immediately summoned Milner back to the control room and briefed him for round two.

'Get your mob under the hatch now. We're going up again in thirty seconds, and I'll be pointing her straight at Jerry. So Mr Milner, quick as you like. Start firing as soon as you hit the deck-plates,' he said, all delivered with the usual piratical glint. Then to Carey, 'Get us up in a hurry when I shout "surface". I'll have us going in the right direction, you let me know the minute the conning tower's clear. Harry, you stick with the plot. Sing out if any new HE or wireless blabber comes up.'

Which is why Harry never got to see them sink the *Räumboote*. But he did get to take part in the toe-to-toe argument with the fishing boat Skipper, and see the bits of dead German sailors floating on the surface among the little patches of burning oil, as they departed the scene of their victory.

Trumble had taken *The Bucket* into another tight turn on slow ahead, and then in the next breath after ordering 'midships' came the awaited command 'surface', and, Carey on the board, blew everything with such alacrity that the sub actually lurched as it started up. The hiss of compressed air could still be heard venting into her buoyancy tanks when Carey, a little more loudly, called, 'Clear!' And Milner was ripping off the hatch clips, and the noise of trapped water on the gun platform could be heard sluicing into the boat. Trumble was still shooting up through the bridge hatch when the report of the first round going off above him, the clang of the ejected casing and the waft of cordite, all reached Harry in quick succession at his position by the chart table.

Harry's ears had been straining for umpteen things at once – a shout from the Asdic compartment, indicating the rating operator had picked up new HE, announcing the presence of new, unknown propeller noises; or that the radio operator had detected new chat on Jerry's radio net, from reinforcements come to bomb or shell

The Bucket out of the contest. And through all of his anticipation had been the sound of the action: the bangs and clangs of Milner's little gang hard at work.

They'd got another round off even before the Skipper managed to start calling down info for Harry's plot: '. . . target moving starboard to port on a ninety-degree track . . . high speed . . . range about . . . bloody hell! A hit! . . . and another!'

And then there was a bloody great *kaboooom!!!!* The flash was so bright, Harry caught the reflection of it coming down the hatch into the red light of the control room. Milner's third shell . . . or had it been his fourth? . . . had hit one of the *Räumboote's* depth charges and blew the whole bloody show to matchwood.

There had still been bits tumbling out of the sky – surprisingly close, too – off the port beam, when Harry had come scrambling on to the bridge, abruptly summoned by the Skipper to 'handle the French'.

He could see the random splashes out of the corner of his eye as they closed on the fishing boat, now hove to, bobbing, looking suspended in the flood of her deck lights against the dark of the night. Trumble had brought his boat burbling up alongside the French drifter and Harry and Leading Seaman Wardell from the twin Lewis mount were quickly on the Frenchman's deck, asking for Gabriel, only to be confronted by an extremely angry French Skipper. His torrent of colloquial Breton had all but defeated Harry's undergraduate French, with him catching only snatches about the atrocity the Royal Navy had committed at Mers-el-Kébir, the cowardice of the British Expeditionary Force at Dunkirk, and the piracy he was now committing against innocent French fishermen.

In the middle of this tirade Gabriel had appeared, but the long-limbed foppish youth seemed more intent on joining in than pacifying the wildly gesticulating French Skipper.

'What are you Een-glish playing at? Why didn't you just send a letter to the Germans, denouncing us? Save all this trouble! The Germans will know it is a rendezvous. We are all marked men now, and our families!'

At least Harry understood Gabriel's French. By that time, however, Andy Trumble, who could hear the row from *Trebuchet*'s bridge but understood no French, had become somewhat impatient. He barked across to Harry to wind it up quick, grab whatever they were supposed to grab and beat it back here right now!

Trying to pacify an increasingly agitated Trumble with one hand, and force some sense of urgency into his requests that the Frenchmen calm down and co-operate, Harry hadn't seen his Skipper stride smartly aft along *The Bucket*'s bridge to Leading Seaman Wardell's twin Lewis guns.

Afterwards they all remarked what a tribute it had been to the robustness of the weapon's First World War design that even after a soaking a hundred feet down in the Bay of Biscay, the damn things had fired right off without the hint of a stutter or a jam. The Lewis guns' four-second burst achieved a number of things right off: it parted the forestay sail and jackstay, splintered the forward gunnel, punched several holes into the bow strakes, and silenced the outraged Frenchmen.

In the pause that followed, Andy Trumble had bellowed, 'Tell that silly arse to get his bloody package here, right now!'

But they'd all stood frozen, and would have remained so if flames hadn't started licking up the heap of collapsed sail on the fo'c'sle. One in six of the rounds Trumble had slammed into the wooden French seine netter had been tracer: white-hot illuminated rounds that generated pretty little arcs of light when fired, and put in a sterling performance as a fire accelerant when placed in contact with tarred rope and canvas.

Gabriel disappeared as the crew rushed to extinguish what had quickly become quite a blaze. The French Skipper and two of his crew were at work with buckets, but the remaining four had equally quickly realised it was too late, and were scrambling to haul alongside the small skiff they'd been towing.

Suddenly Gabriel reappeared out of a hatchway, clutching a battered, bulging academic's leather briefcase, and with a graceful ease stepped off the fishing boat and on to the curve of *The Bucket's* ballast tanks. For one stomach-dropping moment it looked like he was going to slide off in-between the submarine's hull and the fishing boat, but he'd slapped the briefcase on to the deck with one hand and grabbed one of the vents with the other, pulling himself on to the slippery deck. The fire had already got a hold on the fishing boat's rope locker, and a tin of paint had gone off with a bang by the time Wardell and Harry stepped back aboard five seconds later.

The Bucket pulled away as Gabriel clambered up the ladder to the bridge. He stood beside Trumble as Harry and Wardell followed him, and together they watched as the fishing boat's crew, and eventually their Skipper, gave up the struggle and pulled away in the skiff from the now blazing hulk.

'Well, I don't think Jerry will be getting too suspicious about your chums or your families, seeing as I've just sunk their boat and killed one of their crew,' said Trumble.

Gabriel, who obviously had some English, looked shocked, '*Un mort?*' he said.

'You, of course,' said Trumble with an innocent arch of his eyebrows. 'Now how would a dead man fancy a large tot?'

And so they headed home, running submerged during the day, and sweeping along at a handy twelve knots on the surface through the darkness, back into the bigger war. Gabriel stepped on to the jetty at Fort Blockhouse with his briefcase, leaving the coffee and the cheese and the brandy it contained, with his new friends. No one asked about the papers that were also inside, and they never found out who Gabriel really was, or ever saw or heard about him again.

The summer passed. Above them, the air war raged. Churchill gave it a name – the Battle of Britain – and told the nation it would be their finest hour. But if truth be told, it barely broke the horizon for the crew of *The Bucket*, who went on patrol, and came back again, to a Portsmouth that was being steadily wrecked while they were elsewhere.

That they continued to come back increasingly became something of an achievement in itself. Submarine losses were rising at an alarming rate, and each happy return now was being marred by the news that some old chum from another commission, aboard a boat once served on, had been marked up, 'overdue, presumed lost'.

But Harry didn't think too much about that, mainly because nobody else did, and when you lived hugger-mugger with forty-nine other blokes – forty-eight if you didn't count the Skipper because he had a cabin to himself, albeit one smaller than the cupboard under the stairs in his parents' house – you didn't get much time for reflection, morbid or otherwise.

Carey, Milner and Harry shared the wardroom where they ate, slept, coded and de-coded signals, read their books, darned socks and played uckers – which as any submariner would tell you, was a highly complex and cunningly tactical version of Ludo.

Of the cubby's two banquettes, the longer was Milner's sleeping berth. Above it was a fold-down bunk, the one that Gabriel had used, but was normally the preserve of the navigating officer when they had one. At the other end of the cubby was a deck-to-deckhead cabinet in highly polished walnut with little floral curtains masking some of the shelves. This contained all the officer luxuries *The Bucket* could accommodate.

Harry and Carey had two bunks off the companionway forward, Harry on top. The Skipper's little cabin was aft, and on the other side of the companionway, less than a shoulder's width across the way, was the galley for the entire crew. Forward of it was the radio cubby and the Asdic cubby. This was what passed for officers' country on a submarine.

On a big ship, officer country was sacred, but here, all there was between the officers and the crew was four sets of more floral print curtains, one drawn to mask the wardroom from the main companionway fore and aft, and the others for the two bunks and the Skipper's cabin. Doors were deemed to take up too much space. For the seaman ratings there were no bunks, just spaces to sling a hammock for a lucky few, and for the rest, wherever they could stretch out on the forward torpedo room deckplates. The Petty Officers had a couple of cubbies, with bunks and hammock space, forward for the seamen POs, and aft, behind the engine spaces, for the Engine Room Artificers. The Torpedomen electricians and Mechanics' Mates bedded down in-between the machinery.

Space on a submarine was so narrow and so tight that the single long companionway ruled that where you worked was where you lived. A crew quickly became two tribes, with the back afties in the machinery spaces rarely setting eyes on their shipmates forward from one patrol's start to its finish. And one 'heads' for all forty-odd men aboard.

In that space you quickly, easily got to know everything about everyone else, from the peculiar regularity of one man's bowel movements, to how to tell the heavy smokers from the intensity and frequency of their expectorations. And then there was the ever-present, all permeating bouquet of submarine life made up mostly of diesel and cooking and damp, and that special, personal smell of armpit and socks and crotches, all unwashed because fresh water was for drinking.

There was something else aboard a submarine that permeated everything. Except this time you couldn't really smell it, or see it, oil it or polish it. And you never, ever talked about it; it had no specific word to describe it. But if challenged, everyone would agree: it stemmed from the pretty bloody self-evident truth, that for all the boredom, sooner or later there would be times when every man aboard would be scared shitless. No one who had ever experienced a sustained depth-charge attack would ever gainsay that.

The patrols carried out by HMS *Trebuchet* through the late summer of 1940 were a sort of apprenticeship for Harry in his new trade. The fact that they still did not carry a navigator meant Andy Trumble divvied it up between himself and his most junior officer, and as a result Harry actually started to become something of a wizard at the job. Going from being not very good at sums at school to a dab hand on the slide rule came as something of a surprise to Harry.

At the start the Skipper would regularly oversee his work, relentlessly taking the mickey in the process, something he could never resist. He'd watch Harry shoot the sun at noon, when it was visible, with one of the more numerate ratings calling out the precise time on the chronometers on the chart table below, then doggedly follow him down the ladder to the control room to where the almanacs and tide tables were, and hang over him, grinning in a most distracting manner, occasionally tutting and pouting like a fussy schoolmarm, as Harry fiddled with his slide rule in an attempt to complete his calculations.

'Where are we, Harry?' he'd shout, for a smirking control room to hear. 'Ummm. Let's have a look at these sums . . . Oxford Street!' Or sometimes the guesses would be far more colourful, depending on the mood. 'I say chaps, we're fifteen-thousand feet above sea level on the outskirts of La Paz!' Or it would be Tashkent, or 'Three miles south of Diamond Head, at the entrance to Pearl Harbour . . . beers and a bonfire on Waikiki Beach tonight, chaps! Well done, navs!'

Harry would just smile and say, 'I think if you go back over the figures again, sir, you'll find we're a hundred and twenty-seven miles sou'south-west of Valentia,' accurately placing them slap in the middle of the western approaches off Ireland. Or 'Fifteen miles south-east of Hayling Island, on track to enter the swept channel for Portsmouth Harbour. It'll have to be warm bitter in The Red Lion, I'm afraid, as long as Jerry hasn't got the cellar, sir.'

Andy Trumble did it because everyone knew Harry could take a joke, and everyone understood just how important that was, and everything that followed from it.

Around the wardroom table, an unusual friendship began to grow between Harry and Carey. Unusual, but not that surprising, really, since the Skipper, for all his antics, always remained the Skipper, and he spent a lot of his time in his cabin, doing paperwork or sleeping. You could never call him stand-offish; he was always barging in, demanding a quorum for uckers, thrashing all-comers with boring regularity and then goading them with the even more tedious glee with which he celebrated his victories.

It was a habit that never failed to reduce young Milner to impotent, shaking, frustrated rage – the callow youth being just as much a slave to the same rampant competitiveness that afflicted his Skipper. Unfortunate, that, Harry thought, with a mixture of mild compassion and a lot more amusement. There was very little else to say about Milner, except perhaps that for all the world he reminded Harry of Tigger, that creation of boundless energy, random enthusiasms, and an unfettered ability to irritate and amuse in equal measure, that he remembered from the Winnie-the-Pooh books of his childhood. Harry even introduced their tiny wardroom to this notion, and from then on, the Tigger Mr Milner became. Which just left Harry and Malcolm Carey.

To Harry, Carey was beyond exotic. He was from a country so completely different from Harry's own, a place resonant with tumbling images of light and space, not to mention kangaroos and koala bears, but that was only part of it. The bigger part, the unimaginable part, was that he was married. Harry had seen the black-and-white snapshot Carey carried of his wife, Fenella, a gamine creature, the curve of her flanks and legs highlighted by the wind-blown smoothness of a light summer dress, her naturally blonde hair that had never been tamed to the styles so common back in Europe or the USA, laughing directly into the camera, unattainably alluring. Harry couldn't imagine what it would be like to be married to a creature like that. The very idea of it caused an unnameable ache in him. Not that he would ever be so impertinent as to actually ask Carey.

'What's life like in Australia?' was the closest he'd get, and then he'd be entertained with tales of an altogether different existence full of potential and freedom in comparison to the humdrum, predictable and well-travelled rails of domestic existence in the west of Scotland. It never occurred to Harry that Carey, not that much older than himself, might be inventing an idealised land because he was homesick. And if he had, Harry wouldn't have cared; he listened only for the stories involving that wife back in Melbourne. Fenella. He would speak her name, and the very mention evoked mesmerising possibilities no home-grown Scots lass could ever hope to inspire. Harry hung on every word.

Their chats, however, had to be sandwiched between his other junior officer chores. Despite his relative newness to the trade, Harry was expected to stand watches alone. The Skipper wouldn't sleep, mind you, when Harry had the watch, but the sooner he learned to ride this particular bike without stabilizers the better. They were two officers short, and besides, the responsibility was good for Harry's standing among the crew, and good for his own self-respect. The best way to learn something was to do it. That was the navy way.

Then there were Harry's course-plotting duties, or he'd be coding and decoding routine radio traffic; or censoring the crew's mail home, the endless letters, nearly always interminably dull and unimaginative; and then of course writing – and receiving – his own letters: from his mother, the odd one from Sir Alex Scrimgeour, sometimes with a PS or two from other yacht club worthies, from his mates from *King Alfred*, and the odd one from Janis and the many from Shirley. When Carey's reminiscences eased into natural silence, Harry would talk about his letters from Janis and Shirley. There were photographs too to be passed around.

'This is Shirley,' he said the first time. 'She's a friend of the family, just a girl really.' He held out a Box Brownie snap he'd taken on her camera, of her walking towards him on the prom near the Argyll Hotel, carefully clutching two ice-cream cones and laughing; her hair in the breeze, and wearing slacks, which was still somewhat 'avant' for a girl in Dunoon, even in 1940.

They all knew when Janis wrote, however, because the letters – all two of them over the late summer – smelled as if they'd been dipped in perfume. The whiff of them almost overcame the boat's natural bouquet of diesel. Harry showed Janis's photograph without any qualifications. Carey had raised his eyebrows.

'Quite a girl, Mr Gilmour. You are a lucky fellow.'

His eyes had lingered over a studio-posed Janis, sitting pert on a high stool so as to show off her shapely silk-encased calves as they disappeared up into a pencil skirt; her buttressed bosom in profile, straining against an elegant blouse. She was looking into the camera over her shoulder and from behind Veronica Lake tresses, her make-up immaculate and her lips pursed ever so slightly, as if posing a question.

'What does she say?' asked Carey, when the letters arrived, and Harry replied, 'Oh the usual. You know. Girls' stuff.'

But the truth was not even that. Janis's letters were short, with a scatter of endearments to top and tail complaints: how difficult it was to get any make-up, how impossible to get nylons, how ghastly it was to live under rationing, and how only Daddy's 'friends' in business helped eke out their starvation menus. And when was Harry coming home again? And how he should get a staff job, ashore, with some important admiral, or in some hush-hush backroom, which everybody said should be easy-peasy with his languages. A girl couldn't be expected to wait forever, and anyway, Sir Alex Scrimgeour would fix it. All Harry had to do was tell him what was required and why. The only reason she thought so much of Harry was because he wasn't like all the other young men, always thinking of themselves, but now she was starting to wonder. She hated people who always thought of themselves.

Harry didn't know how to reply, so he made excuses. Sorry, but he couldn't answer her questions because of the censor who would never let such answers through. Got to be like Dad, he told her, and keep Mum . . . couldn't discuss anything like appointments or movements or possible postings. Not at all. Sorry. He didn't mention that he himself censored all of *The Bucket*'s mail.

Shirley's letters were different. She wrote often and at length, and replying to her soon became one of his little treats to himself. She wrote about home a bit; about how Hammy and Cammy were faring well 'with the Colours', although she was never so gauche as to mention a regiment or posting. Mostly it was about politics; what did he think of communism? Had that Stalin really turned something hopeful into another tyranny? And shouldn't we be trying to get him on our side? Because we could use Stalin as a useful counter to Hitler. She wrote about books; how she had discovered an American writer called Pearl S. Buck, and she was devouring her. Wasn't China fascinating? She thought she would quite like French Romantic period writers too; Harry would know the good ones having done French at university, could he recommend any? And Tommy Dorsey, and Glenn Miller and swing. Uhh! Heaven! And so sophisticated. Banned in Germany of course. That little rodent Goebbels really was another preposterous little man!

Harry read them as the gushings of a young girl, with a knowing smile on his face; it made him feel mature and so very grownup to compose his considered replies, to be mentoring this lively and really rather intelligent young mind. Which meant he never quite managed to admit that what he was really feeling was pure delight every time one of her letters was waiting for him, which they were – sometimes more than one – on his return from every patrol. He'd read them ashore, with a scotch or a gin in his hand and Tommy Dorsey on the wardroom gramophone, and her photograph propped on the armchair.

Shirley, however, was not the only 'lively' young thing whose welfare he was entrusted with – there were the ratings in his 'division', the slice of crew for which he was personally responsible. Most were callow youths just like himself but there were a few older Petty Officers, career men with varying years of experience between them. Harry's prior deeds aboard *Pelorus* had earned him a certain benefit of the doubt, but when it came to the everyday stuff of life in a blue suit, mere boyish charm and the odd self-deprecating aside wasn't enough to get by this time. He was in a man's world now, and his efforts were frequently met with po-faces.

Harry hadn't been on *Pelorus* long enough to grasp the gap between officers and the lower deck that still existed even in the trade. On *Redoubtable* it had been a yawning chasm you couldn't miss. Under the waves, however, it was an altogether more subtle shift. Harry first encountered it over that most pressing of submariners' concerns: grub.

For grub was very important. It stood to reason; after all there wasn't much else to discuss, in-between the hard work and the boredom of life under water – especially if you didn't want to keep dwelling on the many types of horrific death that lay in wait. This was magnified by the fact that submarines did not carry a designated cook – the job fell to whoever wanted it, or could be coerced into it. It left a lot of scope for trial and error, and much debate over an incumbent's performance. Especially since said incumbent had so much scope to rise to the occasion or bring a crew to the brink of mutiny.

They always got the best of grub in the trade. It was as if, given the risks they ran, the navy treated them like fighting cocks. Stuff like steaks and legs of mutton were impossible to buy on ration coupons ashore, fresh eggs, fresh fruits or jam non-existent, but they were all on the menu aboard HM Submarines. A good cook could create the sublime, and a bad one, an atrocity.

On *The Bucket*, the cook's job had fallen to one of her Torpedomen. He was Able Seaman Vaizey, known universally as 'Lascar', and the occasion of Harry's first brush with him was at a dinner in the wardroom.

It was shortly after 3 a.m. and *The Bucket* was surfaced, en passage to her patrol area off Ushant – mealtimes on submarines on patrol were always day-for-night to allow all cooking to be done on the surface. Milner was on watch, so it was Carey, Harry and the Skipper around the table when Vaizey turned up with a tray of Cheese Oosh, coloured a beautiful golden-brown and looking a lot like a cross between a soufflé and a Yorkshire pudding. He began slicing the deep, piping-hot oosh and dolloping it on to the three officers' plates with absolutely no ceremony whatsoever. But Harry wasn't paying attention to Vaizey's casual, bordering on insubordinate, serving technique. Harry was distracted by the smell. It was wonderful. He couldn't resist a taste, blowing on his fork as he tried to pop the steaming gobbet into his mouth.

'My god, Vaizey! This is . . . delicious!' said Harry. Vaizey's eyes narrowed slightly at the exclamation; anyone watching would have been hard-pressed to tell whether it was irritation or just wind. Anyone apart from Carey and the Skipper, who exchanged knowing smirks.

'Able Seaman Vaizey is well-tutored on the cuisines of the Orient,' said the Skipper, attending to his own plate. 'Aren't you, Lascar?'

'Aye aye, sir,' replied Vaizey in his East London drawl.

'And as such, he is an asset to whichever one of His Majesty's submarines he serves aboard,' added Carey, joining in. 'Isn't that right, Lascar?'

'Aye aye, sir.'

'Is that why they call you Lascar, Able Seaman Vaizey?' asked Harry. 'Because of the spices?'

Lascar was the term universally applied aboard every tramp steamer and on every dock across the Empire for sailors from the sub-continent, and had been so since the dawn of recorded history.

'Yessir,' he replied, bored.

'So what are the spices you use? What's in this?' pressed Harry. 'Apart from the eggs, cheese and tomatoes? And where do you get them, the spices?'

Carey butted in. 'Harry, Harry. So many questions. You're asking the man to divulge his most secret of secrets. Knowledge coveted by hash slingers from Tsingtao to Tilbury.'

Vaizey's face, which until now had worn a look of immovable indifference, actually twitched. The movement was slight, but enough to alarm Carey and the Skipper – a development Harry missed.

'Sir. Ma bruvver gets it dahn the West India docks, 'n' sends it ta us, dunnee, sir.' The words were wrung from him.

Harry pressing on, oblivious, asked, 'And what do you get? It's curry, is it?'

But now, very obviously tiring of the exchange, Vaizey's countenance re-composed itself. ''s two kinds, sir. Brahn 'n' powdery, 'n' dried 'n' leafy . . . sir.'

'Yes, but what are they Lascar? What are the spices called?' entreated Harry. Beyond his vision Carey and the Skipper were rocking with subdued mirth.

'Haven't the foggiest, sir. 'S all foreign names, innit, sir?'

And that was when the Skipper intervened. 'That's all Lascar . . . another kitchen triumph, now back to the galley and get the tea on.'

Lascar departed and Carey and the Skipper made their merriment obvious.

Harry, annoyed at being practiced upon, was curt: 'What was that all about, sir?'

The Skipper went all serious: 'You've upset Lascar.'

'Me, sir? What did I do?'

Carey continued sniggering.

'He'll be looking for a transfer,' said the Skipper gravely.

'Oh god!' exclaimed Carey. 'Don't say that!'

Harry grinned, not rising to it anymore, and assiduously attacked his oosh, but Carey wasn't letting him off.

'There's only one thing worse than not having Lascar on your boat,' he added, 'and that's having Able Seaman Reginald M. Fagg on your boat.'

'Two things, actually,' interrupted the Skipper. 'Having Able Seaman Reginald *Martin* Fagg, *and* Lascar, on your boat.' Then he fixed Harry with a flinty glare. 'Lascar's curries, and "fartin' Martin" don't mix.'

'Don't mix!' Carey exclaimed. 'Put Lascar's cuisine and fartin' Martin's arse together, and you'll contravene several Geneva conventions!'

'A lesson for you, young Gilmour,' added the Skipper. 'Never get on a boat with Lascar or fartin' Martin. And try not to irritate Lascar.'

'We like Lascar,' said Carey.

Harry looked irritated now, so Carey began to explain for the good of wardroom peace: 'Lascar's one of those "Jacks" who somewhat ostentatiously takes no obvious pride in his abilities, and treats the whole world around him, especially the naval world, with an affected contempt. He does this so as to avoid as much as possible his pet hate . . . having to talk to officers. That is why Lascar likes to keep his conversation with the likes of us to "aye aye, sir". You, insensitively, just forced him into a conversation. It's never been known.'

'Words we didn't know he knew,' said the Skipper.

'He'll never forgive you,' said Carey.

'Foreign bodies in your mince, Harry,' warned the Skipper.

Chapter Seventeen

The Battle of Britain had been won, but in the Atlantic it was another matter. The newspapers and the BBC weren't saying much, but the word from the wardroom at the HMS *Dolphin* submarine base to the Fort Blockhouse maintenance shops was that the U-boats were getting more and more active in the western approaches and merchant shipping losses were climbing at a dismaying rate. Everyone knew it must be getting serious, because some submarines were now being diverted to try and disrupt Jerry's hunting sorties.

The mine-laying subs and the smaller S-boats sailing out of *Dolphin* and numerous other small ports up the east coast were being allowed to pursue their traditional targets, heading into the North Sea to attack shipping off the Low Countries and southern Norway, hunting down the blockade runners, but *The Bucket* and the other bigger T-class boats were routinely being ordered west to patrol in huge arcs from the Irish coast to the Bay of Biscay as a U-boat screen. The U-boats were near impossible to find; not only that, it was an extremely dangerous job with little to show for the risks, which bizarrely, mainly came not from the highly trained German U-boat crews. They were usually too wily to become entangled with British submarines, their mission was to sink merchant ships and they tended to obey their orders. No, the ever-present threat was still RAF Coastal Command: if it was a submarine, they reasoned, it must be a Jerry, and so they blasted away.

And while the North Sea boats would come back with growing tallies of sunk merchant ships, boats like *The Bucket* discovered that they were returning from patrol with a full set of torpedoes and without so much as a sighting of Jerry. In the autumn of 1940, *The Bucket* only sighted two U-boats in the course of her three-week-long patrols. Many sported quite a few dents from the RAF, however. And some boats didn't return at all.

By this time it had become quite apparent to Harry and the rest of the crew, that his night vision was not particularly good. 'Lascar' Vaizey could stuff him so full of carrots he'd start growing rabbit teeth, but it was never going to improve by one jot his ability to see in the dark. Night vision was something some people had, like the Tigger and the Skipper. Harry didn't, which made his usefulness as a watchkeeper in the hours of darkness somewhat limited. But he still tried, which was why he was on the bridge with Carey with about an hour to go on the middle watch.

They were quartering their billet, a patrol box about 130 miles west-sou'west of Ushant, on a blustery night in mid September, with the wind coming out of the south-west at about force 6. *The Bucket*, steering one-two-one degrees, was rolling like a pig in the beam sea as she zigzagged her way in the general direction of France – the zigzag course designed to make her a less predictable target for any Jerry who might spot her before she spotted them.

It was an overcast night, so Harry had left his sextant below, and instead of furthering his knowledge of celestial navigation he was straining to peer into the middle water, taking that chore off Carey and the three lookouts dotted round the bridge. They kept their binoculars firmly on the horizon, each slowly panning their slice of sea for distant targets, while Harry's job was close in.

He was wrapped in an oilskin coat and leggings with several layers of vests and shirts below his white pullover against the cold and wet. He had a towel wrapped round his neck to try and keep out the constant slap and spray driven by the wind, but it was by now sodden and so doing little to keep the chill autumn waters of the Bay from trickling inside those oilskins. What with that, and the constant bracing against the rolling beneath his feet, it was all becoming a bore and a strain. It would be fair to say he was miserable, but then so was everyone else on the bridge; although they were just black lumps in the darkness, you didn't need to see them to know.

Except, perhaps, Carey in his flashy Ursula suit, an all in one number with padding and seals and pockets with snap studs all over it, the invention of some other Skipper in the trade called Phillips, and named after his boat. Carey never said much about his kit, unless anyone asked. 'Does the trick,' would be the reply; that, and a smug look, especially when everyone else was peeling off their sopping kit. And, of course, it made him look dashing, which was also very important to Malcolm Carey.

Harry was half-thinking whether staying dry on watch was worth the humiliation and ridicule he'd certainly face if he was to emulate the number one and get an Ursula suit himself, so he was only half paying attention to the dark waters sluicing past a few feet below. He'd been caught out a couple of times being lax on watch and had learned how easy it is to mistake a playful cetacean for a torpedo track, or miss the bobbing of a drifting mine, broken free from a distant minefield, or lifeboats from some far off sinking, whether they still carried survivors, or whether their cargo was long dead. And that was when one of the lookouts said quite matter-of-factly, 'Contact on the port beam, bearing three-two-zero degrees.'

Carey instantly turned his binoculars jerking around the lookout's bearing, and then said, 'Got it!' There was only the barest moment of delay before he opened the voice-pipe to the helmsman in the control room. 'Steer port thirty, bring us on to zero-four-zero! Captain to the bridge!'

Seconds later Andy Trumble shot out of the bridge hatch and was peering into the night with his binoculars. 'Bugger . . . bugger . . . bugger.' Red shift lighting below or no, he still hadn't got his full night vision. 'What do you have, number one?'

'It's definitely a U-boat, Skipper. I've turned us bow on to lessen our silhouette.'

The Skipper flipped open the voice-pipe. 'Diving Stations! Close up for surface torpedo attack!' He turned to Harry. 'Get down on to your box of tricks, Mr Gilmour, and you, Malcolm, on the trim board.'

The now familiar glint of bloody mayhem was in Trumble's eye as he bent to the TBT, a gimbal-mounted device midships on the bridge that was the equivalent to the range and target-bearing bezels on the periscopes. The Skipper was going to take this one at the gallop. Harry went into the hole, no time to climb down, just wrap hands and feet round the vertical rails and slide; Carey hit the control deckplates right behind him. They were in time to see Milner scooting forward, and the balding head of Tubby Tevis, the Quartermaster, slip in to the helmsman's seat. Everyone was at their stations as the Skipper's voice came down the pipe, '. . . flood tubes one through six!'

Six torpedo tubes represented *The Bucket*'s maximum fire power; she used to have two external tubes, but those had been chopped out because they created merry hell with the sea-keeping in rough weather.

'Poor Jerry,' said Carey to no one in particular, 'Skipper's going to make this one pay for all the kippers we've had to haul back home.'

Everyone in the control room allowed themselves a quiet smile.

'Half ahead together,' they heard from the bridge. 'Target is a U-boat on the surface, we are on a ninety-degree track angle to the target.'

Harry, his oilskins in a heap on the deck and his watch cap on top of them, cast his wet towel away and punched in the track . . . ninety degrees. They were on a course to cut the U-boat's course at almost exactly a right angle – couldn't be better!

'. . . I estimate the range at nine-thousand yards . . . she's a homeward bounder . . . and she's got a bone between her teeth' – a bow wave, showing white against the black water – '. . . going at a fair clip . . . twelve knots . . . target's course is . . . one-three-zero. Doesn't appear to be zigzagging. Too busy thinking about beer and bratwurst and mademoiselles. Will engage at six-thousand yards. Give me a deflection angle to the target at that range, Mr Gilmour.'

Harry had all the numbers punched in, and he pronounced with a steady annunciation he certainly did not feel: 'Red-one-six, Skipper!'

'Sixteen red it is.' Then there was a silence as *The Bucket* burbled along on her diesels with Andy Trumble bent to the TBT, looking to port along that sixteen-degrees bearing. Only the noise of *The Bucket*'s diesels could be heard now.

Andy Trumble's voice started up again, echoing down from the bridge, giving a running commentary. The crew, down below, blind, tense and waiting, liked that. It was considerate. It meant the Skipper didn't just dismiss you as a piece of machinery. It was the sort of thing good submarine Skippers did.

'Oh, he's tootling along, not a care in the world. Going to fire one, two, three and four . . . I'm going to give it a spread over two ship's lengths. Then for safety's sake, we'll fire five. Going to give it a track, a length and a half behind her conning tower, in case the bugger sees our torpedoes, decides to slam the anchors on and go full astern . . . bow doors open on one to five,' he said, and then he gave an evil little laugh. Below, another smile went round the control room.

'Tubes one to six flooded,' came Milner's disembodied voice, echoing from the forward torpedo room.

'OK, coming up . . .' said the Skipper, and then, slowly, almost exquisitely, the U-boat crossed the bearing: 'Fire one! . . . Fire two! . . .' he said until all torpedoes had gone.

Carey had the stopwatch in his hand. Seconds ticked away, into the silence of the diesel thump.

'Dive! Dive! Flood Q! Full down angle on the planes!'

The lookouts were plunging into the red glimmer of the control room even before the Skipper had finished yelling.

All at once, from aft, the Engineer's curt orders: 'Clutches out, group up, full ahead together!' And the lookouts were plunging into the red glimmer of the Control Room even before the Skipper had finished yelling.

Harry felt *The Bucket* lurch forward and down, and the deck began falling from beneath his seat. Then from above: 'One clip on, two clips on!' as Trumble secured the bridge hatch, and he hit the deckplates shaking the water from his oilskins, and slapping his watch cap on the ladder. 'Make your depth one hundred and eighty feet, then hard right rudder and all stop.' Trumble's orders were given in a measured tone to Carey and Tevis, then, 'These damn bloody Jerries are getting too damn bloody good at this! Bugger him! He saw the tracks. Piled on more knots then turned towards us and combed them. Damn and blast him. He's up there now chortling away to himself!'

Suddenly *The Bucket* began to heel, and then the hum of her motors died, and she hung suspended, silent, one hundred and eighty feet down below in the Atlantic. Trumble turned: 'Asdic, have you got anything?'

But before the Asdic operator could reply, everyone could just hear the swishing growing, but still very faint. Leading Seaman Devaney, leaning out of the Asdic cubby, had the headset for the device held away from his ear; you could see the sick expression on his face beneath the thick black beard and dense matching thickets that passed for eyebrows. 'Twin screws, diesel, moving fast astern of us,' he said.

They heard the U-boat churn away above them, then there was a series of distant rushing sounds.

'Target diving,' said Devaney, pressing the phones to his ears, listening more intently.

Trumble propped his backside against the chart table. 'He's running. Probably got no torpedoes left.' He turned quickly and looked at the chart. 'Where's he running to, Harry?'

Harry joined his Skipper. They got the dividers out, and the protractor, and they projected courses, *The Bucket*'s and Jerry's, and they drew lines to the edge of their billet, but it was useless. The U-boat had got clean away. There would be no catching him before daybreak, and his rendezvous with his torpedo boat or minesweeper escort, and his air support, there to take him safe home into Lorient or La Rochelle or wherever he was headed. Bugger, indeed, as the Skipper was often wont to say.

In early October they were directed to a billet immediately off Brest. Harry was on the periscope, with about three quarters of an hour to go on the forenoon watch. *The Bucket*, submerged, was ambling along at a battery-conserving three knots, steering zero-six-zero, heading towards the French coast. Above them there was a breezy chop coming from the south-west, which meant Harry had a shallow trim on her to raise the periscope that little higher over the wave crests. Any danger of it being spotted by some sharp-eyed Jerry look-out, however, was reduced by the flying spume effectively disguising any telltale 'feather' from the periscope. Periscope watch was a routine that Harry sometimes did now in his dreams. And in-between sending the scope up and down, and sweeping round the compass, you marked the chart, keeping a constant eye on speed and course, and a finger in the almanac, to factor in tides and known currents; it was all dead-reckoning in deep water, but you had to be as accurate as possible for any number of pressing reasons, like making sure you kept within your patrol box. Straying beyond might take you into the cross-hairs of a 'friendly' submarine in an adjoining box, who would automatically assume that, since no other 'friendly' was operating in his particular bit of sea, you were a U-boat, and would promptly sink you.

Then there was the trim: technically the overall responsibility of the number one, it still fell to the watch officer to ensure the submarine maintained periscope depth – usually about thirty feet – and that she steered level at neutral buoyancy. But then the crew had the irritating habit of moving about, carrying out heavy repairs, shifting stores, making the boat sometimes bow-heavy, sometimes stern-heavy; then there were the surprise little changes in water densities. All of them conspired throughout the day to bugger up the trim, and when that happened it was the responsibility of the officer of the watch to ensure the rating on the trim board was ready to pump little packets of water from one trim tank to another to put everything back in harmony and balance. If it was only minor adjustments to the depth, you could always use the hydroplanes, and the motors; a bit more speed so as the planes bit a little tighter into the water, and a tweak here and there, fore and aft, you could adjust your angle just fine. Except more power drained the battery faster, and that never made you popular, with the Jimmy or the EO.

It was the danger of losing trim that really struck fear into Harry; ending up too buoyant and breaking surface under the nose of a Jerry destroyer, or worse, you went down, too heavy and out of control; too heavy to recover before you hit the boat's crush depth, where the pressure of water outside the hull was greater than her construction could withstand, and then ribs would buckle and the hull would implode. For *The Bucket*, crush depth was supposed to be anything over 300 feet, except everyone knew she would probably take a lot more. How much 'a lot more' was, no one ever found out, or at least never found out and lived to tell.

So watchkeeping was a busy time aboard a submarine; no time to daydream or dwell on matters. No time to think of past lives and who you were now, who you were becoming, and the vast distance travelled from a student's smug Sunday morning lie-in, deep in the quilts with a mild hangover to nurse till midday, to here, out in the Atlantic, conning one of His Majesty's submarines at thirty-five feet, a couple of dozen miles off the enemy's coast, looking for people to kill.

Harry was into the second quadrant of his latest sweep when he spotted an aircraft, way to the north; too far away to be any immediate threat. Harry was pretty good at aircraft recognition, and he reckoned it to be a Junkers 88, a light Jerry twin-engined job; a bomber first, but being a fast, nifty little brute, Jerry had been throwing more and more of them out into the Bay to hunt the RAF Sunderlands that were increasingly making a nuisance of themselves among departing and returning U-boats. When the aircraft began a slow turn to the south-west, its wing shape confirmed it.

'Make a note for the log,' said Harry to the control room rating, without removing his eyes from the periscope. '11.47. Junkers 88 spotted to the north-west, course two-seven-zero approximate . . . range . . . ooh, say ten, no, make it twelve miles.' There; the Skipper would see that and know he'd been keeping his eyes open. He made a mental note to speed up his sweeps, just a little, as he worked through the compass. After a final 'down periscope', he ran his eyes over the trim board, then attended to the chart; then it was time to start again: 'Up periscope!' And there it was, barely five degrees into the start of his next all-round sweep. There was no mistaking it.

'Captain to the control room!'

In the seconds it took Andy Trumble to practically levitate off his bunk, Harry had twiddled the range knob, just to give the Skipper something to get started with. Harry stepped back, and as the Skipper grabbed the handles, he said, 'U-boat on the port bow', and read off the bearing from the bezel above the scope; he also checked the difference in inclination between the periscope's top lenses, the ones he'd used to get the U-boat dancing on its image, as he grabbed the slide rule from the chart table. A quick calculation and: 'The range is twelve hundred yards, sir.'

'Diving Stations!' shouted Trumble, and hit the klaxon twice.

The U-boat was moving fast, and in a straight line. A long, sleek, grey wolf, sporting slashes of rust, worn like battle honours, heading home after a long patrol; and there, a cluster of heads on her bridge, the one distinctive white-topped watch cap; his opposite number, the U-boat Skipper. Again, no zigzag; but this time she had an excuse. According to the chart, they were running close to a minefield, and the U-boat was obviously pointed directly at the swept channel. She was also accompanied by a surface escort, a minesweeper, which had come out from behind the U-boat as Trumble watched.

'Down periscope!' He turned from the scope as the crew settled into their stations. 'Asdic. What have you got?'

The beard and the eyebrows appeared from their cubby: 'Two sets of screws, passing down our port side, range about twelve hundred, moving at between ten to twelve knots.'

Andy nodded, gripping his nose with two fingers, while the other hand rested across his chest. Harry interrupted: 'There's a JU 88 up there too, probably.'

'What d'ye mean "probably"?'

'I spotted it about half an hour ago, away to the north. It could've been doing a sweep for our chum.'

The Skipper leant back and eyed the entry in the log. He grinned his 'murder in mind' grin, and gave Harry an approving pat on the cheek. It was a short reach from where he stood by the search periscope to Harry's seat on the fruit machine, and the Skipper could get quite tactile when his dander was up. He moved to the attack scope. 'Up periscope! Let's start the attack, gentlemen.'

Jerry was going too fast; they'd missed their chance to get to a position where they could turn in on him for anything like an ideal ninety-degree track angle, and they were submerged, and so slow. Every knot they wrung out of the electric motors meant less amps in the batteries, and there was still a lot of daylight left. It wouldn't be good if they ran out of juice and had to surface. Not good at all. Yet Andy ordered a course change, a group up and the throttles wide; they were going to run down Jerry's course.

The U-boat was steering one-three-five degrees, heading right for the charted minefield, with the minesweeper off his port bow. When they got closer, the minesweeper would slip in front and lead the U-boat through, but right now they were both doing what was probably the minesweeper's top speed to get them to safety in the shortest time. Trumble did the sums and laid *The Bucket* on one-zero-zero, then called out the figures to Harry, who punched them in.

In order to get within a decent range to fire, *The Bucket* was going to have to make its approach at a brutal one-four-five degree attack angle, their converging courses like an arrowhead on the chart, with the target all the while moving fast away from her. *The Bucket*'s motors were delivering seven knots, still too slow, but that kind of speed was going to drain the batteries in a very short time.

Harry delivered several solutions, but the ranges were too great for Andy; he wanted a sure kill. It was only after the outside ERA began calling out the charge left on the battery that Andy seemed to return to the reality of his narrowing options; daylight remaining, charge remaining, distance to target. 'Periscope angle now?' he asked, eyes still glued to the scope.

'Nine degrees red,' said Harry.

'Tubes one to four flooded?' he asked again.

Milner's pipe came aft, 'Aye aye, sir, one to four flooded.'

He fired at three-second intervals on the stopwatch, a tight salvo; but firing on such a broad track . . . the target was so, so tight, and moving away.

Four times *The Bucket* lurched, and each time the air pressure jumped as the compressed air used to launch the torpedoes vented back into the boat.

Trumble issued a stream of orders; the motors grouped down and the knots came off; they turned to starboard, and went deep, diving away from the two enemy ships.

The Skipper wasn't interested in the minesweeper. Although it had depth charges, it was small beer compared to a U-boat. And anyway, there was a Junkers 88 stooging around up there, so why tempt fate? Andy Trumble was known as a wild chap in the trade and 'Jack' liked that; but he wasn't a nutter, and 'Jack' liked that even more.

They waited as the seconds ticked away. Carey had the stopwatch and had calculated the running time: torpedo speed, distance to the target, plus speed of the target.

'First torpedo . . . ten seconds to target,' he said, and began counting. Nothing. Then, 'Torpedo two . . .' Nothing. And again, nothing.

Andy's face was a picture of strained insouciance. He stared at the deckhead. And again, nothing. All that tension, and then just silence. Expressions fixed – one rating even managed a quick exhalation – and resigned. The words of some smart-alec remark were already forming on the Skipper's lips . . . but that was as far as they got.

It was as if some giant had struck *The Bucket's* hull with an even gianter hammer. The concussion, when it hit, shot a deep tremor through the whole fabric of the boat. The noise was so great as it reverberated around every plate and bulkhead that Harry felt his vision blur.

Trumble clenched his left fist, and tapped it against the chart table, once; and then he nodded, once, generally, to everyone in the control room. Everyone nodded back, once.

Trumble picked up the mic for the tannoy: 'This is the captain. What you just heard was one of our torpedoes hitting a U-boat, which I think we can fairly claim must now be destroyed . . .'

The beard was leaning out of the Asdic cubby with the phones to one ear, nodding. But no one needed his confirmation anymore; the sound of tearing steel began echoing loud enough for everyone to hear through *The Bucket's* hull; the sounds of another submarine, not unlike theirs, breaking up as she took her final plunge. It was what their deaths would sound like, if or when.

Devaney interrupted the morbid revelry: 'Twin screws, high-speed, moving astern of us, left to right, and closing.'

'The escort,' said the Skipper.

Piecing it together later as they headed home triumphant, sitting round the wardroom table with a scatter of stiff belts from the Skipper's gin bottle, they worked out that the Junkers 88 had probably spotted their torpedo tracks and directed the minesweeper on to them – except that by the time the minesweeper got there *The Bucket* had long gone.

Jerry hadn't given up the hunt that easily, continuing to sprint and stopping to listen on his hydrophones for the sound of their screws. What had followed was a series of leaps and bounds as Jerry picked up their track, and sped towards them while *The Bucket*, hiding behind the racket they made, sprinted off in a different direction, only going silent after Jerry had dropped his depth charges, and again stopped to listen.

Harry had heard depth charges before, when the *Von Zeithen*'s escorts had dropped a few. They'd been a long way off, and although Harry thought them loud, *Pelorus*'s crew barely noticed them. The first depth charges this time, when they came, sounded to Harry's inexperienced ears, very, very loud indeed; and to his bowels, very disconcerting, for they were followed by a shock wave which shook *The Bucket* as if she were a tram going through a well-worn set of points.

Carey counted the blasts out loud, in a bored ritual liturgy, and Harry found it was easiest to curb the first gripe of terror in his guts by looking at the bland indifference on everyone's faces. The Skipper looked bored; Able Seaman Devaney kept up his running commentary on Jerry's various manoeuvrings in his naval monotone. Harry, who initially thought the bangs were two feet above his head, flinched accordingly, enough to provoke an indulgent smile from the Skipper.

Because he was the new boy, Trumble began an inane commentary: 'Oooh, not even warm . . . cold . . . cold . . .' then a bang closer, 'Bloody Norah! That verged on the almost tepid!' And everyone else in the control room responded by smirking, as they concentrated on their duties.

None of it lasted long. Twelve detonations in all was Carey's count. Ten from the minesweeper and when they got round to awarding points on the bangs, they reckoned the other two had been from the Junkers 88.

The Bucket should have remained on patrol for its duration – she still had her six reload torpedoes – but a radio message the very next day summoned them back.

'The King wants to see you about that Jerry you clobbered,' Carey assured the Skipper, as they sat round the *Dolphin*'s wardroom table over one of Harry's donations to the mess fund. 'Wants to award you the VC and Bar, and create you Viscount "Arsend of Nowhere", with bezants and fluffels!'

'Malcolm,' said the Skipper, contemplating his tumbler-full of Harry's single malt. 'Were it but true! Alas, you are a mere colonial and know not . . . of the capricious malice that drives those who run our lives. We are recalled, because they have a better joke to spring upon us . . .' He raised the tumbler and tossed it down, a slam of glass back on the wardroom table, and then: 'Scottish person . . . can I trouble you for another sample of your generous donation to our cellar . . . please?'

In his assessment of their recall signal, it was the Skipper who, not surprisingly, had turned out to be right. *The Bucket* was ordered to join Third Submarine Flotilla, based on HMS *Forth* at the Holy Loch on the Firth of Clyde.

'That's Harry's home port,' the Skipper announced, after passing on the news to their gathering back ashore in the *Dolphin*'s wardroom. 'Harry, you better book a military priority call to your local police station . . . tell 'em to lock up all Dunoon's daughters . . . it's going to be raining "buckets"!'

They all groaned, and the Tigger attempted a witticism of his own. 'But they'll be Scottish . . . and all look like Harry.' That got a laugh.

There had been almost thirty hours of bustle and preparation. A lot of stores were moved ashore, and space was cleared for all the new clutter they'd take on at Holy Loch. Even *The Bucket*'s racked torpedoes were shoved and cajoled up through the loading hatch amid much grunting and blasphemy – she would only keep the kippers already in her tubes, and replenish her empty racks from Third Flotilla stocks.

Although the Tigger was notionally in charge of the manoeuvre, nobody even considered asking him; it was to Harry, who was overseeing everything else, they turned.

'D'you think we'll be getting them new mark eights, Mr Gilmour?' . . . 'The Third Flotilla's a crack mob, sir, they're bound to be first in line for any new uns going, sir, don't you think?' . . . 'You could always fix their Captain (S) up wi' yer sister, sir.'

On a big ship, that sort of remark would have landed the wag responsible with a personal invitation to the next defaulters' parade, but *The Bucket* wasn't big and she wasn't a ship. Submarines. They were like that. And as everyone knew, you had to like a laugh in order to be a 'bucket'.

'I don't have a sister,' replied Harry, with mock formality, 'and if I did, I certainly wouldn't swap her virtue for a set of mark eight torpedoes!'

'You don't have to tell 'im that, sir!'

And all the while the hard graft went on, never losing pace, until it was done, and they were off, on time.

The sullen pewter of an autumn afternoon had leached to darkness before they finally slipped out of Haslar Creek, and then out of Portsmouth Harbour. Off watch, sitting at the wardroom table, Harry had set to one of his many junior officer tasks: decoding all the incoming radio traffic and encoding the out-going.

All the intelligence signals singularly failed to mention U-boat activity in their area, thus confirming the scuttlebutt: that the U-boats had moved farther out into the Atlantic in their search for targets. And the skies appeared to be clear, too. That, at least, was the word; since the end of the Battle of Britain, Jerry wasn't venturing anywhere near their way, at least not in daylight, and a submarine was an absolute bugger to spot on the surface – at night.

The only threat left, it appeared, was complacency. Not that the 'buckets' would ever allow themselves to be accused of that; but as they went round Land's End and began heading up through the St George's Channel the following morning, the passage began to take on a bit of a holiday cruise atmosphere. The stomach-clenched anxiety that was standard issue for a patrol in the Bay was singularly missing. You couldn't stay screwed tight all the time.

The entire passage from Portsmouth to the Holy Loch was completed on the surface, in company with another of those geriatric H-class submarines, and another T-class boat, all three of them escorted by an old sloop of 'last lot' vintage to keep the Brylcreem boys at bay. The sky was typical winter for the Irish Sea: glum, grey, solid cloud, but thankfully with very little wind; just listless airs rarely rising to force 3 from the east, holding the clag static right across the western approaches.

Harry did all his watches on the bridge, doing all the watchkeeper things he was supposed to, but goofing too at the other ships in their little convoy, and enjoying just being in the fresh air away from the interminable reek of unwashed bodies and diesel, their stinky cocktail now augmented by vague wafts of mould, courtesy of the weeks of condensation now making itself felt. You always got a lot of condensation on a sub – heat from the engines and all those bodies in close proximity; no real ventilation; the endless damp clothing and the cold steel of the hull where the fetid air coalesced into rivulets, gathering in tiny pools on pipe flanges, behind control boards and bunks, and every other nook and cranny.

On the bridge there was always a show going on. The lack of rain produced the sudden appearance of washing aboard the sloop; a row of vests and dungarees stretched from the galley pipe to the mainmast, wafting in the cold, clear air. The seagulls soared overhead, and always, at every point of the compass, bobbed fishing smacks with their own personal gangs of seabirds, swooping and harassing like the Stukas from the newsreels of Dunkirk and Norway and Poland.

Off watch, Harry laboured away on the never-ending coding work, and when he finished that, he started censoring the crew's letters. There had been no time to write in their quick turnaround back at *Dolphin*. So they were taking the time now that they had it. Letters to mums, sweethearts, wives, dads, mates, grandparents. Most lumpen, saying nothing, others really quite lyrical, apart from one of the engine-room back-afters, a Stoker called Mottram, whose letters showed an unexpected sensitivity for an 18-year-old from Gillingham. His wistful reminiscences of domestic life amid his mum and sisters and the cat brought Harry up short with a slap of guilt at how little he had even thought of home and the life left behind.

⌣‿⌣

They didn't talk much about hearth and home around the wardroom table. Being short-handed in the officer department, there wasn't that often a quorum even for a game of uckers or cribbage, as at sea each officer often ate alone. Even when Harry didn't, the Tigger had no conversation beyond his precious weapons; Rita Hayworth, whom he was in love with; and rugby.

On the odd occasion Harry ate with Andy Trumble, the Skipper would continuously quiz him on what he'd do in an endless procession of unlikely emergencies:

'Right. You've been caught inshore . . . shoals and islets between you and deep water . . . Jerry is after you with an E-boat and aircraft . . . you've only three hours' charge left on the batteries . . .' – then he would laugh like a drain when Harry fluffed his responses – '. . . dead, Harry, and all who sail in you. Dead-dead-dead. And sunk too. You've lost us the war. Not that you'll care, because you'll be dead.' Etc., etc.

The mundane daily life of a submarine at sea unrolled as they chugged north in their own little cocoon. After dinner on the second night, somewhere west of the Isle of Man, they even had a 'sods' opera' in the disconcertingly empty forward torpedo room. Harry and the Skipper, neither being on watch, were invited. Harry was taught to join in the chorus of 'The Three Black Bastards from Baghdad'. The Skipper didn't need any lessons.

'We are the three black bastards from Baghdad . . . the pox 'n' syphilis we have had . . . we have no fear of gonorrhoea . . .' and on and on around the crush of sailors, each contributing verses vying in extreme crudity with the one gone before, to a squeeze box and a quintet of harmonicas.

Harry reciprocated in his untrained but delightfully melodic baritone with a rendition of 'Ae Fond Kiss' which brought a tear to several eyes among the more sensitive 'Jacks', disguised by extra-deep pulls on their bottles of pale ale, shipped specially at Portsmouth for such a little en route celebration by the bloke who was doubling as supply officer: Sub-Lieutenant Harry Gilmour.

He looked around the press of shiny, happy faces – teenagers and middle-aged POs, the Skipper, red-faced and belting out his filthy ditty – and he remembered the delicate words and the delicate hand of young Mottram, and the drip, drip of the war was upon him. Everything. From the bombed-out houses, the bits of German sailors floating in the Bay, the crash dives and the depth chargings, and the noise of ships breaking up as they sank, from the *Von Zeithen*, when he really didn't understand what it meant, to that U-boat out in the Bay, when he knew only too well.

And the faces: Sandeman at the periscope during the attack; McVeigh, whom he'd thought was going to be his friend, watching his back disappear, not knowing it would be for the last time. And in-between, cradling Ted Pagett's crushed skull as the *Pelorus* sank beneath them . . . and then their ascent, out of the escape hatch and into the perfect black and a cold beyond numb. He dreamt about it now, a lot. And that bastard Bonalleck. What had happened to him? The drip, drip, drip of stuff. He might be heading back home, physically, right now, but inside he was a long, long way from home, and still going.

Chapter Eighteen

Harry could see a number of heads at the kitchen table as he came around the back of the house, so there was definitely someone in, even though it was a Saturday afternoon and his father would be out on the hill somewhere, tramping away, or fishing with his pal in their little clinker-built dinghy on Loch Eck; at least his mother was not away gallivanting among her legion of friends.

'If you get all your requisitions in order, ready to go to *Forth* the minute we're alongside, you can have six hours,' the Skipper had told him after the party in the torpedo room. 'Six. Not a minute more.'

The paperwork was on the wardroom table as they steamed past Paddy's Milestone just after dawn. And so here he was, home in time for lunch.

He opened the kitchen door and stepped into the famil-iar . . . except it wasn't familiar anymore. For a start it was cluttered. Washing on a makeshift pulley hung above the kitchen table – could such an affront have been perpetrated against the good order of the house? And the room was busy . . . with children! Two of them, a little boy and a slightly older girl, were frowning at him with what could only be described as suspicion – especially the girl. Then he noticed a third child, a toddler, coming right at him clutching some rag thing that looked like something he'd seen before; and the wide beaming face of Shirley, standing back in the gloom of the dangling washing, and then his mother coming around the edge of the table in the toddler's wake.

He looked down into the tiny face of a little girl as she hurtled headlong, unsteady, aiming directly at his knees . . . 2 years old? Less? It wasn't the poor, threadbare, washed-out look of her little pinafore, or the fact that she was wearing small yet still too big socks half slid down her little legs. It was the smile on her face; except smile didn't quite encompass it. It stopped him completely as surely as a blow. It was a smile that split her tiny doll-like face with an excitement and an unalloyed joy she could barely contain. He was quite sure he had never clapped eyes on this little girl in his life, yet he had never, ever, seen anyone so happy to see him. His throat closed, his sinuses tingled and, bloody hell's teeth, he could feel the bloody tears starting behind his eyes! After all those months in the company of men, at sea, and at war, the sheer guileless pleasure bursting out of the little mite quite un-manned him.

And in front of Shirley, too? And the other two glum-faced brats and his mother? Surely not! Oh god, he thought, and in panic, he took the only cover he could and swept the little girl into his arms, holding her to his still whiskery face, and spun her so his back was to the gawping crowd.

'Hallo!' He barely managed the words, and even then it was in a daft voice to hide his choking. 'And who are yooo?'

The little girl gave such a gurgle of glee that it almost made matters worse; he had to slip one arm under her rump and whip his cap off and on to her head to give himself more time to recover. His mother was up to him by then, and her hugs finally saved his manhood. What in hell was going on?

'This is Margaret,' said his mother, taking the little girl's fist, and tapping it against the end of Harry's nose, and then gesturing to the other two, 'and that is Archibald . . .'

But the glum girl interrupted. 'Erchie,' she said.

'And Agnes,' continued his mother.

'Aggie,' the glum girl said.

'They've come to stay with us; they're our new family,' continued his mother.

———

'Wu've bin evacuatet,' explained Aggie, in very broad Glaswegian, 'fae Govan,' she added.

'Hello, Harry,' said Shirley, from across the table. 'You look like someone's dragged you through a hedge backwards.' All of them, even glum Aggie, laughed.

Everyone sat round the table and tea was served. The children continued to look at him with a concentrated suspicion, except Margaret of course, propped on his knee, rubbing at the four days growth on his cheeks, and chortling to herself. He sat there in his increasingly greying white pullover, a pair of stiff work trousers and the ex-RAF flying boots he often wore on watch, with the white socks turned over the tops. His salt-streaked watch jacket with its single wavy stripes was draped over the back of his chair, and his watch cap was now pushing out the flappy white ears on Erchie's head.

'Are you aff wan o' they sumbarines, mister?' asked Erchie.

'That's Harry. He's my son,' said his mother.

The boy smiled at her and nodded. It looked like a pat response he practiced to keep her happy. 'Huv ye sunk any Jerries?' The serious, intent little face demanded an answer.

'Oh no,' said Harry. 'We just carry secret messages . . . under-water . . . so that the Germans don't see us.' The very thought of telling this little boy anything approaching the truth didn't even enter his head.

'Whit kinda secrit messages?'

'Oh, they don't tell us . . . they're too secret.'

Erchie sat back, adjusting the cap, then stared silently at his hands folded on the edge of the table in a blatant gesture of dis-belief.

Harry's mother began talking over the awkwardness: 'The chil-dren are here to get away from the bombing, and since we've got all this room . . .' She smiled and opened her hands.

Aggie provided the truth: 'The wummin frae ra corporation sent us. Aw the weans are gettin' sent.'

'The bombing isn't as bad as London but there've been a few raids,' added Shirley, 'and anyway,' she said, turning to the children, 'there was only your mummy to look after you and she was too busy working for the war effort to look after you properly, isn't that right.'

'Wur da's deid,' said Aggie.

'He was in the Argylls,' said Harry's mother, reaching her hand towards Aggie, as if the little girl's father being in the local regiment gave them some kind of affinity. Not like his mother at all to hint at something so meaningless, but what do you say to a child with a dead daddy?

'Saint Valery,' said Aggie, not taking the proffered hand, and concentrating on the two words like they were some kind of expla-nation in themselves. But then she could only have been about eight or nine years old, so what did you expect?

They drank tea, and the women wanted to hear all about Harry.

'We didn't think you'd get here quite so fast,' said his mother, 'otherwise I'd at least have got the washing down . . . children . . . I'd forgotten what you're like,' she said, ruffling Erchie's hair, irritating him. Being Harry's mother, she knew better than to jump up flustered and start stripping the pulley while everyone was sitting at the table.

'You were expecting me?' said Harry. 'How did you . . . ?'

'Shirley saw your boat.'

'I saw your number,' said Shirley. 'It's painted all over the little hut you have on top.'

The conning tower, she meant. And indeed it was. All Royal Navy submarines had their pennant numbers painted on their conning towers.

'Do you look at all the boats coming in?' he asked.

'Of course. P . . . umppity tumppity. Don't want to say it out loud cause walls have ears,' and she gave an arch smile. 'It's your address. When I write. Sub-Lieutenant H Gilmour, RNVR, care of HM Submarine P . . . umppity tumppity, HM Ships.'

Which was true; you only used the number. And she looked for him. Coming in.

'That was lucky,' he said, 'because I'm just passing through. I've only a few hours, then I have to be back on board to load stores and be off; they never tell us where.'

The conversation tootled on; local news, his father's disposition. They didn't press Harry for any of his news beyond the usual platitudes. He was grateful, and so were they. West coast Scots weren't expected to unburden themselves in front of the womenfolk, let alone the visitors. And what could they ask anyway? Stuff like, what's it like being at war? How on earth could you reply to that? Have you killed people? Have you seen people die? Were you brave? Were you frightened?

So they talked about the difficulty of getting clothes for the children. Who'd have thought his old childhood cast offs would have come in so handy? That was when he started realising why some of the children's clothes were familiar, and why he had recognised the rag thing that Margaret continued to clutch; it was a sewn-together representation of some indeterminate mammalian genus, home-made with asymmetrical ears and a bright red velvet grin.

'And I bet you remember Rousseau?' added his mother.

Indeed he did. Rousseau, the rabbit. He had no idea all those things had been preserved. His mum had kept everything. Shoes though; they were the hardest things to get for the kids these days, but when Shirley went up to Glasgow there'd be more shops, and she'd volunteered to keep an eye out. Glasgow? Yes. Shirley was going off to be an ambulance driver, after she'd turned eighteen in January. Of course. He remembered.

His mother took him out to inspect the new vegetable garden while Shirley and Aggie washed up.

'There are children all over, billeted with people who have the room,' she was saying, bent over snatching at the odd weed. 'Your father has a very . . . ambivalent attitude towards them.'

'I can imagine . . .'

'Actually, Harry, I doubt you can,' she said, standing up to look at him. She always defended his father. Always. 'He's happy they are here and not in Glasgow under the bombs . . .'

'. . . but? And where is he anyway?'

'He doesn't know how to deal with small children. He didn't even know how to deal with you. He just sort of looks on in amazed horror.'

'I know the look. Then they grow up, and they go from objects of horror to causes of disappointment.'

His mother sighed, then spotted another weed needing atten-tion. As she bent, she said: 'He worries about you. Every letter you send, he demands I read. Again and again . . .'

'Can't he read them himself?' Harry interrupted.

Rising again, she said: 'Then he rants and raves . . . about you, the war, the stupidity of man, and you, and you, and you.' She paused. 'He won't touch your letters because he says you've got blood on your hands.'

'He's a madman.'

'Yes, Harry, he is. Mad with fear.'

Then his mother mentioned Janis had been round . . . just as Shirley was coming down the garden.

———— ————

He got away with Shirley eventually on a cycle ride through the woods over the back road to Sandbank.

'You told fibs to wee Erchie about sinking Germans,' she said. They were sitting on a mossy bench by the side of a muddy path through the brooding trees, everything October-damp and chill, the birdsong long silenced by the threat of winter, and the light a faerie green.

'Umm,' he said.

'Do you tell fibs when you write to me?'

'No!' A pause. 'Sometimes I don't tell everything.'

'You said you would.' This time Shirley made the pause. 'Is Janis your girlfriend?'

He hadn't thought about Janis in that way for ages. Not in a 'girlfriend' way. Only his loins had really ever thought about Janis, and just because your loins thought about that, it didn't necessarily mean the rest of you actually had to follow. Although as everyone knows, when you're a 20-year-old bloke, your loins have a pretty big say.

But Harry was no longer just your average 20-year-old. While most blokes could still afford to be daft at his age, months at sea as an officer aboard one of His Majesty's submarines had fashioned a somewhat more sophisticated model; sophisticated enough to know that for all the bland casualness of this conversation, pivotal decisions were about to be made, and subtlety was required, as well as decisiveness.

'I thought *you* were,' he said, evading the telling-the-truth-in-letters business quite nimbly, he thought.

Shirley laughed, which was a good sign. 'I'm not sure I want to be the girlfriend of a chap who doesn't tell the truth in his letters.'

Damn, he thought, then said: 'They get censored, Shirley.'

She liked him using her name. He could tell by the smile.

'Who censors them, Harry?'

He stared into the stygian gloom of the dripping undergrowth and saw his future in a wrong answer. It was his turn to laugh. 'Me.'

But she didn't laugh this time. 'Is it really not very nice? Out there?' she said, studiously not looking at him.

'No. It's not.' And that's when he kissed her. He breathed in the fresh air and pine needle smell of her hair, and felt her arms hold him far tighter than he'd expected, and immediately wondered why he'd never done it before.

'You took your time,' she said. 'I was dying for one of those.'

——— ———

When he walked into the Third Flotilla offices aboard HMS *Forth* the first person he met was Jack Twentyman, the flotilla's Commander (S).

'It's Mr Gilmour!' barked Twentyman, offering Harry his hand. 'Nemesis to the *Von Zeithen* and saviour of Padgett. You stayed in the trade . . . and you're still alive! Bloody good show! – Two bloody good shows!'

Twentyman bustled through the tight little space made tighter by the Petty Officer Writers and typing ratings all beavering away.

Against the bulkhead, a leading stoker from *The Bucket* was hovering over a desk watching his paperwork being shuffled.

'Actually, sir,' said Harry to the beaming face, 'I'm here to ask a favour.' A lie. It was happenstance, but why miss a chance to look decisive? 'It's about our torpedo reloads.'

Twentyman's eyebrows shot up: 'Its duffel coats and long drawers you should be a-begging, where you're going, not torpedoes.'

Harry was surprised.

'You're on *The Bucket*, yes?' said Twentyman. Harry's jaw tightened and out of the corner of his eye, so did the leading stoker's, if he wasn't mistaken. Only 'buckets' got to call their boat *The Bucket*.

'HMS *Trebuchet*, yes, sir,' said Harry.

'Hopefully you won't need any torpedoes where you're going,' said Twentyman; which Harry didn't understand at all. What did Twentyman know that he didn't? Stupid question of course; Twentyman knew everything.

'But I suppose if it turns out you do . . .' Twentyman scrunched his brow, then turned to a fellow who looked like a bank clerk, overweight and in shirtsleeves, with steel-rimmed specs, chunky hair slicked down with something greasy and a Lieutenant Commander's two and half rings on his shirt epaulettes. Obviously his staff officer. 'See Mr Gilmour loads with mark eights, and make sure he gets the correct exploders.' And then Twentyman was gone, calling over his shoulder as he left, 'Drop in for a sherry before you slip, if you've got time . . . and wrap up warm!'

The leading stoker caught Harry's eye, grinning. This would be all over the boat by the time he . . . Aw, let's face it, said Harry to himself, it probably was already!

The officers' briefing was fixed for 22.45 in a CO, S/M's cabin which had been allotted to Andy Trumble for the duration of HMS *Trebuchet*'s stay alongside *Forth*.

HMS *Forth* was a new depot ship in the Loch, a replacement for the small *Titania* which had been a mere converted cargo passenger liner of pre-Great War vintage. *Forth*, on the other hand, was built for the job: a huge slab-sided beast of over 9,000 tons, she was a warren of workshops, stores, magazines and messes, to the point where you could be forgiven for thinking she was even bigger on the inside than out. This was no mean feat, given that those grey slab sides seen from the deck of a submarine reminded Harry of nothing more than Lewis's department store on Glasgow's Argyle Street.

Harry and the Tigger were at full trot haring down the passageways, having already got lost twice and fearing being late, when they all but careened into *The Bucket*'s dark, disapproving and notoriously monosyllabic engineering warrant officer, Mr Partridge, standing at ease, cap on, but in a set of blue oil-encrusted overalls, at the entrance to officer country.

'Mr Partridge,' said Harry, 'Are you looking for the Skipper's cabin too?'

Since neither Harry nor the Tigger were wearing their caps, Mr Partridge did not salute, but he did come to attention with a slight incline of his head, and said: 'Fourth door on the left, Mr Gilmour,' and that was it. No explanation, no expression; just the gaunt flat grey planes of his pewtery skin, impossibly stretched over the framework of his immobile face, peering down even on five-foot-ten-and-a-bit Harry.

Harry, with Tigger trotting behind, went down the passageway to a door clipped back to reveal a regulation-perfect naval officer's sleeping cabin: spartan, functional and occupied by a Lieutenant RN, all buffed-up and wavy-dark-hair handsome, looking a bit like Tyrone Power in his number ones, polished oxfords and glittery double gold and so very solid Royal Navy rings on his tailored cuffs. He even had a medal up, but Harry didn't recognise the blue and white ribbon.

'Oh, sorry,' said Harry. 'We were looking for Lieutenant Trumble's berth.'

'Tyrone Power' looked up, then down at Harry's wavy stripes, where his flat gaze lingered for a telling moment.

'This is it,' was all he said as if he owned the place, before bestirring himself to make an affected gesture that said, *come in – if you must*. There was no attempt to introduce himself. The stranger was sitting on the only seat in the cabin, a small desk stool; so Harry and Tigger squeezed in and sat on the single bunk, neatly made up and still unslept in.

Harry thought about introducing himself, but a little voice in the back of his head said, Bugger you, mate! The senior officer always spoke first; always did the introducing. Harry might have had a bellyful of naval etiquette aboard the *Redoubtable*, but it didn't mean to say he'd learned nothing.

That was when the Skipper and Carey hauled up, both bare-headed and in oil-smeared white overalls.

'Ah, the gang's all here . . . no it isn't,' said Skipper. 'Where's Mr Partridge? I left him here five minutes ago.'

'He's standing at the end of the passage, sir,' piped up the Tigger. 'Shall I . . .?' But the Skipper cut him off with a raised hand, as he looked quizzically at 'Tyrone Power'.

'Tyrone' spoke: 'If you mean the warrant officer that was here in oily overalls, on his own, he was a warrant officer, non-commissioned. I didn't think he had any business in officer country. I told him to get out.'

No 'sir', noted Harry. This was going to be interesting.

'I told him to wait here,' said the Skipper, in that level tone his men had learned to fear.

'He was a non-commissioned officer . . . in an officer's quarters,' 'Tyrone' repeated, as if that were explanation enough.

Oh dear, thought Harry.

The Skipper, in the doorway with 'Tyrone' showing no sign of relinquishing his seat, turned to his officers: 'Gentlemen, this is Lieutenant Grainger, he's our new navigator.'

'Terrific!' piped the Tigger. 'We've been one chap short for months, and all busier than a one-armed cabbie with crabs!'

Harry had already noticed the Tigger's recent habit of picking up on 'Jack's' more colourful sayings, and winced at the total inappropriateness of the moment.

The Skipper ignored him, however, and presented each of them in descending order of seniority to 'Tyrone', before turning back to his officers again.

'Fetch Mr Partridge please,' he told Tigger. 'Mr Carey, Mr Gilmour' – the formality boded ill for someone – 'would you mind waiting a moment in the passage?'

They shut the door as they went out. They couldn't actually hear the exact words Andy Trumble said to Lieutenant Grainger, but there was definitely a 'fucking' and an 'ever again' among them, and not even the solid steel of the partition wall was enough to disguise the steel in Trumble's voice.

Well, well, thought Harry, you could always rely on the Skipper to start off as he meant to continue.

They were heading north, a long way north, Trumble told them after they'd all filed back in. The billet would be in the Barents Sea, but for security reasons he was not at liberty to say exactly where, or divulge the nature of their orders yet. What he could tell them was that they would be sailing in company with another T-boat: *Trumpeter*.

'Everybody with duties upstairs is to get fitted with an Ursula suit,' said Trumble.

Harry's first thought was Marvellous! I get to wear one now without getting the piss ripped out me!

Harry was presented with a list of stores he should start requisitioning. Extra rations, especially tinned stuff; and although it was strictly the Tigger's department, the Skipper handed Harry a list of small arms and ammunition he was to secure. And ammunition for the deck gun too. Lots of it. Loading to start forthwith, apart from the engine room requisition list.

The Skipper, Carey and Mr Partridge had just come back from overseeing the start of certain modifications. One of *The Bucket*'s ballast tanks was being plumbed to carry extra fuel instead of ballast water. They were working on *Trumpeter*, too. All stowing in the engine room spaces would be on hold until the welding work was complete. There would be issues affecting *The Bucket*'s trim as a result.

'Harry, give number one a hand on that,' said the Skipper.

Passed over for yet another responsibility; Lieutenant Grainger's already disapproving jaw tightened another knot.

'What charts do you want me to pull?' Grainger asked.

'Don't bother, I'll pull them,' said the Skipper, not even looking at Grainger.

They all filed out and went to work.

A grey dawn and a thin drizzle. Slabs of tinned goods and sacks of potatoes, onions and carrots, and boxes of ammunition started moving down the gangways jutting from *Forth*'s precipitous sides, item by item on the backs of shuttling sailors, down into the submarines. Mid-afternoon, the humping all but done, Harry was summoned to the Skipper's presence in a machine-shop office aboard the depot ship.

'Hand over what you're doing to the chief,' said the Skipper. 'You can have another two hours ashore. Dismiss.'

Harry sought out a chit to use *Forth*'s shore telephone. Mrs Gilchrist, the Dunoon operator, answered after two rings. He gave the number he wanted, off by heart. Everyone knew Mrs Gilchrist, and she knew everyone; and everything about them too.

'Harris,' she said. 'Now, Janis Crumley has been looking for you all day. She knows you're back and she's been telephoning your house. Shall I put you through there instead?'

'No, Mrs Gilchrist. Cowal 235 please. It's Castle Cowal I want.'

Harry prayed it wouldn't be the old bat of a dowager Lady Lamont who would answer. But it was Shirley.

'I've got two hours,' he told her.

She was waiting on the jetty at Sandbank when the duty tender carrying him ashore docked in the fading light.

———

He was back on *The Bucket* barely half an hour before they sailed. The weather forecast was bad. A series of severe south-westerly gales marching in over the past few days had hit the Outer Hebrides and raised the sea state, but hadn't hit this far south. However, the wind was due to swing round to the north-east, rising storm force.

As they cleared the boom, *The Bucket* and *Trumpeter* were already rising and sliding down the swell from the sou'westers. Harry, doubling as usual as *The Bucket*'s pusser, which as he'd learned was 'Jack'-speak for supply officer, was below, sat at the wardroom table, filling in the ship's books for the stuff they had taken aboard in all its ball-breaking detail; trying to ignore Grainger sitting opposite, fulminating behind his scowl.

'Happy in your work, Gilmour?' said Grainger, idly gazing at the deckhead.

Harry ignored him.

Grainger didn't notice. He continued, 'Ah, but of course, you've got work.'

Not looking up, Harry said: 'Skipper's giving you time to get to know the crew, sir . . . that's work, I'd've thought.' Harry had said 'crew' on purpose and not, 'the buckets' – Grainger was a long way from being included in that honour.

'As long as they know I'm the navigator, and number three on the boat. And they do as they're told. That's all I need to know about the crew, and them about me.'

Harry set down his pencil. 'Mr Grainger, sir . . . what brings you to the trade?'

Mr Grainger rose smartly and disappeared through the wardroom curtains.

———

Recreational sailing can be rough from time to time; you get caught out by a wind that suddenly blows up from a brisk force 5 on the Beaufort scale to a blustery force 7, or you'll occasionally miscalculate and find yourself running for port when a full force 8 gale hits you: things can get frisky aboard in one of those. All this Harry had experienced crewing for Sir Alexander Scrimgeour in his determined wanderings all across the Firth of Clyde, and in and out of the Inner Hebrides. Aboard *The Bucket* he'd sailed through a few blows in the Channel and the Bay; everybody knew how bad it could get there. But in all the weeks of patrolling out of Portsmouth, the western approaches had never really bared its teeth, and so none of it had prepared him for the force 10 storm that hit *The Bucket, Trumpeter* and their waddling motor yacht escort late on the second day.

The wind veered round as they battered up the Minch into the teeth of rising seas, with Skye on the starboard beam, beneath grey racing clouds on a grey sea, so that at times the horizon all but disappeared and never any sign of sun or star to shoot. It came out the nor'nor'east, but they were expecting it. In the galley, 'Lascar' Vaizey had stored all utensils and crockery and double lashed the pantry doors with cord. Even the wardroom table fiddles were stored; in a force 10 the nifty little wooden fittings would be useless even if anyone was stupid enough to place a plate on the bucking table and expect to eat off of it. In the engine room, the tools and spares lockers were similarly battened. Fore and aft, men stowed all moveable gear; personal and the ship's. And the Skipper, who'd seen all this before, had a canvas sheet rigged in the control room, like a bird bath, right underneath the ladder to the bridge to catch the deluge from waves breaking over it. Running on the surface, regardless of the weather, the hatch leading up through the conning tower had to remain open, because that was where the diesels sucked their air from.

Harry was wedged in on one of the wardroom banquettes, favouring a steaming mug of galley coffee and a wedge of hot toast slathered with mashed-up sardines, while *The Bucket* bucked. They had passed Cape Wrath in the dark and it was coming time for him to stand another watch. He hadn't tried to sleep, had just sat wedged there against the violence of the boat's pitching and rolling as the seas hit her fine on the starboard bow. Big waves, he thought, until the rhythm changed and *The Bucket* seemed to drop ten feet, then climb it back again . . . and again, and again. After a major wrestle to get into his Ursula suit and sea boots, and wrap his neck with towels and a scarf, he had clawed his way to the control room, stopping by the chart table to check course and position before getting himself to the bridge to relieve the Tigger.

That was when he saw why the rhythms had changed. In the partial lee of Scotland, the storm had only managed to whip up a short nasty sea, but there on the chart it showed when they'd cleared the Cape; and when the full majesty of open ocean rollers had hit them, with wave heights to fall down, from trough to crest, not of ten feet, but of twenty feet and more.

Upstairs was an inferno of wind and water, and pitch black. Amid the shuffles and grunts of the two ratings handing over, Harry and Tigger communicated through yells in each other's ears. *The Bucket* was being conned from the control room below, so there was no course to communicate, just their sailing station. Their little convoy was proceeding line astern; the motor yacht leading, *Trumpeter*, and then *The Bucket*. All Harry had to do was keep *Trumpeter*'s tiny red steaming light in sight, fine on the bow. The Tigger had yelled to him, then, 'Every twenty minutes, *Trumpeter* makes her number by Aldis lamp and we reply,' and that was all Harry needed to know.

The sea got everywhere; waves, unseen in the blackness, broke over the bridge swirling up and in his seaboots, filling them. Sometimes Harry was waist-deep in the black, freezing water. And it soaked his scarf and towels, and poured down his neck, and up behind his gauntlets and into his sleeves. The salt spray stung his face and eyes, and the muscles of arms and legs ached as he held on, leaning back, feet braced as *The Bucket* toppled downhill into a darker blackness, and then leaning forward as she laboured up again, so that *Trumpeter*'s little red riding light would reappear, if she too was on the facing crest before they each fell away again. And if he turned away for a moment, and looked back, even in the darkness, streaks of foam would glow on the flanks of the waves as they powered by, not below him on the bridge, but above.

Then the little blinking red light would come, and it was important he gauge the distance since he didn't want to be responsible for running *Trumpeter* up the arse; important and all but impossible. And he'd reach for *The Bucket*'s little hand lamp, and making sure both boats were in line of sight, and not vanished into another racing valley of water, Harry would key out *The Bucket*'s number in response; just so that they knew they were both still there, and neither had got lost or foundered. Two hours on, four hours off, as Orkney slipped past to starboard. It was Grainger who came to relieve him.

Carey was in the control room when Harry, preceded by the two ratings, climbed down into its red glow, his numb hands hardly able to grasp the rails.

'Watch where you're bloody going!' Carey snapped at him.

Harry had kicked a hose, one end disappearing into a portable pump and the other in the Skipper's canvas 'bird bath'; he looked down and could see it was fighting a losing battle, pumping out all the seawater pouring down from above. He was too cold to apologise, and anyway, he could feel his gorge rise as the smell of vomit hit him. Nearly half the crew were being sick. The two ratings who'd just come off watch were already heading forward by the time Harry had hit the deckplates, which was unusual, but Harry was too cold to notice; he turned aft, where they all should have been heading.

'Where d'you think you're going?' barked Carey, without taking his eyes off the gyro compass by the helmsman.

The deep tremble that the cold had locked on Harry's jaw made talking difficult: 'Engine room. Get out of this. Wet.'

'Mr Partridge isn't playing anymore,' said Carey. 'No more hanging our smalls out on his nice hot pipework.'

'What?' said Harry. This was a catastrophe. All 'buckets' coming off watch with wet gear got to hang it up in Mr Partridge's nice hot engine room, otherwise it would never dry before you went back on watch and you'd have to put them on again wet. It was one of those traditions that held 'the buckets' together; the back-afters and the deck scrubbers.

'He says it is because we are ruining the shine on his brasswork,' said Carey, looking venomously up through the hatch, 'but there are other opinions.'

So Harry went to get out of his sopping gear in the wardroom. Grainger, he said to himself.

The engine room was Mr Partridge's domain. Letting the crew use it as a drying space was his gift to the general harmony. However, if he continued to let the crew use his engine room, then he'd have to let Grainger too; and everyone aboard now knew what Mr Partridge thought of Grainger. Harry could see Partridge's point, but this wasn't good on many levels.

They pounded on through a world of water and wild movement, cold and wet and buffeted while trying to sleep; and frozen, stung and blinded on watch, peering into a wall of moving air that was more water than air, and a sky that only changed in colour from black void to translucent porridge; and with two random flecks for company, *Trumpeter* and the motor yacht. It seemed to take forever, but finally they made it in to the relative calm of Lerwick harbour.

The only pounding now was the racket of heavy maintenance, and the only thing vibrating through the hull was the sporadic judder from machine tools. Harry could feel the gentle bobbing of *The Bucket* through his now dry bum, comfortably resting in its usual spot around the wardroom table. The little overhead lamp with its floral pattern shade and its very own oily smear cast its light over a spread of charts. At last, Lascar, with maximum disruption, placed a stack of corned beef sandwiches, with pickle, and mugs of tea for everyone, on the table – the Skipper, Carey, Grainger, Harry and Tigger; and Lieutenant, the Honourable Bertie Allen-Freer RN, *Trumpeter*'s Skipper, plus his number one, his navigator and his torps – all nine of them in a tight huddle, with notebooks out, interrupted in mid-discussion by the arrival of the grub.

Although their little convoy was at last snug, none of them had made it unscathed. One of *The Bucket*'s engine exhaust mufflers had been stoved in and cracked, and water had been pouring in to the port engine; and her number two torpedo tube bow cap had sprung and kept filling with water: together these injuries had threatened to flood her. Carey had been up for a straight thirty-eight hours pumping water to stop *The Bucket* from either plunging to the sea bed or rearing up and broaching against the terrible head seas.

The 'trumpeters' had similar tales to tell. Andy Trumble, the senior officer present, had them all detailed in his notebook so as to assess his command's readiness for sea. Both submarines were due to sail again on tomorrow's late-morning tide, so all repairs, watering and refuelling had to be done by then.

There was a pause in discussions as they all chomped into their over-sized bread wedges. As a group of young men they were all much of a muchness; the oldest, Bertie's navigator, an RNR officer at 27, and the Tigger the youngest at 18. The same mops of hair, some fair, some dark, except the Honorourable Bertie, who was going prematurely bald; all in their scruffy watch jackets and misshapen, stained and off-white pullovers, and all of them needing a shave; except the Bertie's navigator, who sported a full set. And all of them as whiffy as they should be with no fresh water to wash in.

Trumble broke the sound of chomping: 'Right, what's this all about.' It wasn't a question.

The wedges were set down and the mugs of steaming tea were raised as they composed themselves to listen. This was it: the purpose behind all the hush-hush and faffing about.

'We're going to Russia. And when we get there, we are going to violate their neutral territorial waters to take a look into a small port nearer to the Norwegian border than it is to Murmansk. It's called Bolshaya Zapadnaya, and it's at the head of the Litsa River . . . there,' and he jabbed at the chart, 'but since Bolshaya Zapadnaya's probably too much of a mouthful for our Anglo-Saxon gnashers to get round on a daily basis, from now on we'll refer to it as "Port Boris".'

Everybody leant over to peer at the spot, but it was young Harry who first asked the question on all their minds: 'Why? What's there?'

'Why?' said Trumble. 'To look for Jerries.'

Jerries? Of course. It was autumn 1940, over a year now since Joe and Adolf had become pals. 'Now there's unlikely bedfellows' Shirley had written to him. Unlikely indeed. Any Pathé newsreel would have told you: Nazis hated Communists. But last summer the world had turned upside down: Germany and the USSR had signed a treaty. A treaty that meant when Germany invaded Poland, and Great Britain and France declared war, the Soviet Union would remain neutral. A treaty that had let the Soviet Union grab half of Poland in return and stand aside from the war currently ravaging the rest of Europe.

'It's the Nazi-Soviet non-aggression pact,' Trumble said. 'It's the deal Jerry and Stalin did last August. One of the clauses was a promise from Stalin to hand over a base for Adolf's boys way up north, so that his U-boats could get replenished, and get in and out of the Atlantic way up past Norway, beyond our blockade apparently. But then Adolf's boys took Norway, so it didn't matter; but Adolf's boys still have the base. And we are going in to look because naval intelligence thinks Jerry is putting together a landing force for a descent on Iceland,' said Andy. 'I know, I know. Why don't they just sail from Norway, or are Jerry brass just as perverse as our brass?' A good-natured chuckle round most of the table, and a pause for more tea. Trumble continued.

'The story I have been told is this: Jerry is doing a build-up in Norway; RAF recce is going to catch it. But RAF recce can't over-fly the Soviet Union, because the Soviet Union is neutral. So Jerry won't do a build-up in Norway, but he might do it here' – he jabbed at 'Port Boris' – 'Intelligence thinks Jerry *is* doing it here. So we have to . . . confirm.'

They all sat, glum. Britain had occupied Iceland a few months ago to stop Jerry putting U-boat bases there, astride the convoy routes, because Jerry on Iceland was the end of Britain's north Atlantic lifeline.

The Honourable Bertie was first to ask: 'Um. I know I'm spoiling your soliloquy, dear boy, but what do we do when we get there? If it's all true?'

'Obviously, Bertie, we report back.'

They all knew what that meant: breaking radio silence, even though they'd still be in the belly of the beast.

Bertie nodded and smiled his indulgence for an old chum: 'If there are Jerries there, are we supposed to sink them?'

Sink them in neutral Soviet waters? That was the subtext.

'We've not to get caught,' was all Trumble said.

All discussion on the matter of orders was over so with a few glances all round, they got down to the serious planning.

Communicating between the two boats without breaking radio silence was first up: manoeuvring signals, alert signals all reduced to shorthand Morse, using Aldis lamps from the bridge, or submerged, by Asdic pulses. Then they set out procedures for everything from firing breeches buoy lines to co-ordinating deck gun and anti-aircraft fire. Finally, there was the rendezvous point to be agreed off the Kola Peninsula, where they would meet before proceeding inshore: thirty-degrees east, seventy-three-degrees north, in the middle of freezing ocean.

There was one other problem: the charts. All they had dated back to the 1820s when John Barrow was second secretary at the Admiralty, and he was using the fleet that had defeated Napoleon to check out shortcuts to China for want of something better to do. The only updating done on them since had been the odd 'notes to mariners' from passing tramp steamers engaged in the timber and whale-oil trade out of Murmansk and Archangel. When they got there, there was going to be a lot of 'proceed with caution'.

'One last thing,' said Harry as the Honourable Bertie's lot prepared to rise. It was all to do with something Shirley had said . . . 'P . . . umppity tumppity.'

'You said we weren't to get caught, sir. If the Russians spot our periscopes or a bit of conning tower . . . we're just another submarine. They won't know who to blame. But if they see our numbers . . . they just have to look through last year's *Jane's* and they'll have us as British. Maybe we should paint the numbers out before we sail.'

They all stared at him, more so Trumble. 'You can be a sneaky little bastard sometimes, Gilmour,' he said.

Chapter Nineteen

There was no denying it: it was land. The first good day since they had slipped from Lerwick, they had executed their daily trim dive just before dawn and had surfaced into a clear, cloudless sky; the air still, as if itself frozen, and the waters of the Arctic Ocean rising and falling like a steel-blue lullaby. And there off the starboard bow was land, dancing on a gall of freezing air: snow-capped mountain peaks, eighty miles closer than they should have been.

The Skipper and Grainger were on the bridge. In the control room Harry could feel their consternation tumbling down the conning tower hatch.

The weather they'd endured on the long, long slog north had come at them in varying degrees of awfulness. If the wind abated, fog and mist and rain set in; when the wind rose, so did the sea, and the further north they got, the sea began sticking to *The Bucket's* conning tower, and periscope stands, and gun – ice, in other words – and never, ever a sight of the sun or even a star.

They had battered on using dead-reckoning, working out their progress by speed and course, and frantic fingering of the nautical almanacs trying to factor in the effects of tides and currents when known; and falling back on sheer guesswork when it came to calculating by how much the battering wind might be knocking them off a point here, a point there, from their course. Way point by way point, Grainger had done his sums, and according to his dead-reckoning, the coast of Norway, for surely that must be what they were looking at, should have been a hundred miles to starboard. The evidence of their eyes said different, and now the Skipper was worrying what to do about it. The first worry on his mind was being discovered by enemy air patrols, with the coast of Norway demonstrably a mere twenty miles away. He wasn't apportioning blame yet . . . but the truth was filtering through the boat, and as far as 'the buckets' were concerned, it was the navigator's fault.

The Bucket had not been a happy boat on their long journey to beyond the Arctic Circle. The growing intrusion of Grainger on their everyday lives had hung over all of them. A submarine was too small a space for the effects of such a judgmental ego not to be felt to the furthest reaches. Although in this case, it stopped abruptly at the forward engine room bulkhead. Mr Partridge did not suffer it to come further, and as Mr Partridge reported direct to the Skipper, even Grainger knew better than to try and wander back there, casting his deprecating eye over all he would survey. Forward, the Quartermaster, Tubby Tevis, was ready to kill him. And so was Carey: to rile the Jimmy the way he had was no mean achievement by Grainger. He'd even penetrated the hitherto impervious hide of the Tigger.

Under orders not to waste a minute, they had steamed north on the surface, steering to cross the Arctic Circle at a point five degrees west, before shaping a course direct for the rendezvous point, 600 nautical miles to their north-east on the edge of the Barents Sea, where the north coast of Norway met that of the Soviet Union. It was a course which kept them well away from the coast of occupied Norway and the eyes of any prying Germans. Which was why, on that empty ocean, and while still in company with *Trumpeter*, the

Skipper had been confident enough to arrange a series of gunnery exercises to keep both boats' gun crews tight.

Immediately after surfacing from their dawn trim dives, each boat would dump its gash, unweighted, and the other would blast away until it had sunk the offending sacks. By the time *The Bucket* and *Trumpeter* parted company for the final run in, they were blowing each other's rubbish to bits after only a couple of rounds, even in the crappiest weather.

The Tigger should have been insufferably jubilant – but wasn't, for Grainger had been on hand at every shoot to offer advice. Nor had Harry escaped Grainger's critical attentions; the only difference here was that Harry knew how to deal with him. Navigation was where their paths crossed, and Harry shadowed the new navigator every step of the way.

'I want to pick up your skills, sir,' he'd told 'Tyrone' in tones just this side of fawning.

Every martinet has a weak point reasoned Harry and it appeared that 'Tyrone' was prepared to accept Harry's attentions as his due. As for Harry: his aim wasn't to curry favour, but to open up a dialogue with the man and try to work out what made him tick – and in the process, pick up as many navigation tips as he could along the way.

As the Skipper had already pointed out, Harry could be a sneaky little bastard when necessary. Which was why Harry, down in the control room, was just as concerned as Grainger about this yawning error in their position. According to Harry's dead-reckoning too, they really should have been a hundred miles away from the Norwegian coast.

'Mr Gilmour to the bridge! And bring your sextant!' It was the Skipper.

He was obviously seeking a second opinion on where the bloody hell they were! Harry headed for his locker.

By the time Harry was back in the control room, clutching his instrument, it had actually dawned on him what was happening; if he was right, he was going to feel so bloody smug! Grainger, up on the bridge, must have already been shooting the sun, still low on the horizon to the south-east, calling down his readings to Carey, who was checking them against almanac and chronometer. Even if the whole crew were dying for the navigator to fall on his arse, Carey of all people knew that this was no gloating matter. But then Harry didn't think Grainger had got it wrong. When he got to the bridge he knew it.

It was crowded up there, in the brilliant freezing air, with four instead of two lookouts, summoned upstairs to scour the sea and sky for Jerries, so close to land. Because there it was for all to see and comprehend: a thin, jagged and very solid line along the horizon. Harry could have laughed out loud, but decorum was called for.

'Sir,' he said, by way of innocent preamble.

The Skipper, binoculars fixed on the mountains, said nothing.

'Sir,' repeated Harry, 'I don't think Mr Grainger's position is actually that far out.'

The Skipper leant back and gestured towards the far peaks, with that arch, sarcastic look of faux incredulity he was so fond of.

'They're not really there, sir,' said Harry.

The Skipper just stared at him but you could see his mind working, calculating whether young Gilmour was experiencing a breakdown or picking precisely the wrong moment to discover his inability to tell the difference between a bad practical joke and grossly insubordinate impertinence.

'It's the clear sky, sir . . . the air is really cold. The sea is always that bit warmer, especially in these latitudes, and since the sky cleared last night, it's just that bit more so. That causes a thin layer of moist air to form between the water and the cold air, and it acts as a lens.'

'What are you talking about, Mr Gilmour?' said the Skipper.

'It's a mirage, sir,' said Harry. 'I've seen it before, yachting, in the early spring or late autumn when the air is cold and the sea warmer. The moist air acts as a lens. I've seen the MacBrayne's steamer low-flying on its way to Tobermory, and Ailsa Craig lifted out of the Firth of Clyde when we weren't even up to Toward Point and its peak shouldn't have been above the horizon. Those mountains are probably a good hundred miles away, but the way the light is being refracted through the moist air it looks as if they're just on the horizon. They're not.'

The silence was broken from down below. Carey, who'd heard none of the exchange, called up: 'Mr Grainger's figures put us within two miles, east-south-east of his original estimated position, sir!'

After 600 nautical miles of cloud and fog and gale and unknown currents with never a sight of sun or star, Grainger had brought them to a point that was actually nearer a mile and a half of their aiming point. Everyone paused to consider the seamanship involved, and to reconsider Grainger. Up until now they hadn't much liked what they saw.

On passage, with the routine of the boat fixed, and a standing order to avoid contact with the enemy at all cost, there had been a little more time to spare over meals round the wardroom table for the officers to get to know their new colleague; and submarines being the cramped, hugger-mugger steel tubes that they were, the crew to eavesdrop. But Grainger had given nothing away, and naval etiquette forbade the Skipper from forcing him. They had only learned one thing: when Grainger had been asked where he got his DSC, he merely replied: 'Narvik.'

Harry hadn't known that the dark-blue ribbon on Grainger's chest with its broad, vertical white stripe was a Distinguished Service Cross, but he knew they didn't grow on trees. Or that the man had been in the same waters as he had, probably just a fjord away, exhibiting the 'conspicuous gallantry' the ribbon demanded while Harry had been standing around watching his men 'have a fag'.

Harry decided he was going to get to know Grainger better. But the little he'd found out had filled him with dismay.

Living cheek by jowl on a submarine meant you got to know your fellow crewmen very well indeed, but when it came to what made them tick – that was another matter. Some blokes, you got to know everything about, down to the name of their sister's pet goldfish. Others, rank being obvious, all you got was a name, and sometimes a vague geographic point of origin.

The Skipper wasn't a great one for small talk. They knew he came from Hampshire, where his family were in timber. He was a second son who saw no incentive in going into the family business. There were always girls involved and he was a very good cricketer, liked his beer and was undefeated uckers champion of the boat. Also, you didn't talk to him for long before discovering he was a very witty man – sometimes viciously so – and that there was a steel not to be trifled with.

There wasn't much to know about Sub-Lieutenant Milner, aka the Tigger, beyond an enthusiasm that was itself beyond parody. His family 'had land' in Herefordshire and he had followed numerous brothers to a very respectable prep school before ending up in Dartmouth. He seemed to only vaguely know about his sisters, who were indeterminate in number and collectively referred to as 'les girls'. He liked Rita Hayworth and explosive ordnance, not necessarily in that order, and was cognitively incapable of imagining any existence for himself other than that of a Royal Navy officer.

It was with Malcolm Carey that Harry built up a serious friendship. The tall, angular, impossibly exotic Carey. An intelligent, well-read man, with a precision of speech and movement that bespoke a certain unashamed vanity, which 'Jack' allowed him on account of the fact that he took the care and maintenance of his crew very seriously indeed. He was 'old Melbourne', privately educated and from a family with 'strong interests' in finance down under; who had wanted to see the world but still wanted the respect, and maybe just a tiny bit of envy, from his contemporaries and elders. Oh, and it has to be mentioned . . . if nothing else, Carey certainly looked the part. And of course, he was married to the beautiful Fenella. He and Harry talked about many things, but after the novelty of Carey's exotic background was exhausted, most of the time they talked about books.

And that was the wardroom of HMS *Trebuchet*, until Lieutenant Grainger RN joined. And what did they learn of him? Suffice to say it was some time before they even knew that the Christian name on his papers was Christopher. But that wasn't what he called himself, apparently. For that snippet of knowledge they'd had to wait for Harry's inveigling.

'Kit,' he'd told Harry eventually. 'I answer to Kit.'

Their conversations came in spurts and starts after that. Sudden, spontaneous bursts of chat, always initiated by Grainger, and all singularly failing to inspire any confidence in a bright future together for Kit and 'the buckets'.

'The only point to being in the navy is to command,' he'd told Harry. It was obviously a belated reply to Harry's question of weeks ago about why he'd joined the trade.

In subsequent chats it dribbled out. He'd been on destroyers, usually a berth where responsibility came quickly to young officers. Not quickly enough however for Grainger. His reward for reckless bravery hadn't been a quick bump to Jimmy aboard a sistership, just a pat on the back, a bit of ribbon and a 'carry on, Mr Grainger!'

'It was either light forces. You know, MTBs, motor gunboats . . . or submarines,' he'd told Harry. 'But vroom-vrooming around in plywood bath toys in the Channel isn't proper navy, is it?'

It was a rhetorical question.

285

'So here I am.'

Harry didn't know exactly what that told him about his new shipmate, but none of it gave him a warm feeling. Navigator on *The Bucket* was apparently just another rung on Mr Grainger's rise to command.

But by getting them to here, there was a definite change in the air around Grainger. Not that Harry had any time to properly gauge it. They had just another few hours to the rendezvous point with *Trumpeter*, and since they would be coming up on it in daylight, close in to Russian territorial waters – and by default, the German-occupied Norwegian border – they would be making the approach submerged.

'The buckets' went to work, preparing the boat for action, getting her ready to meet the enemy in whatever shape or form he might come over the horizon. And in the activity Harry noticed something happening among the crew that the short, familiar war patrols had so far not made happen. Up here, so far from home, from support or help, too far for a damaged boat to limp home, on a specific mission, not some opportunistic jaunt to see how many strips of white cloth they could add to their Jolly Roger, they began to change. All these vibrant characters aboard were disappearing before his eyes: their diversity, their personal differences, draining away; their individuality being packed and stowed. He didn't understand what was happening at first, that this was what happened when men long-trained to become part of a machine, finally do so; because this time, more than any other time, their lives depended on it.

⁂

The Skipper had the Tigger and Carey pinned down in the wardroom, idly humiliating them at uckers to pass the time. A pot of steaming coffee sat on the table as a treat, with an opened can of condensed milk on the side. The Skipper was la-la-ing absently to himself as he danced across the board with his quarter-inch nut for a playing piece. The other two looked on, Tigger tight-lipped with irritation and Carey affecting boredom. That was when the subdued shuffling and bumping forward erupted into a full-blown clatter and clang of metal on metal, accompanied by yells and curses, and even a whistle's shrill scream.

The Skipper arched back and leaned into the passageway.

'Good grief, what the bloody hell is going on there?' He turned to the watch messenger in the control room. 'Get forward and find out who's breaking my boat!'

The messenger, a junior rate in overalls and no cap, shot past with a hurried, 'Aye aye, sir!'

Still leaning into the passage, the Skipper heard Harry's voice rise above what was left of the hubbub.

'I do not care if it goes all the way up your arse next time,' he heard Harry annunciate in his slow, fierce, *I'm a grown-up dealing with a child voice*. 'We will keep doing this until we get it right. It's called training. Because if you don't get it right, we'll all be dead and it won't matter where the rifle's gone, or how far. Do you understand?'

The sounds of bodies and stuff rearranging themselves ensued.

The Skipper was readdressing his game when the junior rate came back down the passageway, stifling a grin.

'Report,' said the Skipper.

'It's Mr Gilmour, sir,' said the young sailor. 'He's got his landing party drilling fer getting out the forward hatch wi' their Lee Enfields and the dinghy, sir. G'tting' in a bit o' a fankle, sir.'

'Carry on.'

Carey, brows knotted. 'D'you order him to do that, sir?'

The Skipper smiled his evil smile. 'And upset the hands like that so gratuitously? Of course not.' The smile continued. 'But if they have to go ashore, he's probably just saved their lives,' his eyebrows shot up, '. . . all our lives . . . what an enterprising officer Mr Gilmour is turning out to be, Mr Milner,' he said directly to the Tigger, who was frowning now. '. . . for a schoolboy. You should take a leaf out his book.'

The Skipper sat back, still smiling to himself, his mind no longer on the game.

'Dive! Dive! Make your depth one hundred feet, bring her on to zero-seven-zero!' It was the Skipper at the periscope. The klaxon sounded as he slapped up the handles and the scope shot down. 'Asdic! Pulse to *Trumpeter*. Dive! Dive! Now!'

Leading Telegraphist Devaney, in his cubby, hit the Asdic for the agreed pings. Harry could hear them echoing out as Carey, barking orders, shut all the blowers on his trim board in quick succession, opening the vents, letting the water flood back into her ballast tanks, taking her back down just as she was about to break surface.

'Bloody *Trumpeter* was already up,' announced the Skipper to no one in particular. 'A shagbat. The shaggiest bat ever. Lolloping out of that cloud bank that doesn't know whether it's coming or going.'

'Shagbat' was submarine for a patrolling aircraft, probably enemy but you never knew. Up here it could have been a Jerry or a Russian. One as bad as the other. *The Bucket* reached her depth and as all her pump noises faded, *Trumpeter*'s could still be heard, announcing that her descent had taken much longer than *The Bucket*'s.

'Bugger,' said the Skipper. 'Mr Gilmour to the control room!'

Harry, in his smart new Ursula suit and watch cap screwed tight, scuttled forward through the press of sailors. He had been aft, standing under the engine room hatch with a deck party. Between him and the Tigger's party under the fore hatch, they'd been waiting to go up top for the Tigger to fire a breeches buoy line from his .303 so they could haul *Trumpeter*'s dinghy and Skipper aboard for a quick conference on what to do next. The sun was all but down and by flashing Morse code through their periscopes, both submarines had agreed to risk surfacing while there was still just light enough to complete their manoeuvre, but a low cloud bank to the south-east kept rising and receding, buggering about with the oncoming darkness, and as it had transpired, masking oncoming aircraft until it was too late.

'In five minutes I'm going to stick the attack scope up,' said the Skipper. 'You read all these damn recognition charts. I want to know whose shagbat that is. You've thirty seconds. OK?'

Harry was tempted to say, That's not bloody long enough to find the damn thing in a darkening sky and then work out what it is! But he settled for 'Aye aye, sir.'

'Periscope depth!'

They waited.

'OK, Harry,' said the Skipper. 'Go!'

Harry got into position behind the smaller, second scope. He didn't need anyone to read off bearings or ranges; this was just to be a quick shufti.

'Up periscope!' called Harry, snapping the handles down as it rose, and swivelling the viewer knob; he was already looking through the periscope even as the head was still rising, catching a brief glimpse of dappled surface before the head broke clear. He began to traverse, keeping it slow, counting in his head . . . and there it was. He knew it right away. A smudgy, over-sized orange-crate, with two barn doors tied to its boxy sides by way of wings; and a single biscuit tin on top with a prop on it, held on to the whole rickety structure by a builder's trestle and guy ropes.

'Down periscope!' Harry snapped shut the handles and stood back. 'It's a Russian. A Beriev MBR-2 flying boat. The Soviet navy's equivalent of a Walrus.'

'Twenty-two seconds,' said the Skipper who'd never taken his eyes off his watch. 'Well done, young Harry. A Russian. He's bound to have seen *Trumpeter*. At least! Damn and bugger! Bugger! Bugger!'

They waited until well after dark to convene their council of war, bobbing beneath a clear Arctic sky wreathed in sheets of shimmering green, rippling across the dome of darkness high above the horizon. Two little tin cans in the vastness of the Barents Sea, and dwarfed by a display of aurora borealis as big as space itself. It delivered light enough for the Honourable Bertie and his navigator to make the trip in *Trumpeter*'s dinghy without mishap; any random curses from the ratings charged with their safe conduct drowned in the burble of both boats' diesels pumping charge into their batteries as they rode, stopped on a deep, magnificent swell marching in from the east.

The Tigger on the casing and Harry on the bridge kept *The Bucket* riding a safe distance from *Trumpeter*, and kept Harry from hearing the details of the tactical debate going on below. Every time he looked across at the other submarine, the pale white number daubed on her conning tower glittered a little in the spectral light like a reminder of opportunities lost. Neither boat had managed to paint their numbers out before leaving Lerwick – the rain had stopped them – and neither boat had space to carry that much paint to do the job en route. Ivan in his shagbat had indeed spotted *Trumpeter*; the two boys paddling the Honourable Bertie across had confirmed it. So now Ivan knew there was a submarine sneaking around his twelve-mile limit, and that it was British. But did Ivan know there were two? That question, Harry surmised, must be central to the talk going on below. He wasn't wrong.

———‿———

The Bucket departed the rendezvous point immediately after see-ing the Honourable Bertie and his navigator home, heading to put herself as far inshore and close to the tangle of islets and headlands at the entrance to the Litsa River as possible before first light, when the shortening Arctic autumn days would force her to dive.

'We're banking on Ivan having only spotted *Trumpeter*,' the Skipper had told them. 'And if she continues to bugger about out here, trailing her coat, we're hoping neither Ivan nor Jerry will be looking inshore, where we'll be.'

The fjord leading up to the river mouth was like a huge nibbled kidney running from north-east to south-west. Grainger at the peri-scope had navigated them down the three-mile, narrow dog-leg into its plump middle on a flowing tide, taking bearings on headlands and islets, keeping them to the main fairway indicated on their ancient chart, while Devaney in the Asdic cubby double-checked the depth beneath their keel by frequent pings from *The Bucket*'s echo sounder, sucking the ends of his beard between calling out the feet beneath them.

Harry at the chart table wrote down all the figures and did the sums on his trusty slide rule, marking the chart and noting all the errors between what the chart claimed, and what Grainger was actu-ally seeing and Devaney actually hearing. The discrepancies were depressingly large. But they'd got there in the end, drifting a further two and a half miles to a position behind the south-west bulge of the kidney, hanging at a depth of thirty-five feet with over thirty fathoms beneath their keel, and the Skipper back on the periscope, looking almost directly due east, sucking in his cheeks, then blow-ing them out, like a jazz trumpeter.

'Down periscope!' he said. 'Well, they're there all right. Port Boris is full. Harry, sharpen your pencil and get ready to write fast.'

Harry looked at the chronometer. The final glowing of the sun would be directly behind them, falling on the Skipper's target, while masking their periscope in shadow. Even so, the Skipper wasn't going to have it sticking up longer than was necessary.

'Devaney, what've you got?' The Skipper was leaning back against the main scope, talking over his shoulder, staring at the attack scope's well.

Devaney, headphones stuck to his greasy mop of hair, was also listening in on his hydrophones to the sounds of many small propellors, and to the burbling pumps and other innards of numerous much bigger ships: 'Multiple HE, all inshore from zero-three-eight to one ten. All small craft, lots of movement. Also, lots of background machinery, too many sources to count . . . all stationary.'

The Skipper nodded. 'Up periscope!'

The control room was tense. They were, after all, in a place they shouldn't be and every second their scope was on the surface, there was a chance that some bright-eyed lookout would spot it. Even a docker on a cigarette break might see the thin steel tube. At least they weren't underway; at least there was no danger of showing a 'feather'.

'Three jetties running out at ninety degrees from a long running wharf. From left to right, first jetty; three transports, one on the left, two moored alongside on the right. First transport, two thousand tons; on the right, inboard, big, four, no, four and half thousand tons; out board, another two thousand tonner. Next jetty . . .'

The Skipper described and Harry wrote; eight merchant ships ranging from 2,000 – 8,000 tons; a floating crane and a long wharf curving round from the hump of the kidney, stretching to a point off their beam. A dozen or so lighters moored along the wharf, discharging cargo; numerous small craft plying to and fro; and two small tugboats, also moored along the wharf. On the rising ground away to their starboard a large hut and tent encampment; and beyond that, what looked like the start of another. Between them, a railway sidings. The Skipper also counted eight anti-aircraft emplacements of varying calibre. But nothing heavy, just 20-mm . . . no 88s, thank god . . . and no warships either.

Then there was the vehicle park: lots of military vehicles, lorries, halftracks, at least a dozen light tanks, and several stacks of very large packing cases. And then on the big bugger, the 8,000 tonner, on her aft well deck was an Arado floatplane. And alongside, moored to a floating jetty was another, bobbing on her huge, ungainly floats.

Oh, and there were men everywhere, bundled up in cold-weather gear; working, busy, preparing. And they were Jerries all right, said the Skipper, and no mistaking; Kriegsmarine ensigns on every ship and flagpole; not a hammer and sickle to be seen anywhere. You wouldn't know this was the bloody Soviet Union, said the Skipper.

Then there was the final observation, or rather failure to observe. There were vehicles, there was what must be a barracks, but there were no troops. Harry wrote it all down, and when the Skipper was finished, he allowed Harry a quick sweep around, so that he could more accurately sketch what had been described to him.

He saw a tree-less, blasted landscape of low brown hills, all rock and grizzled brown scrub speckled with snow-filled dips; with Port Boris sitting on it like a scab . . . and then to his astonishment, it suddenly became a floodlit scab. The entire dock area was instantly bathed in a chemical light. It took him a moment to register what had happened: giant lights perched atop metal masts, sparkling in the gathering gloom; but then why shouldn't there be floodlights? The Soviet Union didn't need a blackout. It wasn't at war.

'Dead slow ahead,' called the Skipper, and *The Bucket* began inching towards the jetties. 'Devaney. Keep up a constant pinging on the echo sounder. Keep calling the depth as we move in.'

They were moving against the final flow of the tide, which was complicating Harry's attempts to calculate the speed of their progress over the ground. Grainger was jammed up against him at the table, marking the depths as Devaney was calling them. It would be slack water soon, and then when the ebb was well and truly going, they would ease back out into the middle, then surface in the black night and let the tide carry them down the fjord and out to sea.

Meanwhile the Skipper was obviously testing the approaches to the jetties, making sure the deep water ran clear, all the way up to . . .

Crump.

The dull noise echoed through the hull just a fraction of a second behind the impact. Not that it was much of an impact. Everybody did a little lurch, and the Skipper hissed 'All stop!' distracting everyone from the fact that they weren't moving any more, anyway. He grabbed the mic, 'Skipper here. Forward torpedo room, report.'

There was no damage.

Over the preceding minutes, Devaney's depth chant had been tracing a steadily rising sea bed. It had been getting shallower count by count, but not by that much . . . but then the echo sounder only looked down, not forward.

'A reef,' said Grainger, right by Harry's ear. 'And not on the chart, either.'

'A reef indeed,' said the Skipper. 'Up periscope. Mr Grainger . . . do my readings please.'

Grainger stepped forward and read off the bearing and the angles for range from the periscope's bevels; Harry did the sums and called it.

'Bugger,' said the Skipper. Everyone knew what he meant.

Assuming one might want to fire torpedoes at the assembled shipping, there would be no shot to be had from way out here in the Bay with its deep water and sheltering darkness. The reef was in the way . . . even at the height of the high tide, no torpedo was going to make it over that protective wall of undersea rock.

Before ordering 'Down scope', the Skipper took one last look. He saw a train come around the corner. A troop train.

Chapter Twenty

They're more or less the same the world over: about twice the size of a football, made of cork and painted bright red, with that little rime of green weed to mark the height of their bob above the waves. Fishermen use them to mark the end of a gill net or a fleet of lobster creels. In other words, it was a buoy. And here it was, sat between them on *The Bucket*'s wardroom table, just like any other buoy, in every aspect apart from one: it had a flag sticking out of it. A makeshift flag on the end of a steel rod; a ripped square of sailcloth painted, inexpertly, with the Union Jack.

'She was quite a modern job. Big. About the size of one of our Tribals,' said the Honourable Bertie, describing the destroyer which had been stalking *Trumpeter* since first light, while *The Bucket* had been exploring up the fjord. He kept a proprietorial hand on the buoy. 'I thought she was a Jerry, but my Jimmy said she was definitely a Soviet, and lo and behold, when she whipped round beam on, there it was: a bloody great red flag the size of a boxing ring, flapping from her foremast.'

The Honourable Bertie went on to describe how he'd had *Trumpeter* trail her coat for the Russian; holding at thirty feet with all her pumps and machinery going, cranking up her electric motors and scooting here and there with the periscope up, creating not so much a 'feather' as a bow wave as big as the *Queen Mary's*.

'He came right at us a couple of times,' the Honourable Bertie said, 'swerving away at the last minute. He was big, but he was nippy too. And well handled. Then he just hove to, beam on to us, and started flashing SOS directly at my periscope. I hadn't a clue what was going on. I never saw any chap in less distress. Then, all of a sudden he opened the throttles and was away, and when I did a sweep back to make sure no baddies were sneaking up behind me, there it was, bobbing about in his wake.'

'With that dangling from it,' said Andy Trumble, jabbing a long metal container – the sort they used for keeping flares dry.

The Hon Bertie nodded. 'And with this in it.' He slapped the table and the sheet of stiff cartridge paper unrolled across it. It was a Soviet naval chart of the Litsa Fjord and approaches, its corner adorned with a Soviet naval ensign and lots of tight Cyrillic script. The chart itself showed all the channels, navigation markers and depths from the mouth all the way to the small port facility which *The Bucket* had just returned from scouting.

'Thoughts?' said the Skipper.

The Honourable Bertie, his torps, Harry, Carey and Grainger were sat round the table. The Tigger was on watch, on the bridge, as both submarines lay hove to barely a boat length apart in the shadow of one of the islets at the entrance to the fjord. A force 6 wind was blowing from the east; there was no sky, just the dark, and the moaning of the wind and whipping spray, and sound of the sea beyond the barest shadow of a headland. And it was bitterly cold.

The *Trumpeter's* dinghy was alongside, her two paddlers in the forward torpedo room being fed piping hot ky, the navy's version of cocoa. *The Bucket* had her dinghy in the water, too, aft and being minded by a couple of ratings; in case any vagary of wind or sea drove the two submarines together, the dinghies would act as fenders. Neither boat was running its diesels. The batteries might well have needed charging, but in the pitch dark who knew who was about, and they didn't need all that racket to attract attention.

It was cold in the boat, too, with no engines running. The little huddle sat muffled up in Ursula suits, scarves and mittens, watch caps jammed tight on, hunched in the insipid light seeping from under the lampshade dangling between them. The scene looked like some oil painting of a Jacobean conspiracy in progress.

'It's a trap,' said Grainger.

Harry didn't agree, but didn't open his mouth.

Grainger continued: 'The depths will be all wrong; there'll be hidden reefs. They'll lure us in, then depth charge us to the surface; either hand us over to Jerry or parade us through Red Square in funny pirate hats.'

'Or just shoot us,' said the Honourable Bertie, with a broad grin. 'Us aristocrats anyway!'

The Skipper sucked and blew again, then said: 'We got in and out and only hit one reef. And they've got it marked on the chart. And they don't know we've already been in and out. As for depth charging us . . . from what? There were no warships in there, and anything going in now, we'd hear it. The chart's accurate. But why?'

Now this was Harry the clever clogs's domain. The other grim-faced fighting sailors all sat around, brows knitted to stop any useful thoughts escaping, trying to knot the ones remaining into a plausible answer. But Harry had the drop on them: he knew, courtesy of having had history rammed down his throat from an early age, reading the papers, listening to his father's sneering contempt as he sat by the wireless, railing against the *BBC Nine O'Clock News*, dismantling all the pretensions behind the realpolitik as practiced by men of affairs.

'Stalin doesn't like Hitler any more than Mr Churchill does,' Harry said from his corner perch.

'Stalin has done a deal with Hitler,' said Grainger, as if talking to a particularly slow child. 'They are best pals now, each with a half of Poland to play with.'

But Harry had the Skipper's attention, and Carey's. And the Honourable Bertie, noticing this, leant forward, too. The Skipper knew his Harry.

'Elaborate, Mr Gilmour.'

'Jerry's troopships. There can be only one reason they're here. There can be only one place for them to be going: Iceland. Jerry in Iceland, with a U-boat base right on the convoy routes; it would be all over for us. If that is what Jerry is about to do.'

'It is,' said the Skipper, who sounded like he had a greater knowledge than had so far been shared with this group.

Harry picked his words, trying not to sound like a university lecturer and more like a man of the world. 'Hitler and Churchill at each other's throats means Hitler is otherwise occupied. Stalin doesn't have to worry about Hitler. But if Britain is defeated, that means Hitler's got more time on his hands.'

'They have a non-aggression pact,' said Grainger, still bored.

'Hitler's form on honouring deals won't have been lost on Comrade Stalin,' said Harry. 'And it's happened before, with Napoleon. In 1808 the Czar did a deal with Napoleon at Tilsit; promised to enforce France's continental blockade, keep British ships out of Russia's ports, be a good boy and not get involved in any continental alliances; and in return Napoleon was going to leave him alone. Four years the deal lasted, then in 1812, Napoleon came after him anyway. The Russians have long memories.'

Harry sat back, feeling quietly smug about how useful those 'French nights' round the Gilmour kitchen table continually proved to be. Lascar Vaizey brought in a tray of steaming mugs of ky and everyone leant forward to warm their hands on the mugs and let the steam warm their noses.

'Jerry's presumed upon their hospitality. They can't throw him out, so they are inviting us in to do it for them,' said the Skipper. 'Is that what you're saying?'

'Our mission is to find out what's going on, and report back,' said the Honourable Bertie. 'Much as I've been intrigued and entertained by your young Mr Gilmour's appreciation of the diplomatic state of play, Andy, I think I can say with confidence that their lordships' reaction to anything more than a straight reconnaissance report will not be so sanguine. Shouldn't we be just pushing off and getting our radio antenna up once we're outside the territorial limit?'

'Matters are a bit more pressing, I'm afraid,' said the Skipper. 'I haven't got round to mentioning it before now because I've been wondering what to do. As we were coming out, I took a last shufti around the place. I saw a troop train coming in. They're on the move, or at least, they're about to be.'

'How does that change things?' said Carey.

The Skipper, lost in thought, sat back and pulled the end of his nose. 'I don't know about you, gentlemen, but I find the idea of a little huddle of junior officers stuck out in the arse end of nowhere with no one on the end of the telephone, debating the finer points of the war's strategy, *and* trying to second-guess the thinking of Mr Churchill, and the lords of the Admiralty, on Anglo-Soviet relations, a bit bloody ludicrous.'

The Skipper paused to let everyone finish grinning.

'As far as I can see it, the issue is simple,' he continued. 'This is war and we are serving naval officers confronted with a tactical problem. What do we know? We know Jerry is in there and lots of them. You had a look-see, Mr Gilmour. All that barracks area, the number and size of the transports. I'm not a pongo, so I can't accurately guess the size of the force, but there is probably room for, what? Anywhere between five and seven thousand men? What's that?'

Harry said: 'I don't know how Jerry counts it, but that's almost the equivalent of a British army division.'

The Honourable Bertie said: 'Bloody Norah.'

'So what do we do,' said the Skipper, not asking the question but starting a list. 'Let us assume my briefing before we sailed was accurate and they are headed for Iceland. I don't know our order of battle on Iceland. I don't know if we can repel such a force if it gets ashore. Nor do I know where they might try to get ashore. And it's a big, big island. So, do we just forget about all that, get the antenna up and signal the Admiralty and let them worry about it? Well, what happens then? For a start Jerry and Ivan will know we're here. What will they do?'

They all sat looking at the buoy.

'Well, I can't worry about what they will do. I know what I'm going to do,' said the Skipper. 'Mr Gilmour, run along to the wireless room and get a signal pad and notebook.'

And for the next half hour Andy Trumble outlined his plan for *The Bucket* and the *Trumpeter* to engage and destroy or at least disable the German transports berthed inside Litsa Fjord. When he was finished, he said: 'Questions?'

'We'd have to get out of there fast,' said the Honourable Bertie. 'We couldn't bank on Ivan being best pleased, even if it is what he wants us to do. At the very least he won't be able to look as if he's best pleased if he doesn't want to fall out with Adolf just yet.'

'Jerry certainly won't be best pleased,' said Grainger. 'There might be no Jerry naval escort in there, but there will be one next door in Norway. At least half a dozen destroyers. Maybe even light cruisers. Even after Narvik, they've still got a few left, and they'll be coming after us once we're out of Soviet territorial waters.'

'I fully expect that to be so,' said the Skipper. 'Jerry wouldn't worry about our recce flights picking up warships in Norwegian fjords. He'd know we'd expect them to be there. It's a landing force he'd need to hide. And now we know that is exactly what he is doing . . . in there. If we obey the niceties of international law and wait until he puts to sea, one of two things will happen. We'll lose him, in which case the entire home fleet will have to hunt across the entire Arctic Ocean to try and find the buggers before they get to their objective. Or we don't lose them, but have to fight our way through a substantial naval escort and a lot of air cover to do any damage whatsoever. And how many of them will we get to sink, before the escort gets us? Once he gets to sea, Jerry has the initiative. With him bottled up in there, we have it.'

And what's London going to say about all this, if we actually launch an attack? That was the unasked question.

Harry broke the silence: 'The Soviets and the Germans are already breaking international law.'

'Ah,' said the Skipper. 'It's our own Anthony Eden. You have the floor, Mr Gilmour.'

'If we act now, who's going to complain? It's in nobody's interest. The Soviet Union is supposed to be neutral in this war. Those are obviously military transports in there, and they've obviously been there a lot longer than forty-eight hours. Under international law the Soviets should have interned them all by now, just like Uruguay would've had to do if the *Graf Spee* had stayed any longer in Montevideo. If it comes down to who's broken international law . . . they broke it first. And, will Jerry want to broadcast how badly we'd buggered their plans?'

'Couldn't have put it better myself,' said the Skipper.

There were a few grunts round the table. At least I raised a few smirks, thought Harry.

'So what do we think?' said the Skipper. 'Anyone with anything to say, say it now. Bertie?'

'If we actually manage to succeed, Jerry will be all over us like a ten-bob suit.'

The Skipper looked round the table, fixing the rest in turn. Only Grainger looked like he wanted to speak.

'Mr Grainger. Your thoughts.'

'This is suicide, with no guarantee of success.'

The Skipper nodded. 'Good,' he said. 'I'm glad we're all agreed then . . . we're on.'

Chapter Twenty-one

When you're young and daft, sometimes you don't know when it's smart to be frightened. Sometimes the stuff is all so new and exciting that the mortal danger tends to get overlooked.

Harry had been at war for a whole year now. He'd been at the Second Battle of Narvik, taken part in a successful attack on a German heavy cruiser and had been sunk himself, trapped in the aft section of *Pelorus;* for the first time in his life, close to death. And he had seen the body parts raining down from that exploding Jerry patrol boat in the Bay. A quiet civilian life had been peeled away from him by random acts of war. Shocked and stunned, he had watched it all happen with the kind of immune detachment granted only to the young. Up until now, the war had been something he'd witnessed. But this was different.

Sitting here with his face slathered black with crankshaft grease, with half a dozen ratings around him all similarly blacked up, clutching rifles, with bandoliers of .303 around their shoulders, the bullets digging in to them as they squatted underneath the forward hatch: this was fear. Happening-to-you fear. Fear in all its prosaic blandness: the dry mouth, the constricted throat and the nausea and the gaping void in his bowels; and the concentrated effort to breathe slow and deep to stop himself perpetually yawning like a couple of the younger ratings over there.

They'd all been briefed by the Skipper, then sent off to collect their weapons. Blacking up, they'd all had a shot at nervous bravado; then the lads had politely listened as Harry spoke a few encouraging words to the men he was about to lead. He couldn't remember now what shite he'd spouted. The fear had got in the way.

It was when the rating doling out the guns and ammo had handed him a Webley revolver in its webbing holster, and then the shells, smiling in a grandfatherly sort of way at him, and said: 'Always aim low, sir. That way you'll make sure you get 'im.' That was when the fear started. Right there. With the knowledge of what to 'engage the enemy more closely' could actually mean: putting a bullet in a German sailor's body, or worse, the German sailor putting one in him.

And now their little flotilla was piling on down the Litsa Fjord on a flood tide, in the pitch dark, *The Bucket* leading. The Skipper and Grainger on the bridge, Carey in the control room on his trim board, and the Tigger and his gun crew, blacked up, and the magazine open and the ammunition party all closed up and ready to go. The two diesels sucking down the freezing air through the conning tower hatch behind him, and the boat chill and dark to get their eyes used to the night, the vague reflection of red light from the control room picking out the tangle of the boat's innards: its pipes and cable runs, every nook in its cluttered hull. Everything spectral and claustrophobic, the only connection to any world beyond being the bump, bump as they butted into the sharp chop of the fjord being whipped up by a persistent, vicious south-westerly wind. It was time.

And then they were slowing down, and slewing. Harry could feel the motion through the deckplates. He and his men all shunted up together, too close; he shut his eyes so as not to see all the other white eyes around him, staring out of the cold black faces. Just the sound now of breathing, and low murmuring from the forward torpedo room. The diesels had stopped; they were on motors now. Going astern and moving into the position the Skipper had sketched out on the back of a signal pad all those hours before.

'At least fartin' Martin isn't here,' said a disembodied voice from somewhere in the dark. There were muffled sniggers. 'Fatal in a confined space,' said another, to more sniggers.

'I dunno . . .' Harry recognised the voice: McTiernan, an ERA, one of his deck party; his boarding party. '. . . point that arse at Jerry with a following wind . . .'

'Properly loaded of course with one of Lascar's bum burners.' Another voice: his own, Harry realised, shocked, then pleased with himself, suddenly no longer crippled with fear. There was giggling now.

'Naw, naw, sir.' It was the little Glasgow Stoker called Clunie from the darkness, the one who boxed for the flotilla. 'It's written intae King's Regulations and Admiralty Instructions: Lascar and fartin' Martin arr no' allowed tae serve oan the same boat . . .'

More giggling, Harry thinking, British sailors, and then *The Bucket* lurched and the telltale hiss of air escaping into the boat told them the first torpedo was away and running. They were firing on the surface, from inside the reef. Close in, with clear shots.

Everything moved faster after that. *The Bucket* lurched back, then forward again with the thump of her own diesels, alive again, juddering through the hull. Shouts. Another torpedo, more manoeuvering, forward, then back, then two more torpedoes and two more. All six tubes were fired, and then seconds after the last torpedo had gone the explosions began reverberating through the hull. Hit after hit, more than just six; then other explosions; it must be *Trumpeter* loosing her torpedoes, too. Then Tigger yelling, and the grunts as the ammunition team started slinging shells. Tigger's distant high-pitched squeal again, yelling 'Shoot!' at the top of his voice. Then a *crack!* A 4-inch round on the way; then another.

Harry shut his eyes again, squeezing them tight to look down on it all from a height in his mind, where all the chaos, close up, could now make sense. He saw *The Bucket*, where she'd gone astern into the one-thousand-yard gap between the three jetties and the reef; edging herself closer to the inside wall of the reef, going resolutely astern to where the run of the wharf ended and the steep ridge behind it curved out and down from the shore. He saw the Skipper slowly manoeuvring the boat, so that her bow swung slightly in, opening the angles on the transports where they lay tied up to the right-hand sides of the jetties. *Trumpeter*, out in the fjord; her torpedo tubes pointed squarely at the transports on the left hand.

'We will each have a clear shot at three transports each,' the Skipper had said back in the wardroom. 'The track angles are broad . . . hundred and twenty, hundred and thirty degrees . . . but Jerry's a stationary target. Two kippers each to make sure. Can't miss.'

But two of the transports were 'trotted-up'; masked by the ship moored alongside them.

'We'll use our gun to deal with them,' the Skipper had said. 'I shall bring us up astern of them and Mr Milner will shoot them up the arse. They won't be going anywhere with their rudders and props blown to buggery.'

A voice cut into Harry's mental reconstructions: 'Mr Gilmour!'

It was the Torpedo Gunner's Mate. Harry's eyes flashed open and the white of the man's face glowed dully in the dark barely feet from his own; framed in a set of Bakelite headphones sticking around the torpedo room bulkhead door. 'You're on, Mr Gilmour!'

The Skipper on the bridge took his eye off the Tigger's handiwork yet again to glare down the length of *The Bucket*'s forward casing, slithery bright in the wash from the dockside floodlights, and where the forward hatch remained inexplicably shut. There was too much damn light about. How no one had spotted their dark shadow in that glare he'd never know. And where the bloody hell was Gilmour? He'd passed the order for him to get moving an age ago . . .

Crack!

The Tigger's sixth shot.

The order had been for six shells into the first tub, then six into the next, then back again for another four each. To make sure. But the Tigger's first had sailed into the night and rattled a crane on the jetty, the second had gone through the funnel and blown a lump off the central superstructure's boat deck and the third had merely demolished the poop deck.

'Down a bit, Mr Milner, down a bit.' The Skipper had tried to sound encouraging instead of yelling, because it wasn't the Tigger's fault, it was his. He'd seen the floodlights during their look-see yesterday; he knew he was going to have to take the boat in closer because of the reef, right into the spill of their glare, so he should have known Tigger would be firing right into that glare. He'd ordered the boat darkened to preserve everyone's night vision, but when the gun crew came up they'd been dazzled by the floods that drenched the jetties and wharf in halogen light. He'd overlooked that, hadn't he? Silly Billy Andy – that's how you got people killed.

But as the Skipper squinted into the light himself, the Tigger's fourth shell blew the transport's rudder right off its post. Grainger, out the corner of his eye, saw the Skipper's profile caught between the chemical glare and shadow, in a rictus, a comic gothic gargoyle, manic with delight. Grainger started laughing. The Skipper swung to face him, and became himself again, yelling, 'Where's bloody Gilmour?'

As he yelled, the forward hatch opened, disgorging sailors: Harry, bundling up like the rest of his team in a big, brown watch-keeper's duffel, distinguished only by his watch cap; the sailors in caps, their rifles slung but getting in the way when they went to haul up the semi-inflated dinghy. The Skipper wanted to shout, 'Get a bloody move on,' but they were moving fast and smooth, thanks no doubt to Harry's dress rehearsals. He shuddered to imagine what kind of shambles might have resulted otherwise. And what with all the bloody banging and crashing going on, perhaps the moment called for a bit of Andy Trumble sangfroid. He didn't want his lads flustered. And that young Gilmour, he could keep his head . . . so let him get on with it.

He watched as Harry and his now-practiced deck party swiftly opened the dinghy's compressed air bottle and blew it to its full shape, tightened home the small petrol outboard. Then they started piling into the big black blubbery thing, while Harry and one of the Petty Officers began sliding it over the saddle tanks and into the blacker water, dancing with reflections, before jumping in them-selves. With a splutter barely audible above the diesel thump and the racket of battle, they sped away right below him on the bridge, into the night and towards the wharf and the moored lighters.

As he leant over the Skipper saw a blackened face looking up at him from the dinghy's bows, split silly by a grin of teeth, and a thumbs-up raised high and poking from fingerless mittens. He knew it was Harry by the watch cap. Silly bugger.

* * *

Now they were moving there was a part of Harry still looking on, observing that the fear wasn't quite so bad now; sort of running it through his fingers, testing its quality: the fear for his own hide, yes, but also the fear of letting his men down, of funking it; catching a dose of screaming hab-dabs. But he was OK now, bumping along on the chop, the serious, physical pain of the freezing spray searing into his bare cheeks as they sped towards the shadowed row of lighters: eight of them, trotted up two by two, or maybe there were three together back there, or more; a dozen at most, with a small tug moored to the first two. The tug was not your proper harbour job, all broad beam and engine; she was long and thin, barely fifty feet if she was an inch, with a sweeping gunwhale running high towards the bow, and low almost to the water aft. Her superstructure was a low steel box with a wooden hut stuck on top for a bridge.

'Remember the brief. You're to get aboard the lighters and cut them out,' the Skipper had told them. 'For Christ's sake don't sink them. There's a three-knot current running when that tide is on the ebb. You need to get on to the bloody tug, start her, and tow them out into the fjord after me, casting them loose as you go. I want the whole bloody fjord filled with dark floating objects while we're running for the sea. Got it?'

Harry and the rest of his party had all solemnly nodded.

'I want to see Jerry chasing about all over the bloody shop, after those damn things,' said the Skipper, 'not after us.'

Coming out of the darkness, Harry and his party could see four men lining the gunwhale of the tug, obviously newly rushed on deck, gawping at the explosions and tracer peppering the jetty area; coats hurriedly flung around vests, and long johns disappearing into hastily donned seaboots. They didn't even see the dinghy until it was already under their noses and a mob of duffel-coated matelots were pouring over the low rail and in among them.

Half of Harry's party were up and on the tug roughly handling the stupefied crew before Harry had finished securing the dinghy alongside. There was a lot of low effing and blinding but when the scream finally came Harry knew things were getting away from him. It was turning into a rammy.

'Stop! All stop!'

He had their attention.

The party had been handpicked for what needed to be done. Harry had an ERA and a Stoker – McTiernan and Clunie – for any engines needing started, and a Leading Seaman helmsman for any steering, and three kids, ABs, for pulling on ropes. The scream had come from one of them, Harry couldn't make out which in his balaclava, the front and side of which was quickly matting shiny black – blood, obviously. And anyway, Clunie was in the way, tackling the huge tugboat man who'd done the hitting. The AB had taken a serious belt that looked as if it had flattened his nose across his face. But the tugboat man was on his arse now.

'Clunie!' said Harry. 'I said, stop!'

'Yon bastart Jerry jist banjoed . . .' Then Clunie remembered who he was and desisted. 'Sorry, surr.'

But from the gabble coming from their prisoners, three standing, one sprawled, Harry realised right away they weren't Jerries: they were Russian. French and Italian he could do; Russian he couldn't. He could think of only three words in Russian: *da*, *niet* and *tovarisch*, so he started using them furiously until he had the tugboat crew's attention, shoving his way in front of them, punching his own chest and shouting, 'Tovarisch! Da! Nazi, niet!' It seemed to calm the situation.

But we must get on, his little inner voice was telling him, in a distinctly shrill tone. He sent McTiernan and Clunie sprinting to the engine room, and told the Leading Seaman to drag the wounded and distinctly dazed AB to the bridge with orders to bring the tug to instant readiness.

He turned to one of the remaining ratings: 'You, take this lot into the nearest cabin, shut the door and don't let them out . . . and for Christ's sake don't hit them again . . . wave your rifle about if you have to.' Then he turned to the remaining lad, eyes staring dumbly out of his blackened face: 'And you, come with me.'

———⏜———

The Skipper knew what was wrong even before he leant over the bridge to glare down on to the gun platform.

The air was still getting ripped by steady bursts from the Lewis mount behind him, but the Tigger's gun had stopped firing.

'Slammed the breech before the shell was properly seated,' yelled the Tigger. They'd been working too fast and now the gun was jammed: the shell's base plate not quite home before they'd slammed the breech shut, pinching the thin casing and leaving it not quite in, not quite out and well and truly stuck. And they hadn't even begun pumping shells into the second target.

'Well, get it un-jammed, Mr Milner,' said the Skipper. He looked over the sum of their handiwork so far: all but one of the transports were wrecks. So what if they had missed one? It wasn't enough to lift an invasion force anywhere with just one. So let's get a move on before Jerry pulls himself together and starts shooting back, he thought. If rounds started coming the other way . . . one of those 20-mm anti-aircraft gun rounds through his pressure hull, and they wouldn't be able to submerge. And that was a 20-mm gun on the little headland overlooking the jetties, and another behind it, covering the wharf and tents' encampment; and then there was that other twin 20-mm on the flatbed railway carriage, part of that empty troop train; any of those could put a hole in them. And if they couldn't dive, they were dead.

One good burst, and they were dead. Dead, dead, bloody dead, just like he used to tell young Gilmour around the wardroom table; to annoy him as much as teach him. Not that he'd ever succeeded in annoying him. And where was young Gilmour anyway? He peered back towards the wharf into a dark just beyond the fall of the flood-light glare: too dark to see. Get a bloody move on, he thought, we have to get going, now!

———

Harry, breathless, came scuttling on to the bridge of the tug.

'*The Bucket*'s stopped shooting, sir,' said the Leading Seaman.

'What?'

'Her gun, sir. I think it's jammed.'

Any reply Harry might have contemplated was lost as another burst of light machine-gun fire hit the tug. He wasn't sure where the rounds landed, he just heard the ricochet and saw the flashes of bright-green tracer sailing off wildly into the night.

As Harry and the AB had danced around loosing the light-ers' moorings, casting them off from the shore, small gaggles of huddled-up German soldiers had started appearing on the wharf, popping off at them with rifles and that light machine gun. They'd been forced to duck and crawl behind hatch combings while they went about switching hawsers around, creating a raft of six hulls ready to be towed out into the fjord. It had all taken time – a lot of time – so that the remaining six lighters, triple-trotted at the end of the row, they'd just cast adrift to let them float off free. They had to get going now.

———

The Skipper saw the tracer searching for Harry. The Tigger and his gun crew were still trying to prise the bent shell out of the damn gun – a manoeuvre which called for a blend of brute strength and delicacy. On the one hand it might be a lump of steel that needed shifting, but it still had an explosive warhead, primed and ready to

313

go off at the slightest excuse; and the Skipper certainly wasn't diving the boat with that still up the spout. But then neither was he going to leave without Harry and his landing party.

While he was weighing his options, the twin 20-mm on the train opened up. Where was Harry? That had been another mistake, another failure of judgment. If he'd sent Harry and the boys off earlier, before all the shooting started, let them sneak off in the quiet and the dark; nobody would have been looking for them, they could have been aboard the lighters, cutting them out, before the balloon went up. But he had waited; told them not to go until Jerry was looking at all the fireworks. Now, all this cutting out lark, which had seemed such a good idea, was taking time; and they didn't have time any more. What a balls up.

He waited for long lines of electric-green tracer to find *The Bucket* as if paralysed by the realisation of his own failure, but they didn't. So much for fire control in the famously disciplined German army, he thought; until he realised that Jerry couldn't actually see *The Bucket* from way back there beyond the wharf. So all the hosing around the Jerry gunner was doing was to find some steel for the tracer to bounce off, so he could then start pouring on the fire. The realisation jolted the Skipper back into the game.

'Dead slow, ahead,' he said to the rating on the engine room telegraphs; then he leant down the conning tower hatch: 'Mr Carey. Trim us down to decks awash.'

It was all getting a bit too damn noisy for Harry, and a bit too like the Blackpool illuminations, with all the bloody 20-mm rounds and the tracer flying about; especially as he was standing at the wheel now as they began towing the raft of lighters, straining to move their deadweight. They might be empty steel tubs, but together their drag was very nearly too much for the tug's wheezing engine; and the empty steel tubs were making a hell of a racket as they clanked together. But not racket enough to drown out the bellowing and banging from the cabin below as their four Russian captives registered their displeasure at being kidnapped by strangers.

Harry could feel through every straining rivet of this old rust bucket that the ebb had started now, and it was helping. So imagine his dismay as he saw the shadow of *The Bucket*, just visible to him in the wash of the jetties' floodlights, start to submerge.

'Up!' he screamed at the Leading Seaman, crouched behind the brass stand of the binnacle, as if it might have the power to stop a 20-mm cannon shell. 'Go and get everybody! Everybody! And start casting off the lighters . . . and before you go, what are you going to do?'

The young sailor stared at him with dumb horror. What was he talking about?

'You start at the back! Right? Start at the back! And work forward together! I don't want you casting off willy-nilly, and left like doolies floating about on a lighter each, wondering what time's the next bus back to *The Bucket*. Got it? Start at the back!'

And the rating, nodding, repeating 'start at the back', was off.

As he went out the port wing door, two 20-mm shells came in through the back of the wheelhouse, blasting a couple of wooden splinters into Harry's back. One of the shells ricocheted off the binnacle, lifting the compass off its top and blowing the wheelhouse roof off; the other shattered the wheel, its splinters opening Harry's right forearm, before it exited the front of the bridge, hit the raised steel gunwhale that enclosed the bow and exploded, blowing in the wheelhouse windows and blowing Harry off his feet.

The Skipper watched the tracer find a solid target in the darkness, saw the green rounds skittering away, the small explosions from the shells that had gone home, and he knew Jerry had found the lighters.

'Any time you like, Mr Gilmour,' he said to no one in particular. 'We're waiting.'

The Leading Seaman had turned back immediately after the two shells hit. Amid the splintered wood he saw a mound of duffel on the deck, blood seeping around it. More rounds went into the tug's superstructure below him, so he just lunged for his dazed Able Seaman chum in the corner and dragged him out and down the companionway. There were holes in the cabin where they'd locked the Russians, and screams now coming from inside. The rating ordered to guard them had dropped his rifle and was cowering behind the engine room hatch combing. McTiernan and Clunie were coming up from below. The Leading Seaman yelled Harry's orders.

'Is he still at the wheel?' asked McTiernan.

'He's dead,' said the Leading Seaman; the words like a starting gun, sending them all sprinting aft to release the lighters and get the hell out of there. That was when the first star shell went up, and the entire tableau of burning ships, drifting lighters and skulking submarines sprang to life.

The Skipper, looking aft, could see the figures of Harry's party scuttling about the decks of the lighters now. Everything was in a chemical silhouette, lit by the flares pirouetting delicately down towards the silvered water on their dainty little parachutes in long, languid spirals. The green of the German tracer shells didn't seem so bright and frolicsome now that he could see them, smashing into the lighters and the small tug, now free of its daisy chain and moving erratically towards him. Jerry still hadn't spotted *The Bucket*, hull down with just her conning tower showing.

There was a clank, and then a splash from the gun platform; the Skipper leant over in time to see the Tigger grinning up at him.

'Gun's cleared, sir,' said the Tigger, 'shell's over the side.'

'Secure it, Mr Milner.'

'Dinghy returning!' called the aft lookout.

McTiernan hadn't followed Harry's last orders: he'd unhitched the towline to the lighters and got everybody into the dinghy right away. They'd powered to the back pair of lighters, and two of the sailors had jumped aboard them, dodging the 20-mm rounds blowing steel splinters round their heads, hurriedly unhitching one lighter from the other. It had taken barely two minutes and now they were heading back.

The Skipper caught a new vein of tracer out of the corner of his eye, arcing out to the edge of the parachute flares' spill; the German 20-mms on the headland were reaching out to *Trumpeter*. He ordered the rating on the engine room telegraph to grab the Aldis lamp and make the *Trumpeter* 'return to rendezvous'; that would get her out of the way and moving seawards. By the time he looked back, the dinghy was coming alongside.

But there was something wrong; he was counting the huddled shapes bundled into her when he saw Grainger below him, splashing out along the all but submerged casing to where the Tigger and two of his men were waiting to haul the dinghy aboard. He turned and yelled back down the conning tower hatch to Carey: 'Trim her up a foot, number one! Motors, all stop!'

———⏑———

Harry swayed on to his knees, the two wooden splinters flapping from his back like a matador's swords, looking like a stricken bull in a now empty and shadowy ring. When he moved his right arm, as if to dislodge the splinters, he shuddered with the pain. Around him, the wheelhouse had been scythed away by another burst from the twin 20-mm, leaving just the stumps of steel corner posts, opening out the whole tableau to his swimming gaze.

Harry didn't remember there being a full moon . . . no, there was more than one moon . . . that wasn't right. Then there was that terrible mess out there: at least two of those ships, their backs were broken and they were on fire; and so were those other ones. He had never seen ships close up, so utterly wrecked. It was amazing, mesmerizing. A fantastical sight. But why wasn't someone doing something about it? Where was Mr Fireman?

He didn't notice the splinters finally getting knocked from his back as he slithered down the four steps from the wheelhouse; the big watchkeeper's duffel had stopped them from going deep, leaving just puncture wounds. His bloody head and arm didn't half hurt, though. When he reached the deck he heard moaning, and when he looked into the workshop where he'd told the AB to lock up those Russkies, he remembered what he was doing here.

The walls of the workshop were tattooed with dinner-plate size blast holes and the work benches had been reduced to tangled steel. Everything was covered in dark splatter and scorches. Two of the men were dead, he could tell that right away, because although parts of them were still identifiable as men, where the human-shaped bits ended there was just a mess. In the middle, muttering to himself and trying to get up, was another man; but he was just going round in circles because his right arm and leg were gone. All Harry could see of the fourth man was the dull white smudge of his face in the corner. What damage had happened to his body was masked by wreckage, but his wailing told you the prognosis was grim.

Harry stared, then turned away and slumped against what was left of the workshop wall, looking outboard, towards all the pretty patterns the flares were making on the water. He didn't know how long he'd been sat there when Grainger appeared, clambering around the corner of the cabin.

Chapter Twenty-two

'HE effects. High-speed screws approaching from west-north-west.' It was Devaney's voice. Harry could hear it sharp and clear echoing down the passage from the control room; a blessed relief from the soft, rattling breathing coming from the Tigger, lying on the opposite bunk across the wardroom.

'How many?' he heard the Skipper ask.

'Multiple,' said Devaney, dead flat. 'On a spread; bearing from two-seventy to three-ten degrees . . . four, five, maybe more. Coming line abreast.'

Harry had been lying there for the past six or seven hours since he'd been hauled back aboard, and lowered down the conning tower hatch none too gently as *The Bucket* had headed fast down the fjord. He'd been jagged with morphine, and his duffel coat had been cut off him so that they could stitch his fore arm and slap wound dressings on his back; there had been lots of hot sweet tea for shock.

Like most submarines *The Bucket* didn't carry a surgeon, or even a sick bay attendant. The Tigger's gunlayer, Leading Seaman Titmuss, was the boat's nominated first-aider; delegated to patch up the usual sprains and bruises and fractures and burns until the boat got back to port. But he was lying dead now, wrapped in a blanket in the forward torpedo room. So it had been Grainger, who, it transpired, was a dab hand with a needle and suture, who had sewn Harry up; and Grainger and Tubby Tevis who had pressed and padded the wound dressings to the Tigger's chest until the bleeding had stopped.

Harry wasn't sure what had happened on the tug. He had memories of being lifted and bundled and thrown about, and of a lot of gunfire. Then there was Grainger chucking him into the dinghy. Being hauled out the dinghy and then being half dropped, half lowered into *The Bucket's* control room and the Skipper asking: 'How is he? . . . Oh that's nasty. Anything else up with him?' And someone – was it McTiernan? – saying, 'Aye. Blast. He doesn't know whether it's New Year or New York.'

And in the background there'd been loud bangs, two, or was it three; all close. And *The Bucket* reeling – or had that just been his head catching up with him as unseen hands threw him hither and thither?

He wasn't aware that the transport the Tigger's gun crew had left untouched had a deck gun of its own, mounted on its stern, probably a 3-inch job; or that while the crews of all the stricken ships had leapt ashore, the gun crew on the one they had missed had remained at their posts.

The Jerry crew only got off a couple of rounds before *The Bucket* sped past; the wreckage of the transport moored to their outside masking their line of fire. But one of the rounds hit home, gouging a hole in *The Bucket's* casing just abaft the conning tower before exploding in the sea in a fountain of red-hot metal splinters.

Leading Seaman Titmuss had still been on the deck putting rifle rounds into the dinghy, because they didn't have time to collapse it, and they didn't want to leave it for any other bugger to play with . . . and the Tigger had just turned to tell him to get a bloody move on. And now Titmuss was dead and the Tigger was lying there, breathing in short hiccups, with his chest swathed in gauze and a morphine sheen on his porridge-coloured face; eyes rolled half up into his head.

'Rig the boat for silent running,' the Skipper was saying. 'Shut down all unnecessary machinery and lighting.'

He was saving battery amps; they hadn't had much chance to charge the batteries before the parachute flares had driven them under, and there had been less than ninety minutes on the surface at the rendezvous, before being driven under again by an insipid sunrise . . . heralding four hours of what passed for daylight in the Arctic in late October. And now they were out at sea it looked like Jerry had caught up with them. Multiple high-speed screws, approaching fast from the west: it could only be the landing force escort.

'Four, five, maybe more,' Devaney had said.

Harry got up and eased himself into his white pullover, with its sleeve sliced off to fit over his wadded and bandaged forearm. The watch jacket wouldn't fit. He noticed his pistol was still lying on the table where they'd stripped it off him; he noticed it only because it struck him as quite comic that he hadn't once unholstered it during the action.

The pain in his arm was back, so the morphine was obviously wearing off; that was good because it meant he was becoming clear-headed again, and bad because he didn't know how much worse the pain in his arm might get. That didn't matter right now, because he couldn't stay there anymore, not with the Tigger lying there, and the vision of the four Russians spattered around the deckhouse wouldn't wipe from his mind, nor the fact that Jerry was coming after *them* now.

He gingerly picked his way to the control room and sat down at the fruit machine. The Skipper nodded at him: 'How's Mr Milner?' But Harry couldn't find the words to answer, so the Skipper just smiled thinly and went back to work.

They were going up to periscope depth, and as Carey called off the depths, the Skipper waved Harry over to stand beside him, then called for a bearing on the approaching propeller sounds. Devaney called them and the Skipper positioned the periscope tube before ordering it up.

'Five seconds, Harry. Tell me what they are.'

Harry knelt and grabbed the handles as the tube came up, jamming his eyes on to the rubber eye pad. The surface was quite rough, chopped with spray and white crests, but there they were.

It's amazing what the eyes take in, in the shortest time. The lead ship, angling in on them across the port bow, the long, clean fo'c'sle, with the two shielded single-mount guns, superimposed, one above the other; and that squat, blocky bridge abaft them, with the big bridge wings; and the mast with the single, high cross-tree and that silly little cupola stuck on above the bridge, with its searchlight. And the others all the same. Harry knew them all right. Had even built a model of one as a boy.

Harry stepped back. 'Down scope. Four *Leberecht Maass*-class destroyers, another set of masts to the north, so five ships at least. They've all got bones in their teeth.'

Foaming white bow waves meant they were moving very fast.

The Skipper nodded: 'Fleet destroyers? Big?'

Harry nodded.

'Take her down to three hundred feet, number one. Slow ahead together, maintain this course.'

He's going deep, thought Harry. It'll be 'full ahead' and a turn as they go overhead, their hydrophone sets useless amid all the turbulent water churned up by their own screws.

It was cold in the boat, and the air was fuggy with that second-hand taste. The silence was so complete you could actually hear the odd drip of condensation.

Ra-bumm-rumm-rum-rum!

'Depth charges!' called Devaney, urgent but trying to keep his voice down. 'Bearing three-four-zero degrees. They're quite a way off, though.'

'*Trumpeter*,' said the Skipper.

More depth charges, then Devaney again, tentative: 'Targets changing course. Moving to starboard.'

The destroyers Harry had seen had been charging towards them, strung out like a line of beaters trying to flush their sport. There had been maybe as much as three ship lengths between them and if they'd continued piling on the way they were going they would have missed *The Bucket* completely; but somebody had picked up *Trumpeter*.

'They're executing some manoeuvre, sir . . . it's like they're wheeling away from us; like guardsmen . . . two new targets, baring two-five-zero. Closing us . . . slow,' said Devaney.

Suddenly they could hear a faint noise, like a badly oiled sewing machine, running away: the sound of high-speed ship's propellors. Everyone listened as it got louder. It was the end ship of the line of German destroyers, wheeling north, closing in on *Trumpeter*. But then Devaney was also calling out two more targets: two more surface ships, moving wide, coming at them.

The Skipper ordered: 'Stop together' and *The Bucket* hung there, three hundred feet down; a darker solid mass, suspended in the vast, dark immensity of the Barents Sea, silent, as the bustle of the hunt unfolded way above them.

There was a full load back in the torpedo tubes; all hands had been called at the rendezvous, and while the diesels charged the batteries, they worked like navvies to manhandle the six remaining one-and-a-half ton monsters and make them ready to fire. *The Bucket* could fight back if the Skipper wanted to.

Harry had been lying in the wardroom waiting for his senses to return after that exploding cannon shell had rattled them, wondering how he had got back to *The Bucket*. It was Lascar who told him while he was pouring sweet tea into him, how when the dinghy had first returned, Grainger had jumped from the bridge; how he'd pushed aside the young sailors, all wide-eyed with shock and trembling as they clambered out on to *The Bucket*'s casing; how he'd just grabbed the painter from Clunie and knelt so his face was looming over McTiernan. There were words, but Clunie, who told the boat all about it, hadn't been able to hear them above the din of the action; all he caught was Grainger demanding, '. . . but did *you* check?' and McTiernan, face all black and tight, not being able to answer. And Grainger just jumping back into the dinghy and snatching the throttle out of McTiernan's hand, kicking them off *The Bucket*'s saddle tanks and gunning the dinghy back toward the tug.

Lascar, who didn't talk to officers, had told Harry every last detail; then promised him an extra large dollop of his special oosh once the galley re-opened.

Now Grainger was hunched over the chart table, eyes on the gyro compass repeater and the engine rev counter, with only his head to do the sums; working out how far they had travelled each time the Skipper altered course; plotting as near as dammit where they came to rest each time they moved. As if nothing had happened.

Harry said 'Thanks, Kit' and Grainger gave him a sly wink: 'Don't tell anyone.'

'Don't tell anyone that you . . .?'

'Don't tell anyone that I let you get away with using my first name.'

Harry smiled, and so did Grainger, eventually.

The sewing machine sound had all but faded from their ears, but Devaney's disembodied voice was still calling the shape of the game from out of the gloom: '. . .the multiple targets, ahead . . . moving away to starboard. Other two targets, steady on two-five-zero. Still closing.' And the Skipper, standing by the attack scope, leaning like a spiv on a street-corner light, pinching his bottom lip.

Harry turned in his seat to face the crowded control room, all the bodies crushed together in the space like rush-hour passengers on a crowded London tube, when the *whush-whush* of slower propellors made everyone look up.

'Nearest target moving to cross our bows,' said Devaney, and then it sounded as if someone had thrown a handful of pebbles at the hull; and instantly everyone reached for something to hold on to. The Skipper even stopped pulling his lip.

Harry didn't know what it was at first, but from the looks on the old hands' faces, he realized that this was what it sounded like when Jerry picked you up on his echo location gear; a guess confirmed when Devaney pronounced, 'Nearest target slowing and turning towards us . . . bearing three-four-eight . . . other target's gone to high speed . . . moving fast to our starboard.'

Then a new sound echoed through the hull. Like sewing machine sounds, lots of sewing machines – *rickachiky, rickachiky, rickachiky!*

The propeller sounds became confused now; fast and slow. Then more handfuls of pebbles, lots more, until the high-speed screw sounds seemed to saturate the space around them.

'Second target coming in fast, steady on fifteen degrees, going over our top . . .'

'Twenty degrees down,' said the Skipper, 'full ahead together. Take us down another hundred and fifty feet, Mr Carey, fast as you like!'

Another 150 feet? They were already at 300, their maximum recommended depth. Harry's eyes darted around the control room; until he stopped, not wanting to appear nervous, which he wasn't. He was scared shitless. All fear of the German attack had gone, replaced by a cataclysmic vision of the ½-inch thick plate encasing them crumpling, then rupturing as the pressure of the sea crushed their flimsy life-supporting tube to scrap.

He was so distracted by this vision that he didn't pay attention to the thrum of the German destroyer's screws as she passed above them; his eyes were fixed on the bevel of the pressure hull a mere foot from the end of his nose, instead of looking up like everyone else. He also missed the four ragged splashes of the depth charges entering the water.

Each charge weighed 240 kg and they sank towards *The Bucket* at a rate of fourteen feet per second. Their time fuses allowed them to be set to explode at anything up to about 550 feet; by setting the time, they set the depth. If you were at about 300 feet, and if Jerry could get them to within twenty-five to thirty feet of your submarine's hull when they went off, the blast would rupture your pressure hull. The kill radius got bigger the shallower you were. The only thing that could save you was going deeper: the deeper you went, the more the water pressure acted to contain the blast.

Going deeper also meant it was less likely the damn thing would go off underneath you. The underside of a submarine had lots of holes: vents to let ballast water in and out of the tanks that let you dive and surface; vents that a depth charge could tear apart. Also, more crucially, all the little valve inlets and outlets to the pressure hull were there, from bilge pumps to the WC vent. Weak spots that could be torn open by the shock wave from a depth charge and send you to the bottom.

But *The Bucket* was moving away from the position in the ocean where Jerry had dropped his charges. The destroyer had picked them up first on its echo sounder, sound pulses bouncing back, revealing a big solid shape hanging in the water where none should be. Jerry's other detector device – his hydrophones – were only for listening to machinery sounds, pumps, propellors. But *The Bucket* was hanging there silent.

Once Jerry had started his attack, however, the water became so full of competing noises it didn't matter whether *The Bucket* remained silent or not. Water being such a good medium for sound meant Jerry couldn't tell one racket from another, or what direction it was coming from. So the Skipper had chosen that moment to fire up the motors and dive.

The concussion, when it comes, is stupefying, felt more than heard, although the roaring din makes Harry's eyes swim. Two blows slam the boat laterally, and then down by the stern. Harry is flung from his seat, slamming his back against the chart table and his arse on to the deckplates.

There is the sound of breaking glass.

Harry reaches out to the chart table to steady himself and two more concussions slam into the hull; the solid-steel deckplates seem to ripple beneath his buttocks as if turned suddenly to jelly. The noise hurts and the very air in the control room seems to turn to whisp in the gloom and is left hanging in layers. The crushing sound is replaced by the sound of a waterfall, so that at first Harry believes it to be a rushing in his ears; but it isn't. It is the sound of the ocean rushing back into the flash voids created by the depth charges' detonations.

'Four hundred feet,' Carey says into the stunned silence. They are continuing down. A flurry on the trim panel. 'Steady at four-fifty.'

'Starboard thirty!' says the Skipper. To Harry, dazed and still on his arse, they are behaving as if nothing has happened.

'Mr Grainger,' the Skipper continues, 'mark the time and keep the count please.'

'Fourteen-thirty-eight. One, two, three, four,' replies the navigator.

Harry gets to his feet, and moves to the after bulkhead door and wedges himself in.

'Other target closing fast,' says Devaney, 'from our stern now.'

The sewing machine sounds, *rickachiky, rickachiky, rickachiky!*

Harry hears the splashes this time and he grips the door flanges until he feels his fingers hurt. He keeps on feeling them hurt until the blows land again, so that he feels his eyeballs palpitating and his arse lift from his perch. Lumps of cork insulation fall from the deckhead, and the emergency lighting flickers. The blows once again seem to push the stern down, and this time Harry can see the deckplates jump.

More concussions.

'Five, six,' Grainger is saying, when more blows hit the boat. They are preceded by a distinct *click*. It is barely half a second before the concussion, but Harry knows he has heard it.

The control room goes completely dark. Like a switch into oblivion. Harry cannot see even the shadow of the door rim, inches from his face. Then, when the bucking stops, a torch beam; then two, probing into the whispy air. Someone turns the red lights on, and the control room is revealed again. A single, wire-fine jet of water prescribes a geometric line at right angles from behind the trim board. The outside ERA is there with his wrench, insinuating himself into the pipework. The concussions have loosened a pipe joint. Harry has no idea how vital it is, but the Petty Officer is hard at work tightening the flange-securing bolts when the tannoy rasps into life.

'Control room, engine room. The aft escape hatch has jumped, we are making water.' The voice is that of Partridge, the Engineer. Harry knows about escape hatches, he's used one. And on the one he's used, as long as the inboard access hatch is secure, it would be just another ton or so of water Carey would have to compensate for on his trim board.

The sounds of propellors recede.

'Stop,' says the Skipper, and echoing from aft is the sound of water flooding into *The Bucket*'s hull. With the way off her now, Harry feels the boat tilt beneath his feet, stern heavy. Carey works furiously at the trim board but stops when the Skipper calls 'Stop'.

They are going silent again. If Carey runs the pumps to move water from the after bilges forward and balance the boat, now that all the thrashing about upstairs has stopped, Jerry would hear them. The only other way to restore the trim is to start the motors, and go ahead with the bow planes angled against their forward momentum to keep them level; but Jerry would hear that too. To do nothing means the stern bilges, and all the aft spaces will fill, and *The Bucket* will plunge, stern first, to the seabed.

The sound of propellors return.

The Skipper says to Grainger: 'Lay me a course for the coast. Put me inside the islands and reefs.' Then he turns to Carey: 'Get the bilge pumps going. Take us down to five hundred feet and trim the boat.' Then: 'Group up. Full ahead together, stand by for evasive manoeuvring. Hang on everyone. We are about to become the centre of attention.'

As the prop sounds increase, Devaney calls in the approach of the next attack. Jerry must be hearing them loud and clear, but Jerry has a conundrum of his own to deal with: above a certain speed, his own propellors will drown out the noise of any fleeing submarine, because his hydrophones cannot differentiate between the sounds. But in order to launch a depth-charge attack, Jerry needs to work up to full speed, otherwise he won't get clear in time and the blast from his own depth charges will blow his stern off. So in those few moments, between last contact with the submarine and dropping the depth charges, Jerry is deaf and *The Bucket* is free to dodge any way she wants.

'Target one has commenced his attack,' says Devaney. They can hear her screws begin to whine.

'Steer port thirty,' says the Skipper. Too much noise in the water to hear the depth-charge splashes now; but explosions are a different matter. They are heeled hard over when the concussions, in quick succession, push them farther . . . much farther, as if laying the boat on her side. The crash of unknown objects being thrown around the boat punctuates the diminishing roars of the depth charges. Harry feels his shoulder, cracked and bruised off the door combing.

Grainger counts the detonations: 'Eleven, twelve, thirteen, fourteen.' Then he passes the Skipper heading for the coast, and the Skipper immediately orders *The Bucket* to turn towards Norway. Going flat out submerged at nine knots, they will burn all their battery power; within minutes, let alone hours, they won't have enough amps left to light a Christmas tree. They must go slow; at under three knots it will take the best part of six hours to get there, more if they are constantly dodging Jerry's attacks. But it will be dark soon.

'Target two,' says Devaney, 'closing again from directly astern . . . commencing attack now!'

'Port twenty,' says the Skipper, wedged now between the chart table and the bevel of the port hull. 'Can you risk another fifty feet, Mr Carey? Have you got a grip of *The Bucket* again?'

'Five hundred and fifty feet it is, sir,' says Mr Carey, sounding miffed the Skipper could have thought he'd ever lost the trim of *The Bucket* for a moment, even though he had; even though it had been touch and go. For a moment. 'I'm sure we'll manage,' he says.

And still they press on, pursued by the malevolent whirring of those demented, amplified sewing machines, pulling turns, trying to stay out of the killing radius of the German charges; and again and again, the monotonous thunder of them . . . and Grainger's incantation . . . '. . . twenty-seven, twenty-eight, twenty-nine . . .'

The boat begins to creak now. Groaning, tearing sounds, as if screaming at the pressure.

'It's wooden fittings. The cupboards and panels and stuff,' says the Skipper, not looking at Harry, but obviously speaking to him. 'It doesn't flex as well as the steel, the steel gives a little under the pressure, compresses, which is handy. The wood likes to complain before it cracks.'

Harry smiles, then looks around: everyone pressed up close in the control room, faces so close to his you wouldn't get a twelve-inch ruler between them; the sour smell of fear-heavy breath. No one talking, just the crunch of glass shattered from gauges and dials under foot, the breathing and Devaney's commentary on the men upstairs trying to kill them. And the concussions: '. . . thirty-one, thirty-two . . .'

Then a gun goes off: a pistol shot. Here in the boat. For'ard somewhere. Harry jerks rigid. Two more in quick succession. Someone firing. A scream, followed by low moaning. Harry's eyes search everyone's face, looking for some sign he is not hallucinating. But there is no alarm beyond the tightness of fear they are all etched in. The faces remain the same, until a rating comes aft.

'One of the Torpedomen,' he says, breathless. 'Copped one high on 'is back like. Looks bad, sir.'

The Skipper nods. 'Make him comfortable.' Then he sees Harry's slack jaw. 'Rivets,' he says. 'Hold the section frames together . . . this deep . . . the hull pressure squeezes the looser ones out . . . bullets really. Doesn't do to get in the way.'

Click!

Ra-bumm-rumm-rum-rum!

Ra-bumm-rumm-rum-rum!

And on it goes.

Every now and then the monotonous fear is punctuated by fear of a different flavour; another handful of pebbles hits their hull, or another shouted damage report, followed by the scurrying of feet as crewmen run to fix it.

Another rivet cracks like a bullet. Harry has stopped listening to them now.

He thinks only about the unbridgeable distance between people, even between those within arms' reach. How everyone is so close and yet so utterly alone in their fear.

And again, *rabummm-babumm-bumm!* And again, *rabummm-babumm-bumm!*

'Thirty-seven, thirty-eight.'

They are at 600 feet now. The charges are not as close as before, and detonating a bit further above them now. Being at 600 feet is making a difference, but the boat creaks worse than before, and they still rattle as if being pounded by some giant hammer; and the sound of stuff breaking and the damage control reports follow every explosion.

But Harry isn't paying attention at all; he just stands gripping the bulkhead door combing, wedging himself into the space between the door and its central locking wheel, not even wishing for it to stop anymore; not feeling, thinking. There is only the noise and the blows. *Rabummm-babumm-bumm!*

'Mr Gilmour.'

Harry doesn't hear the Skipper at first. He has to repeat himself.

'Sir?'

'Nip back and see how Mr Partridge is getting on with our errant escape hatch and report back to me, there's a good fellow.'

From somewhere out of his stifling fear, Harry can't help but notice, when matters are getting really sticky, how scrupulously polite the Skipper has become.

'Aye aye, sir,' he says, actually managing to smirk to himself, thinking that if they survive, how he'll make sure to tell the crew.

And the world comes back into focus. Now he has something to do: a task at last, after all the impotent waiting while living in the immediate shadow of death. He clambers aft, telling himself 'give yourself a shake', then realizing that if he would just wait a few moments, Jerry will give him all the shaking he needs. Laughing and grimacing as the pain in his arm and back stabs and dances, lurching and wincing as he goes between the huge diesels, muttering to himself, 'Harry's a real hoot!' And the Stokers, seeing him pass, think he's cracked. Then he catches sight of the water through the aft bulkhead door, spurting down the Stokers' mess at an angle into the pump room; if it had jetted the other way, into the motor room and the boat's electrics . . . well it hadn't, so there's no point in worrying about that.

He slides into the Stokers' mess, where Partridge, even greyer and gaunter, stands with his hands on his hips, scrutinising his handiwork. The centre of the escape hatch is packed with what looks like a hammock, with wooden wedges hammered into the heavy material to keep it tight against the hatch's operating spindle, the device which opens or seals it against the sea. Two Stokers stand below the hatch with hammers, ready to bash the wedges home again should they threaten to loosen. Water still splutters off the gimcrack repair.

Partridge turns to look at Harry: 'One of the depth charges . . . the blast got under the rim . . . the hatch jumped and we took a whole packet of water. It would have blown the whole thing open if the mechanism hadn't held. As it is, the spindle has a crack in it and the packing is all blown. We've bunged it up with a hammock and it seems to be holding. Can't afford to try and stop the leak all together . . . if we keep hammering in the wedges we might end up finishing what the depth charge failed to do. We're still taking water, but nothing we can't cope with.'

'Thank you, Mr Partridge,' says Harry. 'Good work.'

The EO gives him a sardonic look, the sort that a man who knows what he's doing gives a boy who doesn't.

Three more detonations break the moment.

Partridge looks up; the Stokers are about to advance, but Partridge raises his hand. They must have been banging home the wedges every time the detonations loosened them. But Partridge is saying, 'Those were much further away' and even Harry notices that he hasn't been shaken off his feet this time.

'No clicks,' Partridge adds. Then, without taking his eyes off his packed hammock, he asks, 'What's happening in the control room, Mr Gilmour?'

Engine room faces stare at Harry from all around the steering space and the hatch leading to the motor room. Behind him, he can hear the engine room telegraph ring, and before he can answer the motors stop and a crackly voice comes over the tannoy calling for silence in the boat.

'No clicks?' whispers Harry.

Partridge focuses on him this time, and whispers too: 'Jerry uses time switches as detonators. The time switch clicks when it closes. If the depth charge is close, you hear it. What's happening, Mr Gilmour? How are we doing?'

The faces haven't stopped staring; serried ranks of stoicism, hanging on the words he's about to utter. Of course, he realises. It was bad enough in the control room, waiting for the hull to be crushed under the endless patterns of explosions, powerless to do anything; but at least you were able to listen to Devaney's commentaries; hear the Skipper's orders; know he's evading; form a picture of the battle raging around you. Back here, in the engine spaces, they're blind and deaf to everything but the explosions and the concussions. It's bad up forward; it must be hell here.

'The Skipper's heading in shore,' explains Harry. 'There are lots of islets and reefs, but it's still deep water. So we're going to hide.'

He's been frozen; in a blue funk, blocking out everything; too frightened to think. How much worse has it been for these men, in the dark, knowing nothing? Waiting for the next bang to blow the hatch clean open? Harry is learning an important lesson about what it means to be an officer: to be responsible for his crew. If they are prepared to bet their lives on their officers' decisions, it's only fair they know what those decisions are. This is the trade, after all. The deal really is all or nothing.

'He's going to use the clutter to mask their detection gear,' he continues. 'Lose us till the fuss dies down.'

Two more explosions reach them and don't even rock the boat. The engine room crew, all eyes on him, even manage a ragged round of smiles. Harry doesn't know if that is for his news or the fact that the last two depth charges are a long way off. Even Harry knows they are a long way off. He smiles back and returns for'ard to where plans are being finalised.

The Skipper was halfway up the conning tower ladder, with the two lookouts immediately below him, holding on to his legs; his watch cap was stuffed in his Ursula suit pocket.

'Last sweep round, Devaney . . . hear anything?'

There was a pause as Devaney turned the hydrophone wheel: 'No HE . . . clear up top.'

'Take us up, Mr Carey!'

'Surface!'

There was a lot of pressure in the boat by this time; she'd taken on a lot of water. And that was why the ratings were holding on to the Skipper's legs. It wasn't completely unknown for the pressure to blow a careless Skipper or watchkeeper clean out of the boat when the lid came off.

'One clip off!' yelled the Skipper, and the two ratings tightened their grip. 'Two clips off!'

An almighty *whumph* of air and one of the rating's caps shot off his head and out of the opening hatch into the night; and then the tang of fresh air came down into their lungs. The Skipper clambered up and the ratings followed. Harry, standing beneath the tower, could see a circle of stars in blackness yawing above his head as *The Bucket* was hit by the swell.

'Right, Mr Gilmour, damage control party to the bridge,' the Skipper called down the hatch, and up Harry went. There were three of them, manhandling their bullet-ridden and collapsed inflatable dinghy and a tool bag, and they went aft to the bent escape hatch. Harry was striding down the casing when *The Bucket*'s big diesels burbled, and the boat beneath his feet came to life, and the freezing water bubbled up into a serious wake, powering them towards Norway under a frigid starlit sky.

They worked fast; the escape hatch was prised open and two Stokers emerged with a welding set and packing. Harry stood watch as his two men huddled the collapsed dinghy over the hatch to mask the blue glow of the welding arcs as they packed the blown spindle and began welding the crack shut. The noise of the diesel exhaust throbbed in Harry's ears as he shivered and watched, the night sky clear and shrieking with stars. It was beautiful beyond words. Until the star shell burst way to the north-west and the tracer started. He turned to the bridge, and in the pale star glow he could make out the shapes of the Skipper and the lookouts training their glasses.

It took some time for the chatter of gunfire to reach Harry's ear, the sound fleeting against the diesel thump and distorted by the wind; and all the while the green and the red tracer danced back and forward on the horizon, hundreds of little Tinkerbells flitting across a backcloth, with the odd flashes which looked nothing like explosions and more like magic spells cast by dancing faeries.

Jerry had blown *Trumpeter* to the surface.

How do you punish yourself, Harry? For thinking the light show so beguiling when what it means is your mates are dying? Nonetheless, he kept watching. The Honourable Bertie hadn't been so fleet of foot as the Skipper when it came to dodging, but he wasn't dying without a fight.

Later, sitting at the wardroom table, Harry had heard it called down: the loom of Norwegian peaks in the dark, just where Grainger said they would be. Almost there. He took another bite of his gammon and cheese sandwich, followed by more coffee. He wasn't sure if it was right that he should be sitting opposite the prostrate and burst figure of the Tigger, stuffing his face; but he was starving and cold after his work on the casing.

The aft escape hatch was now secured as much as they hope for this side of Holy Loch, and they'd evaded Jerry. All they had to do now was get to Norway. Twenty-four hours, forty-eight at the most, hiding in the maze of islands off the North Cape, until Jerry got fed up and went home; and then they could go home, too. The Tigger was conscious and grinning inanely, just like he always grinned. But he was still the colour of porridge and his breathing still came in hiccups.

'I wish I had one of them,' he hiccupped, eyeing Harry's sandwich and smiling thinly with the effort.

'The book says you're not supposed to eat,' said Harry, shamefully thinking again: Thank god it's not me.

The Tigger shook his head: 'The coffee smells good, though.'

'D'you want one?' said Harry, leaning forward just as the Skipper came into the space and slumped down.

'Mr Milner,' he asked, 'how are you?'

'Topper, Skipper!'

'Of course you are.'

Harry got up and poured the Skipper a coffee and brought it back. Tigger and the Skipper were just sitting there, smiling benevolently at each other. The bland innocuousness of the moment made Harry start smiling, too. He put the coffee down in front of his boss and joined them, and the three of them sat together with absolutely nothing to say. And after a while the Tigger's eyes began to droop and he fell asleep, as if he were still a little boy at prep school.

Eventually Harry found himself asking a question of the Skipper: 'Why didn't they just let *Trumpeter* surrender, sir?'

Andy Trumble was still nursing his coffee, which must have been cold by now. He made no sign he'd heard.

'They were blown to the surface,' Harry added. 'It wasn't a fight any more. There was no shame in just throwing in the towel. So why didn't they?'

Still no reaction.

So Harry tried again: 'Why didn't they just surrender?'

Without looking up, the Skipper said: '*Trumpeter*? . . . why didn't the Germans let them?'

It slowly dawned on Harry what he meant. What he'd obviously seen, through his night glasses from the bridge.

'Bastards,' said Harry.

'I very much doubt it,' said the Skipper, staring at nothing. 'I should imagine they all know their fathers. All of them. Well brought up German lads from nice houses in nice towns, apple for the teacher, *Gott, Kinder und Küche* by the hearthside, *und* apple strudel from Auntie Trudl. Just like us really, but different lingo.' Another long pause. 'It's just the war, young Gilmour.'

The klaxon sounded.

Harry bruised his hip, felt his stitches tearing and was already running when the clutches came out of the diesels, and the boat lurched; the Skipper was in the control room ahead of him, and *The Bucket* well on the way down by the time he got to his Diving Stations at the fruit machine.

'Surface contact approaching from the north, with a bone in its teeth,' said Grainger, sliding off the conning tower ladder.

The Skipper said, 'Flood Q! Two hundred feet.'

They all braced themselves as the boat powered down, Carey calling off the depth . . . interrupted only by Devaney, announcing: 'High-speed propeller sounds . . . coming in fast, bearing zero-seven-zero.'

Down, down, then . . .

'Two hundred feet!' It was Carey on the trim board.

'Port thirty!' said the Skipper, above the demented sewing machine whine. Everyone in the control room looked up. Splash, splash, splash; and it started all over again. The dead hand closed on Harry's innards, familiar now, but still impervious to his willing it to just go away. No matter how much he incanted to himself the majesty of his responsibilities, why he must remain calm, the noise and violence entombed him in fear.

Grainger was counting 'five, six, seven' before Harry heard him, even though that twelve-inch ruler would still have found difficulty fitting between their faces. They made eye contact in the silence that followed the blasts.

Grainger was grinning. 'Is that why you joined?' he asked.

Harry gave a puzzled stare.

'You were humming,' said Grainger. '"All The Nice Girls Love A Sailor" . . . is that why you joined?'

Harry grinned, too; not realising in his fear that he'd been humming. Why he'd joined . . . that was a laugh; and then suddenly through the mayhem he had a vision of Shirley standing on the jetty at Sandbank, hunkered down against the wind, hood up and hands stuffed in her duffel coat pocket; and he wasn't listening to the sound of Jerry's screws any more or the distant splashes; he was watching her spot him in the crew boat, and then her arm in the air and a big extravagant wave; and her smile.

Click!

Postscript

Privilege, as far as Oliver Verney was concerned, was something he and his like should never have to consider. You assumed it as your birthright and lived in its benevolent embrace. It was a simple fact of life. If you had it, all things flowed effortlessly to you. Which was why, if you didn't have it, you coveted it. The trouble with this damned war, however, was that it forced one to reconsider everything.

Now take that scruffy youth, for example, standing out there on the deck of that bloody submarine they'd traipsed all this way to meet, and it looking as if it belonged in a scrapyard, even greyer than the grey, clinging mist that seemed to leach every shade of colour out of the world, and every therm of warmth. That youth, with his improbably scruffy officer's watch cap pushed back on far-too-long hair, and sporting a thoroughly disreputable, tarpaulin-like jacket, all oily, with its left sleeve split halfway to his armpit and held together roughly by some kind of maritime twine, all just to make room for the grubby wound dressing which encased his fore-arm; and the wound dressing slapped half across his right cheek and neck, with its little stain that could only be caked blood.

And this clutch of equally scruffy matelots, in misshapen grubby white roll-necks and ratings' caps insolently crammed on their heads in every jaunty angle, having the nerve to be sharing a joke with him as they prepared to moor the submarine against that ancient mossy stone breakwater, all discipline gone to hell. All aboard for the skylark, wasn't in it. Oliver had no idea who this youth was, or anything about him, except that he was an affront.

He used the word 'youth', but Oliver could see that the young officer was about his own age, except that he somehow managed to look older. There he was, leaning to gauge the distance between the submarine's casing and the breakwater, as if he was berthing a gin palace at Henley, gesturing with his good arm to his men, waiting to receive the heaving lines about to be thrown from ashore; and wearing his honourable wounds, won in battle in defence of his country – their country – with an infuriating lightness. Oliver couldn't take his eyes off him, not out of admiration; never admiration. It was because of the rebuke he embodied.

Like all young men of a certain age, Oliver had had his own notion of how one of His Majesty's ships should return from engaging the enemy. But where was the marine band in gleaming white pith helmets, bashing out 'Hearts of Oak'? Where were the ranks of cheering, hankie-waving sweethearts and wives, snotty brats on hips, the doting parents? Or the 'brass', with their braid and swords and aides clutching medal cases for the distribution of? And the ship: Jack Tar lined up on her deck beneath glorified washing lines all a-flutter with bunting? Or whatever the salty dogs called those damn flags they loved to sport on high days and holidays. Or the crush of press, and the newsreel cameras? Don't forget them, for the love of god. How else would you spread the news?

But no. None of that. Just a drab, forsaken foreshore, plumed and eddied with mist that clung chill and wet to everything, the clutch of RN Bedford three-tonners parked on the hard by the breakwater, and the ambulances, and the score of matelots, off the trucks now and huddled, nursing cigarettes, standing around their kit bags, the collars of their trench coats turned up to their caps in the same useless attempt to fend off the damp.

They were to be the replacement crew.

No one had told Oliver this; he'd heard it over the roar of the engines of the same Coastal Command Hudson which had flown them up from Northolt. Something bad had happened, something to do with the Soviets. The submarine wasn't going to be allowed just to return from patrol with the crew coming ashore, telling stories. The crew was going to be scattered into the fleet, under an oath of silence. The operation had never happened. The submarine was going to disappear somewhere; all very hush-hush. So hush-hush the boss wasn't even telling him. Oliver was affronted by that, too.

And what about Oliver's boss, having to stand in the damp cold, too, just like an ordinary person; his homburg scrunched down to his ears, his yellow muffler between it and the upturned collar of his dark blue overcoat, neither managing to protect the linen flaps his ears made, hanging limp and beaded with moisture, just like the matted strands of grey hair against his skull.

He was talking small talk with the Admiral and a Captain, while their two flunkies stood aside, regarding the submarine and its scruffy officer with the same concentration as Oliver. What were the flunkies thinking? he wondered. Maybe, unlike Oliver, they knew why they were all here; maybe they even knew where 'here' was? Because Oliver sure as hell didn't.

Oliver was being a bit disingenuous with himself. He was on Shetland. Where exactly was the mystery, and why.

He had no idea that the flunkies weren't flunkies. Two RN Lieutenants, submariners both. Neither, however, knew any more than he did, except that one of them was to be the submarine's replacement Skipper, and the other would be the conducting officer for sailors coming ashore. As for what they were thinking: they were thinking about the submarine and what a bloody mess she was in.

She was listing slightly to port, so that when she came alongside you could see the dents on her forward casing deck. The jumping wire that ran from the bow to the periscope stands was gone, and the periscopes bent back as if they'd hit a low bridge at speed. But forward, it was the gun mount which caught your eye. The 4-incher was half lifted from her mount and lying almost athwart the ship, held in place only by a cat's cradle of chain, wrapped around the barrel by a crew obviously desperate to save it. They'd wasted their time – the barrel didn't look quite straight anymore. The conning tower, too, was a mass of dents, but it was aft where the real damage was. The entire casing looked as if some madman had taken a giant hammer to it; the casing plates crushed, and the pressure hull beaten against the boat's ribs, looking more like a series of serving dishes than the smooth lines of a submarine.

The two Lieutenants knew all about the pressure waves that could be generated by depth-charge blast, but they'd never seen the actual results on a boat. Not like this. Boats normally never survived this. It was trade lore that they built them well in Barrow, but they'd obviously bloody well excelled themselves when they'd sent the old *Bucket* down the slips. The Lieutenants thought that very same thought, at the very same time.

***

'I say!' Oliver had said to Miranda, his favourite 'gel' in the boss's office. 'What a marvellous day out!'

He'd never been to Shetland. He'd never been anywhere, really, since he'd come to work for the boss, the senior Foreign Office mandarin to whom he'd been assigned after coming down from Oxford with his first in Classics. Unless you counted Chequers. He'd been there, and met Winston. Twice. Which was pretty damn exciting, actually. He preferred to gloss over the fact the first time the prime minister had been tight, and the second time, in his dressing gown, which hadn't been tied. All those fighter pilots and Dunkirk veterans could go on all they liked about the sights they'd seen, but that was one he'd prefer not to have in his head!

But, all in all, a pretty damn interesting war. You could do a lot worse than be a personal assistant to someone like the boss: a ringside seat to great events; something you could build a career on, carrying the briefing papers, sorting the correspondence, making sure the Mirandas of this world made the tea and didn't stew it.

'We're going to Shetland,' the boss had said. 'There has been an incident in the Arctic involving the Soviets. Very serious. So we are going up to meet one of our submarines to find out first-hand how serious and how worried we should be.'

They had boarded the Hudson with a big pudding-faced admiral called Horton, whom everyone called 'the FOS', and his entourage; then droned north to some god-forsaken airstrip called Sumburgh, conveniently located at exactly the opposite end of the island chain to here; and then Oliver had completed the remainder of the trip – all three hours of it – in the back of a Morris 15-cwt, bumped and bashed and tumbled through a grey, wet fog the driver called 'haar', sitting frozen on the truck's flat bed with nothing between its cold metal and his bum but folded gunny sack, and nothing between the rest of him and the elements but a flapping canvas awning. There had been no room for him in the Humber staff car.

And now Oliver was here, and the submarine was alongside the breakwater. Medical staff had gone aboard, while he stood and stamped his feet against the cold like everyone else, and waited. The youth, as he still insisted on thinking of him, was supervising several matelots while they erected some kind of tripod device above a large hatch on the forward deck, which others looked as if they were having to prise up with iron bars. Oliver didn't know it, but this was the torpedo loading hatch, warped by the depth charging, and up through it would be winched the stretchers.

As he watched, another scruffy officer from the submarine came striding up the breakwater. The boss disengaged himself from the Admiral and strolled back to stand by Oliver, and together they watched the submarine's young CO make his report to the FOS, which turned out to stand for Flag Officer, Submarines.

'The Vice Admiral wants to have a word with his man alone,' the boss had explained through pinched lips, a sure sign that he had been offended in some way. 'A very rude, aloof and vain man,' he'd added, confirming the matter. Then, as if talking to himself, absently almost, the boss continued: 'I shall talk to the officers when Vice Admiral Horton has completed his interview, then the crew is to be dispersed, and I shall report back to the PM. Word of what has happened here must never get out. It could be very damaging. Matters are very delicate with the Soviets. We cannot be linked to any international incident involving them. Who knows what they might do if forced to save face?'

Oliver hadn't a clue what the boss was on about. Usually he would have tried to read between the lines to work out what was going on; maybe a little gentle probing. But Oliver was in a strange mood now. Rather than listen to more, he decided to go and collect his briefcase with all his pens and notepads he'd left in the Morris.

As he turned to retrieve them he couldn't help but notice how the submarine's CO held himself in front of *his* boss. He appeared to be offering no excuse for his crumpled watch cap jammed on his head, or the stained heap of material that made up a watch jacket that looked as if it had been slept in; nor the fact that his two faded gold rings were barely still attached to his sleeves; in contrast to the bright solid and two single rings on Horton's immaculate blue overcoat epaulettes. Completely blasé about it. And the Admiral didn't seem to mind.

God they were cocky bastards, these submariners, thought Oliver, trying to evoke the same shade of puce that he'd once seen as a child on the face of his mother's cousin, an Irish guardsman with his own fair share of the baubles of rank, when *he'd* been confronted with infinitely less military slovenliness.

Oliver returned with the case as the first of the wounded were being carried ashore. In the background, little batches of sailors were going aboard the boat, while the boat's crew, in ones and twos, filed off. Handovers were obviously being carried out below. All very business-like apart from the occasional waves of recognition; former shipmates, Oliver assumed, from different commissions. This added to his irritation.

And there was that youth again, putting a cigarette in the mouth of one of the wounded and lighting it for him as he lay swaddled on a stretcher, waiting to be hoisted into an ambulance. It was such an intimate gesture. Oliver felt his eyes well up. And with it came the thump. My God, he thought. That youth has something you don't, is in possession of something way beyond anything you or your generations of privilege have ever been able to confer on you. And that was when he knew why he was feeling so . . . irritated. Words from his past. From his country's past. He even said the words aloud.

'For he today that sheds his blood with me shall be my brother; be he ne'er so vile, this day shall gentle his condition. And gentlemen in England now abed shall think themselves accursed they were not here, and hold their manhoods cheap whiles any speaks that fought with us upon Saint Crispin's day.'

His boss turned to Oliver with a quizzical look, then followed his line of sight.

'His name is Sub-Lieutenant Gilmour,' said the boss, haughtily. 'I wouldn't be too impressed with him. I understand from the Admiral his previous boat was sunk, and, according to the story being told by his then commanding officer, the only reason this

Gilmour chap survived is because he deserted his post. The boat's loss has not been announced, so nothing's been done. Yet. But there's a big black mark over his name, and those have a habit of catching up with one, sooner or later.'

But Oliver wasn't listening. There was a war going on, and he, Oliver, was carrying somebody else's pencil-case, while that young man over there was fighting it.

His mother's cousin would help him remedy that. He'd get the guardsman's telephone number when he got back to London.

Author's Note

'Port Boris', the name given to a German naval base on Russian territory by Lieutenant Andy Trumble RN, is not a figment of the author's imagination. It did exist, albeit under another name.

Basis Nord was granted to Hitler as part of a diplomatic and economic partnership that developed between Germany and the Soviet Union following the German-Soviet Non-Aggression Treaty of 1939. The secret naval base was located at Zapadnaya Litsa Bay, west of Murmansk, and was to be used to support U-boats and commerce raiding into the Atlantic. German navy supply ships were deployed to the base, but in the event no U-boats or surface units of the Kriegsmarine were ever to use it.

Germany's invasion of Norway in April 1940 would provide bases much closer to the Atlantic convoy lanes for U-boats and surface ships such as the battleship *Tirpitz*, thus rendering Basis Nord redundant.

The Royal Navy Submarine Service

At the beginning of the twentieth century, the idea of submarine warfare was considered by senior Royal Navy officers to be 'underhand, unfair and damned un-English' – that particular quote being attributed to Admiral Sir Arthur Wilson VC, who went on to call on the Royal Navy to 'treat all submarines as pirates in wartime . . . and hang all crews'.

However, those in favour of experimenting with submarine technology eventually won the argument, and the Royal Navy launched its first submarine, *Holland 1*, in 1901.

For anyone interested in finding out more about the service in which Harry Gilmour, the hero of this story, would find himself in 1940, there is the Royal Navy Submarine Museum, situated adjacent to the site of HMS *Dolphin*, the submarine service's first shore establishment on the Gosport side of Portsmouth Harbour, Hampshire.

It is Europe's only dedicated submarine museum and it houses exhibitions covering the history of submarine warfare in general, and the role of the Royal Navy in particular.

The centrepiece is HMS *Alliance*, the UK's only surviving Second World War-era submarine, which has been preserved as an operational boat of the day and is fully accessible to visitors, with frequent walk-through tours conducted by former RN submariners. HMS *Alliance* is also the Royal Navy's memorial to the 5,300 British submariners who lost their lives in the service. Among the other displays are a series of interactive exhibits including a working periscope, and a collection of thousands of personal items, photos and documents detailing the everyday lives of those in the 'silent service'. The other submarines in the collection include *Holland 1* and *X24*, the only surviving Second World War midget submarine, similar to the boats that crippled the German battleship *Tirpitz*.

About the Author

 David Black is a former Fleet Street journalist and television documentary producer. He spent much of his childhood a short walk from the Royal Navy Submarine Memorial at Lazaretto Point on the Firth of Clyde, and he grew up watching the passage of both US and Royal Navy submarines in and out of the Firth's bases at Holy Loch and Faslane. As a boy, the lives of those underwater warriors captured his imagination. When he grew up, he discovered the truth was even more epic, and so followed the inspiration for his fictional submariner, Harry Gilmour, and a series of novels about his adventures across World War Two. David Black is also the author of a non-fiction book, *Triad Takeover: A Terrifying Account of the Spread of Triad Crime in the West*. He lives in Argyll.